THE VAGABOND

THE VAGABOND

A NOVEL

GEORGE WALKER

edited by W.M. Verhoeven

broadview editions

© 2004 W.M.Verhoeven

All rights reserved. The use of any part of this publication reproduced, transmitted in any form or by any means, electronic, mechanical, photocopying, recording, or otherwise, or stored in a retrieval system, without prior written consent of the publisher—or in the case of photocopying, a licence from Access Copyright (Canadian Copyright Licensing Agency), One Yonge Street, Suite 1900, Toronto, ON M5E 1E5—is an infringement of the copyright law.

National Library of Canada Cataloguing in Publication

Walker, George, 1772–1847.
    The vagabond : a novel / George Walker ; edited by W.M.Verhoeven.

(Broadview editions)
Includes bibliographical references.
ISBN 1-55111-375-9

    I.Verhoeven, W. M. II. Title. III. Series.

PR5708.W467V33 2004   839.31'34   C2004-902911-8

Broadview Press Ltd. is an independent, international publishing house, incorporated in 1985. Broadview believes in shared ownership, both with its employees and with the general public; since the year 2000 Broadview shares have traded publicly on the Toronto Venture Exchange under the symbol BDP.

We welcome comments and suggestions regarding any aspect of our publications—please feel free to contact us at the addresses below or at broadview@broadviewpress.com / www.broadviewpress.com

North America
PO Box 1243, Peterborough, Ontario, Canada K9J 7H5
Tel: (705) 743-8990; Fax: (705) 743-8353
email: customerservice@broadviewpress.com
3576 California Road, Orchard Park, NY, USA 14127

UK, Ireland, and continental Europe
NBN Plymbridge
Estover Road
Plymouth PL6 7PY UK
Tel: 44 (0) 1752 202 301
Fax: 44 (0) 1752 202 331
Fax Order Line: 44 (0) 1752 202 333
Customer Service: cservs@nbnplymbridge.com
Orders: orders@nbnplymbridge.com

Australia and New Zealand
UNIREPS, University of New South Wales
Sydney, NSW, 2052
Tel: 61 2 9664 0999; Fax: 61 2 9664 5420
email: info.press@unsw.edu.au

Series editor: Professor L.W. Conolly
Advisory editor for this volume: Michel W. Pharand

This book is printed on 100% post-consumer recycled, ancient forest friendly paper.

PRINTED IN CANADA

Contents

Acknowledgements

I would like to thank the following publishers for permission to reproduce sections of text: Pickering & Chatto (Publishers) Ltd., for extracts from Thomas Robert Malthus, *An Essay on the Principle of Population*, edited by E.A. Wrigley and David Souden, volume 1 of *The Works of Thomas Robert Malthus*, general editor E.A. Wrigley and David Souden (8 volumes, 1986); from Mary Wollstonecraft, *A Vindication of the Rights of Woman*, edited by Janet Todd and Marilyn Butler, volume 5 of *The Works of Mary Wollstonecraft*, general editors Janet Todd and Marilyn Butler (7 volumes, 1989); from volumes 2 and 3 of *The Political and Philosophical Writings of William Godwin*, general editor Mark Philp (7 volumes, 1993); and from William Godwin, *Memoirs of the Author of a Vindication of the Rights of Woman*, volume 1 of *The Collected Novels and Memoirs of William Godwin*, general editor Mark Philp (8 volumes, 1992); Oxford University Press, for extracts from volume 1 of *The Collected Letters of Samuel Taylor Coleridge*, edited by Earl Leslie Griggs (4 volumes, 1956–59); Penguin Books, for extracts from Gilbert Imlay, *The Emigrants*, edited by W.M. Verhoeven and Amanda Gilroy (1998); The Pennsylvania State University Press, for extracts from *The Politics of English Jacobinism: Writings of John Thelwall*, edited by Gregory Claeys (1995). I would like to thank Mr. Kenneth Garlick for his permission to reproduce Sir Thomas Lawrence's drawing of Godwin and Holcroft at the Old Bailey Treason Trials of 1794, and Laura Valentine and the Royal Academy of Arts, London, for providing me with a photograph copy of the drawing. I am grateful to the National Portrait Gallery for permission to reproduce "Copenhagen House" by James Gillray, and to Matthew Bailey, Picture Librarian, for arranging it to be photographed. I would also like to thank the John Carter Brown Library, in Providence, Rhode Island, for permission to reproduce the frontispiece of the first edition of Jean-Jacques Rousseau's *Discours sur l'origine et les fondements de l'inégalité parmi les hommes* (Amsterdam, 1755), and the library's photographic services for scanning the image for me.

I am grateful to the following librarians for their kind assistance: Norman Fiering, and the staff of the John Carter Brown Library, Providence, Rhode Island (with special thanks to Susan Danforth, Lynne Harrell, Richard Hurley, and Richard Ring); N. Sue Hanson, Head of Special Collections, Kelvin Smith Library, Case Western Reserve University, Ohio; John Pollack, of the Annenberg Rare Book and Manuscript Library, Van Pelt-Dietrich Library Center, University of Pennsylvania; A.C. Schuytvlot, assistant curator of Rare Books at the University Library of the University of Amsterdam. More generally, I would like to acknowledge the generous help I have received throughout the project from the staff of the following libraries: the John Hay Library, Brown University, Providence, Rhode Island; the interlibrary loans department at the Rockefeller Library, Brown University, Rhode Island; the British Library; the New York Public Library; the Huntington Library and Art Collection, San Marino, California; the Widener and Houghton Libraries, Harvard University; the Alderman Library, University of Virginia; the University and Arts libraries of the University of Groningen. I would like to thank Julia Gaunce, Leonard Conolly, and Barbara Conolly of Broadview Press for their encouragement and their help in getting this volume through the press. It was also a great pleasure to work with Jennifer Bingham, whose congenial professionalism I very much learned to appreciate during the production stage of the project. Many thanks are also due to the following colleagues and friends, who provided help of various kinds, especially in tracking down some of Walker's more obscure sources and references: Peter Garside, Matthew Grenby, Wessel Krul, Robert Lawson Peebles, Michael Millman, Mark Pollard, Peter Potter, Allison Rich, Stephen Shapiro, Len Tennenhouse, and Nicola Trott. Emma Clery, Phil Cox, Robert Miles, Mary Peace and other (former) members of the Corvey Project at Sheffield Hallam University have provided a most congenial and collegial context for discussing the Romantic-era novel in general, and the anti-Jacobin novel in particular. I would like to express my special gratitude to Gerry Wakker, whose meticulous and expert help with the Greek and Latin sources and citations I could not have done without; to Richard Sher, for sharing with me some of his insights into eighteenth-century printing and publishing traditions and tricks; to Philip Stewart, for guiding me through the writings of Voltaire and Rousseau; to Nancy Armstrong, for giving me the chance to teach *The Vagabond* at Brown University; and to Martin Gosman, for generously funding my many research trips and microfilm needs. I would also like to acknowledge the other sponsors who made it possible for me to get my hands dirty on old books, notably the Royal Netherlands Academy of Arts and Sciences and the John Carter Brown Library.

Finally, I want to acknowledge a long-standing debt to Amanda Gilroy, for putting up with George W. and me all this time, and for much more.

THOMAS HOLCROFT AND WILLIAM GODWIN
AT THE TREASON TRIALS AT THE OLD BAILEY, 1794.

Sir Thomas Lawrence, P.R.A. (1769–1830). Original black and red chalk 8¾" x 7". Private
collection. Photo: Royal Academy of Arts, London. Reproduced with permission.

Introduction

There are several good reasons why the name of the London book and music seller George Walker (1772–1847) should not be familiar to many people today: being known, around 1810, as a "publisher of music at half price and warehouse for Hope's Hectic Pills," might be one such reason.[1] And yet, between 1792 and 1815, Walker wrote more than a dozen books, for the most part multi-volume romances and novels, but also children's tales and poetry. Nor did Walker's work lack contemporary popular and commercial success: several of his titles were republished in Dublin and cities in the United States, while three of his novels were translated into French, with one—*Theodore Cyphon* (1796)—translated into German *and* French. It is *Theodore Cyphon* that has traditionally earned Walker the occasional footnote in literary history, on account of it being allegedly a rather unimpressive imitation of William Godwin's revolutionary novel *Caleb Williams* (1794);[2] in fact, *Theodore Cyphon* is a well-executed conservative *rewriting* of Godwin's influential novel, and its author would for that reason alone deserve a wider readership than he currently enjoys. However, Walker's ultimate claim to fame must be his anti-Jacobin novel *The Vagabond* (1799).

---

[1] *Dictionary of National Biography*. George Walker was born in Falcon Square, Cripplegate, London, on 24 December 1772. At the age of fifteen he was apprenticed to a bookseller named Cuthwell in Middle Row, Holborn. Two years later he started his own business and remained in the bookselling and publishing business for the rest of his life. Thus, although quite successful measured by the number of reprints and translations of his novels, Walker was a writer by choice, not necessity. When he moved his shop to Great Portland Street, he expanded into music publishing; eventually, having relocated to Golden Square, publishing printed music was his main business activity. Toward the end of his life he took his son George Walker (1803–1879) into partnership with him. Walker died on 8 February 1847.

[2] See, for instance, B. Sprague Allen, "The Reaction Against William Godwin," *Modern Philology* 16:5 (September 1918): 65n; Marilyn Butler, *Jane Austen and the War of Ideas* (Oxford: Clarendon Press, 1975), 111; A.D. Harvey, "George Walker and the Anti-Revolutionary Novel," *Review of English Studies* ns, 28:111 (1977): 299; Peter H. Marshall, *William Godwin* (New Haven and London:Yale University Press, 1984), 218; M.O. Grenby, *The Anti-Jacobin Novel: British Conservatism and the French Revolution* (Cambridge: Cambridge University Press, 2001), 200.

Offering a vitriolic diatribe against post-Bastille Jacobinism and sansculotte-style mob rule in Britain in the 1790s, *The Vagabond* immediately speaks to the reader through its highly entertaining true-to-life satirical portraits of many of the radical men and women who fought in the forefront of the "British Revolution." What is more important, however, is that in contrast to most anti-Jacobin writers, Walker had actually read his enemies' speculative tracts and treatises, and had understood them. Thus, *The Vagabond* may be known as a prominent exponent of the anti-Jacobin lobby and "the epitome of conservatism,"[1] slashing away at anything smacking of liberalism and reform, but underlying his satirical humor is an informed critique of Jacobin radicalism seldom found in works of this school. With chief swipes at Hume, Rousseau, Godwin, Wollstonecraft, and Paine among persons; the French Revolution among events; and the noble savage, natural virtue, liberty, equality and romantic primitivism among ideas, *The Vagabond* asks to be read as a cross-section of 1790s radicalism—and the conservative alternative. But Walker does not confine himself to uprooting radicalism in Britain alone. Following depictions of wild scenes of riot and uproar in the streets and taverns of London, and a behind-the-scenes impression of activities of populist leaders and public speakers, is a string of hilarious transatlantic adventures involving the novel's radical hero and his motley entourage. The climax of the book is an excursion to found a backwoods utopia in America, where squabbles, Indian scalpings, and mosquitoes eventually wreck the emigrants' illusions—after which the survivors return home, sadder but wiser.

Ultimately, then, *The Vagabond* is much more than a highly entertaining narrative: set against an expansive backdrop of British history, stretching from the Glorious Revolution of 1688 to the very end of the eighteenth century, the novel is less concerned with knocking over straw men than engaging with the historical figures and ideological positions that they represent. In fact, it would be in vain to look in the novel for anything approaching conventional characterization, or anything resembling a regular plot. In lieu of characters, we find a rich intertextual tissue of

---

[1] Butler, *Jane Austen and the War of Ideas*, 111.

political innuendo, malicious gossip and quotations from a wide range of (mainly) reformist writers; in lieu of a plot, we find a mass of historical events, woven into an idiosyncratic and deliberately anachronistic tapestry of revisionist historiography. The collage offered in the following section is made up entirely of explicit textual references and fictional dramatization of historical events gleaned from the novel. Reading *The Vagabond* is reading two centuries of British history, politics and culture—the anti-Jacobin version, of course; more than any other anti-Jacobin novel, perhaps, *The Vagabond* can only really be appreciated if the reader has a fair sense of that history, politics and culture.

The Vagabond as a History of the British Revolution

Known as the "Revolutionary Decade," the 1790s in Britain witnessed a bitter and decisive clash between the nation's past and its future. Contrary to America and France, where the revolution had involved widespread bloodshed and massive social disruption, the British Revolution—though certainly not free from violent upheaval—was one that was largely fought and decided not on the battlefield, but in the pages of various print media, and in the coffee-houses, ale-houses and reading-clubs, where these texts were distributed, read and debated by a rapidly swelling audience of literate artisans, laborers and shop-keepers. The controversy over the causes and meaning of the French Revolution, and the consequences it might or should have for the political status quo in Britain, had turned the British into "an inquisitive, prying, doubting, and reading people."[1] Book production and consumption had seen a fourfold increase since 1750, but the "Revolutionary Debate" of the 1790s triggered an unprecedented prose revolution in Britain, with an exponential increase in the annual production of novels, pamphlets, sermons, poetry and periodical publications. The British Revolution, then, was first and foremost a print revolution, as well as a revolution

---

[1] Anon., *The Periodical Press of Great Britain and Ireland: or, an inquiry into the state of the public journals, chiefly as regards their moral and political influence* (London: Hurst, Robinson & Co., 1824), 24.

in print. Or, as H.N. Brailsford so aptly remarked, "The history of the French Revolution in England begins with a sermon and ends with a poem."[1] The sermon, "A Discourse on the Love of Our Country," was delivered in 1789 by the leading Dissenter and political pamphleteer, Dr. Richard Price; written not long after the sacking of the Bastille on July 14, 1789—an event which marked the beginning of the populist uprising in France— Price's sermon identified the French Revolution as the natural and just successor of the Glorious Revolution of 1688–89, which had laid the foundation for Britain's parliamentary monarchy, and of the American Revolution, which had ushered in the independence of the American colonies as a sovereign nation. The poem Brailsford referred to was Percy Shelley's *Hellas* (1821), in which, inspired by the same revolutionary fire and hope that had moved Dr. Price, the poet creates a glorious vision of the ideal Republic, but, significantly, founds it beyond the perilous world of fact, in the timeless realm of the muses and the imagination.

Although Price appears to have considerably toned down his claims in the printed versions of the sermon, the "Discourse" acted as a spark that exploded an already highly combustible political atmosphere in Britain. *Pace* Brailsford, it is important to realize— and this is one of the tenets maintained in *The Vagabond*—that the history of the French Revolution in Britain does *not* begin with the fall of the Bastille, but is inextricably bound up with the political reverberations caused by the Glorious Revolution of a century before. It was in the course of 1688–89 that James II was driven from the throne and the Crown was offered to his son-in-law, William of Orange, and James's eldest daughter, Mary. The military campaign that put an end to James II's rule had the backing of the majority of parliament, as well as all those who had opposed James's attempts to impose Catholicism on the country and restore absolute monarchy. In the wake of the armed struggle a number of significant constitutional changes were introduced in Britain. Thus, in 1689 a Bill of Rights was adopted which confirmed the shift of monarchical power from James to William and his wife,

---

[1] H.N. Brailsford, *Shelley, Godwin, and Their Circle* (London: Williams and Norgate, 1913), 7.

Mary; this was followed, in 1694, by the Triennial Act, which provided for parliamentary elections on a three-year cycle, and, in 1701, by the Act of Settlement, which secured independence of the judiciary but, more importantly, limited the Crown to members of the House of Hanover, thereby in effect barring Roman Catholics from the throne.

In the course of the eighteenth century, 1688 came to be regarded by the political and religious establishment as a necessary correction of a constitutional crisis, and the stability of the House of Hanover as a confirmation of the ancient constitutional right of kings. Notably in Dissenting religious circles,[1] but also in the rising middle classes in general, however, there was a growing awareness that the achievements of the Glorious Revolution were slowly being eroded and that the outcome of 1688 put a strangle-hold on a widespread desire for social and economic reform.[2] In the course of the 1770s, a fierce pamphlet war erupted in Britain, as loyalists and reformists attacked each other over what they saw as the only legitimate interpretation of the events leading up to and following the change-over of power in 1688. The rising tensions between the American colonists and the British authorities over commercial and constitutional rights added to the volatility of the political climate, and created an unlikely but important link between these two ostensibly unrelated historical events. This intense political debate reached a peak on the eve of the fall of the Bastille with the centenary of the Glorious Revolution in 1788, which was marked by a flurry of political gatherings, commemorative dinners, and sermons. The political anxiety caused by the revelation of the first signs of George III's insanity in 1788, as well as the violent populist

---

[1] Protestant Dissenters refused to subscribe to the thirty-nine articles of the Anglican Church, and as a result could not take up positions in government or the military.

[2] In his "Discourse," Price, too, tried to reclaim some of the liberties lost since the Glorious Revolution by provokingly redefining "patriotism" as an individual's willingness to defend the "three principles" of the Glorious Revolution: "the right to liberty of conscience in religious matters"; "the right to resist power when abused"; and "the right to choose our own governors, to cashier them for misconduct, and to frame a government for ourselves" (Richard Price, "A Discourse on the Love of Our Country," in *Political Writings*, ed. D.O. Thomas [1789; Cambridge: Cambridge University Press, 1991], 189–90).

protests against the Catholic Relief Act adopted in the same year (see below), added to the general atmosphere of crisis and unrest. Dr. Price's sermon, delivered on November 4, 1789, to the "Society of Commemorating the Revolution in Great Britain," could not have come at a more propitious moment.

It was ultimately not so much Price's plea for parliamentary reform (notably for a more equitable system of political representation) as his passionate and unqualified glorification of the French Revolution as the first step toward the infinite perfectibility of mankind that set the nation aflame. Statesman and thinker Edmund Burke was quick to denounce Price's sermon in his *Reflections on the French Revolution* (1790)—his passionate rhetoric of declamatory rage clearly betraying that "his mission was to spread panic because he felt it."[1] Although Burke's book does not offer a sustained philosophical critique of the French Revolution but relies on superb rhetorical exaggerations instead,[2] it did manage to put the main conservative arguments firmly on the political agenda: the rejection of the ideology of natural rights; the dismissal of a social contract theory; an insistence on institutional continuity (church, monarchy, and common law); the preference of familial affection over reason, and practical experience over speculative rationality. Burke's *Reflections* struck an immediate chord with the political, social and religious establishment in the nation, and soon became conservative Britain's main answer to the Revolution in France and to its growing body of sympathizers at home. However, his eloquent rhetoric inspired his enemies as much as his supporters, thus triggering a "mighty debate" that was to last for a decade and that was to determine the future of Britain—or so the participants thought at the time.

Initially, this national debate was dominated by those arguing for political and social reform. The reformists were encouraged in their campaign by a number of extraordinarily influential radical publications. Within months of the publication of Burke's *Reflections*, the writer, educator and radical feminist Mary Wollstonecraft published a first retort, *A Vindication of the Rights*

---

[1] Brailsford, 18.
[2] For a characteristic sample of Burke's powerful and persuasive rhetoric, see Appendix B.

of Men; this was followed in 1792 by her best-known work, and one of the founding texts of modern feminism, *A Vindication of the Rights of Woman*. A year before James Mackintosh had taken a forceful public stand against Burke in his *Vindiciae Gallicae*. Also in 1791 the pamphleteer and political activist Thomas Paine (1737–1809) joined the fray, having first helped to stoke up the fire of revolution in America. His immensely popular *Rights of Man* (Part I) was in every way a direct answer to Burke's *Reflections*: it not only argued for natural rights, a written constitution, and the right of every generation to govern its own affairs, but it does so in a discourse that is as abstract as it is uncompromising in its hard-hitting logic. 1792 saw the second part of Paine's *Rights of Man*, as well as Thomas Holcroft's radical novel *Anna St. Ives*. But the text that lifted the whole debate to a philosophical level not seen before and whose impact on the age was so dramatic it nearly pitched Britain into civil war was William Godwin's *Enquiry Concerning Political Justice and Its Influence on Modern Morals and Happiness* (1793). "No work in our time gave such a blow to the philosophical mind of the country as the celebrated *Enquiry Concerning Political Justice*," William Hazlitt observed retrospectively in 1825; "Tom Paine was considered for the time as a Tom Fool to him, Paley an old woman, Edmund Burke a flashy sophist. Truth, moral truth, it was supposed, had here taken up its abode; and these were the oracles of thought."[1] With a pen of steel Godwin unrolled his principles towards the Temple of Reason—without any compromise to "natural and generous feelings." "Abstract Reason was taken for the rule of conduct," Hazlitt remarked, "and abstract Good for its end. The narrow ties of sense, custom, authority, private and local attachment were sacrificed in the relentless pursuit of universal benevolence. Gratitude, promises, friendship, family affection had to give way, and the void was to be filled in by the disinterested love of good and the dictates of inflexible justice, which is 'the law of laws and the sovereign of sovereigns.'"[2]

---

[1] William Hazlitt, *The Spirit of the Age or Contemporary Portraits* (1825; Oxford: Oxford University Press, 1928), 18.
[2] Ibid., 20.

Godwin's manifesto of rational anarchy made its author a celebrity overnight. Judging from contemporary accounts, most people in Britain seem to have heard about his anarchist vision of the perfectible society. Godwin was generally referred to as the "philosopher" or the "Grand Master," and many of his supporters dubbed themselves "Godwinians" or "Godwinites." For a little while it appeared to many as if paradise on earth was within easy reach: "Sound reasoning and truth, when adequately communicated, must always be victorious over error: Sound reasoning and truth are capable of being so communicated: Truth is omnipotent: The vices and moral weakness of man are not invincible: Man is perfectible, or in other words susceptible of perpetual improvement."[1] However, when the reaction against Godwin came, and it would come quickly, it came with a vehemence and a fervor equal to the euphoria of its initial reception. When Walker published *The Vagabond* in 1799, the reaction was at its peak; but the roots of the late-1790s anti-Godwin hysteria lay in the bloody events that had been taking place across the Channel earlier in the decade.

Between the fall of the Bastille and the publication of the *Enquiry*, the political situation had gone through a rapid development from democratization and social reform to renewed repression and public violence. The National Assembly, which formed France's effective national government between 1789 and 1791, had adopted the Declaration of the Rights of Men and drafted a new constitution creating a limited monarchy. After Louis XVI had accepted the new constitution in October 1791, the new legislative body, the Constituent Assembly, pushed through major legislative reforms, including administrative and church reform, the abolition of feudalism and economic liberalization. Increasingly, however, the Assembly was marked a bitter struggle between two factions: the moderate Girondists, mainly backed by the emergent middle class and led by Brissot; and the more radical Jacobins, who represented the vindictive lower classes and were headed by Robespierre, Marat and Danton. The Jacobins gradu-

---

[1] William Godwin, *Enquiry Concerning Political Justice and Its Influence on Modern Morals and Happiness*, ed. Isaac Kramnick (1793; Harmondsworth: Penguin, 1976), 140.

ally succeeded in getting the upper hand over their opponents and soon violence once more erupted. In September 1792 the people invaded the prisons and slaughtered over twelve hundred aristocratic prisoners (the September Massacres), on the pretext that the inmates had been plotting a reactionary counter-revolution. Shortly afterwards, the Jacobins abolished the monarchy and put the king on trial for treason. The beheading of Louis XVI on January 21, 1793 sent shudders down the spine of the British establishment; it was followed almost immediately by France declaring war on Britain on February 1. These events are generally regarded as the beginning of the Reign of Terror, during which the Jacobins introduced a series of repressive measures and evened the score with old enemies, sending thousands to the Guillotine, including the queen, Marie Antoinette, and many prominent Girondists, amongst them its leader, Brissot. The Reign of Terror burnt itself out in the course of 1795, with its own leaders Danton and Robespierre falling victim to the Guillotine.

Those British radicals who proudly (and often loudly) styled themselves "patriots," "Jacobins" and "Friends of Liberty" in the years immediately following the French Revolution, soon adopted more modest appellations following the outbreak of war between Britain and France in 1793 and the start of the Terror in France: a "patriot" soon came to mean an enemy of the state, and "Jacobin" became the pejorative by-word for a disciple of Robespierre's *sansculotte* ideology and a sympathizer of the Guillotine—even though unlike their French namesakes, British Jacobins were on the whole reformers, not revolutionaries.[1] During the conservative and chauvinist reaction that erupted in the course of 1794, Godwin was singled out as the prime target for malicious diatribe. In 1795 and 1796 a torrent of anti-Jacobin pamphlets branded *Political Justice* and its doctrine of philosophical anarchism as a blueprint for introducing the Reign of Terror

---

[1] In America, Jacobinism was associated quite early on with anarchy, atheism and, especially, foreign conspiracy—the latter not only in response to the arrival of thousands of French *émigrés* fleeing from the Terror, but also in response to the influx of hundreds of English and Irish radicals and free-thinkers, whose hopes of establishing a Jacobin republic in America clashed dramatically with the spirit of Federalism that had begun to dominate domestic American politics.

into Britain, while Godwin's name became synonymous with sexual license, atheism and moral cynicism. The other two scapegoats for the anti-Jacobin reaction were the London Corresponding Society, and its leader John Thelwall.

The London Corresponding Society (or "LCS" as it was known at the time) was the most notorious of the many parliamentary reform societies or "Jacobin clubs" that sprang up in London and several major towns in the country in the early 1790s, and whose main practical aim was to correspond with other reform societies and exchange radical information with them. The political ambitions of the various corresponding societies differed considerably—some favoring moderate reform, others campaigning for annual parliaments, universal suffrage, and electoral reform. To disseminate their views most societies published broadsides and pamphlets, and held regular meetings and readings in taverns. The membership of the corresponding societies consisted mainly of articulate artisans and shop-keepers, though some societies counted preachers, printers, publishers and journalists among their members. The LCS was founded in 1792 by a shoemaker named Thomas Hardy. With many smaller divisions set up throughout London and low membership fees, the LCS quickly became a political force to be reckoned with: at its peak in 1795 it had between 3,000 and 5,000 members, but its meetings attracted many more. The LCS's publications and proclamations generally derived their rhetoric and inspiration from Thomas Paine's writings on the natural rights of citizens to life, liberty, property, and the pursuit of happiness, but also tapped into an older, non-revolutionary constitutional tradition that tried to recover lost ancient English rights: hence communications from the LCS were often signed as "Citizen" (after the French Jacobin "Citoyen"), but also as "Anglo-Saxon."

Although the LCS's political message was at this stage still rather mild, or at least mixed, the war with France and the radicalization of revolution there had made William Pitt's government increasingly nervous about the activities of reform societies and it had begun an aggressive campaign to repress the Jacobin community. Government-sponsored societies, such as the Association for Preserving Liberty and Property Against Republicans and Levellers, had sprung up all over the country, waging a bitter war against what they called "seditious and treasonable Libels"; government spies were infiltrating reform society meetings, collecting potentially incriminating evidence against its leaders. In May 1792 Pitt's government issued a proclamation against "wicked and seditious writings," and soon after banned Paine's *Rights of Man* and summoned its author to appear in court for seditious libel—not least because cheap editions of the text had led to sensational sales figures, thus spreading its republican arguments in favor of the revolutions in American and France amongst large sections of the population.[1] Hysterical scenes of populist rage and bloodthirsty frenzy against Paine erupted all over the country, effectively forcing Paine into exile in September 1792. He was tried and convicted *in absentia* in December.

Having got rid of the architect of republicanism, it was now time to uproot the network of dissemination. 1793 had already seen the arrest, trial and transportation to Botany Bay of two Scottish reformers—Thomas Palmer and Thomas Muir—for their involvement in the Edinburgh Convention for constitutional change. In December of the same year, along with other members of the LCS, Joseph Gerrald, leading theorist of the LCS and close friend of William Godwin, was arrested during a second Edinburgh Convention. The LCS responded by calling for a British Convention in March 1794, but Pitt was quick to parry: in May 1794 he suspended Habeas Corpus, which meant that the government could arrest and hold suspected criminals indefinitely without bringing formal charges against them. Within days Godwin's friends Thomas Hardy, Horne Tooke, John Thelwall and eight other prominent members of the LCS were arrested on a charge of high treason and taken to the Tower and Newgate prisons (Thomas Holcroft, also a close friend of Godwin, gave himself up voluntarily).[2] During the Treason Trials in the fall of

---

[1] Paine himself estimated that sales of the complete edition of *Rights of Man* reached four to five hundred thousand copies within ten years of its publication. If correct, this would mean that one reader in ten on mainland Britain bought a copy of *Rights of Man*—this is excluding the many pirated and serialized editions. See John Keane, *Thomas Paine: A Political Life* (London: Bloomsbury, 1995), 307–08.

[2] It is an indication of how serious Pitt's government wanted to clamp down on suspected revolutionaries that at one point it had drawn up as many as 800 arrest warrants.

1794, Hardy, Tooke and Thelwall were all acquitted, after which Holcroft was released without charge. It was widely accepted at the time that it was Godwin's *Cursory Strictures on the Charge Delivered by Lord Chief Justice Eyre to the Grand Jury*, addressed to the judge presiding at Horne Tooke's trial, that persuaded the jury to hand down a "not guilty" verdict.

This victory of Godwin and the LCS members over Pitt's government, however, also proved to be the beginning of a serious rift within the LCS between moderates like Godwin, who wanted to achieve their republican ideals by rational argument and by enlightening the people, and hard-line anarchists like Thelwall, who, having replaced Gerrald as the LCS's principal theorist, favored popular agitation to force the government to agree to political reform. A pamphleteer, journalist, playwright, and lecturer, Thelwall was a close friend of the poet Samuel Coleridge, and was no mean poet himself. Initially a dedicated follower of Godwin, Thelwall led the LCS in the post-Trial period away from Godwin's political utopia of perfectibility to a more practical agenda, especially seeking ways to improve the socio-economic conditions of the working man. After a number of Godwin's disciples resigned from the Society out of protest against the new strategy of confrontation and agitation, the radicalized LCS was on a collision course with Pitt's government.

Two main weapons made Thelwall an unusually effective political agitator: rousing speeches and mass meetings. Lampooned in *The Vagabond* as "Citizen Ego," Thelwall was a gifted orator who could incite audiences to a frenzy with his energizing rhetoric—a talent he displayed to great effect at the many political meetings he organized, some of which attracted more than 100,000 people. Thus, on 16 October 1795 Thelwall addressed a meeting in Copenhagen Fields of nearly 150,000 people—an indication that political unrest was reaching crisis levels. Earlier in the year, the country had been engulfed in food riots, after failed harvests had led to shortages and high prices. Inflammatory pamphlets appeared with titles like *King Killing, the Reign of the English Robespierre* and *The Happy Reign of George the Last*. Two days after the Copenhagen Fields meeting, the King's carriage was beleaguered in St. James's Park while on the way to Parliament, with an excited mob of 200,000 people hooting "Down with Pitt!" "No War!" "No king!" A stone was thrown and a carriage window was broken, after which, according to a contemporary pamphlet, the King exclaimed, "My Lord, I, I, I've been shot at!"[1] The carriage was later destroyed by the mob calling for peace and bread. Many people in Britain were convinced that a French-style Revolution was imminent. The government responded swiftly with Lord Grenville's and Pitt's notorious "Two Acts" of December 1795. Better-known as the "Gagging Acts," the "Treasonable and Seditious Practices Act" made it a treasonable offence to incite the people to hatred or contempt of King, Constitution or Government, while the "Unlawful Assemblies Act" gave magistrates wide powers to stop speeches, arrest speakers and disperse meetings. A special clause in the latter Act, aimed at Thelwall in particular, enabled magistrates to close down lecture halls as "disorderly houses."

Although Thelwall for a while continued his political lectures under the guise of talks on Roman history, the Two Acts effectively contained the threat of a full-scale popular uprising in Britain. The LCS itself had virtually collapsed by the end of 1796, although there is some evidence to suggest that some members went underground and continued their activities illegally.[2] In the end the Two Acts were never really invoked in their full force by the authorities: even though Habeas Corpus was to be suspended for eight years, not more than a few dozen people were ever detained for any period without trial. "Fear, spies, watchful magistrates with undefined powers, the occasional example": these appear to have been the main active ingredients of the Two Acts.[3] The post-Trial radicalization of the revolutionary debate in Britain appears to vindicate William Godwin's denunciation of the LCS under Thelwall's leadership in a pamphlet he wrote in response to the Copenhagen Fields incident, *Considerations on Lord Grenville's and Mr Pitt's Bills, concerning treasonable and seditious practices and unlawful assemblies*

---

[1] Anon., *Truth and Treason! Or a Narrative of the Royal Procession* (London, 1795), 3.
[2] The Jacobin underground has been associated with the naval mutinies in the spring of 1797 and the Irish Rebellion of 1798. See E.P. Thompson, *The Making of the English Working Class*, rev. ed. (1963; Harmondsworth: Penguin, 1968), 183–92.
[3] Ibid., 161.

(November 1795). Although he sharply criticizes Pitt's policy of repression (comparing Pitt's "army of spies and informers" to Louis XVI's agents of fear), Godwin is remarkably dismissive of the LCS, describing it as "a formidable machine" and "its system of political lecturing ... a hotbed, perhaps too well adapted to ripen men for purposes, more or less similar to those of the Jacobin Society of Paris."[1]

1795 turned out to be a climactic year for riots, with two distinct political movements converging and joining forces, though not necessarily sharing each other's political agendas: an angry populace trying to reimpose the old moral economy and protesting against the forces of the new market economy, and a Jacobin minority campaigning for reform (spearheaded by the LCS). However, as Walker's novel amply bears out, riotous actions by violent mobs were very much part of the social landscape of England before 1795: in volume I, chapters 6–8, Walker presents a vivid account of the 1780 Gordon Riots, while the riot described in volume II, chapter 4, is based on the attack on Dr. Priestley's house during the Birmingham Riots of 1791. In fact, constituting what social historian E.P. Thompson called the "moral economy" of the disenfranchised laboring poor, riots had been an integral part of British social life throughout the eighteenth century, and would continue to be so well into the nineteenth century—earning the British a reputation throughout Europe for popular defiance and direct action.[2] Generally speaking, there were two different manifestations of riotous action in Britain: more or less spontaneous popular direct action (often occasioned by food prices, turnpikes and tolls, excise, enclosures, press-gangs and other social grievances), and the deliberate use of a crowd as an instrument of threat or pressure by people outside of the crowd (like the riot leading to the attack on the King). The latter kind of mob (defined by one historian as a "hired band operating on behalf of external interests"[3])

---

1   William Godwin, *Considerations on Lord Grenville's and Mr Pitt's Bills, concerning treasonable and seditious practices and unlawful assemblies, by a lover of order*, in *Political and Philosophical Writings of William Godwin*, gen. ed. Mark Philp, 7 vols. (1795; London: Pickering & Chatto, 1993), 2:137, 134.
2   Thompson, *The Making of the English Working Class*, 68.
3   G. Rudé, *The Crowd in the French Revolution* (Oxford: Clarendon Press, 1959), qtd. in Thompson, *The Making of the English Working Class*, 74.

played a curious and often unsuspected role in the British political and legal status quo in the eighteenth century: that is, as an instrument in the hands of the authorities themselves, rather than their opponents.[1] To account for this phenomenon, we must again turn to the Glorious Revolution, as Thompson reminds us: "The 1688 settlement was ... a compromise; and it was convenient for the beneficiaries to seek to confirm their position by encouraging popular antipathy towards Papists (potential Jacobites) on the one hand, and Dissenters (potential Levellers) on the other. A mob was a very useful supplement to the magistrates in a nation that was scarcely policed."[2] The dynamics of this type of mob activity were revealed most clearly during the notorious Gordon Riots of 1780.

Raging between 2 and 10 June, the Gordon Riots led to more property damage in London than Paris suffered throughout the French Revolution; not surprisingly, its traumatic impact was still felt in the late 1790s when Walker was writing his anti-Jacobin novel.[3] The roots of the Gordon Riots go back to religious politics in Britain at the time of the American Revolution. The escalation of the American War came on top of British military engagements elsewhere in the empire, and the contemporary government of Lord North was hard-pressed to find more recruits for its armed forces. One possible source for recruits was the Scottish Catholics, but before they could be won over, some of the major discriminatory measures against Catholics introduced in 1699 had to be removed. In 1778 the Catholic Relief Act received royal approval. Immediately, a "No-Popery" campaign was launched and Protestant clubs organizing local protests sprung up everywhere. In 1779 a Protestant Association was founded in London, and Lord George Gordon was elected as its zealous president. Initially, the protests were carried out by tradesmen and other law-abiding citizens. Yet despite mounting pressure from

---

[1]   Cf. volume II, chapter iv, in which Stupeo distinguishes between "a mob hired by the government" (a "King and Church" mob) and "a republican mob" (a revolutionary, Jacobin mob).

[2]   Thompson, *The Making of the English Working Class*, 74.

[3]   Even as late as 1841 the Gordon Riots were still vivid enough for Charles Dickens to base the plot of his fifth novel, *Barnaby Rudge, A Tale of the Riots of 'Eighty*, on the events of June 1780.

these fanatical Puritan campaigners, the government refused to repeal the Relief Act. Then, in June 1780, as the frustration over this refusal reached a peak, mobs of journeymen, apprentices and some criminal elements, launched the first violent attacks, first on Catholic chapels and houses of wealthy Catholics, and then on Catholic sympathizers as well. During this second stage of the Riots, there was still a general sense that this was a "licensed" mob fighting for a just cause, which was in part caused by the fact that the Whiggish City authorities, eager to show their defiance of George III and his government, conspicuously failed to undertake any action against the rioters. It was only when things got seriously out of hand that the Lord Mayor called in the Horse and Foot; at that stage, drunken mobs had attacked the Bank of England, burnt down and looted scores of private homes as well as a few distilleries, and had sacked several prisons, including the newly rebuilt Newgate Prison, and released the inmates.

The last major manifestation of an eighteenth-century mob was at Birmingham in 1791. Birmingham had long been a center for middle-class Dissent, and to the frustration of the King and Church party, Dissenters dominated the town's economy and politics, as well as its social and cultural life. The riots were allegedly provoked by a dinner organized on 14 July 1791 by well-to-do reformers—including many Dissenters—to celebrate the fall of the Bastille. For three days a marauding Church and King mob caused mayhem in the town, sacking two Unitarian meeting-houses and a Baptist one, looting and burning down scores of houses and shops of wealthy Dissenters, and releasing prisoners from the town gaol. The most prominent victim of the Birmingham mob was the Unitarian minister and Enlightenment philosopher Dr. Joseph Priestley, who appears in the novel as "Doctor Alogos." Priestley gained a reputation as a radical early on, when during the American War he came out publicly in support of the cause of the colonists. Later he espoused the campaign for parliamentary reform and the separation of church and state. It was probably his support for the French Revolution, which he hailed as a harbinger of liberty and reason, that attracted the fury of the Church and King mob.

Having first destroyed his church on High Street, the maddened rabble subsequently attacked Priestley's house. Unable to find any fire, they began to tear it apart with their hands: furniture and other movables were destroyed and thrown out into the street; the scientific equipment from his laboratory met a similar fate, as did his library of books and manuscripts (see Appendix B.4). In the novel Walker has the mob that attacks Doctor Alogos's property shout "liberty and equality," suggesting that it was a republican mob gone berserk, but in reality the cries of the mob that attacked Priestley's house ranged from "Church and King!" to "No Popery!" and "No Philosophers!" In fact, there is evidence to suggest that the mob not only had the protection of several prominent Tory magistrates and clergy, but that the looting was carefully orchestrated by a small number of ring-leaders, and even more carefully targeted, making sure it would strike specific members of the Dissenting community.[1]

It was quite common for anti-Jacobin writers in the 1790s to depict rioters as blood-thirsty *sansculotte* Jacobins, but in actual fact most mobs from 1792 onward were of the "hired band" type, employed by the government to terrorize English Jacobins. Prominent radicals like Thelwall and Priestley lived under the constant threat of physical violence from these Church and King mobs. It is therefore no coincidence that there was a marked increase in the number of radicals that left Britain and emigrated to America, especially after the anti-Jacobin reaction had begun to gain momentum in the course of 1794 (Treason Trials) and 1795 (Gagging Acts). Writing in 1795 in his journal *The Tribune*, John Thelwall reported that the "political and natural calamities" that had recently hit the country had triggered a "rage of emigration"; he estimated that in the summer of 1794 alone some 80,000 people had emigrated to America.[2] This figure

---

[1]   Thompson, *The Making of the English Working Class*, 79–80. Thompson concludes that the Birmingham Riots were "a discriminatory outburst, under the licence of a part of the local Establishment," aimed at taking down the Dissenting radicals a peg or two. See also Mary Cathryne Park, *Joseph Priestley and the Problem of Pantisocracy*, Diss. University of Pennsylvania (Philadelphia: Delaware County Institute of Science, 1947), 5–8.

[2]   John Thelwall, *The Tribune*, in *The Politics of English Jacobinism: Writings of John Thelwall*, ed. Gregory Claeys (1795; University Park: Pennsylvania State University Press, 1995), 69, xxv.

seems somewhat inflated and would in any case have included only a relatively small number of radical activists, but even so, emigration to America was very much part of the spirit of the age and hence became a widely discussed topic in the Jacobin –anti-Jacobin debate. Thus the decision of Joseph Priestley to settle in America in 1794 and build an agrarian utopia in the Pennsylvania wilderness was greeted with much enthusiasm by many a progressive idealist in Britain, including Samuel Coleridge, but it was derided by the anti-Jacobins, most notably by William Cobbett (see Appendix B). Generally speaking, the Jacobin writers tended to depict America as the ideal republic where Godwinian ideals of liberty, democracy, emancipation and the perfectibility of mankind could be realized; however, fearing massive shortages of skilled labor and dire social and economic disruption, the anti-Jacobins vehemently attacked the emigration movement, dismissing emigrants in pamphlets and broadsides as anti-patriotic traitors and vagabonds.[1] In the print-war that thus erupted, "America" became a crucial site of contestation where supporters of the "new philosophy" and detractors of Jacobinism met in discursive battle over Britain's cultural capital—staging, in effect, in America's imagined "backwoods" a British version of the French Revolution, which the increasingly repressive political climate at home prevented from

---

[1]   In its issue for May 1793 the *Gentlemen's Magazine* reported, "Several of our periodical publications have of late abounded with essays written to prove the superior felicity of American farmers, and to recommend our husbandmen to quit their native plains, and seek for happiness and plenty in the Transatlantic deserts" (*Gentlemen's Magazine* 63 [1793]: 401). The same periodicals, however, frequently carried essays warning against the dubious activities of British and American land-jobbers, who were trying to tempt potential emigrants to settle in the New World, and sell them land to which they held the rights. Thus, in September 1793 the *Gentlemen's Magazine* published a review abstract of *Letters on Emigration, By a Gentleman Lately Returned from America*, which, according to the reviewer, "contain[s] much good admonition to the several classes of men who are disposed to emigrate." Commenting on the large numbers of emigrants that returned to Britain destitute and disillusioned, the reviewer can only conclude that "this land of universal promise is the land of general disappointment" (*Gentlemen's Magazine* 65 [1793]: 760). The traveling gentleman himself ends his *Letters* on an equally dismissive note: "But, it may be asked, ought no description of persons to emigrate? The reply is obvious—The guilty *must*, and the very unfortunate *will*, though the prejudices of the natives are too apt to confound the latter with the former" (*Letters on Emigration* [London, 1794], 76).

taking place.[1] With the story set between c. 1780 (when the War of Independence was still very much undecided) and c. 1784 (when surviving members of Dr. Alogos's 'troop of philosophical vagabonds' return to England), *The Vagabond* is one of the most bitter, as well as one of the most entertaining anti-Jacobin diatribes against the transatlantic emigration movement.

A key figure in the emigration print war was the American Gilbert Imlay (1754?–1828?). A self-styled "Captain" in the American Revolutionary army, Imlay crossed the Allegheny Mountains sometime in 1783 to try his luck in the lucrative but risky land speculation business in the District of Kentucky. As in the case of Walker's "Citizen Common," Imlay's job as a land surveyor was but a thin disguise for his land-jobbing activities, which mainly involved tricking unsuspecting emigrants to part with their money in exchange for non-existing plots of land, or land that had already been claimed by other emigrants, or that was too poor to farm. In the early 1790s Imlay showed up in London, where he published *A Topographical Description of the Western Territory of North America* (1792), which described in rhapsodic terms the attractiveness of Kentucky as the ideal site for a reformist immigrant, being—in Citizen Common's words—"the most delectable spot on the face of the earth ... a second Arcadia, a continued scene of romantic delight and picturesque prospects." The *Topographical Description* was one of the most widely-read and influential pro-emigration tracts to appear in the 1790s, and it is therefore no coincidence that Citizen Common should cite a long passage from Imlay's text as the ultimate authority on Kentucky. Cashing in on his success, Imlay published *The Emigrants* in 1793, a novel that presents in a narrative format many of the ambitious claims made in the *Topographical Description*; perhaps most interestingly, *The Emigrants* offers us in its description of the community of Bellefont

---

[1] By the middle of the decade emigration to the New World had become so popular in radical circles that "America" had become a byword for an asylum for radical emigrants. Significantly, in his *A Political Dictionary* Charles Pigott defined the word "emigrant" as "one who, like Dr. Priestley or Thomas Cooper, is compelled to fly from persecution, and explore liberty in a far distant land, probably America"; the word "refugees" Pigott annotated as "English Patriots, as Dr. Priestley and his family, Mr. Cooper, of Manchester, &c. &c. who ... were obliged to quit a country pregnant with bigotry and persecution" (Charles Pigott, *A Political Dictionary* [London, 1795], 17, 113).

a vision of a wilderness utopia constructed on Godwinian notions of social and political justice and Rousseauesque sensibility (see Appendix A). Much of the emigration plot in *The Vagabond* is derived from Imlay's text, most conspicuously the Indian captivity narrative involving Laura. Although by the time Walker's novel appeared, Imlay had disappeared from the public eye and his name had become a by-word for a scheming liar and a con-man, in the middle of the decade Imlay's work had been seized upon by many as a blueprint for building a perfectible society in the pristine wilderness of the New World.

What gave the utopian emigration movement in the 1790s a considerable boost and turned it into a significant socio-political force was the fact that the protests against the suppression of civil liberties had joined forces with an older tradition of transatlantic agrarian utopianism. The idea of America as a modern Atlantis in the west was an old one—the product of the age of the early explorations and circumnavigations of the globe. But it was especially in the course of the eighteenth century that America began to fascinate European writers and thinkers, and, in ever-increasing numbers, travelers of one kind or another—tourists, scientists, traders, missionaries, adventurers—crossed the mountains and traversed the plains of the New World. When their accounts reached audiences in Europe, many recognized in their representations of the American landscape, its wildlife, and its natural inhabitants, the idealist-positivist belief in the perfectibility of life in a pristine environment.[1] Travel books like Captain Jonathan Carver's 1778 *Travels Through America*—the first popular American travel account and an international bestseller—inspired back-to-nature cultists to construct the notion of an American Golden Age. Even more influential was St. Jean de Crèvecoeur's *Letters from an American Farmer* (1782), which popularized the concepts of transatlantic pastoralism and primitivism all over Europe. Characteristically, Crèvecoeur's narrator, James, pretends to be a

---

[1]   For a discussion of the popularity of the American Golden Age in the Romantic period and its influence on the history of Romantic primitivism in general, and on Romantic literature in particular, see Robert Bechtold Heilman, *America in English Fiction, 1760–1800* (Baton Rouge: Louisiana State University Press, 1937), notably chap. 9, "Evolution of the Golden Age."

simple "farmer of feelings," and the book's anti-intellectualism and anti-industrialism recasts the Indians as "children of nature" or Noble Savages—uncivilized perhaps, but for that reason pure and innocent, because uncorrupted by the evils of society. Farmer James in the end prefers life "under the wigwam" to joining the American bid for independence: a choice of life that is echoed— and ridiculed—in Stupeo's preferring imprisonment in a rustic Indian cell to life in Britain.

British transatlantic utopianism from the 1770s through to the 1790s was deeply influenced by Jean-Jacques Rousseau's writings, particularly those on education, in which he defended "natural" simplicity and manly virtue as an alternative to "acquired," corrupt and effeminate aristocratic culture. Rousseau had popularized his ideas on education through his novels *Émile, ou l'Éducation* (1762)—a romance promoting education of children according to the "principles of nature" rather than those of society (experience, observation, physical exercise, and judgment, instead of knowledge and rational understanding)—and through his immensely popu- lar epistolary novel *Julie, ou La Nouvelle Héloïse* (1791), in which he exalts the virtues of sensibility (defined as the physical and emotional capacity for feeling) and the "natural man," as opposed to reason and man's social morality. Rousseau's ideas on education spilled over into the work of many British reformists and their utopian schemes. Thus, discussing the principles upon which chil- dren were to be educated in the American wilderness, Coleridge observed in October 1794, "The leading Idea of Pantisocracy is to make men *necessarily* virtuous by removing all motives to Evil— all possible Temptations."[1] An early convert to Rousseau's cult of sensibility, Mary Wollstonecraft produced a Rousseauesque novel, *Mary* (1788), in which she explores sensibility as both a liberating and a restricting force in a woman's life, before denouncing Rousseau's oppression of womankind through the cult of sensi- bility in her *Vindication of the Rights of Woman*. In the *Vindication* she forcefully dismissed Rousseau's insistence on a separate educa- tion for girls, geared toward what Rousseau saw as their future role

---

[1]   Samuel Coleridge, *Collected Letters of Samuel Taylor Coleridge*, ed. Earl Leslie Griggs, 4 vols. (Oxford: Clarendon Press, 1956–59), 1:65.

in life, viz. to be congenial companions to their husbands; instead, Wollstonecraft insisted on co-education for girls and boys (at least until the age of nine), and argues that outdoor gymnastics and physical exercise in general should be part of a girl's education, as well as a boy's.[1]

When Mary Wollstonecraft met Imlay in France in the spring of 1793, she was impressed by the American's appearance of an unspoiled child of nature—a kind of real-life Émile, grown up. They became lovers and for a while dreamt of acquiring a farm in the American backwoods and of a life of agrarian simplicity and independence—at least, Wollstonecraft did.[2] However, their relationship soon soured, and Imlay disappeared into oblivion, leaving Wollstonecraft behind an unmarried mother, until she met and later married Godwin (in 1797). Nor was Wollstonecraft's the only aborted utopian scheme by a British intellectual and radical. By far the best-known of such ill-fated emigration schemes was Samuel Coleridge's "Pantisocracy"—an experiment in human perfectibility which was to be created in pastoral seclusion in America, and which would be run on the principle of sharing property, labor, and self-government equally among all of its adult members, both men and women. The idea of a Pantisocracy was conceived by Coleridge and his friend Robert Southey in mid-1794, when the two poets were still undergraduates at Cambridge. Trying to decide on a site for the Pantisocracy, Coleridge and Southey thoroughly researched the "American Plan," and enthusiastically read several of the recent reports on the country's topography, including Brissot de Warville's *New Travels in the United States* (1792), Imlay's *Topographical Description* and Thomas Cooper's *Some Information Respecting America* (1794). The two latter texts were in fierce competition with each other, with Imlay tempting prospective emigrants to settle in Kentucky, where his land-jobbing interests were, and the reformer and abolitionist Cooper arguing instead for settlement in the idyllic Pennsylvanian hinterland on the banks of

---

[1] Rousseau's "enlightened system of education" is exposed in *The Vagabond* in the scenes describing the unfortunate birth and death of Laura's baby in the Kentucky wilderness (vol. II, chap. vi).

[2] See Mary Wollstonecraft, *Letters to Imlay*, ed. C. Kegan Paul (1879; New York: Haskell House, 1971), Letter XXXVI.

the picturesque Susquehanna River, which was the region where Cooper and his business associate Joseph Priestley Jr. were planning to found a utopian community (near Loyalsock Creek). It was the emigration of fellow-radicals Joseph Priestley and Thomas Cooper to Pennsylvania that finally persuaded Coleridge in October 1794 to opt for the banks of the Susquehanna. However, in the end the Pantisocratic scheme collapsed before it was put into practice. Rising land prices, disagreement between the two architects of the scheme, and lack of funds caused the "Pantisocratic Plan" to be shelved indefinitely by early 1795 (see Appendix A).

The Vagabond as an Anti-Jacobin Novel

First published in London in 1799, The Vagabond was an immediate popular success. In an age when the great majority of novels never made it beyond the first printing, The Vagabond rapidly went through two editions within six months of its publication, with a third one appearing before the turn of the century (see, however, A Note on the Text). The novel was reprinted again in 1800 (Dublin), and this edition was also used as the copy text for the first American printing (Boston, 1800). A second American edition appeared in 1814 (Harrisonburg,VA), and a French translation in 1814. Although these publication records make it one of the more popular novels of the day, The Vagabond never really made it into the history of the British novel.

Until a decade or so ago, literary histories of the British novel in the 1790s were dominated by histories of the Jacobin novel; that is, by novels written in the service of radical social and political reform, allegedly modeled after changes introduced in France in the wake of the Fall of the Bastille. Jacobin novelists had a firm belief in the perfectibility of society, which was reflected in their commitment to topics like social progress, reason, natural rights, individualism, political justice, liberty, democracy and equality, agrarianism, a written constitution, and separation of church and state. These ideas are reflected most typically in novels such as Thomas Holcroft's Anna St. Ives (1792–94) and Hugh Trevor (1794–97); William Godwin's Caleb Williams (1794); Robert Bage's Hermsprong (1796), and Mary Hays' Memoirs of Emma Courtney

(1796). Despite its traditional preponderance in literary history, virtually no Jacobin novels appeared after 1796. Conversely, the almost complete absence of the anti-Jacobin novel from the pages of literary history (until recently, at least) is in stark contrast to the steady increase of conservative fiction appearing between 1791 and 1805: after a slow start in the early part of the 1790s, the number of anti-Jacobin novels shot up in 1797–98, after which the production remained steady until 1805—totaling more than fifty explicitly conservative novels between 1791 and 1805.[1]

At first sight there is something curious about the timing of the rise of the anti-Jacobin novel, and of the anti-Jacobin movement in general. As Godwin is somewhat perplexed to observe in his *Thoughts occasioned by the perusal of Dr. Parr's Spital Sermon* (see Appendix A), "the flood of ribaldry, invective and intolerance" against his person and his writings had really only been unleashed properly in the course of 1797, when the reformists had all but given up their campaign and virtually no-one in Britain called themselves a Jacobin anymore. "What has happened since the spring of 1797 to justify [the anti-Jacobin] revolt?" Godwin wonders in *Thoughts occasioned*; "Has any new system of disorganization been adopted in France? Have the French embrued their hands in further massacres? Has another Robespierre risen, to fright the world with systematical, cool-blooded, never-satiated murder?"[2] However, even though none of the apocalyptic nightmares of conservative Britain had come true by the watershed year of 1797, there were sufficient reasons for the anti-Jacobins to feel threatened and to come out in full force against the specters of radicalism. Fear of a French invasion, for instance, was real and was kept alive by French attempts to land troops in Wales and Ireland in 1796, 1797 and 1798. Thus, in 1798 the Commissary General for the Southern District of England, Havilland Le Mesurier, published his *Thoughts on a*

---

1   See Grenby, *The Anti-Jacobin Novel*, 1–12. Published in 2001, Grenby's is the first book-length study of the anti-Jacobin novel to appear in print.
2   William Godwin, *Thoughts occasioned by the perusal of Dr. Parr's Spital Sermon, preached at Christ Church, April 15, 1800: being a reply to the attacks of Dr. Parr, Mr. Mackintosh, The Author of an Essay of Population, and others* (1801), in *Political and Philosophical Writings of William Godwin*, gen. ed. Mark Philp, 7 vols. (London: Pickering & Chatto, 1993), 2:168.

French Invasion, with Reference to the Probability of Its Success, and the Proper Means of Resisting It, which he opened with the warning, "The menace of a French Invasion, which formerly afforded a subject for ridicule, cannot now be treated in so light a manner."[1] The naval mutinies in the spring of 1797 and the Irish Rebellion of 1798 brought the threat of revolution closer to home and reminded the British that the nation was still being squeezed in a "Gallic hug."[2] The general feeling of insecurity and threat was whipped into regular paranoia and xenophobia by the publication in 1797 of two highly influential counter-revolutionary treatises, John Robison's *Proofs of a Conspiracy* and Abbé Augustin de Barruel's *Mémoires pour servir à l'histoire du Jacobinisme*, which reported on freemason-like secret organizations infiltrating the democratic institution in Europe.[3] Like these publications, the launch in 1798 of the *Anti-Jacobin Review*, which replaced the short-lived *Anti-Jacobin* weekly newspaper (1797), did more to *stir up* a frenzy of jingoistic fear among its conservative readers than it merely reflected such a fear.

In terms of their ideological outlook, the anti-Jacobin authors aimed to achieve the opposite of what the Jacobins (allegedly) were after: if the Jacobins were—in the words of Robert Bisset— enemies of "Christianity, and natural religion, of monarchy, of order, subordination, property and justice," then the anti-Jacobins

---

[1] Havilland Le Mesurier, *Thoughts on a French Invasion, with Reference to the Probability of Its Success, and the Proper Means of Resisting It* (London, 1798), 1. Fear of a French invasion reached an absolute peak in 1798 and this is reflected in the large number of pamphlets, sermons and treatises that appeared in that year, calling upon the population to be vigilant, prepare for evacuation and siege, and to come forward with voluntary contributions to finance the nation's defense. The anonymous author of *The Invasion; or, What Might Have Been* (1798) even based the entire plot of his anti-Jacobin novel on an imagined invasion of southern England by a foreign power.

[2] As is testified by *The Vagabond*, the bloody insurrection of the slaves against their masters on the West-Indian island of St. Domingo in July 1793 had caused a shockwave of horror that continued to reverberate through the British empire at the end of the decade.

[3] William Playfair had paved the way for these conspiracy theorists in 1795 with his highly successful *History of Jacobinism, Its Crimes, Cruelties, and Perfidies*, from which Walker quotes at several points in his novel. Playfair's influence reached as far as the United States, where his book was republished by the reactionary ex-patriot William Cobbett. Cobbett's own *History of the American Jacobins* initially appeared as the appendix to Playfair's book, but subsequently appeared as a separate pamphlet.

were their champions.[1] Although taken collectively, the anti-
Jacobin novels constitute a historically significant body of social
critique, they in fact reflect a motley array of different conservative aims and ideologies. Thus the early 1790s' focus on political
and constitutional issues shifted to a late 1790s' focus on moral
and religious issues; the social class of the revolutionaries and the
decadence of the *ancien régime* now seemed less culpable than
Reason itself. Most of the polemical anti-Jacobin novels
produced during the peak years of reaction, 1798–1801, satirize
the plot of the sentimental novel by placing their characters in
the context of undesirable contemporary events: as Nicola
Watson notes, the philosopher-villains of these novels are implicated in all manner of insalubrious activities, "from Irish rebellion to Illuminati meetings, from Methodism to methodical
spying-for-the-French, from reading German literature to over-
throwing Christianity" and are "notable for their strenuous
seduction schedules."[2] The characters of Marauder in Charles
Lucas's *The Infernal Quixote: A Tale of the Day* (1801) and
Frederick Fenton in *The Vagabond* (1799) are representative
examples of such villainy. Involved, respectively, in the Irish
Rebellion and the Gordon Riots, quoting to disastrous effect
from *The Rights of Woman* and *Political Justice*, and leaving a trail
of murders, these villains inhabit the sub-genre that A.D. Harvey
has identified as "fully-fledged polemics."[3] This form, which
includes D'Israeli's *Vaurien* (1797) and Elizabeth Hamilton's
Memoirs of Modern Philosophers (1800), is characterized by a high
degree of overt political discussion, and often the lampooning of
individual figures, notably Godwin and Wollstonecraft. Other
anti-Jacobin novels, while dismissive of reform ideology in
general, are not primarily works of political propaganda or
polemic; these include Charles Lloyd's *Edmund Oliver* (1798), Jane
West's *A Tale of the Times* (1799), Robert Bisset's *Douglas, or, The
Highlander* (1800) and Amelia Opie's *Adeline Mowbray* (1805).

---

[1] Robert Bisset, *Anti-Jacobin Review* 1 (1798): 223.

[2] Nicola J. Watson, *Revolution and the Form of the British Novel, 1790–1825* (Oxford: Clarendon Press, 1994), 71.

[3] Harvey, "George Walker and the Anti-Revolutionary Novel," 292, n. 2.

Marilyn Butler once suggested that if there was anything that defined the anti-Jacobin novelists as a group it was that none of them had "a distinctive talent" and that they each wrote "to a formula," using in each novel "the same structure, the same incidents, the same caricatured figures"; it was as if to the anti-Jacobin novelists the world of fiction and imagination "was itself anathema."[1] This so-called lack of aesthetic talent amongst the conservative novelists is certainly one of the reasons why literary history has been less than kind to the anti-Jacobin novel; more recently, however, critics have begun to reassess the nature and significance of the anti-Jacobin novel, and have begun to contextualize and valorize the novel's problematic aesthetics. Notably, present-day commentators tend to read the anti-Jacobin novel's aestheticism in the context of the booming market in the late 1790s for popular literature; the argument being that since the print-hungry and increasingly conservative reading public was eager to absorb large quantities of light-hearted and entertaining prose, that is what the anti-Jacobin hack-writers provided them with. The anti-Jacobin novel may not be an aesthetically innovative manifestation of the British novel, but its significance in cultural-materialist terms as a mirror of the ideological concerns and fears of a large section of British society should not be underestimated. And even while the influence of the market on the rise of the anti-Jacobin novel cannot be denied and a good deal of mere hack-writing was going on, the example of George Walker—a writer and publisher with a keen nose for what sold—suggests that at least for *some* conservative novelists, political motivation was more than skin-deep and anti-aestheticism something of a deliberate strategy.

It is not so much that anti-Jacobin writers had a "deep-seated contempt for novels," as is sometimes suggested,[2] or that they despised Jacobin novels because of their progressive political agenda, but that they had a conventional and fairly strict sense of literary decorum: for them, novels belonged to the realm of Neoclassical *belles-lettres*, *not* that of politics; it was the domain of

---

1   Butler, *Jane Austen and the War of Ideas*, 88.
2   Grenby, *The Anti-Jacobin Novel*, 12.

polite entertainment and moral instruction, not that of rational debate. Notoriously, it was William Godwin who, in his quintessential Jacobin novel *Caleb Williams* (1794), had first jumped the genre divide between fancy and philosophy, between romance and political treatise—as William Enfield was quick to note in a sympathetic review in the Jacobin *Monthly Review*: "Between fiction and philosophy there seems to be no natural alliance:— yet philosophers, in order to obtain for their dogmata a more ready reception, have often judged it expedient to introduce them to the world in the captivating dress of fable.... [*Caleb Williams*] is singularly entitled to be characterised as a work in which the powers of genius and philosophy are strongly united."[1] But in the eyes of novelists like George Walker, the very idea to write a "political romance," to disseminate and popularize *any* political ideas through novels, was suspect; characteristically, in his Dedication of *The Vagabond* to the Bishop of Llandaff, Walker apologizes for having been reduced to choosing *a novel* as the medium for his contribution to "the cause of Religion, Morality, and Liberty":

> but perhaps a *Novel* may gain attention, when arguments of the soundest sense and most perfect eloquence shall fail to arrest the feet of the *Trifler* from the specious paths of the new Philosophy. It is also an attempt to parry the Enemy with their own weapons; for no channel is deemed improper by them, which can introduce their sentiments.

It may then be ironic, but it is by no means surprising, that there should be such a strong resistance in many anti-Jacobin novels *against* being a novel in the first place: indeed, this resistance is so consistent and so deliberate that one could describe the anti-Jacobin novel as a species of *anti-novel*. Thus, in the case of *The Vagabond* the intrusive body of critical comment and polemical asides crammed into the footnotes in the third edition play a key part in Walker's strategy to undermine any reading of his book as a novel, or even as fiction. In one sense

---

[1] William Enfield, rev. of *Caleb Williams*, *Monthly Review* 15 (September 1794): 145, 149.

at least the anti-Jacobin novelist appears to have been bent on eradicating not only Jacobin politics but the Jacobin political romance as well.

If aesthetic excellence was not Walker's aim in *The Vagabond*, nor apparently was financial gain. Walker may have been a hack-writer when it came to churning out Gothic romances in the then popular style of Mrs. Radcliffe, but the writing of *The Vagabond*—his most explicitly political novel—was not motivated primarily by remunerative ambitions, despite what many critics in the past have claimed. Indeed, in the Preface to the third edition of the novel Walker resolutely sweeps aside what he considers to be the preposterous suggestion made to him to reprint the novel in "a *cheap* edition, which might be within the purchase of *all ranks.*" To Walker the mere thought of a cheap edition was tantamount to surrendering to the disingenuous ways of the Jacobin writers and their "Terrorist System of Novel Writing," enriching themselves by stirring up "the shirtless, shoeless *vagabonds*" to roam the country and burn "the castles and title-deeds of the proprietor," not for Liberty's sake but merely to put themselves in the place of the aristocrats they ousted. It is significant, given that he was a professional writer and publisher and with the market for conservative fiction at its peak, that Walker did not follow up on the commercial and popular success of *The Vagabond* with another anti-Jacobin novel. Instead, he returned to romance and branched out into poetry and children's literature.

The anti-Jacobins' intuitive distrust of the fluidity of literary form—particularly of the novel—is directly related to their fear of the mobility of ideas (hence their opposition to the corresponding societies) and of the social and physical mobility of individual citizens (hence their dislike of vagabonds and emigrants). It is this deep-seated anti-Jacobin fear of the new "communication circuit" of the 1790s (to use Robert Darnton's phrase) that prompted William Atkinson to lament in his aptly entitled pamphlet "An Oblique View of the Grand Conspiracy Against Social Order" (1798): "It is a well-known fact, that Hawkers and Pedlars of every description, have throughout Europe been employed to disseminate cheap Editions of Sedition; 20,000 of Paine's Rights of Men, were circulated in this way through the

North of Ireland; and one society ordered 12,000 copies of Paine's Letter to Dundas to be printed and distributed throughout Great-Britain."[1] The anti-Jacobin element in 1790s' British society may have covered a wide range of political and ideological positions (from anti-French conservatives, such as ArthurYoung, to various kinds of Whigs, including Edmund Burke and even Dr. Price), but what united them was their desire for society to be stable and predictable, not mobile, fluid and unsettled. More particularly, the conservatives were convinced that the Jacobins were destroying the "natural" order and time-honored fabric of society; supposedly, this order had been fostered and protected for generations, indeed centuries, by Christian morality (loyalty, trust, charity, faith and hope), by monarchy, and by such aristocratic values as moral and social "obligation," "generosity" and "honor." According to the anti-Jacobins, their opponents were trying to replace this "natural" order of society with a "mechanistic" order, which they commonly referred to as "New Philosophy" or "System." In contrast to the natural order, System was associated with speculative theory, abstract thought and boundless idealism, and was hence seen as unnatural, dehumanizing, and impractical. In terms of national identity, the natural order was identified as quintessentially "British" (being rooted in "common sense" and "experience" and hence "manly"), whereas System was frequently seen as "French" or "Gallic" (being both new-fangled and "effeminate"). Whereas the "systemisers," in Walker's phrase, believed that society, though presently in the grip of injustice and social evil, was susceptible to progressive improvement (man being rational and "perfectible"), the anti-Jacobins considered society in its present condition to be as perfect as human nature (being burdened

---

[1] William Atkinson, "An ObliqueView of the Grand Conspiracy Against Social Order; Or, A candid inquiry, tending to shew what part the Analytical, the Monthly, the Critical Reviews, and the New Annual Register, have taken in that conspiracy, By the author of A concise sketch of the intended revolution" (London, 1798), 4n. It is likewise no coincidence that John Thelwall chose the persona of a "peripatetic" in his three-volume excursion through multiple genres, with debates about the rights of men and women, the politics of class and race, patriotism and nationhood, and the conflicts of modern culture (see *The Peripatetic; or, Sketches of the Heart, of Nature and Society; In a series of politico-sentimental journals, in verse and prose, of the eccentric excursions of Sylvanus Theophrastus; Supposed to be written by himself* [London, 1793]).

with inherent flaws and weaknesses) would allow it to be. If for the new philosophers, liberty and equality were realistic and attainable objectives, the conservatives believed that it was the very *lack* of absolute liberty and equality that helped restrain and discipline human nature and foster moral responsibility and social solidarity through mutual dependency.

Walker's conservative agenda reveals itself in *The Vagabond* as an explicit and deep-seated *anti-modernity*. The novel is not only quite vehement in its dismissal of what it sarcastically calls the "eradicating beam" of the *new* philosophy, but it is also quite self-consciously, and uncomfortably, aware of being set in "this age of reason ... the eighteenth century." Walker evidently despises the age in which he lives; he not only totally rejects 1790s' radical thought and eighteenth-century materialist philosophy as propagated by Hume and the French *philosophes*, but is also in complete denial of the older heritage of Locke's and Newton's "system" of natural philosophy. In the late seventeenth century, Locke's thoughts on human nature and government and Newton's scientific discoveries (notably the principles of gravity and light) had turned the world—or "Nature"—into an oversized but neatly-arranged scientific show-case. This "Book of Nature" contained all that man needed to know and by studying it, he could discover the will of its creator, God, and His laws, the "laws of nature." "Natural law," "natural rights," and "natural philosophy" were the new principles upon which the eighteenth century had reshaped and modernized society. Thus Nature became deified and in the process God was denatured. Walker's universe, however, is that of orthodox Christianity and of the older tradition of "revealed religion," when God was still that slightly unpredictable, sometimes benevolent, sometimes wrathful God of the Old Testament, whose will was revealed through the Bible but who was otherwise basically a big mystery. Not surprisingly, Walker reveals himself to be a creationist and a firm believer in First Cause and divine Providence; in sharp contrast to "systemisers" like Stupeo, who believes in evolution, reason and a "doctrine of chance and skepticism" (of which he is only temporarily cured during a cataclysmic earthquake).

Although Walker's Preface prepares the reader for an attack

upon the doctrines of the *new philosophy*, we actually find him taking on not only people like Godwin, Wollstonecraft, Paine and Holcroft, but also French *philosophes* like Rousseau, Voltaire and Condorcet, natural philosophers like Priestley and De Buffon, and even, oddly enough, the writer, lexicographer and literary nabob Dr. Johnson (who once accused Priestley of "unsettling everything, and settling nothing"). Thus Walker attacks Hume on his skepticism (human knowledge is determined, or "necessitated," by the law of cause and effect; there is no afterlife; man has no soul); Rousseau on primitivism; Paine on republicanism and anarchism; De Buffon on evolutionism; Dr. Johnson on abstruse and artificial language—and Godwin on just about everything he ever wrote (from political justice and perfectibility to his views on education and manners as expressed in *The Enquirer*). For the reviewer in the Jacobin *Analytical Review* this was sufficient reason to accuse Walker of critical overkill (see Appendix C), but in fact what appears to be his encyclopedia of indiscriminate disgust reflects the depth and extent of conservative Britain's angst in the late 1790s.

Yet, although in general terms he certainly subscribed to this anti-Jacobin doctrine, in the final analysis Walker is not the arch conservative he is often made out to be. In his "Godwinian" novel *Theodore Cyphon*, for instance, Walker had already shown himself to be critical of the feudal aspirations, corruption, and immorality of part of the aristocracy, of their abuse of justice and curtailment of the civil liberties of others. The eponymous hero is as outspoken in his criticism of press-gangs as he is in his defense of the laws of the land—even if pulling up one of the local squire's young trees was punishable by transportation to Virginia (after all, he argues, it is those trees that will eventually provide the wood that builds the nation's houses as well as its fleets).[1] Similarly, in *The Vagabond* Walker rejects the activities of *all* mobs—not just Jacobin ones, nor is he entirely dismissive of the Dr. Priestley character Doctor Alogos: the latter may be misguided (having adopted the new philosophy out of frustration over a lost lawsuit),

---

[1]   See George Walker, *Theodore Cyphon; Or, The Benevolent Jew* (London: Printed for B. Crosby, 1796), vol. III, chap. ii.

but he is not evil (like Stupeo/Godwin). Several of Walker's spokesmen in the novel (such as the Justice of the Peace, and the surgeon in the dissecting room) reflect views on society that can be described as belonging, not to the political far right but to the political center—certainly the political center of the day.

Ultimately, the question where to position Walker in the political spectrum, and, by extension, what place in literary history to award to *The Vagabond*, has traditionally been determined more by the dominant trends of literary criticism, notably in the past few decades, than by a full analysis of the intrinsic qualities of either. Of course, Walker's conservatism was permeated with feelings of xenophobic panic and nationalist angst, but they were the feelings of most Britons at the turn of the century; of course, *The Vagabond* was to some extent a commercial venture written to cater for the popular demand for conservative fiction in the late 1790s, but was not *Caleb Williams* a similarly commercial project written to cater for a popular demand earlier in the decade for radical fiction? The recent increase in the critical interest in Mary Wollstonecraft and her circle in the 1970s ushered in the canonization of the Jacobin novel and the concomitant eclipse of the contemporaneous alternative—the anti-Jacobin novel.[1] Much of the rationalization of this critical bias was conceived, theorized and institutionalized in the decades that followed, leading to a one-sided and incomplete picture of what is known as the Romantic-era novel. Establishing a taxonomy for the Romantic-era novel may at this point in time still be problematic, but at least so much is clear, that a thorough revaluation of the anti-Jacobin novel can no longer be left out of such a project.[2]

---

[1] Claire Tomalin's *The Life and Death of Mary Wollstonecraft* (New York and London: Harcourt, Brace, Jovanovich, 1974), Marilyn Butler's *Jane Austen and the War of Ideas* (Oxford: Clarendon Press, 1975), and Gary Kelly's *The English Jacobin Novel, 1780–1805* (Oxford: Clarendon Press, 1976) are among the most influential shapers of the late-twentieth century canon of Romantic-era fiction. Grenby's *The Anti-Jacobin Novel* is part of the current revival of critical interest in the "other" Romantic-era novel.

[2] For a brief survey of the issues involved in mapping the full taxonomy of the Romantic-era novel, see Amanda Gilroy and W.M.Verhoeven, "The Romantic-Era Novel: An Introduction" (special issue of *Novel: A Forum on Fiction* 34.2: 147–62).

A Note on the Text

This edition of *The Vagabond* is based on the "third" English edition of the novel, which appeared in London in 1799, "Printed for G. Walker, No. 106, Great Portland Street, and Hurst, No. 32, Paternoster Row." The conventional phrase "printed for" in this instance appears to be but a thin disguise for the rather more incestuous nature of the publishing history of the novel. Earning a living through the book trade as well as through writing, George Walker was in fact novelist, publisher and bookseller all rolled into one. This fact alone should make us more than a little suspicious of Walker's assertions about the novel's printing record. If we are to believe the claim Walker made in the Preface to the "third edition" of the novel that "Two Editions [had] been sold in less than six months," the popular success of *The Vagabond* was immediate, widespread and sustained. Indeed, the novel was apparently such a commercial success that Walker resolutely swept aside what he considered to be the preposterous suggestion made to him (by fellow anti-Jacobin William Playfair) that he print the novel in "a *cheap* edition, which might be within the purchase of *all ranks.*" However, there are good reasons to be skeptical about Walker's claims.

Close scrutiny of the "first" and "second" editions of the novel suggests that we are in all likelihood dealing with a single edition, instead of two separate ones. Apart from the addition of the words "The second edition" on the title page, the "second" edition is identical to the first edition: nothing has been added or left out, and exactly the same printer's errors that occur in the first edition are still there in the second edition, including the most glaring and conspicuous ones. Given that the first and second editions are identical except for the title pages, it would appear, then, as if Walker was playing games with his readership—which was by no means uncommon in the era's buoyant print market. In the eighteenth century, type was immediately reused after each sheet was printed; it would have been too expensive to leave the type in place while waiting to see whether a first edition sold well or not. Especially because of the relatively ephemeral nature of popular fiction (as opposed to works of science, for instance), this would make it highly likely that the first and second edition of *The Vagabond* were printed from the same setting. The usual way that this trick was practiced was to simply print up a new title page and add it to the unbound copies left unsold in place of the old title page; it could then be readvertised as a second edition in an attempt to jump-start the sale. This type of publication is described by bibliographers as a reissue with a cancel title page, rather than a new edition. The English Short Title Catalogue (ESTC) lists only one copy of the second edition in the world, at Case Western Reserve University Libraries, Cleveland, Ohio (Shelfmark 823.69.W17s v. 1–2), and this suggests that very few copies of the second edition were ever in existence. It would certainly have been very cheap and easy for Walker to print a small number of second edition title pages.

What makes Walker's publishing ruse even more intriguing is that whereas the first and second editions of *The Vagabond* show Lee and Hurst, a legitimate London publishing house, in the imprint, along with George Walker himself, the third edition gives only Walker's name. This may suggest that sales for the first edition were poor, that the second edition trick was then tried, and that Lee and Hurst then bowed out because the book did not appear to them to be a winner. Evidently, Walker believed enough in the commercial potential of his novel to then move ahead with a legitimate third edition, completely reset, with many new notes added, as well as the rather self-indulgent preface.

The third edition corrects some of the printing errors of the first and second editions, but it also introduces new errors, particularly in the second volume; in addition, its punctuation is somewhat erratic, impulsive, and idiosyncratic. However, the third edition has been chosen as copy text for the present edition because it not only adds a number of brief passages to the text of the first and second editions, but, more importantly, it significantly expands the body of authorial commentary contained in the footnotes, in which Walker engages in a polemical debate with some of the novel's reviewers and adds further venom to his anti-Jacobin diatribe. Walker also added a new Preface to the third edition, in which he reaffirms his aversion to the new philosophy in defiant and vitriolic terms. In reproducing the text, this Broadview edition of *The Vagabond* retains the idiosyncrasies, obsolete usage and other irregularities in the original spelling, capitalization, and punctuation, even where these involve inconsistencies or minor errors. However, obvious printer's errors have been silently corrected against the first edition (such as "been" for "beeen"), as well as those idiosyncratic spellings that would otherwise obscure the meaning of the text (such as "olaginous" for "oleaginous"). All of these corrections are recorded in the list of "Silent Corrections." In addition, the eighteenth-century long *s* has been replaced by the modern *s* and the use of quotation marks has been regularized and adapted to modern usage. In the rare instances in which the third edition has dropped material from the earlier editions, this is restored in the present Broadview edition (all such amendments are recorded in the endnotes).

Walker's own notes to the novel have been retained. They are identified by asterisks and daggers, followed by editorial explanation and comment. All other editorial notes are numbered separately.

In all editorial matter (footnotes to the text of the novel, as well as notes to the Introduction and Appendices) full bibliographic details for primary and secondary sources are given only if these sources are not listed in the Bibliography.

List of Silent Corrections

The following is a list of silent corrections to the text of the third edition of *The Vagabond*. Unless otherwise indicated, these corrections have been made on the authority of the first edition. Corrections are identified by page number, followed by line number (in the present edition). Each note gives the reading of the Broadview text before the bracket, followed by the variant reading of the copy-text (the third edition).

VOLUME I

78.3   uttered, had] uttered had
84.6   Frederick] Frederic

90.25   said] "said
95.20   "but] but
97.26   "they] they
98.3   Hanover."] Hanover.
98.16   far."] far.
99.16   war."] war.
104.20 reason,] reason
108.5   "I beg] I beg
113.6   these?"] these
122.14 *universe."*] *universe.*
123.12 "'Tis] 'Tis
129.3   finger.] finger'

VOLUME 2

148.25   Frederick] Frederic
150.28   ayn't] a'n't
160.8   bellows] belows
163.35   bade] bid
167.22   "Oh!] Oh!
174.34   'Not] Not
180.11   spheroid] spheriod
180.22   oleaginous] olaginous
187.33   storm.] storm."
188.26   preserve] proserve
193.31   been] beeen
196.19   than] that
204, note horse] horses
215.4   three] threee
222.35   era] area
226.13   as happy] happy
240.6   species."] species.
240.13   but] "but
240.16   water.] water."

THE VAGABOND

Il retourne chez ſes Egaux.
Voyez la Note 13. p. 259.

"Il retourne chez ses Egaux," frontispiece, Jean-Jacques Rousseau,
Discours sur l'origine et les fondements de l'inégalité parmi les hommes
(Amsterdam, 1755). By courtesy of the John Carter Brown
Library at Brown University, Providence, Rhode Island.

THE

VAGABOND,

A NOVEL,

In two volumes.—Vol. I.

By

GEORGE WALKER.

Dedicated to the
LORD BISHOP OF LANDAFF.[1]

Third Edition, with Notes.

τὸ δίκαιον ἴσον ἀλλὰ μὴ τὸ ἴσον, δεῖν ποιεῖσθαι δίκαιον
Whatever is just, is equal; but whatever is equal is not always just.
PLUTARCH.[2]

The wayward nature of the time, and the paramount necessity of securing
to this kingdom her political and religious existence, and the rights of
society, have urged me to this endeavour to preserve them, by a
disinterested appeal to my countrymen.
PURSUITS OF LITERATURE.[3]

London:
Printed for G. Walker, No. 106, Great Portland
Street, and Hurst, No. 32, Paternoster Row.
1799.

TO THE
RIGHT REVEREND FATHER IN GOD,
WATSON,
LORD BISHOP OF LANDAFF,
THIS BOOK
IS HUMBLY DEDICATED.

My Lord,

In dedicating the present trifling performance to your Lordship, I am actuated by the same pride which glows in the bosom of a common soldier, who feels, and has at heart the success of his General. I am aware how insignificant are my attempts to follow the track of your Lordship in the cause of genuine Religion, Morality, and Liberty; but perhaps a *Novel* may gain attention, when arguments of the soundest sense and most perfect eloquence shall fail to arrest the feet of the *Trifler* from the specious paths of the new Philosophy. It is also an attempt to parry the Enemy with their own weapons; for no channel is deemed improper by them, which can introduce their sentiments.

I should not flatter myself the following Pages would ever be honoured with perusal, did I not know that no branch of Literature is left unexplored by your Lordship; and I might observe with the late Lord Orford,4 that Romances are only Histories which we do not believe to be true, and Histories are Romances we do believe to be true

I am, with the greatest Respect,

My Lord,

Your Lordship's most Obedient,

Humble Servant,

GEORGE WALKER.

PREFACE.

The following work is written with a desire of placing, in a *practical* light, some of the prominent absurdities of many self-important reformers of mankind, who, having heated their imaginations, sit down to write *political romances*, which never were, and never will be practical; but which, coming into the hands of persons as little acquainted with human nature, the history of mankind, and the proofs of religious authenticity, as themselves, hurry away the mind from common life into dreams of ideal felicity; or, by breaking every moral tie (while they declaim about morals), turn loose their disciples upon the world, to root up and overthrow every thing which has received the sanction of ages, and been held sacred by men of real genius and erudition.

Nothing is more easy, if we leave human nature and *commonplace* reason out of the question, than to write a system of jurisprudence, a perfect republic, a body of political justice, or a catalogue of rights: but a close attention to any of these works will readily bring forward glaring and palpable contradictions. What are the various classes of mankind to think, when these men not only *contradict themselves*, but every one has a system widely opposite to the other, agreeing only that every regular order and institution, religious, moral, and political, is worn out in this age of reason, and must be destroyed.

It may be right to apprise the reader, that the words *political justice* are scarce ever introduced, except when the sentiment is taken from Mr. Godwin's Political Justice, 4to. edition.[5]

No doubt those who feel themselves *sore* will endeavour to cast upon the work the charge of exaggeration; but, on this subject it is *impossible* to exaggerate; so inimical are the doctrines of Godwin, Hume, Rousseau, &c. to all civil society, that, when the reader candidly reflects, he will perceive that the inferences I have drawn from *their* texts naturally result.[6]

Can we wonder at the prevailance of adultery, when doctrines such as these men hold out in *fascinating language*, are tolerated? Can we wonder at the vices and crimes of a neighbouring people?

Or, can we wonder that the generality of *shallow*-thinking men, embrace and support them with ardour?

Many of the modern reformists, amongst the most forward, Mr. Pain,[7] asserts, that there is no such existence as a British Constitution. Let those men and their adherents peruse De Lolme[8] on that subject; let all who are repining at their lot read that excellent work, and they will perceive the singular blessings they enjoy, which, because they are familiar, are despised; and let us not act like men in health, who undermine their constitution by excess, till sickness teaches them the inestimable value of what they have unthinkingly and irreparably destroyed.

PREFACE

TO THE

THIRD EDITION.

It has been suggested to me to print a *cheap* edition, which might be within the purchase of *all ranks*, and tend to open the eyes of many deluded followers of the *new* philosophers. But though this work was written from the most ardent desire of warning the world of the intentions and tendency of jacobinical principles, there are *two* reasons for my objecting to this advice:—First, as Mr. Playfair says in his excellent History of Jacobinism, "He who *pleaded* the cause of murder and plunder, *saw his* work distributed by thousands and hundreds of thousands, and himself enriched; while he who endeavoured to support the cause of law, of order, and of the proprietor, had his bookseller to pay, and saw his labours converted into waste paper. It is true that he had the consolation of his own mind, and the esteem of the few to whom his intentions were known; but with regard to effect upon the public mind it produced none: his main object was therefore unattained, and the revolutionary argument remained triumphant.—With energy, some money, and a disposition to make use of it on one side; and on the other, indolence with pecuniary means in abundance, but not the *will* to employ one shilling of it: can we be surprised that things went in favour of those who had the energy and the will? It would have been surprising if it had not: and accordingly we have seen the shirtless, shoeless *vagabond*, burning the castles and the title-deeds of the proprietor, and with an high hand put themselves in the place. Let the rich ask, Which side will have most writers, those who pay, or those who do not?"[9]—Secondly, through the medium of Circulating Libraries, any man may read the work for much less, than though it were printed on paper like the Rights of Man.[10]

In the present instance, however, I cannot speak from what I have experienced, and it gives me considerable hopes that the destructive torpor of the rich is evaporating, and that they begin to take an active interest in the present crisis: I have only to observe, that Two Editions have been sold in less than six months.[11]

Mr. Playfair, when he is speaking of the diffidence, and distrust, and jealousy, and indifference of the different nations, says: "But if they will not prepare seriously to resist, they must prepare to suffer; for France will give law to Europe if she once gets the better, and then adieu to those Principalities and Powers who have quarrelled about useless etiquette, when they should have rivalled each other in MANLY COURAGE: and who will continue in all likelihood to dispute about their rights and privileges, till there remain none for them to dispute about."[12]

It is here that the conduct and character of Great Britain *deserves well* of mankind. But for the energy of this nation, Europe would, ere this, have been *squeezed* to pieces with the *Gallic hug*: and this country would have swelled its bloated pride.—But the VOLUNTEERS[13] have saved the nation. They have told France, that before she can *plunder and burn London, that selfish and shop-keeping city*, according to the threat of Barrere,[14] she must float in the air, and march through a forest of pikes and bayonets. They have told the French Propagande that we are not to be cajoled with flatteries and lies to believe a people, who conquer more by these means than by the sword; and they have told the idle and rebellious, that they cannot hope for success. While we remain firm to ourselves, we may suffer much, but cannot be brought under the yoke of France.

CONTENTS.

THE

VAGABOND.

CHAPTER I.

THE MEETING OF TWO REPUBLICAN PHILOSOPHERS.

One fine summer evening Doctor Alogos walked out to the banks of Wynander Meer, to enjoy the beautiful scenery surrounding, and reflected in the mirror of the crystal lake.

"This is charming," said he to himself, as he walked onward; "the harmony of nature is visible in every object round me; the clouds form a majestic and ever-varying canopy; man alone deviates from that pure state of existence he knew in the golden age; man alone is unhappy; his passions and his appetites in society know no bounds short of attainment; and why? because he will not copy the example of unerring nature in her conduct of animals. These never deviate into rapine and outrage—they live free, and are happy."

At that moment he heard a noise in the air, and, looking round, distinguished an hawk in full pursuit after a lapwing. The harmless creature fluttered, and appeared nearly exhausted, while the bird of prey redoubled his exertions.—Doctor Alogos, who usually walked with a fowling-piece for his amusement, brought the hawk down at a shot; and the lapwing, as if to thank him, settled near upon the ground. In a little time it recovered from its fright, and a fine worm creeping before it fell a prey to *instinct*.

The Doctor mused on this subject as he continued his walk.—"At worst," said he, "this is only a partial evil, and does not interrupt the harmony of the universe; it is only matter changing form, and making room in the great field of nature for new existences; if we had no hawks, in twenty years the whole surface of the earth would be covered with lapwings; and if we had no lapwings, the whole globe would be so over-run with worms, that, like a Cheshire cheese filled with mites, the crusting would crumble away. It is necessary the stronger animals should prey upon the weaker, and quite in the order of things: but for men to murder each other is very different, and arises from an unjust accumulation of property. Oh happy times when *property* was unregarded, when no tyrant could plant his foot upon an acre of ground, and repulse his fellow from the sod! Property! property! thou art the bane of earthly good, an ulcer in society, and a cancer in the political œconomy."

As the Doctor stamped his foot on the ground in the attitude of an orator, heated with the idea of revolution and equality, a young man in a very ragged dress leaped from a thicket of hazels, and, holding a pistol to the Doctor's breast, demanded his money.

The Doctor's piece was unloaded, or his benevolence for the human species might have been lost in the agitation of surprise; but making a full pause, and gazing at his antagonist—"This," said he, "is not right in the nature of things; force tells me that your argument is wrong: you should have first convinced me of your wants, and then my purse would have been your just property."

"All property is a monopoly," cried the young metaphysician, "and the most laconic arguments are best: these rags which I wear are sufficient vouchers for my wants; and unless you can prove that some other has a greater claim to your property, I must have the contents of your pocket."[15]

"You are a philosopher," said the Doctor.

"Yes," replied the youth; "my dear Stupeo used to tell me so: but philosophy is not rewarded in the present detestable system of things; virtue is ridiculed, and vice rides in gilded coaches."

"How much do you need?" said the Doctor, in transport. "You are a pupil of the *new school*; come along with me, and you shall find me a man who will esteem you exactly according to the quantity of merit you possess; your talents ought not to be thus lost."

"Stupeo was perfectly right," said the youth, "he told me that all men are equal: I will go with you."—"Who is this Stupeo?" inquired the Doctor, while the young man walked by his side. "He was a very great philosopher, a mythologist, a metaphysician, and a scholar: he was my tutor at college."

"You a collegian!" cried the Doctor, in surprise; "how came you in this miserable condition, and how could you commit such an act of dangerous outrage?"—"From the most natural reason in the world; all crime, my dear Sir, arises from some possessing what others want: but in fact, there is no such thing as crime; it is a mere chimera, existing only in the law, like John Doe and Richard Roe."[16]

"There surely are crimes," interrupted the Doctor, "crimes against political justice, and the liberty of the individual: as for instance, I have, as a willing animal, a right or power to take a walk; but if I am to be assassinated every time I go out, my liberty is restrained, my house becomes a prison, and I might as well be in a dungeon. I think crimes of this nature ought to be punished."

"How? By coercion or restraint?—My dear Stupeo used to say that punishment is a specious name, but is in reality nothing more than force, put upon one being by another who happens to be stronger. How can truth be promoted by this? If I am hanged for what is called a robbery, how am I convinced of my error? And it is the reform of the individual you should seek, and not the punishment of an action partial in its nature."[17]

"You are wrong," said the Doctor; "the offender ought to be restrained as long as the safety of the community prescribes it; for this is just: restrain him not an instant from a simple view to his own improvement, for this is contrary to reason and morality."*

"But, my dear Sir," cried the youth, warmly, "Stupeo, who was a philosopher and a metaphysician, says—"

"Says a fiddlestick," retorted the Doctor, "it is the good of the whole we are to seek; what signifies individuals? they are as mites in the universe. Truth, truth must be propagated, and I glory to see we are making such rapid progress."

---

* See page 132 and 161 of Political Justice, where the two last contradictory absurdities will be found verbatim. [Editor's note: The "verbatim" citation from page 132 of the first edition of William Godwin's Enquiry Concerning Political Justice (1793) occurs in Book II, Chap. vi: "Punishment is a specious name, but is in reality nothing more than force put upon one being by another who happens to be stronger" (Political Justice, ed. Philp, 78). There is no verbatim parallel between Walker's text and Godwin's on page 161 of Political Justice; instead, Walker in this paragraph loosely paraphrases parts of Godwin's text.]

They were by this time arrived at the gate of a neat-looking mansion, with high chimneys and heavy cornices, which declared it to have been erected in the time of William the Third,[18] a flower garden spread before it, in which a beautiful young woman was gathering flowers. She appeared about eighteen, with all the innocence of that period, and the beauty attending upon health and good nature.

"Your daughter, I suppose?" said the stranger.

"No," replied the Doctor; "do you think I would belie my principles by uniting myself for life to any object, when the human mind is of so changeable a nature?—She is my niece; her parents, who were very poor and very ignorant, are dead. I attempted to educate her on my plan; but she is of a perverse disposition, she will not exert the divine privilege of resistance, and throw off the shackles of domination: she persists that the very difference of sexes should teach us that they are designed for different pursuits."

"Laura," cried the Doctor, "have you set my room in order? I have brought home a stranger."

"No," replied Laura, blushing; "I was obliged to visit a poor old woman in the village; and I intended, as soon as I had gathered some flowers, to arrange your apartment."

"The d—l take all the old women in the universe," cried the Doctor, in a passion, "with their diseases and their wants! What had you to do, you idle slut, with gathering flowers, when all my room is covered with litter? What a wretched state is society!—every thing thwarting the temper, and spoiling our reflections."

"In a state of nature," said the young stranger, "we should certainly have fewer wants. The pleasant spring would supply us with drink, and the mast of the forest with food. How happy would it be if all mankind, by universal consent, would destroy every vestige of society, and return to simple nature!"

"Nothing more true," cried Doctor Alogos, taking his hand and leading him towards the house; "you seem a youth of profound intelligence, and I glory in having discovered such a gem. All the children of men are dear to my heart; and my indignation boils when I hear that our brethren of Africa are urged to labour with a lash—torn from supreme felicity—carried from the yellow sands of Guinea to the burning furnace of the West-Indies—and all for what? to supply us spices and sweetmeats. I could hug a Tartar to my breast, and divide my little property with a Greenlander."

A wounded soldier at that moment accosted them from the gate, entreating a morsel of bread, or a farthing to buy it with.

The Doctor's countenance reddened, and turning round— "Go," cried he, "to your parish; for what do I pay so many poor's rates,[19] if my purse is to be always open to such vagrants? In a state of nature there is no necessity for soldiers; and I am determined I will not support the present infamous system." So saying, he slapped the door in the soldier's face; and leading his new friend up stairs, they entered an elegant apartment, the furniture of which was in a style of the greatest luxury.

"Is supper ready?" inquired the Doctor of a servant girl, who entered the room to place his chair.—"It won't be ready this half hour," replied she, pertly: "if you want it sooner, you must come and help to get it yourself."

"Go along, you baggage," said the Doctor, laughing. Then turning to his guest, "This," said he, "is a girl of independent spirit, the genuine equality for which I admire her. If my niece were a little more of her disposition, I should be extremely fond of her—not for herself, because I am above all those false notions of relative connection, but for her virtues."

Supper was soon after served in a style that would have gratified an epicure. The Doctor declaimed, between every bite, on the virtues of temperance and the beauties of nature.—The young man ate little, being engaged with the beauties of Laura: and the latter was much abashed by the company of a stranger, who, though in a garb that declared present poverty, had yet a nobleness of physiognomy, which shone forth beneath the cloud that enshrouded him.

Having sufficiently satisfied the demands of nature and appetite, the Doctor ordered his niece to retire; and having replenished the table with wine, which he observed was taxed in an infamous manner, he requested the stranger to relate the outlines of his history.

CHAPTER II.

THE PROGRESS OF TRUTH AND PHILOSOPHY
IN AN IGNORANT MIND.

My name is Frederick Fenton. I might perhaps be ashamed to mention my family, when you see me in these miserable garments; but truth must be spoken without regard to those false prejudices, which call folly by the name of honour.

My parents have great landed possessions, that is, are great tyrants, in the county of Kent. They educated me in all the superstitions of the Protestant church, and my whole study was to conform to their desires, and restrain my wishes to the line of what they called rectitude and religion.

I was so grossly ignorant, as to believe that disobeying them was displeasing to the Almighty; and I considered religion as a sure means of leading me to a better world, and making me hereafter happy: but these were the dreams of unenlightened imagination, impressed upon me by education.

Learning appeared in my eyes the greatest object of human attainment; and my parents delighting in my progress, my whole powers were bent to the acquirement of what they called valuable knowledge.

I did not then know that profound ignorance is the real and only state in which men can enjoy felicity; and that every advance from this is so far diverging from the intention of nature.

I was never easy under the neglect of a duty, because I either feared the censure of my parents, or the vengeance of an offended deity: and I refrained for these reasons from committing any of those actions false morality particularly considers atrocious. So eager was my application to study, and so tenacious my memory, that at fifteen I was judged capable of commencing student in form.

I took leave of my parents with tears; and my bosom seemed to lose its tranquillity at parting with a youth nearly my own age, and who had been my friend and companion from infancy. Vernon was not less affected; and we vowed eternal amity at our separation.

At the recommendation of a nobleman, the divine Stupeo[20] became my preceptor. He was a person of mean birth; but that distinction I despised, seeing in him only a man of talents.

He began his plan of education, with starting[21] bold truths, which shocked and dazzled me with their lustre, without confounding my perceptions. "I will not," said he, "overwhelm you at once with the whole blaze of knowledge, though I would as little wish to lead you step by step, as though I would surprise you to an acquiescence with truth: immortal truth can never lose by being seen; it bears down every barrier; it is a mighty torrent; it may be stayed for a while, but the acceleration of its rapidity will increase in equal ratio."

At first I ventured to observe, that the human mind is too often led into error by a deception of the senses, which are ever ready to adopt any new object however absurd. His eloquence, which was like the torrent he described, soon overcame my weak objections, and the first gleam of truth and philosophy dawned upon my soul.

He lamented the profound obedience I paid to my parents. "My dear pupil," said he, "what is this bondage you call duty? And what right have these beings you call father and mother to direct your actions, and controul the inborn vigour of your soul?"

"By the claim of nature; by the trouble they have taken for my preservation; and by the love they bear me in particular," said I.

"Unjust in extreme!" cried he. "Do your parents love you for your real value?—No! it is aristocracy, self-love, and family pride that teach them to set a value on you. No human being ought to be preferred because that being is my father, my wife, or my son;* it is the good of the whole we should endeavour to promote. And what is your claim of nature? Are not all men born free? Children can be no longer connected with their father, than while they stand in need of his assistance. When this becomes needless, the natural tie is of course dissolved, the children are exempted from the obedience they owe to their father, and the father is equally so from the solicitude due from him to

---

* Political Justice. [Editor's note: See Godwin, *Political Justice*, Book II, Chap. ii ("Of Justice"), *passim*.]

his children; both assume a state of independence respecting each other."*

"But gratitude," replied I, "would seem to inspire reverence and esteem."

"Gratitude!—Nonsense," answered he; "I ought to esteem a benefactor, not because he has done a kindness to me, but because he has done it to an human being."†

"But if what my parents request is for my own advantage, surely there can be no crime in obeying?"

"Of that you are the best judge: if the action be good, it should be done because it is so, and not because certain persons have requested or commanded you to do it. But even this you ought to doubt: to doubt is the first step to be a great philosopher, and the more you doubt, the more real knowledge you are possessed of. For instance, you will call that an apple lying on your table because it appears so: but you must doubt it; your eyes, your taste is fallible—it may be an orange, or it may be nothing—it may be any thing."

"It may not be a church or the Alpine mountains," said I.

"But you must not believe it to be neither, for those who believe *any thing* certainly are fools."‡

"I am convinced," said I. "I doubt whether I ever had a father, or ever was born: I will no longer be held in the leading-strings of obedience."

Youth has a natural passion for entertainment; and having now cast off the trammels of parental admonition, I determined to enjoy those moments which my dear Stupeo taught me would never return. "How few are our years, and of those years how few are allowed to pleasure!" would he say. "Grasp then, my pupil, the moments as they fly, for all beyond this life is annihilation and non-entity: dry and barren study is well enough for muddy souls, but not for those who know how to live."

*   Rousseau. [Editor's note: These ideas are expressed in Jean-Jacques Rousseau's *Social Contract* (1762), Chap. II ("First Societies"), 46.]

†   Godwin. [Editor's note: See Godwin, *Political Justice*, Book II, Chap. ii ("Of Justice"), 51.]

‡   Hume on Human Nature, vol. i, page 168. [Editor's note: See David Hume, *Treatise of Human Nature* (1739), Book I, Part iv ("Of the Sceptical and Other Systems of Philosophy"), Section 2 ("Of scepticism with regard to the senses").]

It is surprising with what conviction truth flashes upon the mind:—Stupeo's axioms were unrefutable, and I found the superiority of pleasure over all the laborious and musty researches of learning, which never satisfy a doubting philosophic mind.

I confess I ran into a few eccentricities, such as breaking the leg of a waiter in a drunken frolic—getting a fever by a surfeit—and spending my salary before it became due: but these are the necessary attendants on this miserable system of things. We are so enervated with *drinking tea*, that we cannot withstand the power of fixed air in fluids: and the monopoly of property prevents our spending more than we can acquire.

These reflections naturally led me to abhor tyranny of every kind. It is singular how we imbibe great truths, when once the mind doubts of every thing. The genius of liberty shone resplendent in mine eyes, and I groaned at the sufferings of my fellow men. I saw that no possible right could bind any man in slavery. What power had any generation of men to sell their posterity (no matter who bought them)? When had I *given my consent* to the government I lived under? Never; and therefore to me it was as *absolute* a despotism as any under the sun.* It was no consequence to me that it might be just and well administered; to me it was a tyranny. I confess there seemed a trifling argument against this *new truth*; for it seemed a matter of difficulty, that the government should be sending to every individual, as he attained certain years, to know if he approved their establishment. But in the best of systems there is always some little defect, and surely Voltaire, Rousseau, Tom Paine, and the metaphysician Stupeo, knew which was for the best.[22] "I even doubt," said the latter, "whether the very article of our birth be not a great breach of political justice, since our consent was not required."

He was a most exquisite reasoner; I remember him expatiating one day on the happiness of natural liberty: he kindled into enthusiasm on the subject. "War," cried he, "that destroys our vitals, and in one moment silences eloquence, genius, and every virtue with

---

* Pain. [Editor's note: Thomas Paine, *Rights of Man: Being an Answer to Burke's Attack on the French Revolution* (1791), "Miscellaneous Chapter," 144-45.]

the howlings of misery, murder, and despair, would never exist but for the machinations of monarchs. When did you ever hear of republics going to war? what have they to fight about?"*23

"Did the Tyrians, the Grecians, the Romans, the Carthaginians never go to war?" said I. But Stupeo knew his ground too well to be stopped by so *trifling* a question: he continued—"The reciprocal relations of mankind, while living together in their primitive independence, were not sufficiently durable to constitute a state either of peace or war, so that *men* cannot be naturally enemies. It is the relation subsisting *between things*, and *not between men*, that gives rise to war; which arising not from *personal* but *real* relations, cannot subsist between man and man, either in a state of nature or in a state of society, in which every thing is secured by the Laws.† Thus it being evident, that as men never can be at variance with men, for as much as no savages in a state of nature ever fight; it follows, that war never could happen, but for the

---

* It may not be unworthy observation, that the French *Republic* has conquered *all* the little *republics* round them, and only the two monarchies of Sardinia and Naples [remain unoccupied. (text corrupt)] [Editor's note: This is a reference to France's territorial expansionism in the 1790s, when several neighboring independent states and republics were systematically occupied and later annexed by the French. Among the nations that met this fate were the Dutch Republic (which became the Batavian Republic in 1795); the Republic of Genua (which became the Ligurian Republic in 1797); and the Swiss Republic (which became the Helvetian Republic in 1798). In addition, the Austrian Netherlands were annexed in 1795 and the Dukedom of Milan was transformed into the Cisalpine Republic in 1796. The Kingdom of Sardinia, mentioned here by Walker as an independent nation, was overcome in stages. It had already lost the provinces of Savoy and Nice to France in 1796 when, in 1798, the Kingdom's central province of Piemont (including the capital Turin) was brought under French military rule. The last remaining part of the Kingdom, the island of Sardinia, remained independent. The Kingdom of Naples, apparently still independent when Walker added this footnote to the third edition of the novel, became a satellite state of France in the course of 1799.]

† This inconsistent sentence makes a brilliant figure in the Social Contract. The reader is not to be surprised if he finds these great men contradict themselves in the course of the work; if they did not, they would not be modern philosophers. [Editor's note: The alleged inconsistency in Rousseau's *Social Contract* appears to exist in the English translation Walker was citing, rather than in the original. A modern translation of the passage reads, "It is the relationship of things, not of men, that constitutes a state of war, and since the state of war cannot be engendered merely by personal relationships but only by relationships between things, a private war between man and man cannot exist—either in the state of nature, in which there is no permanent possession of property, or in the social state, in which everything is controlled by laws" (*Social Contract*, 51).]

quarrels of a set of tyrants, who lead men into the field of battle to butcher each other with their eyes shut." "Then man becomes a mere machine?" said I.

"Man a machine!" said he, with ardour: "man is a sublime animal; the great lord of creation: 'tis true his soul is nothing but an heap or collection of different perceptions, or objects, united together by *certain relations*, and supposed, though falsely, to be endowed with perfect simplicity and identity. If any one, upon serious and unprejudiced reflection, thinks he has a different notion of himself, I must confess I can reason with him no longer: he may perhaps perceive something simple, and continued, which he calls *himself*, though I am *certain* there is no such principle in me. But setting aside some metaphysicians of this kind (who believe they have a soul), I may venture to affirm of the rest of mankind, that they are *nothing* but a bundle or collection of different perceptions, which succeed each other with inconceivable rapidity, and are in a perpetual flux and movement."*

"But," said I, "you tell me you are *certain* you have no soul, and yet you lay it down as a maxim, that we are not to be certain of any thing. This is sure a contradiction. Beside, if this bundle of ideas is always changing, and never the same, what is memory? How am I conscious that I ate my breakfast this morning, and got drunk last night?"

"'Tis merely in idea," replied he; "you cannot be certain you did either. All ideas are only slighter impressions than realities, and there is no other difference between reality and idea."†

"Then," said I, "the idea of an inch, must be an inch long, and

---

* Hume on Human Nature, vol. i, page 361 and 438. [Editor's note: The passage, "is nothing but an heap or collection of different perceptions, or objects, united together by *certain relations*, and supposed, though falsely, to be endowed with perfect simplicity and identity," is a verbatim citation from Hume's *Treatise of Human Nature*, although Hume is talking about the mind, not the soul (Book I, Part iv, Section 2, 206). The passage, "he may perhaps perceive something simple ... in a perpetual flux and movement" is also a verbatim citation from Hume (Book I, Part iv, Section 6, 252).]

† Hume on Human Nature, vol. i, page 361 and 438. [Editor's note: Despite the page references, this is a non-specific reference to Hume's "general proposition" concerning the origin and nature of ideas, viz. "That all our simple ideas in their first appearance are deriv'd from simple impressions, which are correspondent to them, and which they exactly represent" (4).]

of a mile, a mile long. If I have an idea of a roaring lion, or a thunder storm, I shall hear the sounds, only in smaller degree. I have an idea of two bottles of brandy, and the impression will surely equal the effect of two bottles of wine; but do I feel any actual difference between an idea of the frozen pole or the bowels of Mount Etna? am I colder or warmer for either? Does the idea of a bombardment lay me dead upon the plain? which it must do if it were as you say, that reality and idea are in every respect the same, except that the former strikes with more force than the latter."*

"You will *believe* every thing I have said," he answered, "if you *doubt* your own understanding; and nothing is more fallible than human reason, or more certain than immutable truth."

In this new path of philosophy I made so much progress, that I soon ceased to trouble myself with the jargon of the schools; Aristotle, Grotius, and Puffendorf appeared as so many children, and even the great Locke, but an infant in science.[24] Latin and Greek became the most insipid of studies; and in fact my moments were too precious to be wasted on such trifles.

My father wrote me several letters expressive of his grief at my change of principles, and hinting that he would discharge Stupeo, if I attended to his infernal doctrines.

"And so," cried the great logical metaphysician, "you will stoop to the domination of this man, who wishes to cramp the divine impulses of your soul, to torpedo your faculties! Other tyrants would be content with governing your body; but this man, who calls himself your father, would depress the energies of your soaring spirit, and tear it down from beholding the splendid sun of reason and truth, to walk in the common track of plodding men."

What reasoning could be more just, or delivered in more eloquent terms? I wrote in reply, that my mind was free, that I detested controul, and would not submit to the directions of any tyrant, however distinguished by name.

My father returned me an answer in the mildest terms: he requested me to consider how much attention he had bestowed

---

* See Beattie's excellent Treatise on Truth. [Editor's note: James Beattie (1735-1803), professor of moral philosophy and logic in Aberdeen, from 1760 to 1793. He gained national fame (as well as clerical sympathy and a royal pension) with his *Essay on the Nature and Immutability of Truth* (1770), a blunt attack on David Hume's doctrine of skepticism.]

upon me in my early years. He asked how I should think of the man, who should return any favour I did him, with equal neglect and contempt. He entreated me to consider if any of his former advice had been in any ways detrimental to my own welfare; and to reflect, that no possible advantage could arise to him from my proceeding in a virtuous life, except that of beholding one whom he had been a means of bringing into the world, an honour to his country, to human nature, and to himself. He concluded with entreating me to meet him at a certain house upon the road, where he would communicate to me matters of great importance; and should set out from home (though very unwell) the moment he received my promise to meet him.

Stupeo was on a party of pleasure when I received this letter. I am almost ashamed to own the impression it made upon me, though it is all in the old-fashioned style; but we cannot at once wholly overcome every prejudice of education.

I wrote immediately, that I would attend at the place appointed. I delayed till Stupeo arrived. He was surprised to find me ready for a journey, and more so when I informed him of the particulars.

"Weak, puerile, and inconstant man," cried he, "you resolve in one hour what you undo the next. It was either fitting that you should yesterday have bowed to the commands of your father, or it is not fitting to-day: time cannot change a moral action. What is it he requires? To bend you to his will—to make you the passive tool of his power: He would persuade you all he has done was for your sake. Who are you? an individual! his property!—A master gives physic to his slave, and pretends he has no interest in doing so. Nonsense! it is the good of the whole he should seek."

"But I have *promised* to meet him; and I would not willingly forfeit my word."

"All promises are morally wrong, and ought not to be kept. The action to be done, is either right or it is wrong. If it is right, it should be done without an eye to a promise; and if it is wrong, no promise can make it right. For instance, I send word to a merchant I shall meet him on 'Change, and I find more pleasure in some other excursion, or some action of greater good (in my mind) appears for me to do.[25] I ought not to meet the merchant;—his inconvenience I am ignorant of, and I can no more be said to be accountable for any thing he shall suffer from the disappointment, than I am guilty of murder for not being on a trial at Newcastle, when I knew of no such trial, though my evidence should have saved the man. All that can be said is, that people would then in these cases depend more upon themselves, and less upon others."[*]

"But," said I, "how is business to be done, if no man has a certainty of meeting with those he has to transact some concern of the first importance with?"

"What is business, what is commerce, when compared with moral virtue and political justice? 'Tis the good of the whole, my dear Frederick, and not the petty interest of individuals, we are to consider. We ought never to do an action without first calculating the resulting good, and considering if some greater good may not be done.—You are dressed, and to tell you the truth, for we ought always and in all instances to speak truth, I this night am going to Mrs. Ell's, where you will see a charming girl: she has not been introduced a month, and you will not regret the loss of——. Come, my dear fellow, shake off all these old superstitious notions, and taste real and genuine liberty."

CHAPTER III.

THE NEW MORALITY OF FRIENDSHIP, HONOUR, AND PHILANTHROPY.

Some days after, I received a letter from my father, informing me, that the disappointment he had received, with the fatigue of the journey in his weak state of health, had so much raised his fever, that

---

[*] Political Justice. [Editor's note: Here, and elsewhere in the novel, Walker offers an incomplete and distorted reading of the famous Book III, Chap. iii of Godwin's *Political Justice*, "Of Promises." In a nutshell, Godwin argues that far from a moral duty, a promise is a "fallacious mode of binding a man to a specific mode of action" since it must under all circumstances give precedence to the "great principle" of *justice*, which dictates that "all private considerations must yield to the general good" (93-94).]

he had little hopes of recovering his health; and that if I yet retained the smallest spark of filial piety, I would instantly hasten to him.

I was at first shocked with the event; but it was evidently not owing to me, but to the improper journey he had taken; for to say the disappointment could have such an effect, was talking like a nervous old woman. I was easily convinced by Stupeo that it was all a trick: and indeed I was in no condition to undertake a journey into Kent; the charming girl who had not been a month introduced, having given me sufficient reason to remember her innocence.

"What a shocking effect!" said Stupeo; "but you ought to doubt its reality."

"To doubt it?" cried I: "No, no, I have no reason to doubt."

"But it may only exist in your idea, and that idea affects you."[26]

"Affects me! How?" said I. "What, if I have an idea that my throat is cut, shall I find the blood streaming about me?"

"It all arises from the present miserable system of things," said Stupeo; "a despotism is the very worst of governments."

"But what has despotism to do with it?" cried I peevishly; "am I not burning with all the flames of a volcano? and should I not have been well at this moment if I had attended my father? Pray how does this rise from the government?"

"I'll maintain," said Stupeo with metaphysical coolness, "this and every thing else that is bad arises from it. If genuine liberty were established, all the female sex would be within our choice; we should not have to venture———. What business has one man to monop olise a woman to himself? Affection and love is as various as any other passion. What are the names of mother, and wife, and daughter, and sister? In a state of nature men pursue their own inclinations, and not each grasp a female being to himself, the slave of his caprice, and the object of his disgust.—Over this imaginary prize, men watch with perpetual jealousy; and one man will find his desires and his capacity to circumvent as much excited, as the other is excited to traverse him:—as long as this state of society continues, *philanthropy* will be crossed and checked in a thousand ways."*

---

* Political Justice. [Editor's note: On Godwin's views on a monogamous marriage as "the most odious of all monopolies" (453), see the extracts from *Political Enquiry*, Book VIII, Chap. vi in Appendix A.6.iii. The passage, "Over this imaginary prize ... checked in a thousand ways" is an almost verbatim citation from *Political Enquiry* (453-54).]

"That must be a very admirable state of things," I replied; "but at present what are we to do, when our philanthropy must be practised in private? for it is a very dear article at Westminster Hall.[27] I am almost tempted to think it a judgment of Providence upon illicit connection."

"Providence!" repeated he; "is it possible you can really be such a child in science? In the eighteenth century to talk of Providence, is a mark of the profoundest ignorance. Do you think then that there is a great and omnipotent Being who cares for such a bundle of atoms as you are? All priestcraft and lies. Does any thing tell you that you shall live hereafter?"

"I have an idea that I shall; and all ideas must be realities, only in a slighter degree, if the doctrine of the *fashionable* Hume be true."

"Not in this case. Your existence will terminate when the lobes of the lungs are no longer inflated, and the blood ceases to beat in the arteries. The union of the spirit with the body is a mere fortuitous connection, happened wholly by chance, and will terminate in like manner."[28]

"But," returned I, "nature seems embellished with a thousand beauties, that surely are not the result of chance. In the formation of one single flower, how insensibly does the stem increase, the leaves unfold, and the flowers expand! Were these the effects of chance, we ought to see the particles which form the component parts, settling from the air into the shapes of plants, trees, horses, and geese; nor should we ever see two animals or plants of the same species."

Stupeo paused a moment, but he never wanted resources in the extensive stores of his mind. "All this," said he, "proceeds from physical *necessity* and the nature of things: you impell a ball along a smooth surface, and it must proceed in a fixed progress; so nature has given to all things an impulse which never ceases to act.[29] The same quantity of matter and spirit exists now that did exist at the first, though it is ever varying in form. In the first kernel, in the first egg, was contained the germ of all other kernels and eggs, of all the plants, and all the chickens, requiring only the progress of time to unfold them: and the first man contained in him all the men that ever did or ever will exist."*

"But how that first could ever exist without a creating power, is to me incomprehensible. We do not see new species of animals produced by nature in our time; we never find men with their heads just rising above ground, like the children of *Deucalion* and *Pyrrha*, or the teeth which *Cadmus* set in the mud.³⁰ It would be a convincing argument, if we were ever to find the horns of animals rising like plants before us in our walks. Indeed, my dear Stupeo, you must allow a great first cause."³¹

"Nature is all powerful," said Stupeo.

"But what is nature? To be a powerful cause, it must have *will*; it must be a Deity; and I care not whether you call this mighty being Nature, Providence, or God."

"Those who believe any thing are fools," replied he: "matter and motion may be regarded as the cause of thought:† every thing arises from matter and motion."

"But what is motion? And what is the cause of motion?" said I.

"Priests," he replied, "have led the mind, through their knowledge of its passions. They have introduced Hell to controul us by the horrors of future punishment. But the burning-glass of truth has struck the temple of prejudice and priestcraft; the fabric totters to the base, it will shortly fall, and crush all tyrants in its ruins."

I could not but observe, that he had evaded my questions, but that was an effort of his exquisite wit and talent for disputation. It was impossible any one could resist the torrent of his eloquence; and my imagination was warmed by the glorious and

---

*   Buffon. [Editor's note: Comte George Louis Leclerc de Buffon (1707–88), French naturalist, best-known for his *Histoire naturelle* (36 vols., 1749-88), *Théorie de la terre* (1749), and his *Epoques de la nature* (1779). Anticipating the work of Erasmus Darwin (1731-1802) and of the latter's more famous grandson Charles Robert Darwin (1809–82), Buffon laid the foundation for a scientific description of the earth, minerals, animals, and man. Thus he was the first to write a history of the earth in terms of a series of successive geological stages and his work on geographic zoology paved the way for Darwin's evolution theory.]

†   Hume on Human Nature, vol. i, page 468 and 434. [Editor's note: Despite the page references, this appears to be a non-specific reference to Hume, although Walker may have been thinking of Hume's observation in Book I, Part iv, Section 5: "And as the constant conjunction of objects constitutes the very essence of cause and effect, matter and motion may often be regarded as the causes of thought, as far as we have any notion of that relation" (250).]

brilliant idea of the temple of superstition tumbling down, and crushing tyranny in its ruins. I forgot my sufferings in the prospect, sighing alone in the fear that mankind were not yet sufficiently enlightened. Indeed I have to lament, that I find too many self-interested people, who prefer the *misanthropic* way of living in families, watching their wives and daughters like so many dragons guarding the Hesperian fruit,[32] and hoarding up that wealth which thousands would be rejoiced to share. But the time will come, when knowledge is disseminated in all ranks; when the ploughman shall sit on his plough reading the Rights of Man, and all books of law and religion shall be burnt by the magistrates.[33] Then, then, my dear Sir, liberty shall triumph! and aristocracy and property vanish together!

It was a long time before I recovered my health and strength; and my father finding he could not bully me into his narrow principles, sent a dismissal to Stupeo. That great and good man could not bear to take a personal farewel of his pupil, but departed in the evening, two days after his discharge, taking with him a gold repeater of mine, which his delicacy would not let him ask as a memorial.—The loss of my dear Stupeo would have been dreadful, had I not imbibed sufficient knowledge to proceed without a guide; the light of nature being sufficient for those who will follow her impulses, unbiassed by vulgar errors.

I endeavoured to *spread the truth** with all my powers; but the old fellows thinking their places in danger, and alarmed at the thunders of reason and the fulminations of science, expelled me the college, and I returned to my father's house.

There I resolved to live as much as possible in conformity to reason, without stooping to the forms of custom. Nature is the best regulator, and I was not obliged to eat and drink because the hand of the clock pointed to such a set of figures; or to eat pork, when my appetite preferred mutton.

My mother, who was a weak silly old woman, was always crying at my whims (as my father called them); and if I had not steeled my heart against that foolish failing, *pity*, I could not have persisted in the line of truth.

---

* A cant phrase of all Reformers.

Vernon, the friend of my youth, resided at this time at our house, having finished the studies necessary to a mercantile education; and he now only waited for a vacancy, to go abroad on some adventure.

I endeavoured in vain to open the eyes of this bigoted youth, who was nearly my own age. I put into his hands books of religious controversy, in hopes of catching his mind by some insoluble question. I demanded of him frequently, an explanation of all the articles of religious belief. I read to him the admirable writings of Voltaire and Hume: but he had the impudence to say, they contradicted each other; that Voltaire frequently asserted falsehoods as certainties, which three-fourths of his readers had not means to detect; and that Hume was so contradictory and unintelligible, that the reader was lost in a jargon of words.

He had taken a strong fancy to a very elegant girl, the daughter of a farmer in our neighbourhood, and was never happy but when writing verses in her praise, or teaching her, what he called, the Christian virtues. He was so jealous of this fancied property, that he was for excluding all others from their natural right. Had I attended to the old-fashioned doctrine of *honour*, I might have refrained from desiring the girl myself; but our enjoyments are very transient in this world, and none but fools will think of the next.

Your church people, who believe that they have souls, might indeed be deterred from violating innocence and plundering the weak; but I rejoice to think these notions are growing obsolete; and not being troubled with such qualms myself, I resolved to gratify the pure and natural desire I had, at least to divide with Vernon the affections of Amelia.

The girl herself soon perceived the difference; for, having a quick understanding, she became enamoured of the new doctrines I daily discoursed upon, for they carried self-evident proofs in the latitude they allowed for the passions and weakness of human nature.

Vernon was of too jealous a disposition not to perceive her growing coolness towards himself, and that all his sanctified religious notions were unattended to. His vigilance was roused, and he soon discovered that I had not only supplanted him, but even gained those favours he durst not in idea think of: a glorious proof of the superiority of truth and the new morality.

In the narrow spirit of self-love, and the old times of chivalry,[34] he sent me a challenge with all the fire of a madman, and all the reproaches he could have uttered, had I injured him in the most infamous manner.

Determined to preserve the dignity of conscious innocence, I replied to him in a letter, "That it was the offspring of despotism, to bring any argument to the sword;—that his appeal to force was palpably wrong, as he should have convinced me, by rational tenets, that I was not right. I also begged him to reflect, that my mind, being infinitely more illumined and more liberal than his, I was so much more valuable in the scale of moral virtue. That his death would, in the eye of political justice, be a matter of insignificance, but that mine would be a great detriment to society in general, for whose benefit I even durst not use the self-command of my person, by risking it against his."*

I happened to meet him the same evening, on my way to Amelia. His eye kindled the moment he saw me; and standing firmly in my way, he waited my arrival.

"Execrable coward!"† cried he, "monster of human depravity! you have for ever ruined the tranquillity of my existence, and you deny me the *honourable* satisfaction of a gentleman. Were there not others less worthy than Amelia, whom you might have contaminated with your detestable maxims? But none other than the beloved darling of the soul of your friend, the girl whom he had doted on from infancy, you must defame!"

"*Friendship!*" said I, when his passion allowed him to pause; "we ought never to form *particular* friendships with any one, to

---

*   The modern doctrine of Godwin and Co. [Editor's note: In his *Political Justice*, Godwin describes the custom of settling disputes of "honor" by means of dueling as a "detestable practice ... originally intended by barbarians for the gratification of revenge" (see Book II, Chap. ii, Appendix ii, "On Duelling," 57). Although widely attacked in the second half of the eighteenth century by a host of legal writers, novelists and moralists, the practice remained part of the upper classes' aristocratic code of honor until well into the second half of the nineteenth century. Dueling was one of the topics in the realms of morality, religion and law in the Revolutionary period where feudal, chivalric ideals of class and justice (often embraced by conservative and anti-Jacobin elements in society) clashed with more modern, egalitarian ideals (often entertained by reformers).]

†   I have been accused of pleading for duelling. Let any man who calls himself a gentleman judge. [Editor's note: Walker is probably referring to a remark by an anonymous reviewer in the *Monthly Magazine*, Supplement, 7 (20 July 1799): 542 (see Appendix C).]

the exclusion of the whole species: every man ought to be our friend; but before we enter into confidence, we ought to inquire carefully into the worth of our object, that we may not bestow upon him a regard which his abilities do not deserve, or we shall act unjustly. We ought to be sure, after a certain allowance for the fallibility of the human judgment."*

"Perish such infernal doctrines!" cried he, interrupting me: "such cold-hearted and diabolical systems would unhinge all society in the universe!"

"True," cried I, "true, most true," raising my voice, determined to be heard in the cause of truth. "It were well for mankind, if society were this moment abolished: we should then be free from its vices; virtue would spread her celestial banner over the children of men; science would dart the rays of its fecundating beams to the bosoms of all men; and liberty would spread her reign from zone to zone, and from one pole to the other."

"What is this jargon?" said he, with a look of calm contempt: "Is the liberty you wish, the right of ravishing your friend's mistress? Is this virtue you blaze forth—the committal of outrage, and slinking from the punishment? And what is your state of nature, but a state of anarchy and bloodshed?"

"You misname every thing," said I. "If the great metaphysician Stupeo were here, he would soon convince you. As it is, I would ask how I have injured you? Is Amelia any way injured but in your romantic fancy? What claim had you to her more than I? Should I at this moment oppose you, if you were to supplant me, or even divide with me her affections? No; so much *philanthropy*, so much *friendship* do I feel, that though I was now going to her, you shall go in my place."

"Villain! monster!" cried he, nearly choking with passion; "this moment I would tear your soul from your body, did not

---

* Political Justice, page 86. [Editor's note: This is Walker's—partially verbatim—rendering of Godwin's, "Is the general good promoted by falsehood, by treating a man of one degree of worth, as if he had ten times that worth? or as if he were in any degree different from what he really is? Would not the most beneficial consequences result from a different plan; from my constantly and carefully enquiring into the deserts of all those with whom I am connected, and from their being sure, after a certain allowance for the fallibility of human judgment, of being treated by me exactly as they deserved?" (*Political Justice*, Book II, Chap. ii, 51-52; see also Appendix A.6.1).]

gratitude for your father prevent me. Live then! live to be a curse to yourself and society!"

"Do you not know," said I, "that *gratitude* is a crime? because—"35

"Because, d–n–n!" vociferated he. "Begone, monster! The man without gratitude is a companion alone for the blackest fiends of hell. The affections of angelic mind are lost on his callous soul. He may talk as he will of benevolence, but *self* is the centre of all his actions; and because he will not *return* a favour, he would meanly seek to destroy the obligation.—Frederick," continued he, in a voice supernaturally solemn, "remember this. Nothing can be more fallacious than the philanthropic principles held out by modern philosophers: they paint themselves as the most benevolent of the human race; they lament the horrors of West-Indian slavery; they groan at the sufferings of mankind, which arise from the nature of man and mortal existence. But look yourself, and let others dispassionately look into the conduct of these worthy patriots, and I challenge you, or them, to bring me *one* man in an hundred, who will, or who has bestowed one single shilling *voluntarily*, either to relieve the distresses of the poor, or to aid the support of their country. In the one case, they shuffle off, by saying, the poor have a *right to demand* the property of the rich; we are determined not to give a penny to a set of cowards, who will not rise and cut the throats of aristocrats and placemen.36 In the other case, they exclaim, *I* give any thing to support a set of ministerial minions! No, it is contrary to my principles, I will oppose them in every measure; and if a foreign enemy should come, I will either be neutral, or rejoice to see the day that shall make us free. What is the meaning of this cant, let your own sense dictate. Were these men to come forward and pay the regular taxes, there would not require above half that are now ostensibly demanded, the burden would be more equal, and the honest part of society would not be crushed with more than their portion. This, Frederick, is probably the last time I shall converse with you: it is *gratitude* which impels me to desire your reform; and I would have you look at those men, who have always the word *morality* in their mouth: look at the private life of any one of them, and you will find the liberty they seek to be no other than the right to practise every licentiousness, unchecked by the *law*, and unstig-matised by sober and religious men."

I was going to repeat some of the arguments of the profound metaphysical Stupeo. I was going to prove, that we ought to doubt whether two and two made four, or the greater was larger than the less: but he turned from me with a look of superiority, and I could not for my soul but muse over his sermon, which was sacrilege against the cause of reason and truth; it being well known that our political demagogues, our brethren in the cause of universal man, live in the most abstemious manner, that they may give the surplus to the poor. Will they not with true patri-otism make the meanest subterfuges to evade a tax, by which means a double burden is thrown upon those who cannot flinch, and mankind are forced to open their eyes? Do they not print cheap books to enlighten their understanding, and let them see how they are plundered and robbed?* For it is no argument to say, that from those who have not, nor ever had any thing, noth-ing can be taken:—for what is more clear, than that I commit a robbery on a man if I with-hold his just demands? and the rich have no more real claim to their wealth, than a farmer has to the product of the ground he has cultivated; and which ought to be divided equally to all the people on the surface. No man has a right to monopolise the fruits of the earth.

The arguments of Vernon might have weight on some minds; and I trembled to think that he was counteracting all the good which I hoped to produce in the vicinity. So dangerous an enemy to liberty and reason ought to be removed; and when I returned home, I immediately went to my father, desiring him to withdraw his coun-tenance from Vernon, who was a man that abused his generosity.

"I can hardly believe him capable," said my father; "and even if he were so, the hopes I have inspired him with, render it in me a sacred duty to provide for him. I have educated him superior

---

* It is to be lamented that the Government party do not endeavour to counteract this method of propagating French principles, by distributing books of religious and moral duty. [Editor's note: On Walker's disgust of radical writers like Thomas Paine printing cheap editions in order to spread republican arguments in favor of the revo-lutions in American and France amongst large sections of the population, see Introduction, and Walker's Preface to the third edition of the novel above.]

to his fortune; I have given him, as I may say, a mind equal to a great employ; and I should deem it injustice to cast him down, and to destroy all the talents he has acquired, and the schemes he has indulged, beneath my influence."

"But," cried I, "your influence may be employed to better purpose, and it is the greater good we ought to prefer. What is the tenderness to which you are bound? This expectation you dare not disappoint. Has his expectation altered the original purpose of his life, engaged him in undertakings from which he would otherwise have abstained? Be it so: he and all other men would be taught to depend more on their own exertions:* they would be taught never to rely on vain expectations, but act from the noble energies of independence."

"What language is this?" cried my father. "What would society become, if no human being could depend on the promise or the protection of another? And what is this greatest good? A term without meaning, a cant phrase to avoid a duty. The greatest good is, to be upright and sincere before God and man; and not, because my present convenience may suit, to turn the whole life of a dependent into a different channel; break all his connections, and dissolve his plans at my will. This indeed is despotism with a power superior to the mandates of Persian plenipotence."37

"I wish," said I, "the divine, mythologistical, metaphysical Stupeo were here; he would shortly convince you that you are in a palpable error."

"He could never," replied my father, "sophisticate the common-sense dictates of a mind wishing to do right."

We were interrupted by the entrance of Vernon, who paused, and trembled at seeing me. I did not wish wholly to confound and embarrass him with my presence, and therefore withdrew.

I know not what passed between him and my father; but the next morning he departed by break of day, and my father shut himself up in his closet, in a gloomy fit.

---

* Political Justice, vol. i, page 156 to 160. [Editor's note: See Godwin, *Political Justice*, Book III, Chap. iv ("Of Political Authority"), in which Godwin argues that "to give each man a voice in the public concerns comes nearest to that admirable idea of which we should never lose sight, the uncontrolled exercise of private judgment" (92).]

CHAPTER IV.

THE GREATEST GOOD FULLY ILLUSTRATED BY A STRANGE ACCIDENT—ANECDOTES OF PATRIOTISM.

I continued my connection with Amelia, and had the satisfaction to perceive that another human being would be added to the race of men. My father, by some means, became acquainted with the circumstance; and I was catechised for having followed the dictates of nature. Family pride did not permit his requesting me to marry her, though he pretended that his only objection was, that no union could be happy after so great a lapse of discretion. He proposed that I should, for some time, quit the country; and he would provide for Amelia and the child, when it should be born.

"Let the parish provide for it," said I: "all children ought to belong to the public. The great, the immortal, the virtuous, and illustrious Rousseau sent his children to be maintained by the Founding Hospital at Paris:* and shall I be ashamed of copying so great a master, whose actions were all sublime?"

"And how do you reconcile those principles with morality?" said my father.

"Morality," I replied, "is political justice, which prefers the good of the whole to the good of a part; suffering partial evil,

---

* Rousseau's *Confessions*. [Editor's note: Written between 1766 and 1770, Jean-Jacques Rousseau's idiosyncratic autobiography, *Confessions*, was published posthumously (Part I in 1781 and Part II in 1788). Relating the details of Rousseau's erratic and rebellious life, the *Confessions* are an attempt to justify himself in the eyes of his numerous enemies. One of the issues his detractors attacked him on repeatedly was his decision to send the five children he had with his mistress, the linen-maid Thérèse Levasseur, to the Paris foundlings' hospital, rather than to raise them himself. Rousseau thought the arrangement "so good, so sensible, so legitimate" that he told everyone who knew about his relationship with Thérèse (348). In all fairness to Rousseau, he later expressed his regret about placing his children in the Paris orphanage, characterizing it as "a misfortune for which I should be pitied, not a crime for which I should be reproached" (qtd. on 662). Typically, however, he regretted having broken his promise to Thérèse not to divulge the secret to anyone much more than having abandoned children he had "never seen" (349).]

that the great work of truth may go forward, and liberty and reason be paramount over selfishness, pride, superstition, and priestcraft."[38]

"Excellent!" cried my father, breaking into a loud laugh: "a speech worthy the humble copier of Rousseau, and the great metaphysician Stupeo. Let me ask you one question, Frederick—Do you understand yourself?"

"Do I understand myself? Yes; and what I say is as legible as the broad beams of the sun at noon day: it is written in the great book of Nature."[39]

It was evening when this conversation took place: and we were startled by a sudden blaze of light, which darted across the hemisphere; at the same moment the servants cried out, Fire! and we could perceive the farm in a blaze.

My father and I, together with the servants, hastened to the spot, where we found a scene of deplorable distress. The farmer had forgot his children in his endeavours to save his property, which he threw out at the window.

His wife had fainted away; and the younger children were screaming in an upper story. My father, without any reflection, darted up the flaming stairs, and descended with the two little boys in his arms; in doing which, he was considerably scorched. Meanwhile, I snatched a ladder from one of the men, with intention to rescue Amelia, who had been sleeping in her room, and now appeared terrified at the window. I was going to apply the ladder, when part of the roof fell into the room where her father was employed, and drove him to the window in danger of suffocation.

In this dilemma it was impossible to save both:—"Were Stupeo here," cried I, "he would tell which is the most deserving of life; but I shall commit some injustice, if I save the life of the one with the lesser merit." ("Let go the ladder," cried several; "why do you keep it useless?") I, at that moment, remembered a parallel case, quoted by the excellent philosopher, Stupeo, in support of the new political justice.—"Suppose," said he, "the Archbishop of Cambray and his maid are both in danger of perishing in flames, which ought I to save? The maid, a stupid creature, little better than a brute;—the Archbishop, a man of eminent virtue and

learning, and the author of Telemachus.* To save the one, at the
hazard of my own life, is scarce more virtue than to save a dog;
but to save the Archbishop, is an act of the highest virtue; because
all actions are to be esteemed in exact proportion to the merit of
the person receiving benefit. Now the difficulty is, in the present
case, to know whether the farmer or his daughter is of most value
to mankind. The farmer cultivates the earth, and provides for his
family in a gross kind of way: the daughter is young, and may add
many to the human species: but then——"

I was calmly proceeding, in spite of the struggles of the men
to wrest the ladder from me, when a tremendous crash and a
large column of flame ended my discussion, and I had the horror
to see the farmer and his daughter both overwhelmed in the
burning ruins. I was shocked at so dreadful an accident, which
would not have happened had Stupeo been there: but in this
present rascally system of government and society, virtue will not
always succeed; and no man can be condemned, if evil should
result from a good intention.

It was, however, a very deplorable circumstance, and I regretted deeply that I was not better versed in the great book of
Nature and Man, as I should then have known instantly how to
appreciate the several degrees of merit.

Another unpleasant circumstance resulted. The common
people, who are like a swinish multitude,[40] and cannot perceive
reason, (how indeed should they, when they are held in profound
ignorance?) insisted upon it, that I had retained the ladder
purposely to suffer them to perish; by which I expected to avoid
the consequences of my connection with Amelia. My father
himself was inclined to believe the report; and unless I had the
logic of Stupeo, and the effrontery of Voltaire, (who being asked
how he could insert falsehoods so glaring in his history, replied,
"To one half of the present generation they will be facts, and the

---

* Godwin's Political Justice, page 84. [Editor's note: François de Salignac de la Mothe
Fénelon (1651-1715), Archbishop of Chambrai, a liberal in politics and in his educational theories, tutor of the duc de Bourgogne, grandson of Louis XIV, and author
of the didactic romance Télémaque (1699). Godwin introduced his notorious hypo-
thetical choice between the relative worth of the archbishop and his chambermaid
in Political Justice, Book II, Chap. ii ("Of Justice"). See Appendix A.6.i.]

next will not possess the means of detection.")[41] I should have found it impossible to prevent their reproaches.

A committee of stupid farmers met to inquire into the cause of the fire. It began in a back stable, where I had been on some business in the course of the day: their suspicions appeared facts, and a warrant was sent for to apprehend me.

I was very much astonished when my father mentioned this with tears in his eyes, and told me the corroborating circumstances were in every point against me: that my retention of the ladder was too evidently to prevent the rescue of two wretched persons whom I had in fact murdered: that he shuddered at being father to so profligate a son; but that his consideration for my mother prevented his assisting to detain me himself, as I should most assuredly be hanged, unless I possessed incontrovertible proofs in my favour.

"I maintain it," cried I, "that in a state of nature the fire could not have happened: I even doubt that it has now happened. Did you ever read the great, the fashionable Hume, in his Treatise on Human Nature? In all incidents of life, we ought still to preserve our scepticism. If we *believe* that fire warms, or water refreshes, 'tis only because it costs us too much pains to think otherwise: nay, *if we are* philosophers, it ought only to be on sceptical principles."*

"You will believe," said he, "when the rope is tightened round your neck."

"I know not whether there be reality in that," said I, "it may only be an idea: we cannot be certain that any man was ever hanged; because, if we proceed upon hear-say evidence, upon tradition, ever-varying; upon chronicles and annals, which are half interpolations; I say, if we believe all those sort of testimonies, we may as well believe the authenticity of our bibles; for, in fact, we have as little real proof of the burning of the farm-house, the hanging of John the painter, the revolution of Massanielo, and the existence of Alexander,[42] as we have of a book, which is merely the laws and history of people, preserved in their synagogues by *themselves*: our senses are the most deceiving things in nature."

"You speak lightly," said my father with a deep sigh: "had you

---

* Vol. i, page 469. [Editor's note: "In all incidents of life ... on sceptical principles": an almost verbatim citation from Hume's *Treatise* (Book I, Part iv, Section 8).]

the common feelings of a man, the loss of Amelia would rend your heart; but you are callous to the ties of nature: if, however, you cannot prove your innocence, you would do well to fly; and this purse will supply you the means."

"Give me a few moments," said I, "to deliberate. I would march rejoicing, with a firm step and steady countenance, to meet the axe of the executioner, if it would promote the cause of truth: but I have yet to consider how my death will benefit mankind, whether it will impress a conviction of the omnipotent power of truth, or whether——"

"Are you indeed mad?" said my father, gazing at me sorrowfully.

"Mad!" cried I. "No; I repeat the sentiments of all enlightened men: I have the power to escape, and the power to march to the gibbet, and I only balance between the resulting good of either action."

"You are not fit to be a member of civil society."

"I know it; I glory in the idea: were I fit to live in society, I should be no real and genuine philosopher. Society is a fungus, reared in the hotbed of luxury."

"Fly!" cried he: "the mob is coming across the green—it is dark, haste through the garden!"

I really did not see that any good would result from my being hanged; for how could I know what yet remained for me to perform on the great stage of life? and accordingly I hastened from the house.

I continued to cross the country, chagrined at the effect of consideration. I must confess, the new philosophy involves one in situations that require all the energies of the human mind; and indeed it would be almost impracticable, were it not for that fundamental and happy maxim of disbelieving every thing past, present, and to come.

I detested disguise, because it is inconsistent with the spirit of truth; and I know not but all sorts of stratagem are blots on the dignity of virtue. It was, however, very awkward, that a philosopher should be hanged for such a trifle as the death of a farmer and his daughter.

I proceeded forward the whole of that night, and the next day I remained to rest at a farm-house, again setting out at the commencement of evening. I had not advanced above seven miles, when I heard a considerable noise in a barn, like a tumult of applause, which again subsided into a calm; and I could hear a voice pronouncing a declamatory speech. I hastened to the door, which was guarded by some ill-looking fellows, and, having paid sixpence, was ushered into a crowd of gaping farmers and cottagers. A little dark-complexioned man, with a most hypocritical countenance, and a grin of self-applause mingled with contempt, was instructing the clowns in their rights. His voice was elevated to the pitch of raving, and the idea of liberty gave volubility to his tongue, which he rolled about with the energy of enthusiasm.

"Citizens," cried he, "citizens and fellow brethren of the human race, this is a glorious sight: this is a display that shall strike terror into tyrants. The prisoners rattle their chains, and will soon dash them in pieces on the heads of their jailors.—Germs of my love! how it gives satisfaction to my soul, to see you assembled and determined in the good cause! What shall we do? Shall we pray, like a set of canting methodists? No, we will do something better. (Here he made signs of fighting.) Yes, citizens, we will rally round our rights; we will claim something else besides mouldy parchments and rotten charters; we will demand the Rights of Man! (Can any citizen furnish me with a morsel of fruit, for I am exceeding thirsty?) Well, brethren, let us reflect upon the horrid times we live in; I don't mean to say this country, and I don't care how many Government spies there may be amongst us; I am speaking as if I was in Rome.[43] Let us remember the times of our forefathers:—hear it, citizens! In the time of good Queen Bess, every ploughman could, with his day's wages, carry home a sucking pig, or a turkey, to his family at night:* which of you can do so? Won't you believe now that the times are bad?

---

*   This very assertion, amongst many others, was made to a *London* audience by a London Political Lecturer. [Editor's note: The "London Lecturer" is a reference to John Thelwall (1764-1834), a radical political orator who had claimed in a lecture he delivered on 29 April 1795 entitled "The Present War a Principal Cause of the Starving Condition of the People" that "in the golden days of Queen Bess" (i.e., Queen Elizabeth I), "*the wages of a single day would have bought the poor labourer a fat pig, a loaf of bread, and some good ale to drink for himself and his family*" (*The Tribune*, 142-43).]

that you are slaves? that Old England (mind I mean Old Rome) is ruined, and that, without some energetic exertion, we shall never redeem ourselves from perdition?—Brethren! germs of my love! this is a meeting for the cause of universal man: no real citizen would refuse to give—What! slinking away through the gate when we talk of giving? Aye, aye, the minister has drained your pockets, not left you a farthing:—however, the box is held at the gate.* Well, citizens, I am the man that stands forward to defend your rights—and what do you think the Government will do with me? I'll tell you: they will put me in a dungeon, where I shall look through the grating at you; or they'll hang me on a gibbet, where I shall dingle dangle before you like a scare-crow. But let them—I am willing to suffer for your sake.†

Here he descended from the rostrum, amidst the loud applauses of the multitude; and I pressed eagerly forward to get a sight of a man labouring in the cause of philosophy and truth.

"Citizen," said I, seizing his hand, "were the great, the metaphysical, the oratorical Stupeo here, he would honour you for your noble speech."

"Which of my speeches?" said he. "You may get the last philippic44 of the doorkeeper for a shilling."

"My dear friend," said I, "I am a disciple of the wonderful Stupeo, whom you must have heard of. Tell me how I may be of service in the cause of human nature."

"Have you subscribed?" demanded he: "Are you a member?"

"I am a stranger, but I pretend to some little philosophy." He

---

* Meeting at Chalk Farm. [Editor's note: A reference to a general meeting of the London Corresponding Society, held at Chalk Farm, near Hampstead, London, on Monday, 14 April 1794. The meeting, which attracted upwards of 2,000 people, was attended by John Thelwall. According to a report of the meeting by one of the government spies present at the meeting, "Every person delivered his Ticket at the Garden Gate, which was torn & one part returned to be placed in the hat in order to prevent any person getting in, or remaining there without a Ticket—The Example was set by Thelwall" (Mary Thale, ed. and intro., *Selections from the Papers of the London Corresponding Society, 1792-1799* [Cambridge: Cambridge University Press, 1983], 136).]

† Meeting at Copenhagen House. [Editor's note: A reference to what was possibly the largest political gathering organized by the London Corresponding Society on 16 October 1795 in Copenhagen Fields, near Copenhagen House, in Islington, London. On that occasion John Thelwall addressed a meeting of nearly 150,000 people (see Introduction).]

gazed upon me; and some friend stepping up, I was parted from him by the crowd.

He is too much a philosopher, thought I, to have his reflections interrupted by idle curiosity: he will now retire to meditate on the subject of his undertaking, and I will endeavour to see him in the morning.

I proceeded towards the next village across some fields, and, as I went slowly, was overtaken by two countrymen, who were in high argument.—"I tell thee," said one, "it be's a thing impossible as a labouring body should yearn a pig in yan day. Why, doan't I know as how, thof we pays dearer for an article in name, we do have more money in *proposition*, as our Parson say."

"He say!" cried the other: "he's a right to stand up for himself, and make folks believe any thing. Why, I tell thee now, atween mon and mon, that Ould England be gone to the dogs, as we heard Citizen Ego say; and it will never be as it ought to be, till we have another Aldermon Cromwell, and no tithes."45

"Alderman Cromwell!" repeated the first. "Why, thee be's an arrant ninny-hammer:46 he were Oliver Cromwell, an our Parson did tell us about him last Sunday, as how he did tax the people, when he got fixed, as much or more than they were before."

"I will be stringed up," cried the other, "if it were not Aldermon Cromwell now. Why, I did hear a deel about un from a paper Citizen Ego did give away for nothing."

"Like a montabank to catch fools," said the other. "You'd a deel better go and mind your master's business, and not trouble your thick head about nation affairs."

My blood began to rise in the cause of truth.—"What," cried I, "would you have the human soul bound down and fettered in bonds of superstition and ignorance? Give the intellectual faculties play, and then the great day of universal emancipation will soon arrive."

"Mensuration!" cried the first: "who be you, to talk of mensuration? Ayn't the country divided enough, without more mensuration?"

"My good friend," said I, "learn that emancipation is the freeing of all mankind from their chains; when neither priests, nor kings, nor Oliver Cromwells will be wanted."

"Thee lies," cried one in anger: "Alderman Cromwell were the only good man in the land, and I wish we had an hundred at this present."

"Who are you," said the other, "that abuse your betters? You shall go to the stocks if you talk treason."47

"The stocks," cried I: "you would do well both of you to go there, and learn your alphabet; then you would know a little more."

The champion of Alderman Cromwell was too much irritated at this reply to enter deeper into the argument; and being also in a quarrelling disposition from the speeches of his adversary, he instantly struck me over the head a blow which nearly brought me to the ground. I returned it in an instant with a good cudgel, and he fell at his length before me. His antagonist attempted to collar me; but, darting my fist in his mouth, he stuck up to me in a more scientific way; and though I beat him black and blue in about six rounds, I was myself so bruised, that I crawled with difficulty to the next inn.

Having procured some vinegar, or rather sour beer, I retired to the chamber allotted me, which was on the upper story, the roof admitting the sparkling of the stars as they passed over. I lay down on a dirty piece of a bed, which the maid told me was all they had to spare, the rest of the house being engaged by the London gentlemen.

I was grieved at so fair an opportunity being lost; but my bruises paining me, I found little inclination to enter into political discussion.

I endeavoured to sleep, but a loud noise in the room beneath effectually prevented me. I arose after some time, and through a chink in the floor could perceive the same little dark Citizen Ego, and two others, the one in green-and-buff, and the other in black.

"We shall make a decent harvest, citizens," said Ego; "the germ of freedom begins to shoot, and we shall reap the benefit."

"How much," said Green-and-buff, "shall we divide to-night? This is but a poor place. I am about a work that shall bring more money, and set the nation more together by the ears than all your lectures and debates. I shall demonstrate by a ratio, clear as the angles of a triangle, that the whole kingdom is beggared; and every man will buy the book to see how: it will be torn from the press; the very Government will buy it up. I shall prove to every man, if he has any common sense, that all the property in his warehouse won't fetch him half-a-crown in the pound."

"Drink about, my boys," said the man in black. "Citizen Pepper reminds me of the froth of a porridge pot, if you go to wipe it off with your hand, you will scald your fingers.[48] If we had but three nice pretty little *rogues* here, I would recite my ode to the best of kings—'tis a d—d clever thing, citizens; Pepper's book will be nothing to mine: I make out every man to be a rascal or a fool; there's nothing like it: the more you abuse people, the more eager they are to buy. I've found out the secret, and I take care to lay it on thick enough; true or false, 'tis no matter to me, not a pin.—There was the other night I was at the Opera, and there was my Lady ———. Oho! here comes the supper."

The papers before them were rolled into their pockets. Roast fowls, and other articles of equal luxury, attracted their attention; and jests at the folly of mankind filled the intervals. "Damn it," said Ego, "do you know I had a devilish difficulty to get on to-night! I thought I was a little too far out; but I thundered it away, and they gulped it all down for gospel. If I mention a Government spy, I always set the room in a roar."

Having eat till they could eat no more, they were again left to themselves over a bowl of punch.—"Here's," cried Ego, grasping the bowl and lifting it to his mouth, "Here's the dignity of human nature, and may the blood of ruthless tyrants flow like this punch!"

"Bravo! citizen," roared out the man in black; "down your throat you mean. Well, but now we must to business."

"We have letters to write," said Ego, "from Edinburgh, from Liverpool, and from Portsmouth. Our club in London is grown so fearful, that we shall not keep them together without some flaming correspondence from some of the large towns. Which will you take, Pepper? will you write from Liverpool? Talk a great deal about virtuous poverty, the dignity of human nature, and a thirst of knowledge; tell them of the converts my speeches daily procure: and you, citizen, you write from Edinburgh; talk about the Scotch tree of liberty:* for myself, do you know I'm assassinated!"

"Ha! ha! ha! how, pray?"

"Why, the enemies of Liberty, the hirelings of Government have stabbed me at Portsmouth. D——n it, citizens, it will be a blow up, better than a mine in a counterscarp:49 when I get back to London, I may shew myself for a wild beast."

"But it won't do," cried Pepper; "John Bull won't be gulled so. D——n it, keep the broad way; tell him that there is a mine of dormant good sense in him, which, if not brought into action, will die with him.† Talk about revolutions, taxes, ropes, and axes, till you set his brains a-whirling, and then you may pick his pocket with all the ease in nature."

"Right, right, right!" shouted Ego. "But what are all these trifles? When our clubs are properly established we shall govern the nation, we shall ride upon the heads of the people, superior to law or human controul."‡

I was so agitated with this dialogue between the pretended

---

* The conductors of the Corresponding Society will perfectly remember the *genuine* letters read to the society from places where no clubs existed. But there are secrets in all trades. [Editor's note: Also known as "radical societies" and "Jacobin clubs," corresponding societies were organizations that sprang up in London and many provincial towns in the 1790s and that campaigned for social and political reform; as part of their effort to spread this reformist agenda, they maintained an intensive correspondence with other national and international groups (although Walker here suggests the letters were faked). The London Corresponding Society (LCS) was the largest of these societies in Britain (for more information on the aims and activities of the London Corresponding Society, see Introduction). In November 1793, delegates from many reform groups gathered at a "Convention" in Edinburgh to formulate their claims for constitutional change and to canvass popular support for their cause. In an attempt to nip this bid for liberty and reform in the bud, the government arrested a number of delegates and, after show trials, sentenced several of them—including Thomas Palmer and Thomas Muir—to fourteen years' transportation to Botany Bay.]

† Rights of Man. [Editor's note: The reference is to Paine's *Rights of Man, Part II*: "There is existing in man, a mass of sense lying in a dormant state, and which, unless something excites it to action, will descend with him, in that condition, to the grave" (198).]

‡ No man who has the smallest affection for genuine liberty would for a moment wish the establishment of affiliated clubs, under whatever pretence. The Jacobine club has deluged France with blood. But not to mention what every one knows, and to suppose that their *ostensible* motives were good, still they have no right to dictate to the nation at large: and it is well known that a few daring and needy men may by this coalition domineer over a whole people. The words of the Emperor Trajan to Pliny may here be applied. When the latter requested permission to institute a company of firemen, the former consented with these words: "But it is to be remembered, that this sort of

friends of liberty, that I started up, and cried aloud, "Hypocrites! will you sully the beauty of truth by such actions? Will you bring her into disgrace with mankind?"

"Blood and murder," roared our Citizen Ego, "where are my pistols? Citizens, we are betrayed! Let us fly! The spies of Government are come upon us, thick as the locusts of Egypt."

"A despotism," cried Pepper, "is the worst of all governments; no man is safe in his own house: formerly, an Englishman's house was his castle; but since we have opened the eyes of mankind, we are daily more and more restrained."

"Sit down, citizens," said the man in black. "Drink away, and laugh at the devil: it was only a false alarm."

"I won't stay another hour in the house," cried Pepper; "I will be off through this window."

"Who is paying the reckoning?" said Ego.

"Pugh! What's the reckoning to us?" said Pepper. "We will tell the world that we were pursued by the blood-hounds of Government, and somebody else will pay the score. We have been here more than a week, and the bill will be some pounds." So saying, he gently opened the window. I stamped aloud with my foot upon the floor; they were again alarmed; and, not waiting to look behind them, all three descended into the lane.

I raved about the room, lamenting the depravity of mankind, and

---

societies have greatly disturbed the peace of that province in general, and of those cities in particular. *Whatever name* we give them, and for *whatever purposes* they may be founded, they will not fail to form themselves into assemblies, however short their meetings may be." So political clubs, for whatever purpose instituted, will not fail in the end to produce anarchy, and take the reins of government into their own hands. [Editor's note: The Paris Jacobin Club was a political club initially named the Club Breton and formed by liberal members of the National Assembly of Versailles (1789). Later, after they had started to meet in the hall of the ex-convent of the Jacobins in Paris (hence their name), they became increasingly radical and were thus a major force behind the escalation of the Revolution from 1792 onwards. Among the best-known members of the Jacobin Club were Jean-Paul Marat (1743–93), Maximilien François Marie Isidore Robespierre (1758–94), and Georges Jacques Danton (1759–94). Pliny the Younger (full Latin name Caius Plinius Caecilius Secundus, AD 62-113), nephew and adopted son of Pliny the Elder. He rose to a high rank in imperial Rome, and his friends included the emperor Trajan (AD 52?-117). His collected letters give a vivid account of the political, social, and literary life of his times. The citation appears in *Epistulae* 10, 34.1 ("Sed meminerimus provinciam istam et prae-cipue eam civitatem eius modi factionibus esse vexatam. Quodcumque nomen ex quacumque causa dederimus iis, qui in idem contracti fuerint, hetaeriae praegraves fient").]

almost afraid that some of the principles of the new philosophy were erroneous: but I remembered that truth could not be injured by the abuses of some of its professors, except they were hypocritical priests, there being a wide difference between religion and politics.

In the morning I found myself too stiff to remove with pleasure. The whole inn was in an uproar about the fugitives; and the landlord consigned all politicians pell mell to the devil. To refresh my spirits, I walked down into the garden, where I had not stayed long before I was alarmed by the cries of a lad, and, hastening to inquire the accident, found it the son of the innkeeper, who was suffering a severe flagilation with an horse-whip; his father seemed to lay on in vexation for his late loss.

"What," cried I, seizing him by the arm, "what are you doing? What has the poor lad done?"

"What I'll murder him for if he repeats," answered the angry innkeeper: "he has been robbing an orchard, and will bring himself to the gallows."

"But you should advise him—you should convince him of his error by reason and argument, and not use coercion."

"I don't know what you mean by coercion?" said he: "but I have already sufficiently talked to him, and now his hide shall suffer."

"You are wrong; all coercion is wrong," cried I: "at this moment your son feels a sense of insult and injury; he feels himself right, and that you are a tyrant."*

"Who are you?" demanded the innkeeper. "D—n me if I don't think you are a partner with those that bilked the reckoning, and go about the country teaching children disobedience, and the poor people to knock the rich on the head for feeding them."

"Softly," said I: "if you ever heard the mythological Stupeo, you would have thought differently. The rich plunder you, tax you, and drive you."

"That's as bouncing a lie as ever was uttered," said he bluntly: "we don't plunder them to be sure, because its all in the way of business, but we tax them pretty soundly, and my ostler drives them."

---

* Political Justice. [Editor's note: An allusion to Godwin's thoughts on the disadvantages of coercion in punishment. Reason and argument, Godwin asserts in *Political Justice*, are more effective in promoting virtue and morality than penalties and threats. See *Political Justice*, Book VII, "Of Crimes and Punishments."]

"You don't comprehend," said I: "I speak of political evils."

"What have I to do with politics?" said he. "Let every man mind his own business, and I'll be bound for it the nation will run very well. Why now, there's a canting set of mealy-mouthed vagabonds, preaching up rebellion and setting people by the ears, and what good comes on it? Why, the minister, to keep his seat, pulls the reins tighter, and the steady horse is pinched for the restiveness of his companion."

"But," said I, "these are only partial evils: we ought to consider the good of the whole, and the benefit mankind will receive."

"Benefit! what, to talk politics when their families are starving, and about the Rights of Man when they are drinking their children's maintenance, and about clothing the negroes of Africa, when their own family is in rags. I tell ye, master, I've seen enough of these here rotten politics in my ale-room."

I found his conceptions so gross and stupid, that I determined to remain no longer under his roof; and, though I could scarcely walk, I took a place in a stage-coach for London.

CHAPTER V.

THE VAGABOND MEETS WITH VARIOUS ADVEN-TURES—A DUEL IN THE REPUBLICAN STYLE.

In the stage were two female passengers, a young man well dressed, and two persons with the appearance of substantial tradesmen.

"Well, Mr. Adams," said one of the tradesmen, as soon as the stage had cleared the town, "Is there any news from London? Have the rioters in St. George's Fields dispersed yet?"[50]

"Dispersed! No," cried Adams, "nor I hope ever will, till they have cut up popery root and branch, and established liberty."

"So you would establish liberty by religious persecution? That would be like the Americans fighting for freedom with one hand, and rattleing the whip over their slaves with the other."

"You and I never agree, Master Ketchup; you have read so

little, that you are quite ignorant of all the wheels within wheels that set the great crane of government in motion."

"I never heard that government was like a crane," said the young gentleman; "Pray, how may that be?"

"Why, it lifts heavy brains into the cockloft of honour," retorted Adams, with a loud laugh. "You thought, I suppose, you had caught a green one: it is not for ignorant people to talk politics."

"You are right, my friend," replied the young gentleman; "and I can give you another simile:—government is like a crane, because it lifts all the rascals it catches out of this world."

"Gentlemen," said I, "this is idle punning, and beneath the discussion of men who think on the glorious dawn of liberty that is breaking from the shores of America."[51]

"And blazing in the destruction of houses in London," said Ketchup. "I have, however, little doubt yet, but we shall be able to reduce the Americans to obedience."

"Never," cried Adams, "never: the French will pour in troops upon Canada from the Baltic; and I had it as a private fact, that they were at this moment marching from the Spanish settlements in South America, and intended to take our Hudson's Bay factory in their route, and to ruin our Newfoundland fishery.*[52] Then, what shall we do for whale-bone and lamp oil? The streets of London will be involved in darkness, and I shall never go to club without loaded pistols."

"Be not alarmed," said the young gentleman, laughing at the geographical error, which was a mere trifle: "they never will do

---

* A postmaster's son at Louvain, of the name of Wolfe, whose intellects were deranged, had for many years imagined himself to be a prince. As his madness was harmless, his friends did not confine him, and he used to sign his name the Prince de Wolfe, and to wear stars and ribbons of different orders. This Prince wrote a letter to the *Assembly*, testifying his admiration of the wisdom and philosophy of their decrees, and promising to imitate so great and good an example in his own territories.—The letter was received, and read with enthusiasm in the Assembly, and the president was ordered to write an answer to the Prince de Wolfe.

One would be apt to think the ignorance of the twelfth century was returned, when the geography of Brabant was unknown in France.

PLAYFAIR's History of Jacobinism, page 346.

[Editor's note: Walker's footnote reprints the bulk of a footnote in Playfair's *History of Jacobinism* (1:346 n.). Brabant was a province of the Austrian Netherlands, which were annexed by the French in 1795.]

it. There is news arrived within the last twenty-four hours, that the whole expedition has been wrecked upon the flats, off the coast of Hanover."

"Indeed," cried Adams, "I lament it from my soul; but I hope yet that liberty will prosper. If they would take my way, they would run no danger of these horrid tempests. But people in office are always too proud to take advice from those who are in low situations, or they might listen and learn."

"Well," said the youth, "let us hear your advice, if it be no great secret."

"Why, now, this is it, and can any thing be clearer?—Is not France a continent? and is not America a continent? and is not a continent, as Johnson's Dictionary says,[53] land not disjoined by the sea from other lands? What then should prevent them from marching over land to the relief of the Americans? We hear every day of journies by land to the East-Indies, and America is not half so far."

"Did you ever look at the map of the world?" said the youth; "you would then see a trifling objection."

"I'll bet you a bottle," cried Adams, "it is so in Johnson's Dictionary, and that's the best book of the sort."

I sat in some little pain for the well-meaning Adams, who seemed to have a clear sense of truth and reason; and what after all does it signify to know the relative situation of countries, it only conduces to extended oppression. Had Alexander known of China, he would not have lamented the want of other worlds to destroy.

"Mr. Adams," said I, "you seem a man of a true mind, and so far as you wish the Americans success in the cause of universal man, I honour you; and were the profound politician Stupeo here, he would press you to his bosom as a brother of the human race. But, my dear friend, when shall we see an end of this detestable butchery of our species? When shall we cease to worry and devour each other?"

"In a republic," said Adams, "no man has an inclination to quarrel—war always originates from kings. If there were no kings, there would be no wars."

"I am tired of this eternal babble," said the young gentleman. "I abhor war from my soul as much as any man; but is it possible mankind can be dupes to so glaring a lie? What were the republics of Greece and Rome, but a company of banditti, who over-ran all the countries which could not oppose them? These very Romans pretended to emancipate the people they went to conquer; yet, when they had reduced them to the state of dependent provinces, so heavy were the taxes they imposed, that Rollin informs us in the tenth volume of his history, page 136,54 that the people of Asia frequently sold their children of both sexes to pay these republicans for procuring them freedom. What were the so much boasted Spartans? who were too imperious to till the ground, and had all things in *equality*. Were they not worse than the most cruel despot that ever breathed, to a whole people, whom they compelled to every servile employ? What were the refined Athenians, but a company of boxers and prize-fighters, on a par with our porters and draymen?55 But let us look coolly into the subject, and we shall find, whatever be the ostensible reason, all sorts of governments, and all the tribes of the earth have ever engaged in war."

"You are right," returned I. "Mankind has hitherto been in a state of childhood, but the new philosophy will teach them to go without leading-strings. Stupeo has demonstrated, that when men are sufficiently enlightened, their chains will drop off as by magic; every man will hail his fellow as his brother, and the copper-coloured Indian will clasp in his arms the white European. Can any heart not beat with rapture at the idea? Can any mind resist the torrent of omnipotent truth?"

"Your ideas are very strange, I must confess," said he, "but they are morally impracticable. If you destroy the arts, and return to pure nature, how will you teach men the new philosophy? How will you prevent them sinking into barbarous ignorance?"

"That is not my business," said I, "it is the greatest good we are to prefer, and not to be staggered by apparent and trifling evils."

"You are as far wrong, my dear Sir," said he, "in true maxims of political jurisprudence, as this learned gentleman is in his knowledge of geography. One thing let me however observe, and I have done. When we see the infinitude of principles and ideas on subjects of religion and politics, ought we not to be careful how we destroy all the establishments which time has sanctified?"

"Truth," cried I, "cannot admit of error: alter it, and transform it as you will, it is still in its essence the same; and the divine Stupeo—"

"Was for aught I see," interrupted he peevishly, "an arrant fool."

I saw it was in vain to attempt reclaiming bigotry and prejudice so firmly established, and I attached myself to Adams, who seemed to have made some progress in real knowledge.

After dinner, we were proceeding over a fine cultivated track of country, and passed by several weather-beaten and aged countrymen, who were mending an hedge.

"See," cried Adams, "the effects of aristocracy and luxury. It is from thence all the miseries of the poor arise. Why is one man to wallow in wealth, while another is labouring in an hedge for a scanty existence? No man can give a reason for this."

"Would reasons convince you," said the young man, "I would endeavour to give you them, for I am grieved to see any entertain such strange doctrines.—Luxury is a vulgar phrase for every thing possessed by another of which we could make use; but in reality it is like the manure to the ground, which causes every thing to bring forth double increase; it gives invention to the ingenious, it fosters arts and sciences, it employs the mechanic, the shopkeeper, and the merchant; without luxury, none of these could meet employ."

"But the lands would feed all who dwelt upon them; mechanics would not waste their health in the noxious fumes of various processes, and the poor would have less to do."

"It is true, the ground would feed all who cultivated it: but if we infer from facts, we shall universally find agriculture keeping pace with what we call luxury. You will find, that though on calculating upon paper, this country of England, if cultivated like a garden, would feed thrice the number of inhabitants it contains; yet, unfortunately for political romances, the people would inevitably diminish, and a poor half-starved system of husbandry infallibly ensue. It is by calling forth variety of inventions, giving employment to all kinds of genius, that every thing is urged to perfection, and the multiplication of mankind forwarded."

"But virtue and talents," said I, "do not meet their rewards, while vice rides triumphant: you surely cannot say that is politically right? Why should a man be despised because in a mean garb? And why are riches alone honoured?"

"For this reason:—riches are only the means of gratifying our desires, and increasing our conveniences. A wise man, and a man of genius will endeavour to do so by laudable means. In the present constitution of society, it is in the power of every man possessing real abilities to rise to a station equal to those abilities; and therefore we reverence the exteriors of wealth, tacitly bestowing it upon all the possessors, because indiscriminate intercourse will not admit of time to distinguish the truly worthy. It is rare, very rare, to find a man of genius in a wretched situation, without having brought himself so by imprudence; but it is by no means rare to find those, whose self-love has taught them a wrong value to their abilities, and who, therefore, repine at the success of others, and their own failure, as the greatest injustice; and originating in a depraved government, and a profligate generation."

I was extremely chagrined that the sophisms of this youth should pass unrefuted, for his arguments and volubility had so confused my senses, that I did not recollect any retort, and nothing can be more shocking than to lose the last reply in an argument.

The fineness of the road invited the coachman to drive forward with celerity. "The poor beasts," said the gentleman, "feel for our riding at our ease. I am astonished any of our modern nervous philosophers make use of carriages."

"Why," cried Adams, "what are the beasts to us? They want human understanding to free themselves. Let us first emancipate man, and then we shall not need the aid of animals."

At that moment the coach overset in a waggon rut; and several countrymen came from their labour, in a neighbouring field, to assist to right it. Fortunately none were hurt; but Adams snatching up a whip, made at the coachman, cursing him for a careless scoundrel. "Who the devil are you," cried the coachman, "that give yourself such airs?"—"And who are you," cried Adams, "a lousy, stupid, drunken coachman, with not half the sense of your beasts. I'll enter an action against you, Sirrah. What am I! a gentleman, a citizen, and housekeeper, to run the danger of having my neck broken by you?"

"Peace, friend," said the youth, "you have forgot that you are usurping all the airs of imperious aristocracy: come, and help to right the carriage."

"I help to right the coach! dirty my clothes! and work like a porter! Sir, you mistake me."

"I do, indeed," said the youth. "But what right have you to be exempted more than your fellow men? If there was a revolution to-morrow, your lot would be a ploughman." So saying, he turned indignantly away, and helped the peasants to replace the coach, I being engaged in comforting the women, who were very much frightened.

It was discovered that one of the wheels were broken, and the next inn at the distance of some miles. The countrymen finding they could render us no more service, begged something to drink.—"Come," said the youth to Adams, "you would not work yourself, let us see your generosity in rewarding the labour of others."

"For what?" said Adams. "It is the duty of every man to help his fellow men; in fact, those in distress have a right to demand it. To reward a man for doing his duty is unjust, because it is a bribe to do what ought to be done: beside, the money may be wanted to some act of charity, and the greatest good is always to be preferred."

"You are right," said I, "in theory, but the present state of things frequently infringe upon political justice: for instance, I employ a workman to make me a set of chairs, for which I appropriate ten pounds; this man is rich, and another who is poor, comes and tells me his case; political justice commands me to give the ten pounds to the poor man, and let the other go without."[56]

"I profess," said the youth, "that is a most admirable argument; no wonder so many are enamoured of the new political justice."

The affair of the countrymen being settled, by the youth giving them a crown to drink his health, we were proceeding towards the inn in full cavalcade, when a post-chaise driving up with a single gentleman, he ordered the driver to stop, and calling to the youth—"My Lord," said he, "is it you? What in the world are you now upon? Some frolic, I suppose?"

"My dear friend," replied the young gentleman, "this is a fortunate meeting, a little accident has happened to our vehicle, and I will trouble you for a lift."

"Upon my soul," said Adams, bowing profoundly, "I humbly beg your pardon, my Lord, I hope nothing I have said will prejudice your Lordship; and if you will honour me by taking one of my cards, no man in the trade shall use you better."

I was confounded at this abjection of soul, and walked forward without taking the smallest notice of the young nobleman.— This is a strange world, said I to myself; and it is plain, as Stupeo said, that half mankind are fools and slaves to commerce, with all its train of selfish affections. Poor Adams has a weak soul, he sees clearly what is right, he feels the invigorating rays of truth, but his habits of trade drag him from the daring height, and sink him again into all the prejudices attached to property.

The inn where the stage was to stop was not the general rout for the stages; and it being only three in the afternoon, I determined to proceed on foot without waiting for the coachman, whom I had not paid for my journey (but that was nothing); I was not to be prevented by prejudice and common-place rules from following that free-will, which I possessed in my breast, for the direction of my actions.

I still felt the pains of my bruises, and walked forward slowly, admiring the beauty of the country, and reading the great book of Nature. I fell into a profound trance, and began to doubt my own existence, which is very necessary, according to all philosophers, as we thence proceed in synthetic order to erect hypothesis as upon a base. The fashionable Hume doubted whether he thought he existed;[57] but I went farther, I doubted whether I doubted that I thought I did not exist, and from thence proceeding to establish the axiom, *Cogitas ergo sum*, I think therefore I am.[58] I began to think that I did not think, that I thought at all, when I was awakened by the sound of several voices; and looking up, I perceived coming along the road a man on horseback, with several people surrounding him; one held the reins, and two others, with constables staves, held him on each side.

A sight so shockingly shameful to human nature, and the natural freedom of man, aroused me to attempt some noble exploit. I darted forward, and brandishing my cudgel—"What right," cried I, "have you to imprison your fellow man? This is a shameful abuse of power, it is all society hunting down an unfortunate individual, who has ten thousand chances against him, especially if brought to trial."*

---

* Godwin. [Editor's note: Walker is here alluding to Godwin's arguments against coercive punishment, notably imprisonment, such as: "The most common method

"He is an highwayman and a murderer," replied several, "and you look like a madman."

"That is nothing to the purpose," cried I, kindling into patriotic frenzy, at recollecting some of the arguments of the great Stupeo, and the maxims of political justice. "The man who professes himself ready to commit murder, seems to be scarcely a less dangerous member of society than he, who having already committed murder, has no apparent intention to repeat his offence.*—Unless this man appeared ready, and in a situation to repeat his offence, political justice requires him to be left at his own discretion. He is no more likely to repeat the crime than any man here, for aught you can tell; and no man ought to be deprived of his liberty on presumption."

"Pelt the madman," cried several clowns. "Whoever heard such nonsense? A murderer is not to be punished for committing the crime, but appearing ready to commit it."

"Certainly," cried I, "could you hear the mythological, metaphysical, philosophical Stupeo, you would not hesitate a moment bowing before almighty truth and moral light; but if you are like stupid beasts, deaf to the voice of reason, I insist that you liberate the prisoner."

So saying, I seized the bridle from the man who held it, and the highwayman sticking his spurs in the beast, rode over the constable, and would have gained his liberty, had not a sturdy clown levelled a stone at his head, which brought him over his horse. I was seized by several at once, and notwithstanding a stout resistance, I was dragged like a slave, and forced against my will into an inn upon the road.

Are these the laws, the detestable maxims of society? cried I,

pursued in depriving the offender of the liberty he has abused is to erect a public jail, in which offenders of every description are thrust together, and left to form among themselves what species of society they can. Various circumstances contribute to imbue them with habits of indolence and vice, and to discourage industry; and no effort is made to remove or soften these circumstances. It cannot be necessary to expatiate upon the atrociousness of this system. Jails are, to a proverb, seminaries of vice; and he must be an uncommon proficient in the passion and the practice of injustice, or a man of sublime virtue, who does not come out of them a much worse man than he entered" (*Political Justice*, Book VII, Chap. vi, 403).]

* Godwin's Political Justice, page 761. [Editor's note: "The man who professes ... to repeat his offence" is a verbatim citation from *Political Justice*, Part VII, Chap. vii, 408.]

Am I to be confined here as a prisoner of state, for attempting to rescue an injured man from the tyranny of the law? O that the glorious day were come, when every man shall act from the divine impulses of his will, and reason and liberty be acknowledged as the presiding deities.

While I was exclaiming to myself, a constable entered, and informed me, that as I was deemed either intoxicated or touched in the head, it had been agreed, that on my paying five pounds as a compensation to those I had wounded, they would not enter an action against me, otherwise I should be sent to the county gaol for attempting a rescue.

"Society," cried I, "I detest thy barbarous maxims and rights: what times! what country is this! where a man shall be imprisoned for an act of moral virtue in the eye of political justice, and be obliged to pay for his liberty? Dear, dear liberty! what are five pounds to thee? Here, take the money, and permit me to fly from the whole herd of mankind. O, my dear Stupeo, would that I could discover thy retreat; some philosophic retirement conceals the brightness of thy genius from mankind."

"There is a return chaise for London at the door," said one of the waiters, "are you going that way?"

"Any way," said I; and following him, I entered the chaise, and was driven rapidly towards London.

I always make it a rule to read the great book of Nature, and philosophise as I go along the road; and I could not but be delighted to see the great book bound in green, with variegated edges of trees and flowers. Now, thought I, is this chaise an idea or a reality; I cannot prove it by argument to be real, it is therefore an idea, a whirling idea: now I have a very strong impression of this whirling idea; I wonder if I was to step out into what seems an highway to my eyes (but which may be in fact the Red Sea), I should still continue whirling to London. This was a very metaphysical problem, which nobody but the fashionable Hume, the conundrumic Berkely,[59] or the great Stupeo could resolve.

The cries of *No Popery*[60] roused my attention, and I perceived we were entering the metropolis. *No Popery* was written upon every house, and a parcel of ragged fellows, with No Popery chalked upon their hats, stopped the chaise, and demanded money.

"For what?" said I, "I don't care any thing about Popery; a wise man will have no religion at all, because the prejudices and narrow principles of religious sects will prevent his mind expanding to the broad beams of truth."

"No gammon!—Tip us the grub!"[61] cried several greasy fellows. "He's a Popery man! a Roman Catholic! and an enemy to the church!" roared out others, while the words "Go it! go it!" sounded around me, and a shower of mud and stones nearly overwhelmed me, smashing the glass of the chaise, and almost knocking down the driver.

"You are a set of rascally cowards," cried I: "will any man of you fight me: I will die in the cause of freedom."—A ring! a ring! was shouted and formed; and stripping off my coat and hat, I threw them into the chaise, which drove away from the fury of the mob.

There is something generous in a mob; we there see the first germ of justice, generosity, and magnanimity; we see that a giant of a man shall not be allowed to annihilate a little one. 'Tis true, that the love of novelty often inclines them to promote a quarrel where it might be reconciled: but no man should be ashamed to box in a just cause, especially if he remembers the value of the pugilistic science at Athens and Sparta:[62] and why, because I am better dressed should I refuse to enter the ring with a dirty antagonist, whom I may have injured? Whoever has read the novels of a very great dramatist, must be struck with the beauties of boxing;[63] an art, which I hope will supersede the use of pistols between jealous lovers and injured husbands.

A champion being found, he came forward with an aspect horridly ferocious. He was a great-boned Irishman, and all the vile passions of human nature were written in his countenance. His savage appearance inclined the mob in my favour, who uttered a long roar of applause when I intrepidly determined to stand the contest. I had taken several lessons at College, and knew the most scientific motions, so that the difference was not very great, and we immediately fell to.*

After six or seven rounds I marked an opening in his right

---

* See the elegant reasons for boxing in Anna St Ives and Hugh Trevor: two Novels, which the democratic Reviews hold up as samples of virtue and morality. 'Tis true,

guard, and with a well-placed side stroke, cut a long rip in his fore-head, from whence the blood streamed into his eyes, nearly blind-ing him, at which the mob (who are always generous) roared with a tumult of admiration and pleasure. I now had considerable advantage, and though I had three teeth jammed into my mouth, I broke one of his ribs, and levelled him with a full blow upon the ground, where he turned black in the face, and was left for dead.

A hackney coach was instantly pressed into my service, and I was conducted by the mob in triumph to a public-house, where they drank themselves half drunk in the joy of my having conquered.

Though I had at first been in considerable danger of being murdered, yet my subsequent valour had rendered me dear to them all; so true is it, that pure human nature can discern truth when it descends to the level of their own ideas.

I was here cleared of gore, and refreshed with some cordials. I had lost my coat and hat, and had not paid the chaise, which I knew not where to find; but these were mere partial evils. A generous blacksmith accommodated me with a coat, and a butcher insisted I take his red and blue cap for love, for he had never seen a better cock in his life, as tough as bull-beef. My dress was completed by a pair of trowsers, and a large cockade of blue ribbon.[64]

It was now near eight o'clock. The mob who were drinking in the street were more than a thousand strong, and the shouts and vociferations of No Popery! Lord George Gordon for ever! rent the air.[65]

---

if blasphemy and curses are virtue and morality, these offsprings of the new school have an ample claim. [Editor's note: *Anna St. Ives* (1792) and *The Adventures of Hugh Trevor* (1794), two popular Jacobin novels by Thomas Holcroft (see note 62). Echoing much of Godwin's doctrine of political justice, Holcroft's novels are vigorous satirical attacks on various aspects of late-eighteenth-century English society, including the Church, the law, the university and reactionary politicians. Walker is right in asserting that Holcroft wanted literature to serve a moral purpose—in Holcroft's case, expunging corrupt social institutions. And the heroes in both novels do get involved in boxing fights: Frank Henley faces the Irish thug and experienced pugilist Mac Fane in *Anna St. Ives* (Vol. VI, Letter cx), while Hugh Trevor gets involved in a fight in which he nearly kills his opponent (Vol. IV, Chap. ii). Both novels present boxing in the context of a sort of raw justice-of-the-street as favored by English mobs. While he does not quite condone boxing as a mob-orchestrated people's court, Holcroft is very dismissive of the "chivalric" alternative to boxing, viz. dueling, which was the preferred way of settling scores amongst aristocrats (see Walker's footnotes to Chapter III).]

A man, dressed like a chimney-sweeper, with No Popery gilt on a blue ribbon round his hat, came familiarly up to me, and taking me by the hand, led me into a corner of the room.—"Are you engaged?" said he.—"No," I replied, "I know of no engagement."—"I beg pardon," he returned, "I thought, by the clothes you wear underneath, you were one of us."

"I am always for the greatest good," I replied; "in seeking a magnificent object, we are not to regard the means."

At these words he clasped his arms round me, nearly smothering me with soot.—"I know," said he, "you are a man of education—all London will shortly be in flames, and the cause of mankind will be successful. We have cast aside prejudices and human frailties; it is necessary in the great labour of a revolution. We have at our command some thousand insurgents, who, with a little more discipline, may be brought to face the regulars, and then despotism will tumble with a tremendous crash; the very earth will be split by its fall, and the gulph of hell yawn and swallow it up."

"O glorious!" said I, "then the great day is dawning. But what are those cries of No Popery?"

"It is our watch-word. The ignorant believe they are fighting for religion, but we guide them and direct where the storm shall fall. The passions of men must be raised, their rational senses must be confounded with terrific reports, before the mass can be roused; but there are always a sufficient number of profligates and vagabonds to join in with any thing.—You appear one of the true men; you will be a great man in the new system of things. At this moment the mob are plundering Newgate; I am wanted in another place; I beg you will direct the mob to Snow-hill, for I am certain you may lead them any where.[66] I have studied the mobs of different nations, and they are all alike. Go then and prosper."

I was on fire at the glorious idea of emancipating the victims of tyranny and oppression, of opening the cells to the heart-sick offender, who could not hope any redress from those laws which condemned him.

"Copenhagen House" by James Gillray (November 1795). By courtesy of the National Portrait Gallery, London.

CHAPTER VI.

THE VAGABOND ACHIEVES SEVERAL NOBLE EXPLOITS—AN UNEXPECTED MEETING IN THE CELLS OF NEWGATE—A SLIGHT IDEA OF A REVOLUTION.

I descended amongst the mob, and grasping a pole with blue colours, and the words *No Popery* inscribed upon it—"Let us go," cried I, "my dear boys. No Popery! Lord George Gordon for ever!" A loud and repeated huzza rent the air, and the prodigious mass of people pressed after me towards Newgate. I was astonished in myself at the change of my fortune: I had but an hour before been in danger of being stoned by the very mob that, under my commands, would have made no scruple of setting London on fire. But such is always the reward of great talents in moments of popular commotion; it is then great men are brought forward from obscurity.

Thousands were already assembled before the august deposit of trembling victims: our reinforcement was received with the triumphant shouting of the patriotic bands, who felt the energy of liberty pulsating in every artery. The air was crimsoned with the flames of the jailor's house, and his furniture was cast into a bonfire, which sparkled in my eyes like an offering to the Goddess of Reason, or like that glorious flame which consumed all bonds and engagements when equality was established by Lycurgus[67] at Sparta.

I hastened to second the attack upon this grand fortress, by leading my followers into Newgate-street, where, with sledge hammers, crows, and iron pallisadoes,[68] we soon broke an entrance into these detestable abodes, where the poor criminals were panting for freedom. With an high ladder, and in the sight of thousands, I scaled the lofty walls, exulting as I rose at the glorious prospect before us, and waving my colours as a trophy of conquest.

We soon penetrated into the wards of this almost impenetrable building, which short-sighted politicians might have supposed capable of repulsing an invading army: but the energies of the people are unresistible when determined on emancipation, and *unopposed.*

Fire-balls and fire-brands soon set the timbers in flames. I ran from one ward to the next, and from cell to cell, sounding the tidings of liberty, and receiving a thousand blessings from those tongues which had too often been turned to curses and execrations. Pickpockets, cut-purses, shop-lifters, and felons of every denomination, hailed the dawn of returning freedom, and sprang forward to a glorious consummation, helping us to destroy this dreadful tomb to all who depise the laws, and claim the natural privilege of dividing property.

The flames raged and ran with rapidity among the thick oak planking, which cracked with the noise of thunder; the smoke and heat was nearly suffocating, and many in their over eagerness to clear the dungeons, fell martyrs in the glorious cause. In a cell which I had nearly overlooked, I found a miserable wretch half naked upon the ground. I had broke open his door with an iron crow, and the first object he saw was a tremendous blaze of light, which proceeded from the opposite wainscot on fire. He had long heard the shouts of exulting thousands, and the burstings of the fire. "Heaven and earth," cried he, "is the day of judgment come? Or have I alive sunk into hell? Are you a fiend?" said he, staring wildly, and starting from me. "Are you come to pitch me into everlasting flames?"

To say truth, my figure was not a little hideous, for I was covered with all sorts of dirt, swelled in my face from the different bruises I had received, and streaked with blood from a cut in my head by the falling of a plank: but how was I astonished to perceive by the light of the fire, the great Stupeo, the wonderful philosopher, in chains.

"Exult," cried I, "you are revenged, my master, my tutor, liberty has reared her standard on these walls, and the fabric of selfish tyranny is tumbling about our ears. Haste, get these irons off, and join in the noble cause of liberty and man."

Stupeo immediately started up, uttering incoherent expressions of joy. I hurried him from the chamber of his studies into the press-yard,[69] where his detestable fetters were knocked off, and being refreshed with a large goblet of wine from the cellars of the gaoler, we went into the street to enjoy the exultation of the surrounding multitude, and the most tremendous sight that can well be conceived; a sight which awed the military into inaction, and struck the magistrates into a panic of the most pusillanimous nature: but cowardice is ever allied to terror, and I stood considering how best to exert the force now in action, that the greatest blow might be struck to the present detestable system of monopolised property.

Part of the army of pariots remained upon the walls, and dancing round the ruins to prevent every attempt at extinguishing the flames: the rest followed Stupeo and myself, who encouraged them to persevere and be free. The crowd would have destroyed Langdale's, a large distillers, in Holborn,[70] but I represented that this was a paltry business, when we had yet to open the doors of so many gaols to the liberation of our brethren; besides, we had already near four hundred felons amongst us, and the augmentation of this force was a grand point, for who could fight for freedom like those who had experienced its loss? Or who would level property like those who had nothing to lose, and all to gain.

As we proceeded, every passenger was stopped and plundered, and from every house was collected, two or three times over, considerable contributions. I would have remonstrated, but a fellow, who had been confined on a charge of murder, and whom I had liberated, swore he would rip me up alive if I attempted to prevent it; and indeed, though his argument was not in the line of reason, Stupeo reconciled me to the practice.

"In revolutions and public commotions," said he, "no man in Athens was allowed to be neutral: every man who does not fight for us, ought to be considered as against us; and if we follow the new philosophy, we should shew no mercy to those who support the system of despotism."*

Having liberated the prisoners in Clerkenwell,[71] our forces were divided to objects of less moment. That division under our direction proceeded to Lord Mansfield's;[72] and there liberty and rational principles received a complete triumph over all regular order. The musty records of precedents, cases and law, made a fire to warm the people they had so long enslaved: I own I wished to have preserved

---

* An article in the Jacobin Creed. [Editor's note: Not identified.]

several works of curiosity and art, but Stupeo would not suffer a thing to be taken.—"Let them all perish together," said he, "we have yet remaining too much of art to be happy; let us not stain the cause with the appearance of selfishness."

"But why then," said I, "are we to plunder the poor inhabitants? Surely it were better to supply ourselves from stores like these?"

"No," answered he, "can you not perceive that the destruction of property must be the grand aim; from those who have little we must take that little, and the hoards of affluence must be utterly destroyed. As long as one single cart-load of property remains in any country, there will be no genuine equality."

From these ever-memorable exploits, I and Stupeo, with several select leaders, retired to an obscure public-house, to contrive and arrange the undertakings of the ensuing night. I already fancied myself as great as the immortal John the Painter.73

At our meeting, several foreigners of *liberal principles** were present. A plan was proposed for organizing the body of the people, and urging them to throw off the yoke of dependence, and declare themselves free. A paper, titled *The Thunderer*,† was drawn up by Stupeo, which he hoped would kindle the glow of enthusiasm, and awake the people to their rights.

The prisons were condemned to destruction, that none of our brave followers might be deprived of their liberty. The New-river

---

* The cant word for no principles but those of profligacy, irreligion, &c.
† See the Political Magazine for 1780. [Editor's note: *The Political Magazine and Parliamentary, Naval, Military, and Literary Journal* was a monthly periodical published in London by J. Bew between 1780 and 1791. The issue of June 1780 was devoted almost entirely to the Gordon Riots, and, aside from analyses of the background and causes of the riots, descriptions of the life and ideas of Lord George Gordon, and his speeches in Parliament prior to the riots, contained day-by-day accounts of the riots, as well as reports of debates in the House of Lords, the King's speeches on the subject of the riots, an account of Gordon's arrest, and an assessment of the number of people injured and killed. *The Thunderer:* a political pamphlet by William Moor (fl. 1780), published at the time of the Gordon Riots (London, 1780). A handbill advertisement announcing the publication of Moor's pamphlet was distributed by the alleged publisher, C. Thompson, around that time ("England in Blood. On Thursday morning the 8th inst. at nine o'clock will be published, in one sheet and half, folio, price only three-pence, by C. Thompson, No. 159, Fleet-street, The Thunderer: addressed to George Gordon ..."; ESTC CN44770), but no copy of "The Thunderer" has been located. The affair of the "diabolical handbill" announcing the publication of Moore's pamphlet is reported on page 434 of the June issue of *The Political Magazine*.]

water[74] was to be cut off, that we might have the town effectually at command, and compel those weak and obstinate people who were afraid of joining our standard. The Museum[75] we fixed upon as a good deposit for stores after all that trumpery should be burnt, which gives edge to a childish employment of time. The toll-houses on the bridge we condemned, because bridges ought to be built without subjecting individuals to expence. The East-India warehouses and the Custom-house we considered as large lumber rooms for monopolising property that belonged to every body.[76]

The Tower and the Bank were two grand objects, behind which we could entrench in defiance of the troops which were drawing towards the town from every quarter;[77] and indeed our plans were too extensive and grand for me to detail in minutiæ.

In the attack upon the Bank I was severely wounded in the hand by a musket ball, for there the soldiers recovered their thirst for blood, and fired upon the innocent people, who were gloriously fighting for liberty. We determined there to conquer or die, being strongly reinforced by the Borough[78] patriots, who had burnt the toll-houses on the bridge in their rout. To place a just sense of our cause before them, an horse, loaded with the chains of Newgate, was driven through the crowd in place of colours, and every breast beat with throbs of vengeance at the sight.

A body of savages on horseback cut down several with their swords, and the infantry made use of their infernal muskets, which severely galled the unarmed patriots. It was shocking to hear the tremendous roar of exulting rage sink after every platoon,[79] as if it was exhausted.

Poor Stupeo, who stood beside me encouraging a band of those whom the ignorant call felons to an attack on the infantry with iron spikes and bottles, received a shot that laid him dead beside me. The mob, who now began to faint from the unequal contest, trampled over him, and hurried me along with them. I endeavoured to rally them, and one of them dashed a link[80] into my face, which I returned by shooting him with a pistol, for I had found a very good pair in an house we had gutted, and nothing could be more proper than turning the weapons of tyrants against themselves.

I was confounded at the fickle disposition of a mob, which

can only arise from their want of instruction; and so long as what is called civil order and police exists, I very much fear the people will never unanimously rise: but, however, truth is making a rapid progress, and it must irresistibly break forth into a glorious day.

The mob would have executed summary justice upon me for the murder of the link-bearer, had I not escaped through the narrow streets into Holborn, where Langdale's (the distiller) was on fire. Torrents of spirits ran in the streets, and being played upon the neighbouring houses for water, augmented the danger and the flames.[81]

Here the military destroyed a great number of patriots, who were dancing round the fire, or tumbling the furniture out the windows; while many others fell victims to the half rectified spirits which ran in torrents through the streets.[82]

I saw clearly it was a lost cause, for want of a more regular organization, and I lamented that we had not made better use of the time allowed by the timidity (they called it humanity) of the government; we should then have reduced the whole city to an heap of ashes, from which liberty, like a phœnix, would have arisen in ten-fold splendour: the mass of luxury and of wealth would have been annihilated, and the partial injury individuals might have received would have been amply compensated by the new order of things which must have arisen.

It would have been, as Stupeo often said, talking of revolutions like the fermentation of anarchy, which from all the rage of lust, of revenge, of murder, of cruelty, of rapine, and unheard-of distress, sinks into a glorious and heart-soothing calm.*

Indeed, nothing could be more dreadfully great than the appearance of London on that glorious night. The large body of fire issuing from the different conflagrations of the Fleet Prison, King's Bench, Toll-houses on Blackfriar's-bridge, Mr. Langdale's two immense warehouses full of spirits, and a vast number of small fires, together with the illuminations,[83] which of themselves would have rendered the streets as light as day, all ascending into the air, and consolidating together, formed an atmosphere of flames, impressing the mind of the spectator with an idea, as if not

---

* Pain and Godwin on Revolutions and Anarchy.

only the whole metropolis was burning, but all nations yielding to the final consummation of all things. But how much greater must have been the sight, amidst which even the soul of a modern philosopher might tremble, would it have been to see the flames chasing the distracted people from street to street; to see the enemies of liberty perishing in heaps before the burning sword of retributive justice; to see the rage of lust despoiling those disdainful beauties, whose love heretofore was only to be won by crying; to see trembling tyrants biting the dust, and drinking their own blood as it mingled in the kennels; to hear amidst all this uproar the thunder of cannons, the whistling of bullets, the clashing of swords, the tumbling of houses, the groans of the wounded, the cries of the conquerors; and see, amidst the blazing and red-hot ruins, the sons of Freedom and Liberty waving the three-coloured banners dropping with the blood of their enemies, and hailing the everlasting Rights of Man!!!

Ah! how dear must such a scene be to the *friends of liberty* and *universal man*; nor should the paultry consideration of two or three thousand being massacred, to satiate private revenge, be taken into account of so great, so immortal a consideration.

CHAPTER VII.

HUMANITY OF A MOB—THE VAGABOND IS UNFOR-
TUNATELY PREVENTED ATTAINING A MARTYR-
DOM—GAMING DEMONSTRATED TO BE THE ONLY
LIBERAL SCIENCE.

I was so agitated by the failure of our glorious cause, that I was nearly putting a period to my existence, especially when I recollected the shocking and infamous system of a constitution, which none but fools can see *any one* virtue in; and this was, that every man who had suffered by this effervescence of liberty, would receive satisfaction for his losses, and thus the people would be made to pay for what they had destroyed; so that our failing in the ultimatum was worse than if nothing had been done, and we had in fact been strengthening the lash for ourselves. To be sure, there was this alleviating reflection, that the cowardly and selfish citizens would have to contribute equally with the patriots.

I wished myself away from such a detestable country as England, where property is guarded with as much vigilance as if it were a deity; and no man, however obnoxious, can be plundered, without a right of retribution from the parish or county, a thing totally unknown in other countries, and quite inimical to genuine liberty.

My wound, my bruises, and fatigue had nearly exhausted my strength; for till mind shall overcome matter, the human frame stands in need of repose and cessation from action, though it is astonishing what exertions we are capable of, when the mind is engaged in great exploits; and I have little doubt but when the new system is established, we shall have no need of what is called *sleep*, nor shall we require *food*, both of these being superfluous to *spiritual substance*. In fact, as my dear Stupeo says, why may we not one day become immortal?*

I did not regret the loss of this prodigious great man any other than as society lost an invaluable member, for I had strengthened my mind to the case, and should, with the immortal Brutus,[84] have looked with indifference on the death of any relation or friend, these being mere partial evils, and not to be separated from extensive designs.

It is not politically just that a wise man should expose himself carelessly to martyrdom for the sake of liberty, till he has well weighed whether the human species will be most benefited by his life or death. To run rashly on the point of a bayonet was wrong, because I might yet live to illumine the world, and catch some glorious crisis—while truth would not receive any promotion by my death at the present instance: I therefore retired unnoticed amidst the universal alarm.

---

* One would be tempted to suppose the man insane, who should maintain that the human soul was a material substance, and had no existence after death, but that he had no doubt when we had cast away our prejudices, we should become *immortal* in this present world. Such consistency is the doctrine of Godwin, Holcroft, &c. &c. [Editor's note: This appears to be a very loose reading at best of the new philosophy.]

I was very little acquainted with the town, having been there only upon one or two vacations; but the light of the fires and the brilliance of the illuminations were sufficient guides. Several watchmen looked as if they intended to stop me, but awed by the dignity of my countenance, though covered with blood and dirt, they all slunk away, so powerful is the effect of innocence and impressive resolution.

I arrived opposite a bonfire, where the furniture of a Roman Catholic milliner was blazing; it made but a paltry light, compared with the many others that gleamed in the air; and the noble band that danced around it being ashamed to be out-done in their patriotic exertions, in the goodness of their hearts dragged the bed from beneath two infants[*] and a woman in labour, which gave a great but transient addition to the fire. To be sure, the poor woman died of fright, but that could not be helped in such a case; and it is the ill-education of women which introduces all sorts of nervous affections.

In a little back alley I met an old woman carrying something in her apron; at my approach she appeared very much frightened. "What have you got there?" said I. She replied, trembling, "Only some trifles, your honour, that I have preserved from the fire." I required to see those trifles. Accordingly she opened her apron, displaying some gold fringe, a silver censor, and two cups, which she had taken from a Romish chapel. "You are heartily welcome," said I, "to these spoils of superstition; I wish you had as many more: but now, can you tell me where I may sleep securely from unwelcome intruders?"

"Aye, and that I will: come to my little lodging, my dare babe, you need not be frighted at nobody there."

Accordingly I followed her into a miserable house, up three pair of stairs, into a back garret. A crucifix stood on a chimney-piece, and a string of beads hung upon a nail, by which I soon discovered that this good lady, who had been plundering a

---

[*] Political Magazine, 1780. [Editor's note: Walker's description of what happened to the hapless Catholic milliner is based on a similar incident reported in the June 1780 issue of *The Political Magazine* (436), which is also the source of the scene following this, of the old Roman Catholic woman hoarding valuables looted from a sacked "Romish chapel" (429).]

chapel, was a Romanist; and I rejoiced to find that knowledge had reached even into a back garret, and taught an old woman to discern the cause of mankind from the bigotry of priestcraft. With this hospitable creature, who was an Irish woman, I determined to reside. Being extremely jaded and pained by my bruises, I went immediately to bed, and she hastened to procure me some refreshment. She would have fetched a surgeon, but I utterly detested the whole crew of leeches, who deal in a cant jargon (like the priests of Cybelle)[85] which nobody understands.

When the fermentation of my spirits began to cool, in spite of all my efforts I became nearly distracted. I had lost three of my teeth, and my whole body was bruised: the cut in my head, to be sure, was only an inch and a half long, and a finger deep; but I had a musket wound in my hand, which had taken off half my little finger, and grazed the rest, so that I was not in the most comfortable situation. I raved like a madman at the loss of the noble opportunity, which might not occur in a whole generation.

Before morning I became wholly delirious, burning with a violent fever; and now it was the old woman introduced a lame apothecary from the neighbourhood. I was tortured, blistered, and blooded, and underwent worse than a thousand deaths in the course of three weeks, when I recovered my senses, and awoke as from a dream. I then learnt, to my infinite regret, that the kind old woman had been taken up and hanged, adding another to the long list of victims to despotism. The apothecary pretended that the old woman had attempted to criminate me respecting the stolen articles, and that I should have been taken up had he not sworn I had been under his care prior to the riots; and it turned out, on the trial of the old woman, that she had been seen alone entering the chapel.

I reproved him severely for his falsification of truth.—"Truth," said I, "ought at all times and in every situation to be spoken. Friendship—every thing should bend to omnipotent truth. Stratagems of all kinds are detestable, even in war they are unjustifiable; and I hope tactics will be so simplified, that they will be reduced to a few general maxims, and then no man will need the experience of a long life to become a general; it will then

become a generous, manly, and open system.* Beside, in concealing the truth, you have done me an irreparable injury, you have
sunk my name in obscurity, you have deprived me of the honour
of a public death."

"It is not too late yet," replied he, "if you have an ardent desire
to swing; but I thought you had the appearance of a gentleman."

To this observation I made no reply, being agitated with the
loss I had suffered.—"All mankind," cried I, "would have seen
an example of magnanimity in the cause of freedom. Oh, my
beloved Stupeo! had you been alive, you would have gloried in
hearing the name of your pupil in the same sentence with
Massienello, William Tell, Oliver Cromwell, Cato, Leonidas,
Jaffier, and Judas Maccabæus."[86]

"We must take at least three more ounces of blood," muttered
the apothecary, and went out of the room.

I now plainly perceived that I had a rascally, ignorant, aristocratical apothecary, who meant to bleed me to death out of spite,
that my name might for ever be lost to mankind. I therefore
searched for my pistols, which I had thrust under the bed; and
that never having been disturbed since I laid down upon it, I had
the satisfaction to find them. The apothecary soon after entered,
with a ragged attendant, and made preparations to tie my arm,

---

* See Godwin's Political Justice. In one page he declaims against war, with all the fire
of words, and in another he tells us he hopes it will one day become a generous,
manly, and open system. So much for consistency.—It may not be unworthy to
remark the eternal babble kept up by the new philosophers concerning war. War is
savage, war is inhuman, war is despotic, &c. &c. Granted. Who does not know this.
But there are wars which are *inevitable*, in which, to be passive, would be tame submission to destruction. The people fortunately begin to open their eyes, and see into the
hypocrisy of these friends to the human race. They see that a republic can outstretch
the farthest stride of kingly ambition, and grasp at *universal* dominion. [Editor's note:
Godwin puts the case against war in *Political Justice*, Book V, Chap. xvi, "Of the Causes
of War," arguing that war was contrary to the nature of democracy. According to
Godwin, the only legitimate wars were defensive wars, aimed at safeguarding the
values and principles of a democracy against an invading force (see Book V, Chap.
xvii, "Of the Object of War"). Godwin nowhere expresses the hope, as Walker
suggests, that war might one day become "a generous, manly, and open system";
however, he does argue that should a defensive war be unavoidable, it should be
conducted with "firmness" and with "frankness, and an open disclosure of our
purpose, even to our enemies," while the "utmost benevolence ought to be practised
towards our enemies" (Book V, Chap. xviii, "Of the Conduct of War," 286–87).]

when grasping one of my pistols, I drew the trigger, and should have terminated his practice had the piece been loaded.

"Do you mean to murder me," said I, "with all this bleeding? Does Nature ever bleed her patients? and her you ought to follow in all things.You think I am mad, but I have sense enough to tell you never again to come in my sight."

"Who is to pay my bill?" said the frightened dealer in drugs. "I saved you from the gallows, and from dying raving mad."

"How could I have died both ways?" said I. "As to your bill, I have more need of the money myself, and the greatest good is always to be preferred."

"But my attendance and medicine must be paid for."

"What is your attendance? Ought not every man to labour for the good of his fellow men? I should be guilty of political injustice were I to reward you for doing your duty."

"But, Sir, I have dedicated my life to the practice of medicine: I have no other means of gaining a living, and cannot afford to practice for nothing."

"That is not my fault, it is the ill-construction of society. In a state well ordered, no man would receive wages, but every one would do what he esteemed the greatest general good. Had you ever listened to the lessons of the great, the immortal Stupeo, you would have been convinced of what I say, and you would have disdained a bribe to perform a duty."

"Sir," said he, humbly, in a vile depending tone, "when you reflect, you must observe that you only exchange one benefit for another. In society all must mutually hang together, and if any part be disordered, the whole organization must suffer. Men have a variety of genius, and what would become of the world if those who were willing to work gave all their labour for the benefit of the idle? All human genius would then be cramped, and directed merely to the providing of food."

"Peace, peace," cried I, "will you, an ignorant apothecary, a pounder of drugs, pretend to talk philosophy with a disciple of the everlasting Stupeo?—Why, Sir, I could talk with you on this subject for seven years, and in five minutes you would not have a word more to say. Is it not, therefore, demonstrable that you are in the wrong?"

"Well, Sir, pay me the trifle I require; it is only three guineas, and I have a numerous family."

"A family!" replied I with indignation, "and what business has such fellows as you to get families? In the present system, it is only bringing into the world a parcel of slaves."

"But population is the riches of a country."

"Granted," cried I, "in a good government, where the children are public property, and no one knows his relations; but in our system children introduce all the infamous train of selfish and family connections, and shut up the bowels of compassion against the dear suffering Chinese, who eat rotten meat and pounded rice."

"Sir," said he, "give me leave to say you talk in a very singular manner; your sentiments would *unhinge the universe*."

"Come here," cried I with transport, "you own then the power of my arguments; I knew they must carry conviction; I should die contented if I could only unhinge society. I detest a claim, but you are a man of understanding, and in want. At present, I do not know on whom I could bestow five guineas to do a greater good; take them—but remember that I shall always regret your having prevented my execution."

"A very singular gentleman," exclaimed he, overjoyed, "give me leave to attend you in future for nothing."

"As long as you please," said I, "that is, the natural way, but I will not be blooded. The art of medicine is to follow nature. If the patient is sick, 'tis a sign nature wants to discharge, and you should dose him with emetics:[87] if he is delirious, you should apply strong stimulants to increase the frenzy, as the sooner it arises to the height, the sooner a calm will ensue."

I continued to take his drugs by way of experiment; but I am satisfied I owed my recovery alone to the natural strength of my constitution. I had daily accounts of the sufferings of the persecuted patriots; and I debated with myself what line of life I should pursue as the most rational, and in harmony with my principles.

I resolved not to stoop to my father; I could as ill cringe to any man in power, and I detested every thing in alliance with trade as a debasement of the human soul. Surely, thought I, I am born for something more noble than to measure goods, or sort the articles of commercial exchange: low and base minds may find satisfaction in such employ, but the intelligence which learned to soar into the realms of science, must not be chained down to such groveling undertakings.

To amuse my mind, I visited a billiard table which was at no great distance from my lodging, and I found some entertainment from the exertions of skill. I there became acquainted with the most good-natured man in the world, whose name was Williams. I soon discovered that he was an advocate for the new philosophy; and he protested that he could not in conscience accept a living in the present system of things in any other way than by gaming. "'Tis true," said he, "the prejudices of mankind have stigmatised it as ignoble, but it is of all sciences the most natural; it brings lords, and all those titled trumpery, down to a level with the most insignificant of men: it introduces a freedom of discourse, it detaches the mind from all those bigoted notions called religion: it equalises property, by taking from the rich to give to the poor; and in one word, it is the most eligible way of living with honour and independence."

"You charm me," said I, "I once thought gaming was a foolish method of spending time, and calculated merely for the introduction of vice and dissipation; I now see better, and it is to me singular how naturally the mind transides from one truth to another: but so it is with human nature. The progression of knowledge is going forward with rapidity, and the wisdom and experience of ages is discovered to be nothing at all in the eighteenth century."

Williams proposed, that as I was what he called new to the town, we should divide our gains, to which I readily agreed, and we were for several nights very successful, so that I had to my share near two hundred pounds. The transient state of human existence loudly urged me to grasp at the present; and my college habits returning with force, I frequently spent whole nights with drinking parties.

CHAPTER VIII.

MR. HUME'S ARGUMENTS FOR ADULTERY, WITH PRACTICAL CONSEQUENCES— THE NEW MODE OF BENEVOLENCE.

I was charmed one evening at the play, by a beautiful young woman, who was in company with an ill-humoured, jealous-looking, *illiberal* man. I attempted several times to address myself to the lady, but his severe looks and lowering frowns compelled her to restraint, and I did not wish to be the cause of increased domination.

I was extremely well dressed, for in these trifles one may as well appear like the rest of the world, though I had more than once an intention to adopt the Roman Toga, on purpose to attract attention, for these matters go a great way with little men. I found that I gained the attention of the lady, who appeared uneasy under her restraint, and I made a secret vow, to emancipate her from the bondage under which she groaned.

I discovered, on farther inquiry, that she was the wife of a citizen, who had married her when she was extremely young, and extremely giddy; that they had two children, and were as happy as a tyrant and a coquet can be in wedlock.

I read over the Essays of the fashionable Hume, where I found that adultery was one of the moral virtues, and perfectly agreeable to political justice. In volume 2, page 409, of his Essays, edition 1767, are these admirable words, which, singly, and unconnected with his other excellent principles, would be sufficient to raise the book into public notice.—"Adultery," says he, "must be practised, if men would obtain all the advantages of life, if generally practised, it would soon cease to be scandalous; and if practised secretly and frequently, it would, by degrees, come to be thought no crime at all."—"Immortal Hume,"[88] cried I, "though thou doubtest whether thou hadst a soul, I doubt whether it be possible to doubt that thou hadst a body."

I determined to follow so great an idea, and it was not long before I contrived an interview. It is needless to say the lady soon became a convert to the prevailing principles of reason and nature; she was disgusted with her slavery, and wanted only an opportunity to exert the inborn freedom of her sex. I engaged very neat lodgings for her, and began to enter into that state, so congenial to the feelings of human nature and rational beings. I found her a very singular character, within a truly feminine form; she had a soul of a masculine energy; every thought of her mind seemed received by intuition. She was often right by this means, only in matters of mere speculation; she adopted one and rejected another, *by a sort of tact*, and the force of a cultivated imagination; and yet, *though upon the whole she reasoned little*, it is surprising what degree of soundness was in all her determinations.* My disposition frequently led me to waver in the practice I had adopted: I doubted, and I sometimes feared; but my oscillations and scepticism were fixed by her boldness. When a true opinion emanated in this way from another mind, the conviction produced in my own, assumed a similar character. She did not descend to all the frivolous softness of her sex, which custom has rendered general. She saw in woman, a being in no point inferior to man, except in personal prowess; and she disdained all those attractions, which poets and mankind have generally combined in perfecting the female character.

---

* The reader may find many of these sentiments in the Life of Mrs. Wolstonecraft. [Editor's note: Walker's text is in part a loose rendition, in part a citation of remarks made by William Godwin in his biography of his deceased wife, the English feminist writer Mary Wollstonecraft (1759-97). See Godwin's *Memoirs of the Author of A Vindication of the Rights of Woman* (1798): "The strength of her mind lay in intuition. She was often right, by this means only, in matters of mere speculation.... She adopted one opinion, and rejected another, spontaneously, by a sort of tact, and the force of a cultivated imagination; and yet, though perhaps, in the strict sense of the term, she reasoned little, it is surprising what a degree of soundness is to be found in her determinations" (121). In *A Vindication of the Rights of Woman* (1792) Mary Wollstonecraft had put the case for feminist social reform firmly on the radical political agenda, much to the chagrin of the conservative side of British society. However, it was Godwin's intimate portrayal of Wollstonecraft's life and passions that triggered the vitriolic response from large sections of the press that still reverberates through Walker's novel. Notably Godwin's candid account of her love affairs and her suicide attempts were received with outrage by both friends and critics alike. Walker's crude, even callous parody of Mary Wollstonecraft as Frederick's companion "Mary," is characteristic of the scorn and loathing that were heaped upon Wollstonecraft in the wake of Godwin's *Memoirs*.]

Our connection was that of friendship; we only met when mutual inclination prompted; and she has frequently lamented, that the customs of the world prevented her mingling in all the pursuits and undertakings of men.—"Is there any sex in soul?" she would say, "if not, what right have those tyrants, the men, to exclude us from the senate, the bar, and the army? *Do we not pay taxes in every article we consume?—And who are our representatives in Parliament?*— It is an outrage against the inborn Rights of Women."[89]—"Why," I would ask, "may not a woman be as capable of leading troops into the field as a general? Are they not perpetually playing cunning tricks? Soldiers and women I maintain to be equally alike: the officers are perpetually attentive to their persons, fond of dancing, crowded rooms, adventure, and ridicule: like the fair sex, the business of their lives is gallantry: they are taught to please, and they live only to please; yet they do not lose their rank in the distinction of sexes, for they are still reckoned superior to women, though in what their superiority exists, beyond what I have just mentioned, it is difficult to discover."*

A woman of these sentiments was congenial to my soul; our discourses were a feast to the mind, in which the senses had no share. She frequently lamented the evils to which nature had necessitated her sex in the article of children; a subject which she never could discuss with patience, it being an evil to which man was not subjected, and a badge of bondage not to be overthrown.

"Oh!" cried she, one day to me, in a fit of enthusiasm, "what signifies all the freedom of our souls, all the exaltations of our intellects, if we are to be confined for months to carry a burden which we have no means to lay down, and when the little wretch appears in the world, what a dreadful idea:—with intellects that soar beyond the firmament, are we to be confined to swaddle and dandle an animal that has no ideas, and must at every

---

* Rights of Women, part 1. [Editor's note: Walker's text is a partial citation of Wollstonecraft's *Vindication*: "It may be further observed, that officers are also particularly attentive to their persons, fond of dancing, crowded rooms, adventures, and ridicule. Like the *fair* sex, the business of their lives is gallantry.—They were taught to please, and they only live to please. Yet they do not lose their rank in the distinction of sexes, for they are still reckoned to be superior to women, though in what their superiority consists, beyond what I have just mentioned, it is difficult to discover" (24).]

moment destroy itself if we do not preserve it? Oh horrid! that Nature did not provide some middle, some stupid, lumpish being, to rear and take care of the human progeny: why not make man an oviparous animal?[90] Then we might have hatched the eggs in tempered stoves, as they do chickens in Egypt."

I could not but admire this flash of idea, which was bold and grand, and new; indeed, all her speculations were sublime, *though she reasoned little.** I had nearly overlooked an unpleasant incident, which would have very much grieved me, had it been occasioned by me: but it was another dreadful consequence of the present organization of society, and gave me an additional reason to execrate the prejudices of mankind.

The husband of my Mary had expected to find in her that softness, complacency, and modesty, which none but idiots ought to require, and which are merely calculated to fit a woman for a seraglio, or a play-thing to a voluptuary. He had taught himself to desire a female, who might solace him after his business, with the endearments of a mind that had no will but his own, and sought to oblige the man who preferred her to all her sex. But Mary was of a different nature—her soul was not to be confined in a gilded cage, and she would not bow to the bashaw[91] dictates of a master.

The poor wretch became distracted at her loss. In place of taking another, he was perpetually raving about conjugal affection, the claims of children, the duties of wives, and such ignorant prejudices, till his senses failed him, and his friends sent him to Bethlem Hospital.[92] The children, who had none to provide for them, were sent to the work-house, to be educated by the public, where they caught the small-pox, and died; an event, which ought naturally to have been expected, when they had not been inoculated,[93] and could not throw any blame upon the conduct of their mother.

After this incident we continued on the most harmonious footing, for though Mary allowed herself the conversation of many of the opposite sex, I did not experience the smallest uneasiness, for she had as much right as myself to all the *eccentricities of fancy*; and

***

* We are told in the Life of Mrs. Wolstonecraft, that she reasoned little; those who reason much will easily believe the fact. [Editor's note: "she reasoned little" is Godwin's phrase. See earlier footnote above.]

I never thought her the worse for having contributed to the happiness of other human beings.

About a month after this, the poor husband died delirious, one of the most stupid deaths a man could die for the loss of a woman: and Mary, thus freed from the shadow of a tie, appeared with me openly in public. Our neighbours made their usual rude comments upon our intercourse; and because several gentlemen pressed some handsome presents upon Mary, they circulated the calumny, that I kept my wife as a prostitute.

I despised all this; I was not to be frightened into any act because of scandal, and I had long regarded marriage with so well grounded an apprehension, that, notwithstanding the partiality for Mary that had taken possession of my soul, I should have felt it very difficult, at least in the present stage of our intercourse, to have resolved on such a measure; thus, partly from similar, and partly from different motives, we felt alike in this, as we did perhaps in every other circumstance that related to our intercourse.

The human mind delights in variety. It is impossible we should be for ever attached to one particular object. This change Mary experienced before myself, and she parted from me for the protection of my friend Williams, who certainly possessed very powerful attractions, and was an athletic figure.

I regretted this separation, but was not fool enough to repine; and I determined, according to the maxims of the great Stupeo, instantly to select some other; though it was difficult to find one with such an understanding as to march forward to the high goal of reason, trampling down prejudice, superstition, and character, in its career.

While I was in search of such a female, I wrote, by way of amusement, a little tract, proving that girls ought to receive the same education as boys; that the same exercises ought to be pursued by each, and that beauty was not of the smallest value, when compared to a robust constitution, that feared neither wind nor weather. I proved, beyond contradiction, that every thing called the graces, such as music, singing, dancing, timidity, delicacy, and bashfulness, ought to be exploded.[94]

I know not how it was, but my book was only bought by a few; and the aristocratic critics condemned it, as the work of a man who paid no regard to truth, provided he made himself singular; which was an absolute libel, for I had lost in the cause of truth, three teeth and half my little finger.

I confess I did not understand the subject. When a man writes a book of *methodical* information, he does not write because he understands the subject, but he understands the subject because he has written. He was an uninstructed Tyro, exposed to a thousand foolish and miserable mistakes when he began his work, compared with the degree of proficiency to which he has attained, when he has finished it.* In like manner, no man understands poetry or architecture, till he has written a poem or built a house.

Frequently, by way of amusement, I attended the six-penny debating societies,95 where truth is propagated in every branch, and religion and government attacked from behind a masked battery.96 A debate on the beauty of a coquet, or the merits of a beau,97 was sufficient to introduce annotations on despotism, and satires on nobility, to the edification of the ignorant and young, who are thus prepared to receive all the enlightened principles of the new school. It is astonishing what energy reason possesses, when adorned with all the flowers of oratory: and it was in vain that a man of narrow opinions should endeavour to be heard; for let him say what he would, he was unattended to. I was however, disgusted at a little trifle, for I could not endure the smallest duplicity, which is beneath the dignity of man, and ought not to be permitted even in the promotion of general knowledge. This trifle, was a quarrel between Citizen Cow and Citizen Calf, about which side of the question they should take; the one insisting that he could declaim best on the side of liberty, and the other declaring his own talent lay in discovering faults. I was ashamed that such great men should wrangle about the parts they were to act, like the performers of a country barn; and I could not but consider, that the cause of liberty must suffer, when garbled by the palsied efforts of men, whose object was a dividend of sixpences, to be spent the same evening in a debauch.

---

* Godwin's Enquirer, page 27. [Editor's note: *When a man ... finished it*: a verbatim citation from William Godwin's *Enquirer: Reflections on Education, Manners, and Literature, In a Series of Essays* (London, 1797), Essay IV, "Of the Sources of Genius," 27. *Tyro*: novice.]

One evening, at the hazard table, a young man, who had been sitting near six-and-thirty hours, attracted universal attention by the extravagant execrations he uttered, and the agitation of his mind. He protested that he was ruined and undone to all perdition.

My feelings are ever peculiarly alive to the sufferings of my fellows, and though I endeavour to guard against false pity, I am frequently melting at the distresses of my fellow mortals. I followed the poor wretch home at a distance, and entering his room abruptly, I found him sitting in a chair, with a fine young woman hanging on his shoulder weeping, and a child sleeping in a cradle.

He started up confused at my entrance, and would have made an apology, but I soon tranquillised him, and pressing him with the irresistible arguments of truth to rely on my services, he confessed that he had wronged an excellent master to a considerable amount, under the fallacious hope, that by hazarding it at the gaming table, he might acquire an independence, his salary being too small to enable him to keep a family and appear as he must; that he had now lost the means of concealing his crime, and should bring shame on his wife and his relations by a public death.

I was affected at the dreadful situation, for though his feelings were false, he having a just claim on his master's property, yet, in the present system of things he would have all mankind against him; I therefore determined to let him have two hundred pounds, the whole amount of my cash, which would cover his affairs for the present.

Returning home, I met with Williams at the door of a tavern, and acquainted him with my purpose.—"You know my senti- ments," said I, "and you know of what little value I esteem prop- erty when it is conducive to good. I have not *promised* Jackson, because promises are criminal, but I think at present it is the greatest good I can do, and I have raised his hopes from the edge of despair, by my assurances of succour."

"But shall you not want it yourself, and how shall he repay it?"

"Hear," cried I, "the profound sentiments of the infallible Stupeo, that most exalted of philosophers.—My neighbour is in want of ten pounds which I can spare: there is no law to transfer my property to him, but in the eye of simple justice, unless it can be shewn that the money can be more beneficially employed, his claim is as complete as if he had my bond in his possession, or had supplied me with goods to the amount. If two persons should offer, I must balance between them; it is therefore *impossible for me to confer upon any man a FAVOUR, I only do him a right*."*

"Stupeo," said he, solemnly, "was a man of the most exalted intellect, he was a prodigy amongst men, a meteor in the path of science, which blazed for a time, but was too brilliant to be permanent. His language was superior to all the grovling maxims of men, and his eloquence must have rivalled the persuasion of Cicero."98

"I might say," answered I, "as Æschines said of Demosthenes,99 if such be the effects of mere repetition, what would you have said had you heard himself?"

"We regret," replied he, "the decease of great men; but when their principles are practised by their pupils, we ought to be content. At this moment I was searching for you, to throw myself into your protection, well assured that the justice of my claim will convince you. I have lost this night every farthing I possessed, and I am now under immediate apprehension of an arrest for two hundred and fifty pounds: I am even told the bailiffs have been after me. To be deprived of liberty, is more dreadful to me than death; I never will support it: I am determined in my purpose, and it remains for you to consider whether the saving of a rational being is worth two hundred pounds."

I felt myself in a distressing situation, and pressed on both sides by very urgent claims, the merit of which required reflection.— "My dear Williams," said I, "more than ever I lament the death of the illuminated Stupeo; he would with one word have relieved our embarrassment; but, tell me yourself, without any bias of prejudice or weakness, which will be the greatest resulting good."

We walked several paces in silence. "At length," said he, "I would not appear selfish, I swear it by my love of truth and political justice, that both these cases are severe, but I do think that mine has the greatest claim upon you."

"It is sufficient," said I, "you are right." He accompanied me home, where I delivered him, within a guinea, of all I possessed.

---

* Godwin's Political Justice, page 89. [Editor's note: *My neighbour ... do him a right*: an almost verbatim citation (compilation) from Godwin's *Political Justice*, Book II, Chap. ii ("Of Justice"), 88–89.]

It was useless to visit the young man when I could not relieve him, and I had no inclination to insult distress. I was happy in having saved Williams from imprisonment, though the disappointment Jackson must endure in the failure of my offers now and then intervened, but I remembered that no man ought to place dependence upon any but himself.

I cannot remember the conclusion of this incident without regret, and the reflection that philosophy cannot always direct us amongst the doublings and mazes of human affairs. The young man was apprehended the next day, and his wife running forward to the most sinister conclusions, cast herself into the Thames, where she was unfortunately drowned.

I grieved, but grief was useless, after the event; I execrated the custom of mankind, and drew some comfort in remembering that I had probably saved Williams from equal calamity.—I hastened to his lodgings, to pour out to him and Mary the tumults of an agitated soul, but I was informed that they had departed before break of day, nobody knew where; and that a warrant was out against him for having cheated a gentleman with cogged dice.

I was struck dumb at this account, which informed me that I was a beggar; and the woman of the house hinted that I was implicated in the business. My mind was, however, clear of this aspersion; it was too manly to descend to other finesse than that of skill; but I could not reconcile the behaviour of Williams to any maxim of truth or political justice; for if there be not *common honesty* amongst those the vulgar call rogues, how are the affairs of life to be conducted?

The accidents I had witnessed resulting from gaming, had startled my mind, yet I preferred it to binding myself a slave to the caprices of any man. This resource was now become dangerous. No man, from persuasion would render me a portion of the superfluities he enjoyed, and in the midst of society which calls itself polished, I must either labour in employ, beneath the dignity of a rational being, or perish unpitied or unrelieved.

Occupied with these reflections, I returned to my lodgings, absorbed in a gloomy melancholy. Mankind appeared to me a set of selfish, solitary animals in the midst of society, and so far from being associated for mutual protection, they seem only to live for themselves.

I remembered, in all its brilliance, the state of nature, described by Rousseau, and enlarged by Stupeo. I repeated again and again *Il retourne chez ses Egaux*;[100] and I determined to make the wilds of America my asylum. In this intention I sold every article of value, and changed my dress to that of which you see the remains, the better to pass unmolested, having many reasons to fear personal detection, for no man can be truly great, till he is become an object of hatred to nine-tenths of mankind.

CHAPTER IX.

THE OMNIPOTENCE OF MODERN TRUTH— MEDITATIONS ON A GIBBET— AND THE CONSEQUENCES.

I determined to cross the country of England to the North-West, and proposed to make observations upon man in my journey; for, as some writer[101] has said, that ought to be the object of all voyages and travels; and, as Pope says, "The proper study of mankind is man."[102] Indeed, man may be said to compose the first chapter of the great book of Nature: and before we pretend to a knowledge of all the chapters of that large book, we ought surely to be masters of the first.

On the sixth day of my journey, for I walked on foot, towards the evening I arrived on the borders of an extensive waste; a large crowd of country people were assembled, and in deep debate about some new enclosures,[103] which had shamefully infringed upon the common right. Some gentlemen were endeavouring to persuade them, that by cultivating the useless ground, larger crops would be produced, which would create greater plenty, and render the articles of life cheaper.

All my patriotism was aroused at the glaring imposition, and taking advantage of a mound of earth, I requested to be heard.

"Can you listen patiently, citizens," cried I, "to this detestable doctrine? Do you not know that the ground which now scarcely sustains a goose, will then fatten an ox, and thus your oppressors will be enriched, and you will be starved? You have an undoubted right to the whole surface of the earth, but if cultivation goes forward, you will be penned up in the highways: you will not have so much as a path left through a meadow; your very highways will be taken from you, and made into canals, by which every waggoner in the kingdom will be ruined; and what will you get by this spirit of improvement as they call it? Will they give you the surplus of what they cannot devour? No, they will pile it up in barns to rot, and make manure for a double crop. Open your eyes, citizens, and you will see the falsity of their speeches: they tell you provisions will be cheaper; I tell you they will not; and ask yourselves which you are to believe, those interested men, or I, whom you never saw before: I tell you, you ought to have provisions for nothing.—Awake, citizens! remember that when you are driven from the highways, you will be like frogs in a gutter. Now is the time; a moment's delay, and you will be too late. Unite and tear up the fences, level the hedges before the cultivating spade has turned up the sod. Would to heaven there was not a single acre cultivated, and the then imperious rich would not monopolise provisions. I see impatience in your eyes—I see the rising flame of liberty and truth flash in your countenances.—Come then, down with the boundaries, those badges of slavery, and tell all the world that you have as much right to the surface of the earth as you have to the air."

This speech was like an electric shock, every man confessed its truth, and the triumph of patriotism was complete. In vain the gentlemen endeavoured to argue down the storm; *no one wou'd hear them*; a plain demonstration that their *arguments* were false. I tore up, with my own hands, one of the stakes, and in an instant the aristocratical enclosures were laid open again in a state of nature. Oh, cried I to myself, Oh that Stupeo could witness this effusion of reason, this march of philosophy. But, alas! the great mythological, metaphysical patriot, was first killed by a musket bullet, and then trod to death by his friends.

While I stood witnessing this transient start of energetic freedom, I was suddenly seized by three of the gentlemen, and though I made a strenuous resistance, was soon overpowered. I called aloud for the country people to rescue me (but the disposition of a mob is always fickle), those who a few minutes before hung with rapture on my words, now seemed to rejoice in the new object raised to their attention.

I was chagrined, and as they led me on, I exclaimed aloud, "Rascals and cowards, is this the manner to treat a pupil of the great and immortal Stupeo? Is this treachery to be reconciled with political justice? For myself, I am not concerned, I glory in the martyrdom I shall suffer; but remember, that the axe which sunders my head from my body, cuts at the same moment all your liberties."

"Who the world are you?" said one of the gentlemen; "you surely are not in your senses, or you would not utter such incoherent absurdities."

"Did I not tell you," said I, "that I am a pupil of the great Stupeo, a man who, if he had been here, would have confounded you with his eloquence, and shaken all the prejudices and habits of your mind like an earthquake, which, at one trembling, overwhelms all the proud puny structures of ignorant and tyrannical men."

A gentleman on horseback advancing towards us, stopped at the sight of so tumultuous a procession; and I knew him to be the same I had met in the stage. He recollected me, but seemed not to know me.

"How does your Lordship?" said one of the gentlemen. "We have here one of those seditious imposters that go about the country destroying its peace, and telling palpable lies in a flowery language, which warms the passions, and runs away with sober reason."

"My Lord," said I, "I am glad to see you, because you shall be the judge of the subject in dispute, and for which I am dragged along the public road like a traitor and a slave. What is truth? Can any circumstance change the immutability of its nature? Is it not like those mathematical axioms, which we only require to hear to understand? Think you that the senses of the people are so dull, they do not comprehend the light of truth when it flashes in their eyes? Or, as the sublime Stupeo would have said, when truth, like a volcano, bursts forth and the darkness of night—its thunderings shall awaken the dormant senses of mankind—its lightnings shall glitter in their eyes like the brilliant morning of science—its lava shall bear down all opposition, overwhelming all the puny barriers of state—its cinders will scatter destruction upon its enemies, and the devastation it spreads (like a revolution) shall be momentary, giving place to a tenfold fecundity."

"But," said his Lordship, "not to question the *truth* of your bombastic metaphor, you forget that this *devastation* would sweep away all the then generation."

"And what is one generation," I returned, "or what are ten generations to the resulting good? Are we always to be as imbecile as infants? I have no doubt, that when reasons acts in all things, we shall live to the age of the primitive parents of mankind, and then we shall not tremble at revolutions."

"Oh that the glorious days were come!" said he with a sneer, "when the dagger and the rope shall lose their destructive qualities, when the musket, the sword, and the pike shall rebound from the bosom of the patriot, and the cannon ball, in place of flying onwards, winged with death, shall fall harmless to the ground—then, and not till then, ought we to rush into revolutions."

"But truth," cried I, "truth is omnipotent, of which this very day is an example."[104]

"Which way?" said he. "I know you have sense, though at present it is warped. You call by the name of truth that which stimulates ignorant people to outrage: but you forget that all men are not cool philosophers, that the great mass of mankind are enamoured of novelty. The very bustle of a riot or a revolution has for them equal charms with a horse-race or a bull-baiting, and the merits of the subject are never discussed till they smart under the consequences. What can be more easy than to lead people to desire to live without labour, to plunder the rich, and pay no regard to those laws which were made purposely to restrain the passions? And because this is easy to be done, you call it truth and liberty, and patriotism. But I would ask one sober question, and would to God the whole world could hear me. If simple nature, poverty, and equality is the natural state of man, why do reformers wish to deprive the rich of their wealth, to render the poor unhappy? A plain argument that all they want is to plunder the rich, and, under a mask of mock patriotism, destroy all those sacred bonds which give energy to genius, and encouragement to virtue. If they have the real welfare of mankind at heart, in the establishment of equality, and detest (as they are always pretending) cruelty and bloodshed, it would be very easy to establish themselves in America."

"But monopolisers," cried I; "are they to be suffered to prey on the entrails of society? What right has one man to eat a pine-apple, for which he gave a guinea, when another is starving for want of an half-penny worth of bread? Answer me this—."

"Few things can be more easily done," replied he. "In the first place I would observe, that the incident never happened but in imagination, drawn for the purpose of casting an odium upon the rich, they do not in general deserve. Secondly, the accumulation of individual property is the natural and certain consequence of society. It is to be seen in the state of savagism, where an industrious Indian shall possess good arms, while an idle one shall be almost without. In the state of equality, that is, ignorant barbarism, no pine-apples would be cultivated. How many depend for their share of the guinea paid for the pine-apple? The fruiterer, the gardener, the glazier, the carpenter, the bricklayer, the smith, the coal-merchant, the mariner, the miner, with all the crowd of others who supply each of these individuals with materials; and when you shall have divided the guinea between all these, I think the gentleman may eat his pine-apple with a good conscience, unless you can prove that he ought to give half of it to the vagabond, who will not work to provide himself food.—To state your question right, you should ask which is the greater good, to aid all those tradesmen and their dependents, by encouraging the luxury, or to give the superfluous guinea to the support of unproductive idleness? There is another question frequently asked— What right, they say, have the rich to tax the poor? What right have they to live by the labour of the poor? The real fact is, that they do not live by the labour of the poor, but *vice versa*; for were there no high people to pay the poor for working, there would be no work done. What bricklayer would build a house without being paid? What labourer would work for him without hire? *The benefit is reciprocal to both parties*; but, to speak a truth, the rich, wrapped as they are in ease and indolence, would do much better without the poor, than the poor without them. As to taxes, the poor in this country pay very few in proportion to the rich; their cottages are exempt, they are not vassals who work without pay (as in most countries in the world), and those who wish to live in peace, may do it with as much security as a lord; their persons and their little all are equally sacred in the eye of the law, and except in the article of game, *equally free*. It is the drunken, the idle, and the vicious, who have their families starving, and a burden to the parish. But such is the singular constitution of the country, that no Englishman can die of absolute want, if he will appeal to the charitable institutions. In fact, it is the middle class of people who bear the great burden of the state: the poor are exactly the same as they were a thousand years ago, and were, and will be always the same under every form of government, with the exception of personal freedom and protection. It is to be remembered that taxes ought never to be murmured at, provided they are applied to public affairs. I am, however, grieved when I reflect that the upright, peaceable, and loyal citizen pays at least one-third more than his just portion, to make up for the deficiency occasioned by the sneaking, miserly part of the rich; and by the mock patriot evading every impost he can flinch from—thus stabbing the country he pretends to weep over."

"But," replied I, "it is a gross and ridiculous error, to suppose that the rich pay for any thing: there is no wealth in the world except this—the labour of man.* So that when a man of property pretends he is rewarding the labourer, he is cheating him, he is giving him a bauble, and cajoling him. If he employ them in erecting palaces, in sinking canals, &c. it will be found he is their enemy; he is adding to the weight of oppression, and the vast accumulation of labour, by which they are already sunk beneath the level of brutes."

"From this doctrine," said Lord B———, "it follows, that the less employ given to mankind, the greater is their happiness, and the greater your benevolence; and the Eastern Bashaw,[105] who grasps every accumulation of property, destroys the speculations

---

* Enquirer, page 175. [Editor's note: *It is a gross … the labour of man*: a verbatim citation from Godwin's *Enquirer*, though the original phrase is actually on page 177.]

of commerce, arts, sciences, and agriculture, reducing men to the happy station of providing no more than just sufficient to support existence, is, in your system, the benefactor of the human race."

I know not how it was, I felt all my ideas unorganised, and I endeavoured in vain to reply: though what could be more *trite*, illiberal, and common place. The country people who had listened to this discourse, one and all protested they were grieved at their offence, declaring, that they now saw plainly how much better it was to receive the wages for their labour in cultivating the ground, than to keep it barren, and of use to nobody, at the same time offering, the next day, to replace the hedges they had thrown down.

"And to conclude this adventure," said the young nobleman, "let this unfortunate man be liberated; and I hope he will yet be convinced of the folly of destroying one system, which has *some faults*, with *many beauties*, and in its place proposing another, which has not one single *practical beauty*, but is pregnant with the most detestable and dreadful evils."

Being at liberty to proceed on my journey, I left Lord B—— and his train of slaves. Continuing along the road by moon-light, and having leisure to recollect the apophthegms[106] of Stupeo, I was angry with myself that I had not contradicted every assertion made by Lord B——, and proved that his reasonings were false in *toto*.

I was roused from these reflections by the creakings of a gibbet on the highway, and could not avoid shuddering at the inhuman spectacle.

"O property!" said I, "this is one of thy blessed effects—what a dreadful exhibition of injustice glares upon the thinking mind, that death shall be the fate of the man who by force exerts the rights of nature. In the Principles of Penal Law,[107] we are told near an hundred persons anually are executed. Oh ye victims of this infernal monopolising scheme, the whole amount of the goods (vulgarly called stolen) is only three-fourths per cent. upon moveable property, yet they hang you up on the highway. Perhaps you were obliged to shoot somebody in self-defence, and must ye die for that? Can we wonder at the miseries of society, when luxury and trade are risen to so enormous an amount, that the aggregate of property brought to the city of London, and moved in floating bottoms only, is annually seventy millions, out of which only about four millions are taken in plunder, only four millions reduced to the laws of equality. There is, indeed, a bright gleam breaking through this dark picture, which enables the private patriot to tax the property of these dealers in wealth; this is the article of *base coin*, amounting, it is true, to no more than one million a year.* Let us a moment contemplate this mighty Colossus of property, which threatens to devour up the Rights of Man, and resist all the open and secret attacks of philosophers, and we shall see how necessary it is by every means to render property less secure. Let us reason calmly, and without prejudice, and to any man of liberal ideas, what is the moral turpitude of robbery? It is no more than taking by force what I have a natural right to: it is an heroic and generous way of exerting the claims of nature and Agrarian justice; and the hazard I run is the same as every patriot must lay open to, who excites revolutions, and proclaims the glad tidings of universal emancipation. The one, as well as the other, is detested by all men who are blinded by religion, and the prejudices of the old school. It becomes, therefore, the part of every patriot, who would nobly resist oppression, to begin by counteracting the unjust distribution of property; and were they all to a man boldly and heroicly to set out on the high road, they would soon render wealth less secure, and its possessors less arrogant. It may be objected, that this would not be so manly as at once throwing off the yoke of bondage: but till the *march* of sentiment has proceeded to universal conviction, the next greatest good ought to be preferred to listless inactivity."

Such were my reflections while I stood gazing at the gibbet: I ridiculed the idea that it would act as a restraint: it was in my

---

* See the excellent Treatise on the Police of the Metropolis, which, though certainly exaggerated in some of the calculations, deserves the attention of every man. [Editor's note: The reference is to *A Treatise on the Police of the Metropolis, explaining the various crimes and misdemeanors which at the present are felt as a pressure upon the community; and suggesting remedies for their prevention* (London, 1796) by Patrick Colquhoun (1745-1820). Colquhoun's book went through many editions, both in Britain and North America, and was revised and enlarged several times. Walker's data are accurate and are lifted from Chapter VII ("On the Coinage of Counterfeit Money") and Chapter IX ("On River Plunder"). As for Walker's reference to the staggering production of and trade in counterfeit "base coins" (coins made out of base metals, as opposed to precious metals), Colquhoun observes that "the trading in base money has now become as regular and systematic as any fair branch of trade" (182).]

eyes like the mangled body of Cæsar,[108] which only stimulated to revenge. I considered the poor victim as unjustly massacred by the iron-fisted law, for though he had committed murder, that was no reason for coercion in the code of political justice.

My mind was impressed with a majestic and independent tone, resulting from those ideas. I felt myself aroused to some arduous exploit, and a post-chaise driving towards me, gave me an opportunity to emulate the valour of an Alexander, or a Charles the Twelfth.[109]

I drew out my pistols, and marched forward along the middle of the road, which the postillion perceiving, spurred his horses, with an intention to ride over me. With a stroke of my oak-stick I brought him down, and grasping the reins, retained the horses. The gentleman immediately fired, and missing me, I returned the shot, and a loud scream from a female caused me to think it took place. The horses taking fright, tore away from my grasp, and rode over the postillion, who was much bruised, and had one leg broke.

This unfortunate accident extremely chagrined me, but I consoled myself as much as possible with remembering, that partial evil will ever attach to general good. The *immortal* Stupeo, before he died, used to observe, that Nature, in her fecundity, produced all things in superfluity, that much might be spared for the destruction of accident. As in the produce of animals and vegetables; and man, being nothing but a brute, who also supplied in greater numbers than sufficient; in fact, that the death of two or three hundred thousand was a matter of no moment, and absolutely unworthy to fill the mind's eye a second in the contemplation of a great event.

These arguments were clear as the broad base of truth; for what man could walk out on a summer's day, if he feared crushing the insects in his path? Or who could look coolly upon a revolution, if they valued the lives of individuals, who must be crushed by the ebullitions of the moment.*

---

* The reader must observe the difference of the Vagabond's sentiments, which is the exact language of modern Jacobins. If one of their own party suffers for his crimes, it is a massacre, and must be revenged by the most sanguine examples; but if thousands are murdered by their own party, it is then a petty ebullition of liberty—nothing, compared to the great object they aim at.

I rejoiced that my mind was superior to prejudice, and continued forward, after this little accident, with an high flow of spirits. I was on foot, and walked slowly on, forgetting, that by this outrage (as it is vulgarly called) I rendered myself liable to account, when I heard behind me the clattering of horses. It was totally dark, and stepping a little from the road, that they might not run over me, I stuck in a muddy ditch on one side.

The plashing I made to clear myself caught their ears, and they quickly surrounded me ordering me to surrender. I was in no situation to contend, for I could not extricate myself. I threw my pistols over the hedge into a thicket of whins,[110] and replied, that they might use me as they pleased, for death was infinitely preferable to slavery.

I was conducted back on horseback several miles, to the nearest inn, where I was ushered into a large kitchen. It was now very late, being near three in the morning, so that only two maid-servants were there, with the three persons who had caught me. One, who had the appearance of a gentleman, turned me to the light to examine my features, when I instantly knew him to be my father.

"Great God!" exclaimed he, "who do I see? What dreadful fate is this? Why did I not die before I had beheld this hour? But for a trembling hand I should have killed my son! and that son would have been spared the guilt of murdering his mother!"

A cold damp sweat gathered on my brow. I was unmanned in a moment, notwithstanding every effort I could make to preserve my resolution.—"Was it not imprudent," said I, "to travel at this hour? What business had you upon the road? And how could I know you in the dark from another?"

"Ill-starred boy," said he, shedding tears; "Providence directed your arm against your parents, that you might behold, in full light, the horror of your actions, and repent!"

"Nonsense," cried I, recovering at this impeachment of truth. "Do you not know, that, in the eye of a man of sense, relations are no more connected than the greatest strangers? Would Rome ever have been a republic, had Brutus recoiled from ordering his own children to execution? Would Cæsar have fallen, had the second Brutus been tied by the name of friend?[111] Or would any revolution happen, if brothers, and fathers, and sons, feared to plunge the dagger in each others bosom? The mind which cannot leap over these paultry and prejudiced considerations, is not inspired with genuine patriotism: we must learn only to appreciate persons by their intrinsic value, and not by their titles, nominations, and connections."*

My father, during this speech, had thrown himself upon a chair, holding his head in an agony of emotion, which I did not wonder at, considering his prejudices; and I regretted myself, that so little good had been produced by an action, which, had it occurred in a full day, amidst a tumultuous people, and in the bustle of a revolution, would have rendered me eternally immortal, and handed my name down to the remotest posterity as a dread to tyrants, and a *text* to all declaimers on the sufferings of human nature: as it was, it was only like seed scattered in sterile ground, unproductive and obscure.

"What shall I do?" cried my father, suddenly starting up. "Shall I, for the sake of severe, but immutable justice, become the instrument of vengeance on my son? Shall I adopt his own maxims, and rend at once all the tender ties of nature? Shall I burst all those fine bands asunder, and consign him to public execution? O heaven! can such a sacrifice be required of me, for having given existence to such a monster? No, no, get from my sight! fly! fly to the desarts of the world! beyond the boundaries of society, lest the earth open and swallow you alive."

"See," said I, calmly, "what it is to be agitated with all these puerile feelings of kindred; they unman the soul, and when we should reason rationally, overwhelm us in a vortex of passion. I am not so prejudiced as to refuse that portion of liberty you offer me: I will go, because I do not think that I have yet fulfilled the great mission I have undertaken. In the present instance, I do not see how the good of mankind can be promoted by my death: till we can see this, we ought never voluntarily to march to the scaffold, or, as the immortal Stupeo said——."

"Perdition strike him to the centre," cried my father, flaming with fury.

---

* I would observe, that *I* never personally knew a republican who did not support this doctrine; there may be those who do not, but I never found them.

It is a folly to attempt reasoning with madmen; and seeing the two countrymen debating whether they should allow me to pass, I put on a determined air, and walked calmly out of the house. There is something imposing and aweful in the frown of a determined man, conscious of his *innocence*; and I have little doubt but an hundred would have suffered me to pass with equal impunity.

I soon shook off the chagrin this little incident had occasioned, and having recovered my pistols, I thought it a matter of common precaution to strike from the high road.

END OF THE FIRST VOLUME.

THE

VAGABOND,

A NOVEL,

In two volumes.—VOL..II.

By

GEORGE WALKER.

Dedicated to the
LORD BISHOP OF LANDAFF.

Third Edition, with Notes.

τὸ δίκαιον ἴσον ἀλλὰ μὴ τὸ ἴσον, δεῖν ποιεῖσθαι δίκαιον
Whatever is just, is equal; but whatever is equal is not always just.
PLUTARCH.

The wayward nature of the time, and the paramount necessity of
securing to this kingdom her political and religious existence, and
the rights of society, have urged me to this endeavour to preserve
them, by a
disinterested appeal to my countrymen.
PURSUITS OF LITERATURE.

London:
Printed for G. Walker, No. 106, Great Portland
Street, and Hurst, No. 32, Paternoster Row.
1799.

CONTENTS.

THE

VAGABOND.

CHAPTER I.

THE VAGABOND CONCLUDES HIS STORY—
THE EFFECTS OF REFORMATION IN A COUNTRY
PARISH—THE VAGABOND'S REASONS
IN FAVOUR OF SEDUCTION.

On the following day I stopped a post-chaise in a cross road, which contained two ladies, and was driven by a lad. One of the women fainted away, and the other was excessively frightened. I took nothing but her purse, informing her, that she mistook, if she supposed me a common robber; for, though I was willing to equalise property, I did not wish to monopolise. So saying, I quitted her, that she might assist her insensible companion.

I could not but execrate the whole system of female education, which thus enervates the human body; it being an eternal fact, that were women educated to all the exercises of men, and, as my dear Mary used to say, so mingled with the world, that every action would be performed promiscuously, (sex out of the question) we should not have women fainting on sudden emergencies, and as imbecile as infants.

What a glorious thing would it be, if the whole female sex would emancipate themselves from those tyrants the men, and enter equally into every concern of life! We should then no longer admire a beautiful idiot, but value them according to their mental charms and personal prowess. It would also be a very great advantage in the article of love, it being no inconsiderable trouble to a philosophical mind to bend to all the frivolities of declaring a passion.

By the exertions of my independent principles, I acquired a sufficient subsistence; but I always made it a rule never to put in my claim to a part of the universal stock, till necessity (which has no law) in some sort compelled me. It was one of those occasions I had the good fortune to meet you, and I only lament that the immortal Stupeo was killed with a musket bullet.

"I lament too," said Doctor Alogos; "I should have delighted in the conversation of so great a man, who has introduced so enlightened a pupil to the world. But let us now retire to rest; the clock has struck three, and tomorrow we discourse further." So saying, they separated for the night: Frederick rejoicing that he had at length found a man illuminated with the irradiating principles of the new philosophy; which he the more wondered at, considering the Doctor's *property*, for he had found the pupils of the new school, in general, a little short in financial affairs.

The next morning the company met to breakfast. Laura was extremely lovely; and the eyes of the philosopher frequently repeated the observation. Susan sat down familiarly to breakfast with them; and the luxury of the times was ably descanted upon.

Tea and chocolate, new bread and fresh butter, with a relish of cold ham and eggs, composed the breakfast of these practical philosophers.

"Luxury," cried Doctor Alogos at every mouthful, "will be the bane of this country; every thing rises to so enormous a price, that a poor man cannot absolutely get an existence; we shall be starved!"

"'Tis a dreadful thing to think of it," said Frederick; "I have often considered what could occasion such a rise in meat, for instance; formerly we used to have the best beef at one penny a pound, and now it is six-pence."

"I apprehend," said Laura, "that there are two reasons: the increased consumption, and the increased quantity of money. Formerly, a farmer, before he killed a ox, had to contract with so many families as could purchase the whole, not being able to place a dependance on chance custom; a fact that must give the lie to the tales of some people, who would make us believe that day-labourers fed upon roasted beef."

"You are a little perverse jade," said the Doctor, "to dare contradict a man like me. Pray, how should you know what used to be, who have not yet seen eighteen summers?—You are a moth in the creation yet. I insist upon it that our peasants are starved and famished: Are not potatoes and bacon half their support?—Answer that."

The Doctor enjoyed the triumph of rhetoric over common sense; but Laura, with becoming deference, replied, that it might be true, but that was even better than skimmed milk and oatmeal cake, which was formerly the general food, with a change of barley and rye. "The people of England, then," said she, "were subject to leprosy and cutaneous diseases, which have vanished since the introduction of tea. I grant that they live hard, but it is what they have ever done; and were it possible for them to see the peasants of other countries, they would rejoice at being people of England. Not to mention the powers of life and death, possessed by most landed gentlemen on the Continent, let us look at the Eastern nations, whose lower orders live upon nothing but rice, and particularly the Chinese, supposed, in the Annual Register for 1789, to contain *two hundred millions* of people, whose lower orders, in-land, taste nothing but rice and water, and on the sea-coast a little fish."[112]

"Rice and fish!," said the Doctor, "I am persuaded they are both primitive dishes. Rice is the food of more than half the human species, and savages on the sea-coasts universally eat fish. I am determined my table shall be furnished with these productions of all-provident nature; and suppose, for the second course, you give us a brace of roast capons and a few tartlets."

"For my part," said Frederick, laying a slice of ham on his bread and butter, and putting three lumps of sugar into his cup of chocolate, "it is to me a matter of the greatest indifference what I eat; I eat merely because it is right to eat for the keeping our bodies in order. A family physician proves, that one half the necessity of eating is to distend the intestines; for which purpose, any farinaceous paste is sufficient; and I have an intention to try a pudding of *marble flour*,[113] for, if this proves true, what great exploits may be performed without the trouble of carrying bread!"

"For heaven's sake!" said Laura, laughing, "forego the experiment, or the images of Jupiter[114] and Juno, in the garden, will be made into hasty-pudding;[115] and the arm of Venus will have as much temptation as an haunch of venison."

After breakfast, the Doctor requested Frederick to walk in his garden, and help him to weed some beds of herbs.

"Do you think," said Frederick, "after what I have told you, that I will degrade my dignity by a menial employ? that I will become a slave to till the ground?"

"No," replied the Doctor; "you are a philosopher: I do not propose to you any such thing; but husbandry is a primitive art, and no disgrace when practised for exercise. I propose that we shall live together on a footing of equality, and that we shall endeavour to enlighten the people in our neighbourhood, erecting to ourselves a little republic."

"The idea is grand and noble," said Frederick: "had we Stupeo here, his whole soul would enter into the subject. Let us begin this very day—only let me observe, I will be entirely independent."

"Of course," said the Doctor. "Though I very much fear we shall never bring them to the standard of nature. This island is the sink of slavery. The very elements won't let the people go naked like the Indians of America. What shall we do first towards bringing about the freedom of man?"

"The first great action to be performed, is to convince them of their wrongs—to shew them they ought to govern the state; and that, if they do not recover their rights, they will be starved and enslaved; and that all distinctions are badges of tyranny, and not rewards of merit."

"But in that point," said the Doctor, "it appears to me cheaper to bestow titles and ribbons than pensions—if there were no titles, the pension-list[116] must increase."

"And suppose it did," cried Frederick, "ayn't we going to do away all profits and rewards? Every man should labour for the resulting good."

"Right, right," answered the Doctor. "But should we not say something on the article of marriage? We shall never introduce real liberty till we can do away that Gothic barbarity. There's Susan, a good deserving creature, just such another as Rousseau's Teresa:[117] to own the truth, we, that is, she and I——You understand me—but the opinions of the world have hitherto prevented my living with her in a manner congenial to my wishes, and as nature and reason point out."

"Hear," said Frederick, "the sentiments of the great philosopher Stupeo: When the distinctions of society shall be confounded, and men shall cease to appropriate a whole female to themselves—*two men might easily enjoy one* woman, because it would be *her company* they desired, and the *sensual* gratification would be considered as a trifle. *Reasonable* men will propagate their species; not because a certain pleasure is annexed to this action, but because it is *right* the species should be propagated, and the *manner* in which they exercise this function will be regulated by the dictates of reason and duty. It cannot definitively be affirmed, in such a state of society, who is the father of the child; but it is of *no consequence.* I ought to prefer *no* human being to another because that being is my father, my wife, or my son."*

"What a glorious doctrine!" cried Alogos: "one might then have as many concubines and children as they could procure. This very reason alone ought to make us detest monarchical government, where what is called sacred engagements are obliged to be in some sort preserved. I will, this very day, tell the world that I disregard its prejudices, and Susan shall appear in her proper character."

Poor Susan, who was an ignorant, vulgar girl, was so intoxicated with the elevation from the cookery, that she resolved to exert the inborn Rights of Women, disdaining any longer to superintend the kitchen; and the Doctor frequently cursed society, which had introduced luxurious dishes.

Mean-while these two great men exerted their endeavours to reform the parishioners, and it was not long before the excellent effects of their doctrines became visible. The churches, those temples of priestcraft and ignorance, were soon left without visitors; and even the elocution of a popular preacher could not assemble an audience.

The two philosophers rejoiced at this dawn of reason, and, the better to *spread* the truth, erected a large barn into a Hall of Reason, where they undertook alternatively to read moral lectures.— Frederick there clearly proved that all religion was the offspring of ignorance, resulting from ideas, mingled with impressions, mingled

---

* Godwin's Political Justice, 4to. page 852. [Editor's note: *Reasonable men ... or my son*: an almost verbatim compilation of Godwin's text.]

with realities, and that the first idea of the Deity was taken from a howling wind on a stormy night: so that, if he did not convince, he confounded his hearers. He, however, proved beyond a doubt, that religion was not of the smallest benefit to mankind. "'Tis true," said he, in one of his lectures, "that *architecture* was first carried beyond the unpolished beam, and the unshapen stone, by the enthusiasm of people to honour an unknown Deity; but could any thing be more absurd than to raise great piles of magnificence to nobody knew who? And what was the consequence? Why, the great men then would have great houses, and no longer live, as they used to do, in hovels of mud. 'Tis true that *astronomy* was first studied for the sake of tracing the power of God in the creation; but what has been the result? We have learnt to traverse the ocean, and send people from Europe to tyrannise over the people of Africa. Religion indeed gave birth to all the *arts and sciences*, because it was supposed the Architect of worlds must delight in grandeur, and every costly ornament was deemed too little an offering to his abode. But, in my opinion, this would better have been given to the starving poor—no doubt the priests had their tithes out of it. (Here a loud burst of applause broke forth.) It is in vain to say that monks have been the preservers of *literature*; for, at the time they promoted it, they had no intention to benefit mankind, and it is the intention which makes the merit. You are told that religion teaches social duties; that it is wrong to injure your neighbour, for you shall be hereafter punished. Who told you all this? A parcel of priests, whom you pay to hold you in darkness. Are you to believe them, or I who instruct you for nothing? I tell you then that there are no future rewards and punishments. I am certain no man can prove that there are; and if you read the great book of Nature, it does not say a word about it. That's the book you ought to study, and burn your Bibles, if you would enjoy the world without those shocking reflections about fire and brimstone."

Moral lectures like these could not but influence the minds of the country people, who wondered they had been so long imposed upon. The Curate was under the necessity of suing for the tithes, and the parsonage was threatened with destruction.

Corn had been dear and scarce, owing to a wet season; and to render it cheap, a mob of patriots burnt down several stacks and barns, for which one was hanged, and three transported.[118]

The Principles of Universal Equality, and The Catechism of Nature, the one written by Frederick, and the other by Doctor Alogos, were printed and distributed gratis. The public-houses had each a club, where the newspapers were subscribed for, politics discussed, and ale consumed with genuine liberty; by which means those heretofore-ignorant people became *warm advocates* for freedom, and declaimed about the inborn reason of the human soul, till all reason was suspended in hilarity, and the whole company *levelled* to a state of *swinish equality*.

They now clearly perceived that the times were the worst that ever Old England had witnessed; for they every day found themselves less able to maintain their families; and so far from being capable to pay their rents, they had scarcely money sufficient to support the club, on which depended the salvation of their country.

In vain the gentlemen of the parish endeavoured to stay this torrent of philosophy. Man only requires to be told his rights to know them. The young men copying the example of Doctor Alogos, were not to be bubbled out of a fee by the priests, and the wives became what is vulgarly called lazy and slovenly, but which, in the language of refined philosophy, is independent, and superior to prejudice.

Things proceeded thus admirably in a parish, where, but a little time before, all had gone on in the old track, where contented and ignorant families depended on their own labour, and were so proud of their childish title of Englishmen, that they detested the work-house so long as health and strength remained. But now they saw clearly, that, according to the *Rights of Man*, every one had a just demand for support from the community after a certain age, and therefore to work for a rainy day was as absurd as it was old.

The poor-rates multiplied so fast upon those who still continued to support the Gothic prejudices of their ancestors, that several heretofore flourishing families were obliged to quit the parish, and their farms remained unoccupied.

Frederick, in the mean time, had endeavoured to cultivate the affections of Laura; but though he gained upon her heart, her head resisted all the arguments of his philosophy. It was in vain he traduced the custom of marriage; she remained wedded to the blind principles in which she had been educated. "For," said she, "were I to become your *companion*, or that of any other man, when I shall perhaps be surrounded with two or three children, a moment's disgust may leave me without a partner. Till it is the fashion for men to maintain the children of others, no woman in her senses would permit the passion of a man unmarried, because, though he could range and select another, she must remain forlorn and abandoned."

"The supposition," said Frederick, "that I must have a companion for life, is the result of a complication of vices: it is the dictate of cowardice, and not of fortitude: it flows from a desire of being loved and esteemed for something that is not desert. The institution of marriage is a *system of fraud*, and men who *carefully mislead* their judgments in the daily affairs of their life, will always have a crippled judgment in every other concern.—Marriage is law, and the *worst of all laws*. Whatever our understandings may tell us of the person from whose connection we should derive the greatest improvement, of the worth of one woman, and the demerits of another, we are obliged to consider what is law, and not what is justice. *So long as I seek to engross one woman to myself, and prohibit my neighbour from proving his superior deserts, and reaping the fruits of it, I am guilty of the most odious of all monopolies.*"*

"Do you wish me," said Laura, "to suppose you speak seriously? You are dreaming, Frederick, or you are mad, or worse. To say nothing of the *moral* turpitude of such infamous and *brothel* doctrines, I should like to know if there is one single republican in the kingdom, who, however he might wish to indulge *himself* in such licence, would permit his mother, his wife, his sister, or his daughter, to live promiscuously like beasts of the field?"

"And are men not by nature brutes, as the mighty Rousseau has proved to a demonstration?"[119]

---

* After such a sentence as this, which is in Godwin's Political Justice, 4to. page 851, the reader will not accuse the author of exaggerating facts. [Editor's note: *The supposition … monopolies*: a verbatim compilation drawn from Godwin's original text (though on pp. 849-50, not 851).]

"Let us take it so," said Laura, with a sigh: "what will be the result? We should see half a dozen throats cut for a pretty woman, for then the law would be no check on licentious appetites. But, Sir, reflect if what I say be not true. Your reformers *in general* are men of broken fortune, fiery passions, or eccentric dispositions. You would cast aside restraint, because you are too great tyrants yourselves to submit to the government of others; as, for instance, Doctor Alogos was one of the best-tempered, humane men in the world, till he took to these whims from the loss of a law-suit; and now, though he is always telling us we are slaves, and have as much right as the men to every freedom, yet, if every article in the house, to the smallest trifle, is not in exact order, we hear nothing but execrations, which once he was afraid to utter. But, in the present case, I do sincerely believe, that those men who preach up promiscuous intercourse of sex do it merely to cover their own depraved desires, and avoid the stigma of the world by rendering it common."

"I am very sorry," said Frederick, "that you argue as if you had never heard the great doctrines of philosophy. Had you heard my Mary on this subject! persuasion hung upon her tongue, and the self-demonstrated axioms of moral science flowed from her lips. 'It is difficult to recommend any thing to indiscriminate adoption, contrary to the established rules and prejudices of mankind; but certainly nothing can be so ridiculous upon the face of it, or so contrary to the *genuine march* of sentiment, as to require the overflowing of the soul to wait upon a ceremony, and that which, wherever delicacy and imagination exist, is of all things most sacredly private, to blow *a trumpet* before it, and to record the moment when it has arrived at its climax.'"*

---

* Memoirs of Mrs. Woolstonecraft Godwin. A Democratic Review says, my treatment of Mrs. Godwin, in these volumes, *is brutal*. If repeating verbatim her own sentiments be brutality, then I am guilty. But if they mean that such sentiments brutalise a woman, I cannot help that. [Editor's note: *It is difficult … climax*: verbatim citation from Godwin's *Memoirs* (105). This "sheer bombast," in Laura's terms, is actually therefore Godwin's, not Mary Wollstonecraft's. The "Democratic Review" Walker is referring to in this footnote is the *Analytical Review*. It was founded by Mary Wollstonecraft's publisher, friend and literary patron Joseph Johnson (1738-1809), in partnership with Thomas Christie (1761-96), and ran from May 1788 to 1799. A member of the Society for Constitutional Information, Johnson positioned the periodical firmly in the reformist camp. The *Analytical Review* was the first British literary monthly aimed at the general

"Excellent!" cried Laura, breaking into a laugh; "this is sheer bombast, and putting into hyperbolic language what might have been said in simple words. Can any thing be more *impudent* than for a woman to *marry*, because by marrying she tells the world that she has conformed to its customs in following the purpose of her creation? Whereas, if she despised all its rules, trampled down those barriers to lust, modesty, and morality, and became a *prostitute*, she is *modest* in extreme, because she did not tell the world before-hand she was going to be ruined. With regard to the trumpet and the climax, it is not a practice in our country, where marriages are frequently performed with that decent secrecy which eludes even the questions of friendship."

"There is no reasoning with women," cried Frederick in a pet; "they have no souls capable of receiving the new light of irradiating science, which is breaking through the mists of super-stition and ignorance. How few are like my Mary, free in thought and in action! She was a wonderful woman, and despised the jests of the world: she knew, that in reality there was no difference of sex in souls, but that education made women fools and idiots."

"You have often," said Laura, "talked to me in this strain; you have told me that women are no otherwise inferior to men than by education; but to me there appears an humbling difference.— Have they not to bear and bring children into the world? Are they not then tied down to the routine of a nursery? Are not all their employments necessarily domestic? And does not Nature seem to have pointed to this end in the disposition of their frame?—Men, in all countries, take upon them the ruder employments, and it is only an eccentric soul that would wish, in the frenzy of imagination, to blend the sexes."

"But women, with their present *weakness of intellect*, are not capable of teaching children their duties and rational philosophy."

"I will quote you a passage," said Laura, "from the droll book of reveries my uncle lately bought, called The Rights of Women.

reading public, and was made up almost entirely out of book reviews. Wollstonecraft was a regular contributor to the *Analytical Review*, and it was through her reviewing that she came engaged into contemporary intellectual and political debates. In a review of *The Vagabond*, which appeared in February 1799, Walker was accused of heaping "indecent and *brutal* sarcasms upon Mrs. Godwin" (see Appendix C.1).]

In page 148, I will believe you will find these words:—'The management of the temper, the first and most important branch of education, requires the *sober, steady eye of reason*: a plan of conduct equally distant from tyranny and indulgence. I have followed this train of reasoning much further, till I have concluded that a *person of genius is the most improper person* to be employed in education, either private or public.'[120] From this quotation we may infer two conclusions:—First, that a person of *genius* possesses not the *steady, sober eye of reason*, and therefore all your pretended philosophers, reformers, and men of profound genius, have not one jot of reason, consequently, are *fools*. Secondly, allowing women to be pretty idiots, they are the most proper to give education, and the less genius they possess, the greater is their qualification: and indeed I might draw a third inference, that persons writing palpable contradictions are unworthy notice on either side."

"Oh!," cried Frederick, "were the great Stupeo here, he would bring arguments that would incontrovertibly prove——"

"Prove what?" said Laura, "prove himself a greater fool than his pupil."

"No," cried Frederick, "prove that you are the charmingest pretty idiot in the world."

Thus the great copyist of one of the greatest philosophers that have glittered in the eighteenth century descended from the pinnacle of intellect to tell a girl what her glass told her every morning. But, as Voltaire has admirably proved, by a few arguments, in about a hundred different places, and Rousseau demonstrated by practice with the idiot Teresa, it is a fact, that great heroes, great poets, great philosophers, metaphysicians, and ballad-makers, have all become fools to please foolish women.

CHAPTER II.

REASONS FOR PEOPLING THE WORLD—SPECIMENS OF THE SUBLIME—THE CONSOLATIONS OF PHILOSOPHY IN DISAPPOINTMENT— THE IMMUTABILITY OF TRUTH.

Frederick was discomposed beyond the dignity of a philosopher at the perverseness of Laura: he began almost to think that women were beings made expressly for the pleasures of men, a gilded toy, which a great metaphysician and philosopher might condescend to play with when he quitted the Hall of Contemplation, and ventured from the paths of intellectual rambling to the gross pavement of life.

His mind was perpetually bent upon the great work of reformation, and the perfection of jurisprudence, *except* when he mused upon the pretty lip of Laura, which frequently dimpled with an inimitable smile, and that smile was not the vacant smile of childishness—it was a smile of meaning, expressive of some fine sensation of mind, brightening the whole countenance, and lighting the eye with the intelligence of good sense.

"I know not," said he to himself, as he rambled over the fields, "what to make of this girl; she reasons as if she had reason, but it is quite in the old style. What is this love? What would my dear Stupeo define it? A passion, that, like an optic glass, inverts its object. Ah! now I am satisfied she does not in reality possess any good quality: it is my passion which deceives me, and she is no more an angel than the rest of her sex. All her virtues are only like colours in objects, merely rays pressed in different angles upon the eye. She herself is a blank, a mere white sheet of paper; and it remains for me to stamp upon her any character I please. As to beauty—what is beauty? Ask a negro of Guinea what is beauty, the supremely beautiful, the το καλον (to kalon),[121] he will answer you, a greasy black skin, hollow eyes, and a flat nose. Consult the philosophers, they will tell you some unintelligible jargon for answer—they must have something correspondent to beauty in the abstract."

Having thus used the light of human reason in rational argument, Frederick determined that Laura must and should be his, not for his own sake, but for the promotion of freedom, and the *spread of the truth.*

"It is the universal good and greatest resulting benefit we are ever to have in view," continued he: "all the great men of the eighteenth century tell us we must not regard any contingencies, these being only partial and unavoidable evils. It is plain the world must be peopled; for if it is not peopled, we philosophers would have nobody to revolutionize, and reason, and logic, and ignorance, would be tantamount to the same. This then is the self-demonstrated hypothesis: this then is the grand basis to build upon; and as all things depend upon peopling the world, it follows, that to people the world is the most meritorious action of life. But how am I to contribute to this greatest good, if Laura persists in her notions of matrimony? It is impossible. I should then surrender my freedom, and freedom is even a *greater* good *than life* itself. Some middle-way must be devised; and though I abhor giving pain to any creature under the heavens, yet I must not be deterred from peopling the world, by the tears, faintings, and frettings of a woman who even does not know the great maxims of philosophy. What are tears? Mere bubbles of water emitted from a particular stimulus of the nerves of the eye: women have weaker nerves than men, therefore tears from them are more common.—As to fainting, that also depends on weak nerves:—some will faint at the sight of a rat. Well, I can't help the irritibility of the nervous system:—A charming idea indeed! that, because women have weak nerves, the world is not to be peopled! Besides, am not I a philosopher? Yes: I have, and I will rise far above human nature.—Have I not seduced the mistress of my friend? Have I not been the means of a pretty girl and her father perishing in the flames? Have I not led a mob to burn down the metropolis of Great Britain? Have I not induced a wife to betray her husband, which caused his own and his children's death? Have I not lost three teeth and half of my little finger in the cause of liberty? Have I not murdered my own mother? And shall the tears and lamentings of a girl prevent my marching forward in the high road of all-irradiating science and peopling the world?"

"O Philosophy! how few can contemplate thy sublime and terrific features: thy feet stand upon the poles of the world—thy head is cinctured round with nubilated exhalations, whose volcanic entrails emit thunderings and lightnings that scatter all existence around thee, and hecatombs of infidels and surdous men are reared or dispersed by the cataclysms of thy scientific fulminations. When shall the catenas of mankind be decrepitated by the furnace of truth, ignited by the bellows of reason? When shall the ignannations of prejudice be delacerated, and the catachrestical reasonings of facinorous aristocrats be disbanded by the zetetic spirit of the eighteenth century?"*

From this prodigious flight of the true sublime and unintelligible, Frederick suddenly descended to the consideration of more common action: simply, how he might promote the increase of mankind. It appeared no very easy task to do away the qualms of conscience in a modest girl, unless indeed he could prove to her that there was no such thing as conscience, which was a task of no great difficulty for a modern philosopher to undertake. Another small reflection occupied him, for he saw that he must proceed upon the principles of deception, and what then became of immutable truth? But, on weighing over the maxims of *political justice*, he found that deception was extremely moral in affairs of love, and he was more than ever enamoured of the new philosophy, which seemed calculated for the comfort of man.

He began with Doctor Alogos, whom he soon convinced of

---

* For the sake of the *English* reader, these words may be found in Johnson's Dictionary. [Editor's note: The prose style of the lexicographer Samuel Johnson (see note 52), marked by a frequent use of Latinate and abstract words and phrases, is often referred to as "Johnsonese"—a quality that Walker evidently associated with the new philosophy's penchant for abstruse thought and scientific discourse, even though Johnson was far from radical (in fact, he was an orthodox Christian and staunch defender of traditional values). In plain, modern English, *cinctured around* means "encompassed"; *nubilated*, "cloudy"; *hecatombs*, "large numbers"; *catenas*, "chains, strings"; *decrepitated*, (of a salt or mineral) roasted until it no longer crackles in the fire; *delacerated*, "torn in pieces"; *catachrestical*, from catachresis, "improper use of words or metaphor"; *facinorous*, "extremely wicked, grossly criminal, atrocious, infamous, vile"; *zetetic*, "inquiring, investigating" (annotations based on those in *OED*). *Surdous* and *ignannations* do not occur in Johnson's *Dictionary*, nor in the *OED* and appear to be Walker's inventions. "Surd," however, does appear in both dictionaries (defined in Johnson as "deaf," but here used by Walker in its figurative meaning, defined in the *OED* as "irrational, senseless, stupid").]

the non-entity of conscience; that reason was the only guide to truth, and passion the index to pleasure. Laura, the blind prejudiced Laura, was not to be wrought upon by the profoundest of his reasonings and the subtilty of his logic.—"Though I feel myself unequal to answer you," said she, "that by no means is an approval of your arguments; for I well know that by argument we can neither prove nor refute many things which yet we feel to be or not to be. For instance, you may tell me I am ten feet or only ten inches high; that my sight deceives me; and you may confound me with arguments to prove your assertion. But all those arguments will not change my opinion that I am only five feet high, nor will you persuade me that I have no conscience."

One fine glowing evening, when the country was yellowed over with harvest, and the birds chirped amongst the hedges, which were hung with stalks of loose corn, Frederick and Laura took a walk to some distance, and, as it is very natural, discoursed on love by the way.

Frederick exerted all his eloquence upon the usual subject; but feeling that he made no impression, he *transided* into the more natural language of common-place, such as has been the practice of all lovers since the flood, and such as will continue to win the hearts of the fair, till philosophy shall introduce a new set of ideas and sensations.—"I will," said he, "charming Laura, adopt your side of the question, for really metaphysics do not altogether satisfy the heart."

"Were you to forsake your wild opinions," said Laura, "you would become an agreeable member of society."

"It is you," he replied, "who must make me so; it is you I shall look up to for instruction; but remember the sentiments of Rousseau in his Emilius.[122] If woman be formed to please, and be subjected to man, it is her place doubtless to render herself agreeable to him instead of challenging his passion: the violence of his desires depends upon her charms; it is by means of these she should urge him to the exertion of those powers nature has given him. The most successful method of exciting is to render such exertion necessary by resistance, as in that case self-love is added to desire, and the one triumphs in the victory which the other is obliged to acquire."

"These sentiments were worthy a voluptuary," replied Laura: "they came, no doubt, warm from the heart of Rousseau."

"Yes," said Frederick, "from the author of Eloisa[123] we should expect strong expressions, but they are nevertheless true. You have read, Laura, that charming romance. What did you feel at the *first kiss of love?* In a word, did not the whole performance set your soul on fire?"

"No," replied Laura; "I saw through the sophistical jargon of rhapsodic language. I beheld only a man who *kept* a milliner, endeavouring to justify his actions to the world by drawing a fiery picture totally untrue. Do you think there is a man in the world like Wolmar? And what was St. Preux but a precious sentimental rascal, who, under the sanction of the most sacred friendship, plunders a believing love-sick girl, and talks all the while about virtue and celestial innocence?"

Frederick found by this discourse that he should not easily contaminate the purity of her mind by the introduction of voluptuous subjects, for he knew of no book more likely to introduce a desire of dissipation than the celebrated Eloisa of Rousseau:* he therefore resolved to supply his want of persuasion by violence, beginning with those liberties often allowed, till his passions throwing him off his guard, he exerted that prowess which men are endowed with for other purposes; but here he was again deceived, Laura not being one of those puny slips of fashion which shrink from the touch.

The philosopher was confounded at a resistance he had not expected from the delicate figure of the maid. He hung down his head in silent *vexation* at her keen reproaches; for *shame* he knew not, unless it was in stopping short of his heroic and patriotic intentions. He proposed, in a tone of voice much beneath the dignity of manhood, to accompany her home, but she refused his offer with superlative disdain.

---

* To this may now be added the Monk. [Editor's note: *The Monk* (1796), by Matthew Gregory "Monk" Lewis (1775-1818), was one of the most scandalously salacious Gothic novels of the period. A sensational success when it first appeared, *The Monk* was reviled in the conservative press, which regarded it as an exponent of Jacobin moral depravity—causing Lewis to discretely but rigorously bowdlerize later editions of the novel.]

He turned away to philosophise, and call to his aid the doctrines of Stupeo: so chagrined was he at his disappointment, that he almost resolved never again to present himself before Doctor Alogos—but again he reflected, that it was unworthy a great man to stoop to accidents, it being more in the order of Nature that accidents should bend to them.

As he walked forward, wrapped in *musing melancholy*, a gleam of satisfaction darted across his mind—"Why," said he, internally, "am I so grieved at a trifling disappointment?—I, who am a being independent of the Universe, in how few years will age destroy the appetite for pleasure, and I shall then regret not having made more advantage of the fleeting moments. Did I bow down to the idols of priestcraft, I might be deterred from many actions *called crimes*, by the dread of future punishment; but it is the height of monkish blindness to suppose there is any such thing as future punishment, and I am persuaded, I am certain, half mankind do not give credit to such shocking doctrines, or it would be impossible they could act as they do. What lawyer would undertake a wrong case? What guardian would ruin the orphan under his care? What wife would betray her husband? What son would disobey his father? What father would ruin his family with variety of excess? And what young man would, for the pleasure of half an hour, cajole, with false oaths and professions, a fair, believing, tender-hearted girl into a misery that can end only with her life?—No; I am certain, if people believed any thing of revealed religion, none of this could happen. Then shall *I* be trammelled by such considerations? O philosophy! divine light of the soul! thy consolations never fail in the hour of distress. Beware, says St. Paul, lest men spoil you through philosophy and vain deceit; but Paul was an old woman, Paul knew nothing of *eternal sleep*."124

Having thus confirmed his mind in these delectable principles, he felt re-assured to his purpose, and inclined his thoughts to suggest the means of subduing Laura.

Laura informed her uncle of the great designs of the vagabond philosopher; but that disciple of the new school only coolly bade her be cautious, for nothing in nature could be more natural.

Frederick was surprised to find the Doctor in good spirits; and no hint being dropped concerning his recent attempt, he already concluded Laura in his possession. He retired early to bed to digest his plan; and not being able to sleep, he tumbled about till midnight, when he was alarmed with a grating noise at the window beneath him. He listened, and fancying he heard footsteps, arose, and was proceeding down stairs with a poker in his hand, when two men ascending, presented pistols at him, with threats of instant death, if he alarmed the house.

"Am I to be deterred from speaking the truth?" said Frederick: "a truly virtuous man will proclaim the truth, amidst an host of foes."

"D—n my glims,"[125] said one of the ruffians, "you are a rum quiz; but I suppose he's dreaming."

"If you will tell truth," said the other, "tell us where the old codger hides his cash."

"Truth," replied Frederick, "is invariable: the great Stupeo declared that no circumstance could change its effects, and that it must be spoken at all times."

"Well, out with it then, and no qualms."

"In love," continued Frederick, with *sang froid*, "we may conceal the truth, because it is an allowable deception to deceive a girl to her own benefit, and the augmentation of mankind. But, for the sake wealth, dross, trash, rubbish——"

"D—e," cried the first, "you are a devilish rum one: only tell us where we may find the rubbish, and less of the gab."[126]

"This rubbish," cried Frederick, "the bane of society, the cause of all unnatural accumulations, of all the miseries of suffering man; what is this to truth, eternal and immutable truth?"

"Blow his brains out," said the robber, "if he don't instantly tell us where the possibles[127] be."

"We are not to be compelled to speak the truth," said Frederick; "we should speak it for its own sake, and not to avoid any evil, or to promote any independent good: for instance, I could now, to avoid the evil you threaten, tell you that in the front palour there are bank notes to the amount of fifty pounds, and that would satisfy you; but that is an equivocation, because you ask where *the money* is concealed, implying *all*. (Aye! aye! All! all!) Well, that being the case, and an equivocation being a lie, according to Dr. Paley,[128] I continue to tell you, that under his bed in the back room, on the second floor, is an iron chest, where you will find the remainder, and thus it is clearly demonstrated that——"

"Aye, aye, clear enough," cried the thieves, "don't say a word more—go back to your own bed, and sleep in a sound skin."

I am not obliged, said Frederick to himself, to run hazards in proclaiming truth when it is not required. Perhaps these patriots intend to murder the old Doctor: well, suppose they do, what will be the resulting consequences? Ignorant, unillumined people, in stating this fine and metaphysical argument, would talk about gratitude—that's totally exploded in political justice. A servant might urge his being obliged to serve his master, but I am no servant; and a servant would be condemned if he did not assist to destroy his master in the cause of truth, by the new system. But what possible good will result to mankind by the death of the Doctor? Is he not one of us? Is he not an enlightened philosopher of the eighteenth century? He has already created three or four riots in the parish, and rendered the people so dissatisfied, that they will neither work nor play. A revolution seems maturing in this little spot, that shall light the torch of liberty all over Europe: and shall this man be cut off by men who seem unorganised to systematic depredation—men who do not seem to plunder upon principle? No; the whole human race would suffer in his loss.

These arguments were convincing, and he hastened with the poker in his hand to the chamber. The robbers had drawn out the chest, and emptied its contents, when Doctor Alogos awaking, began to call aloud for assistance, and the robbers swore they would cut his throat if he was not silent. At that instance Frederick burst into the room, and one of the thieves fired, but missed him. A blow of the poker tore off the rascal's ear, and shook his arm so rudely, that the pistol fell to the floor, and the Doctor having reached a blunderbuss, they hurried away, carrying with them the notes and cash, with which they filled their pockets, swearing they would shoot whoever attempted to follow them.

"My dear Frederick," cried the Doctor, embracing him, "you are a brave fellow, and this favour shall not go unrewarded: you may always rely on my friendship."

"Friendship!" exclaimed Frederick. "Has fear clouded your intellects? Friendship is well enough for boarding-school girls, who are plotting intrigues. You must esteem me for my intrinsic value, and not because I have done *you* a service. No man ought to return favour for favour—that is an old obsolete doctrine, done away entirely by the new political justice.—Hear the great sentiments of the great Stupeo on favours:—It may be objected, said he, that a mutual commerce of benefits tends to increase the mass (or cube lump) of benevolent action, and that to increase the *mass* of benevolent action is to contribute to the general good: indeed, is the general good promoted by falsehood, by treating a man of *one degree* of worth, as if he had *ten times* that worth? or, as if he were in any degree different from what he really is? Would not the most beneficial consequences result from a different plan, from my constantly and carefully inquiring into the deserts of *all* those with whom I am connected, and from their being *sure*, after a *certain allowance* for the infallibility of human judgment, of being treated by me exactly as they deserved? Who can tell the effects of such a plan universally adopted?"[*]

"Not even the profound Stupeo himself," said Doctor Alogos. "I very much fear we shall never arrive at that perfection of knowledge, so as to be *sure* and yet *uncertain* of the quantity of merit: had that great man lived, he would, no doubt, have made a barometer, which, upon being applied to the object, would instantly settle to the exact degree of worth."

"The idea is original," cried Frederick, "and I am persuaded he would have attempted its completion, for mind in that case would

---

[*] Godwin's Political Justice, page 86. [Editor's note: *It may be objected ... universally adopted*: Walker's citation from Godwin is rather inaccurate, and reads more correctly: "It may in the second place be objected, 'that a mutual commerce of benefits tends to increase the mass of benevolent action, and that to increase the mass of benevolent action is to contribute to the general good.' Indeed! Is the general good promoted by falsehood, by treating a man of one degree of worth as if he had ten times that worth? or as if he were in any degree different from what he really is? Would not the most beneficial consequences result from a different plan; from my constantly and carefully enquiring into the deserts of all those with whom I am connected, and from their being sure, after a certain allowance for the fallibility of human judgement, of being treated by me exactly as they deserved? Who can describe the benefits that would result from such a plan of conduct, if universally adopted?" (85-86).]

overcome matter.—Alas! what has the world lost by the death of such a man, who only was rescued from the gallows to be shot in a riot. O Fortune! what a jilt art thou to men of genius and science."

"Nothing more true," said the Doctor, with a sigh. "Here is an end of our great projects of reformation, for my rents come in very slowly, the wretches declaring they have a right to the ground-rent free, and here I have lost five hundred pounds."

"It is the vile government we live under," said Frederick; "a monarchy is a mere excrescence, and a disease in the body of society: the wars it occasions, and the lavish revenues by which it is maintained, make it unbearable. Ah! if we could fly from its evils and re-assume the primitive simplicity of mankind—if we could shake off all sorts of governments, and live to ourselves as independent and rational beings, we should then pay no taxes: Laura should be my companion, and Susan yours:—there, beneath vine trees of our own planting, we should sit and talk of love: beneath the date tree and the olive we should sing hymns of peace, and in the sylvan shades should we be united in harmony and celestial affections. Our children would promiscuously grow up untainted by the world, and no tyrant should violate the chastity of our daughters at his imperious will."

"Oh! charming," cried the Doctor, dressing himself. "Go and wake Laura instantly, and before to-morrow's sun raises the blue mists of the lake, we will be on our journey to this terrestial paradise."

Frederick, impressed with equal rapture at the romantic idea, and repeating to himself anathemas against the tyrants who have debased unthinking innocence, he hastened to the chamber of Laura. He found her half dressed, having been alarmed at the cries of her uncle. She blushed at being thus exposed to the eyes of so great a philosopher, and that blush drove all the tyrants from the mind of Frederick. He clasped the fair maid in his arms, and at that moment Doctor Alogos entered to tell his niece the service he had received from the interposition of the virtuous hero.

Frederick, in such a situation, would have been confused if he had not been a very great man; but he was arrived at so much perfection, that he could listen to his own praise in the moment he wishes to perpetrate what with half mankind would have rendered him an object of detestation; but this attainment could only be acquired by a steady attention to all the enlightened doctrines of the eighteenth century, and is called the bold, unblushing front of manly truth.

Laura rejoiced at the escape of her uncle, for her bosom was only too susceptible of gratitude, and she almost forgave the attack upon herself. She, however, objected to the plan of emigration, as a wild-goose chase after happiness; and the arguments she used almost convinced the Doctor that all pleasure was ideal, for, as to dates and olives, not a single tree grows in all North America, which obliged Frederick to own he meant only *figurative* expression.

Frederick was too candid to conceal his discourse with the robbers, and Doctor Alogos could not refrain observing, that, though truth ought to be spoken at all times, yet, if it cost five hundred pounds, it was as well to be silent.

CHAPTER III.

THE INTRODUCTION OF A VERY GREAT MAN— MATTER AND SPIRIT DISCUSSED—THE RAISING OF THE DEAD BY NATURAL MAGIC.

The harmony of the family once more restored, the public good became again their chief care, but an accident happened that very much checked their proceedings. A countryman had been detected offering one of the notes which had been stolen, and was carried before a Justice of the Peace, where he was identified by Frederick and the Doctor. He pleaded very much in his own favour, protesting that it was his first crime, and that his accomplice had carried away the whole booty except that single note.

"And how," said the justice, "could you be guilty of so great an offence when you could not be ignorant of the law?"

"That be very true, your honour," replied the man: "but I did hear Doctor Alogos in his pulpit reading a great book of political justice, which did say as how no law ought to punish *offenders* for a crime that be done, because as that it were not likely, please your worship, that any man should commit the same again, and no man ever committed the same offence in all its sarcumstances, as the law do mention.[129] So, your honour, I thought that I did see clear enough, that if I did not do the action as the law did forbid, I were not guilty. Beside, and more, your honour, I were near starving, having lost my playse because I would not tend church on a Sunday, nor work like a neger, as the Doctor did tell us we all were, as laboured for the rich; and so, your honour, I had nothing to do but to starve, and the day were once, when I would have starved rather than do a dishonest act:—but Doctor Alogos did tell us that there were no such thing as dishonesty; that it were all a tale to cheat us out of our right; and that the poor ought to have the lands of the rich divided: so, playse your honour, I were in a strange quandary, and though my heart did misgive me, I were persuaded to begin with the Doctor, as it were but proper he should practise what he did preach."

"Doctrines like these," said the Justice, "are certainly of the most pernicious tendency, and, in fact, Doctor Alogos, this man appears to me less guilty than yourself. You know I must commit him if you prosecute, but I should suppose you would not wish to appear in such a situation; and I hope this will be a warning to this simple man, and teach him to follow the track of his fore-fathers."

"Such," cried Frederick, "is the blessed effects of property! The great philosopher Stupeo used to say, that the fruitful source of crimes consists in one man's possessing in abundance that of which another man is destitute. This day gives us proof of it; for this poor man would not have attempted the robbery, notwithstanding the beam of truth which flashed on the obscurity of his mind, had it not been from want."

"It is not my place," said the Justice, mildly, "to attend to arguments; my business is with facts: but, for the good of my countrymen who are round me, I will observe, that this is the general topic of modern reformers, but, like most other of their pernicious principles, it is erroneous. Thieves, ninety-nine out of the hundred, are idle and dissipated, and in general possess that ingenuity which, rightly employed, would raise them to considerable eminence.— Drunkenness and lust are their great incentives to outrage, and *not* the want of food and raiment, the latter being, with a very small exception, in the power of every one who is willing and who has strength to work. It is likewise to be remembered, that, in the professed system of equality and property, no man is to enjoy or possess more than food and raiment, all else being luxury. It has been urged, that some have been starved to death for want of encouragement, *who had genius* and talents; but let this be remembered, that it was owing to their employing those talents in a wrong way. Chatterton,[130] for instance, starved as an author, but he might have maintained himself well as a schoolmaster: but, you will say, can any man of feeling speak so coldly of so great a genius? We will not talk of feeling, but reason.—When I speak of Chatterton, I mean it of *all others*. Chatterton knew his abilities, and he wished to force the world to acknowledge him at once—but this must always be a work of time. Placing his whole dependence on *one* foundation, he was too proud to stoop from the high throne of poetic exaltation; whereas, had he become a schoolmaster, he might have lived and watched the progress of his productions to the climax which awaited them. Again I would seriously observe, and would to heaven I could be heard by all mankind:—this man here accused of robbery tells you one means of losing his place was disregard of Sunday—mark with your own eyes the difference of those who do attend the service of God and those who do not!—I will not mention sects of religion; but look at those who pay a reverence to holy things, sobriety directs their way: they have no taste for profligacy, and they rarely sink into ruin from their own vices. But let us see those men who despise the formality of church, and spend the Sunday in drinking and gaming: idleness and debauchery powerfully seize on the mind in these vacant moments, and thus it is from the cottage to the mansion that we may in general draw a man's moral character from his attention to Sunday; and we need none of us look far round, without as it were, perceiving that even, in the transient prosperity of this world, God has distinguished those who obey his commandments."

The attention of the numerous company assembled was arrested by the approach of a crowd of people. The poor labourer was discharged (for in the interior of the country, justices of the peace are extremely arbitrary.) Frederick hastened into the yard, where, amongst a troop of women and country people, appeared a thin, sallow complexioned man, with one eye, and a large gash on one side of his face, which added to the deep gloom of his countenance a trait of horrid ferocity and malignant expression. Frederick gazed upon him a few moments with a look of surprise.—"Is it possible," cried he, "I behold the profound and immortal Stupeo? Are you resuscitated, or were you not hanged nor murdered?—Can I believe my eyes?"

"It is I," cried the great philosopher himself: "I have escaped these evils by accident, but I have lost my eye in the cause of freedom. How, my dear Frederick, are you here? How could you possibly escape the vengeance of that glorious night?"

"Another time," answered Frederick, "I will tell you every thing: but why are you deprived of your liberty?—Have you fallen at last under the gripe of that many-fanged monster—the Law?"

"This is a mere trifle," said Stupeo: "I am accused of marrying *three* wives, and as it is not a criminal process, I shall escape with finding bail to maintain them. So much for the glorious uncertainty of that profound abyss—the Law."

"But is it possible," cried Doctor Alogos, "that you, Sir, the great and powerful opponent of matrimony, should be married to *three* at once? This strikes me as a contradiction."

"That is, Sir," replied Stupeo, with a look of superiority, "because you are but little versed in the sublime doctrine of political justice. Sir, you would there find that contradictions are nothing in the way of truth:—but here there is no contradiction. The excess of an evil is always a remedy; as, for instance, when the militia of Europe shall exceed the standing armies, and all the citizens become soldiers, the evil of standing armies will cease, as the power of directing them to the destruction of the people will be gone.* In like manner, a man who has three or more wives may live as free as though unmarried, for he has only to go to the altar with any female whom he judges capable of adding to the stock of general or resulting good."

---

* I believe this is an observation of Hume, in his History of England, but only quoting from memory, cannot be certain. [Editor's note: David Hume's monumental, multi-volume *History of Great Britain* (1754-62) was for many years the most authoritative text on the subject. The citation (if that is what it is) has not been identified.]

Frederick was struck with this profound argument; and the company being now ordered before the Justice, he paused to reflect whether, after all means were tried of subduing Laura, he might not adopt this plan without infringing the principles of liberty.

Doctor Alogos, who, had he not imbibed the new philosophy, would have been a man of benevolence, agreed to pay a stipend for the maintenance of the young woman at whose suit the great philosopher had been detained, and, proud of having so celebrated a man for his guest, (though at present a little in disorder) he invited him to the mansion-house.

Laura started with surprise at the sight of so shocking a being in human form, and not being able to discern the wondrous patriot beneath his unseemly habit (for females are strangely impressed by exteriors), she concluded it one of the robbers of her uncle, and scarcely knew whether to run away or stay.

The name of Stupeo, which she had often heard, arrested her attention, and when she gazed more minutely on the master, she ceased to wonder at the eccentricities of the scholar.

When they were seated and refreshed, the Doctor inquired in what state Stupeo had found the people of England in his excursions?—"In what state!" cried he, "why, absolutely starving and undone: the whole country is in a rapid consumption, and no efforts of man can save it. I may say, without vanity, I have done my endeavours. I have had twelve illegitimate children, but not one of them could bear the air of this foggy climate. I have had three wives, but still the people decrease—population is rapidly declining. What with emigration and the prevailing taste for celibacy, I am convinced this island will, in a very few years, become an howling wild, and its sea shores a place for fishermen's nets. The sun of science is hastening Westwards from these benighted lands, and it becomes every rational man to follow its beams."[131]

"I have long meditated on the subject," said the Doctor: "I would not proceed rashly, but I find the people of this country so tenacious in their support of an old rotten constitution, so wedded to old principles, that we are thwarted at every motion by some cross accident, and they are such gross fools, that the most palpable facts they invert to contrary tendencies."

"I am on fire," cried Frederick: "I am determined to breathe a freer air; and let me tell you, the man who remains voluntarily in a despotic country, lends his countenance and support to the measures of that country."

In the evening Stupeo and Frederick took a walk, when the latter requested his tutor to inform him of the accidents he had met with since their first separation, their meeting in London having been so momentary, and their minds so employed on great exploits, that they had no time for private relations.

"It would be impossible," said Stupeo, "to detail all the actions I have engaged in; I must therefore briefly enumerate them in a sort of catalogue. The life of a philosopher ought to be perpetually changing.—First, then, I was appointed tutor to some young ladies, one of whom I took a fancy to (for I am not very difficult of choice), and the father having prevented me from starving, it was impossible I could do less than instruct his daughter in the new philosophy of political justice. He was, however, such a bigot to the old school, that he kicked me out of his house, and I remained for some time nearly starved, when I had an undeniable right to dine at the richest table in the kingdom. A trifling forgery I had been induced to commit, not for any purpose of self-interest, that would have been morally wrong, but merely to take a little from the fortune of a man who wallowed in wealth he could not consume, was the means of introducing me to the cells of Newgate: such is the present detestable system fencing round property, with capital punishments, so that it is next to impossible to reduce the horrid amassments of wealth into more equal channels.

After I was shot and trod down, I lay some time insensible, when a surgeon's man dragged me into a bye alley, and whipping me into a sack, carried me to his master's dissecting-room.— Having prepared himself for a grand experiment, he was surprised to find that I was not wholly dead, and applying some powerful stimulants, I opened my eyes.

I was astonished to see, stooping over me, an haggard figure, dressed in a brown stuff gown streaked with blood;[132] in a belt hung a parcel of instruments, and round the room were various preparations of anatomy, with saws and skeletons hung upon nails. I inclined my eyes to see my own situation:—a wet cloth bound my head, and I found that I was lying naked upon a large table clotted with morsels of skin and flesh. I fancied myself in the Inquisition.

'Fiends!' said I, 'is this your way of promoting your superstitions? You would make me believe the immortality of the soul; but matter is eternal—and as to the soul, it is like the sap in vegetables, when it leaves one form, it goes to impress motion on another: it is a bundle of ideas perpetually changing, and never is the same two moments together, and yet this fleeting something you would make me believe is immortal.'

'Are you an atheist?' said the surgeon.

'No,' cried I, 'I am no atheist, I am a new philosopher. Helvetius says, he is no atheist who says that *motion is God*, because, in fact, motion is *incomprehensible*, as we have no *clear* idea of it, as it does not manifest itself but by its effects, and lastly, because by it all things are performed in the universe.'133

'Then you call *motion* God?'—'Certainly,' said I, 'because it is *incomprehensible*.'

'Then whatever is incomprehensible is God?—But, what do you say of the *cause* of motion?'

'That must be motion itself, because passive power cannot act, and active power is action or motion.'

He took a lancet, and making a slight incision in my thigh, dropped upon the part a few drops of elixer, which threw me into such intolerable pain, that I started on my legs and made at him like a fury.

'Is it a Deity?' cried he, 'that acts on you? You are under some strange impression.—Do you *comprehend* the *cause* of your motion?'

'That fluid,' said I, 'has cut to my soul, and stimulated my nerves to a convulsive motion.'

'How say you? What then is *motion mechanical*! If so, how is motion God? But, do you comprehend the reason why this elixer ran like fire to your brains?'—'No.' 'Not comprehend it? Why, then this elixer is your God: it is an *incomprehensible cause of incomprehensible motion*.'

'I might reply in the words of Mr. Hume,' said I:—"If you do not believe as I do, I must confess I can reason with you no longer."[134] But, however,' continued I, 'to give you a *clear* idea of this grand doctrine of motion:—The internal organization of abstract principles coming in contact with tangible substances, forms a concatenation of resulting consequences, demonstrating the powers of loco, impinging motion, resulting from the chance arrangement of ponderous bodies, subsiding in concocted masses, and assuming a form of vacuo.'[135]

'My dear Sir,' cried the surgeon, 'I can form no clear idea of your *incomprehensible* discourse, and yet I should not take you for a Deity—at least you must be one in disguise.'

'You must allow, however,' said I, 'that chance has produced every thing and directs every thing.'

'So far the contrary, that chance produces nothing, and cannot direct any thing: this elixer acted on you as it would on a thousand others. What appears chance to us is only an invisible cause, of which we see the effect. In some cases we may trace up the effects to a great First Cause, who must, from our very nature, be to us incomprehensible; but not for that reason non-existent, or, on the contrary, because many things possess this *one* attribute to us, are we to call them Deities? For if so, every phenomenon of nature would become a Deity, and the philosopher of the eighteenth century would have more gods than the ancient heathens.'

I saw by these arguments that he was so wrapped up in the midst of the old school, that it was no use attempting his reformation, and finding I was not in the Inquisition, I rejoiced at having escaped the muskets of the soldiers and the fangs of Jack Ketch,[136] not for my own sake, that was out of the question, but for the sake of universal man.

After my recovery, with the loss of an eye, I lived some time with this anatomist, being frequently employed *raising the dead*, which to me was a matter of indifference, because I knew that all things in nature were merely modifications of the same matter, there being no difference between a putrid carcase and a bank of violets, except in the perception of our ideas.

The surgeon frequently lamented the necessity there was for this barbarous practice, as he called it.—'Were we allowed,' said he, 'all unclaimed bodies which die in hospitals, all malefactors, of every description, and all suicides, we should not need to disturb the repose of sacred bodies, whose places affection laments and visits, when perhaps they have been mangled to pieces in our lecture room, or sold piecemeal, at fixed prices, like butchers' meat, to any person.* The dissection of suicides would be a greater preventive to the action than all the laws of *felo de se*,[137] because the plea of insanity would not abrogate the consequence.'

My practice of plundering the church-yards at the most solemn hours, under danger of detection, and what was worse, under the fear of infection from diseases nearly advanced to putrescence before the interment; to break open a coffin, and carry in my arms a naked body, whose scent was sufficient to ferment a plague, was an undertaking that required all the resolution of philosophy, and fitted me for the event of any revolution or combustion of nature.

One day I observed to Dr. Cuticle, that it was to me a plain demonstration from the structure of the animal œconomy, and its tendency to putrescence, that it was like every other material substance; that the derangement of any one part affecting an immaterial, impalpable something, called the soul, was a gross bigotry; for, were the soul an immortal spirit, it could not be affected by matter—it could not feel pain in disease.—He replied, 'Place a man in perfect health in a circular room, glazed round, some of the windows shall be green, some red, and some blue: you will grant that in looking through these windows he will see objects of different colours and shades, but yet his own sight shall be clear and perfect. If the windows are dirty, he will see objects obscure; and if they are painted black, the surrounding scenes will to him be invisible; so the human soul, placed in the body, like the man in the room, can receive no external impression but through that body. His reasonings will take various shades—his passions and affections will be variously combined: but this does not deduce from his perfection as a man, but proves that the soul

---

* It is a know fact, that every part of the human body has a regular price. No person can deny the necessity of dissections, but as at present conducted, they are a disgrace and an outrage on society;—nor are the jests and levity of some of the young surgeons becoming, over the body of an human being. [Editor's note: The 1790s' spirit of reform and progress left the medical profession largely untouched; as a result, the procuring of bodies for the dissecting theaters of medical schools was still unregulated, and the practices described here by Walker were common.]

may be immortal, and yet *obliged* to partake of every accident which touches or acts upon its habitation.'

To this I replied—'Modern philosophers define the soul to be an immaterial substance, in the strict use of the term, signifying a *substance* that has *no extension* of any kind, not any thing of the *vis inertia* that belongs to matter: it has neither *length, breadth,* nor *thickness,* so that it occupies no *portion* of space; on which account the most rigorous metaphysicians say, that it bears no sort of relation to space any more than *sound* does to the *eye,* or *light* to the ear: in fact, that *spirit* and *space* have nothing to do with one another, and it is even improper to say an immaterial being exists in space, or that it resides in one place more than another, for, properly speaking, it is *no where,* but has a mode of existence that cannot be expressed by phraseology appropriated to the modes in which matter exists.'*

Cuticle bowed profoundly at this observation.—'You have proved to a demonstration *in words,*' said he, 'that we have no soul: to answer you *in words* would be an easy matter. I must confess that modern philosophy has something in it sublimely unintelligible: it is like the definition you have given, a *substance without substance,* a cube long, broad, and wide, but occupying *no place,* and has no more relation to reason and sense, than *nothing* has to *something,* and *something* to *nothing.* It is even improper to say philosophy exists *any where,* or that it is *here* more than *there,* for, properly speaking, it is *no such thing:* its mode of existence cannot be expressed in any language utterable by the human tongue. Such an argument as this may be applied to any thing, and would disprove the existence of the whole universe.'

So saying, he turned away to pursue some anatomical preparation, and I saw clear enough that we have no souls at all.—My present employ was not congenial to my desire of benefiting mankind. I was like a gem hid in the mud, and I resolved to quit my situation. Indeed, the house-maid had been a little troublesome, for in teaching her some of Monro's anatomical comparisons,[138] we were naturally led from theory to practice, for she

* Priestley on Matter and Spirit, vol. i, page 74. [Editor's note: *Modern philosophers .... exists:* an almost verbatim citation from Priestley's *Disquisitions on Matter and Spirit* (Section VII, Part i, "Of the Presence of the Soul with the Body").]

had so much of the modern spirit of inquiry, that she frequently attended dissections promiscuously with the other sex.*

I rambled over great part of the country under different professions, and gained a great deal of money from a certain medicine that was an infallible cure while I staid in the town. Wherever I went I disseminated the new doctrine of universal emancipation; I made many converts *from* religion, and taught the ignorant peasant to read the great book of Nature. I may say that mankind are infinitely obliged to me for the knowledge of various grievances they never so much as dreamed of till I pointed them out."

"My dear master," said Frederick, "you are a martyr to your virtues; but here you may rest for a time."

CHAPTER IV.

THE FORMATION OF THE WORLD—A STRANGE
EVENT RESULTS FROM A POLITICAL LECTURE,
WHICH DISGUSTS THE PHILOSOPHERS
WITH SOCIETY.

The following day Frederick, in the garden, informed his tutor with his passion for Laura; that he debated with himself as to the resulting good, and found a sort of hesitation to use her with too much violence.

"I will let you into a mystery," said Stupeo. "The great mass

---

*   One of the pursuits pointed out to females: vide Rights of Women. [Editor's note: Walker is referring to a passage in chapter 12 of Wollstonecraft's *Vindication*: "In public schools women, to guard against the errors of ignorance, should be taught the elements of anatomy and medicine, not only to enable them to take proper care of their own health, but to make them rational nurses of their infants, parents, and husbands; for the bills of mortality are swelled by the blunders of self-willed old women, who give nostrums of their own, without knowing any thing of the human frame. It is likewise proper, only in a domestic view, to make women, acquainted with the anatomy of the mind, by allowing the sexes to associate together in every pursuit; and by leading them to observe the progress of the human understanding in the improvement of the sciences and arts; never forgetting the science of morality, nor the study of the political history of mankind" (177).]

of mankind are fools, and no better than the callous sod on which we tread. It is the part of the great men and philosophers to mould them as they please; and when we have shaken off the influence of every thing called principle, are satisfied we have no portion in eternity, and that the fable of an avenging Deity is an old woman's tale, what power, I ask, can control us? We become almost too great for the world; mind seems to rise superior to matter; crime becomes nothing; all that men call murder, incest, lust, and cruelty, is trifling, not more, in fact, than changing the form of passive matter, or cutting down the trees of the forest; for, remember we cannot *destroy* any thing, we only change its form: and suppose a woman dies under our hands, her death makes room for another; the same as plucking a turnip makes room for the planting of a cabbage."

"I feel," cried Frederick, "I feel I am now free. I shall render my name immortal, for no human tie—no moral check shall stay the purpose of my power. But it seems true, after all, that a society of atheists could not exist, they would murder and be murdered: no trust could be placed upon any man: the king would assassinate the man who affronted him; the courtier would assassinate the man who opposed him; the wife would assassinate her husband, when disappointed in meeting her lover; no girl would arrive at the age of maturity; and the human species would soon become extinct."

"And what then?" said Stupeo.—"The same spirit which now actuates our bodies, must then actuate something else:—you cannot annihilate that subtle gas; and if it does not give motion to men, it may to some new species:—who knows but it may animate the trees and plants with rational faculties*—it would make this world a very different place."

---

* Let the reader reflect upon this. Nothing is annihilated, though the form may be changed.—What then becomes of the soul?—And the laws of nature suspended in this one instance? If not, the soul must still exist—it must be somewhere. [Editor's note: Walker appears to be alluding here to Priestley's *Disquisitions Relating to Matter and Spirit*, in which Priestley proposed the thesis that matter was not an inert substance requiring the impression of an external force, but a substance in which force was inherent. Priestley's natural history was therefore thoroughly materialist— even man's soul and the Deity had a material existence. Because of this, the soul cannot be immortal, and when the body dies, it, too, is returned to God, for Him to

"I should like to see it," said Frederick. "Metaphysics are surely the most useful of sciences; but here comes Laura and the Doctor. We have been discoursing," continued he, "on matter and spirit, and it appears plain that matter is eternal, and spirit mere fermentation."

"I wonder," said the Doctor, "how our world was so admirably formed, unless it was by the power of an omnipotent Being."

"Our earth," cried Stupeo, "was once a part of the sun, a molten mass, when a large comet brushing too near that luminary, dashed off a considerable portion, which flew till the natural motion formed it into a spheroid, and it began to cool. The atmosphere round it formed the ocean, and the friction of this vast body of waters upon the scoræ and cinders,[139] which composed the great skeleton of the world, formed the sands of the sea, which subsided into large beds, rising by degrees to the surface, where the action of the sun hardened the superfices. The heat of this luminary upon the putrid particles of the sea generated shell-fish, which are evidently most allied to stone of any animal we know. These possessed the whole of the ocean for some thousand ages, and being, by the gravitation of the earth, thrown into large chains of beds, in the progress of time decaying and cementing together with the oleaginous substance they contained, the shells became stones, forming mountains. Thus we always find shells in every body of rock, and on the highest mountains.—Every great change produced a revolution, and from the soft slime of shelly mountains, vegetables were produced. This new form of matter decaying and fermenting, animals, such as lions and tigers, bulls and monkeys, were produced. The latter was man in his original state. It was some thousand years before he learnt to walk upon his hind legs, some

---

resurrect, if it pleases Him. As the "intelligent first cause," the Divine Being permeates everything, from the physical to the spiritual, so that without His power, without His energy "we are, as well as, can do nothing" (241). Therefore, if a man dies, he will in some shape or other remain part of God's creation, "for no particle of that which ever constituted the man is lost. And ... whatever is *decomposed* may certainly be *recomposed*, by the same almighty power that first composed it, with whatever change in its constitution, advantageous or disadvantageous, he shall think proper; and then the powers of thinking, and whatever depended upon them, will return of course, and the man will be in the most proper sense. *The same being that he was before*" (334).]

thousand more before he pulled off his shaggy coating; but it is not material for me to trace him in every improvement, till he acquired a full face from the effects of a change of climate, and learnt the articulation of sounds by imitating the babbling of a brook, for he is to this day a creature imitating every other animal, and nothing is more clear than that he was originally an ouran-outang."[140]

"It strikes me," said Laura, "that your system is a little preposterous; and one is led to inquire where you stood when the earth was a liquid stream of melting fire? But, with regard to man, I would observe, that had he *ever* been a mere brute animal, he *never* would have changed his nature: he never could have acquired perfectability, for we never see the least progression in animals, nor are monkeys, at this period, one single degree advanced beyond what they were three thousand years ago; but, nevertheless," said she, with a look of irony, "when one sees some people, they are apt to acknowledge the relationship, and when they hear the chatter of jingling, unmeaning sentences, they are apt to cry out, that the ouran-outang is the better man."

Stupeo could not but feel this sally, but it was beneath his philosophical metaphysical dignity to regard, or even reply to this reasoning of a woman who was not illumined with the splendid rays of intellect.

Frederick often sought an opportunity to accomplish his schemes, but sought in vain, the vigilance of Laura precluding a possibility of success. He more than once attempted to infuse a drug into her drink; but whether she suspected him or no, she always avoided any thing from his hands which would admit adulteration.

Peace was about this time established with America, and the whole country rang with exultation.[141] During the war, no one had more execrated the system than the Doctor, and every lecture concluded with an apostrophe to peace.—He now mounted the pulpit in the Hall of Science, (the name of the lecture barn) and to prove that he was a very great philosopher, could find fault with every thing, and was staunch in all times and all seasons against government. He declared that the peace was the most disgraceful that could possibly be made; that it would not continue a twelvemonth before we should be driven from Canada. He declared, that, like Milton's devils,[142] mankind were only born for rebellion and revolution, that all their joy was to riot in destruction, murder, and violation.

A number of soldiers who were returning to their families, hearing these great truths, swore the Doctor was insulting them. A sailor, with one leg, threw a crab cudgel[143] at the head of the Doctor, which narrowly escaped him. Frederick leaped upon a bench, vociferating, "Citizens! the cause of all mankind is involved in this dispute: we ought to know whether these vagabonds are to insult us in our halls, and in our temples. Truth is sacred, and I will speak it, though a legion of spies were around me."

"Citizens!" roared Stupeo, "you are under military government; the Philistines are upon us; the freedom of speech has departed, and you are all slaves, bound in chains, and rivetted by your own supineness."

Anarchy and confusion now reigned in the Hall. The benches were broken in pieces, and served for clubs. A desperate battle ensued, as some few of the country people stood by the Doctor; but they were soon completely drubbed, and fled in different routes. Doctor Alogos and his two companions found a temporary shelter in the mansion, and, to their utter astonishment, saw their principal hearers the most violent.

"What shall be done?" cried the Doctor, trembling most philosophically: "This enraged beast, this many-headed monster[144] will devour us."

"Reverence the divine majesty of a mob," cried Stupeo; "all their motions possess energy, and all their actions justice. This is a mere momentary fermentation, the effervescence of popular frenzy, and will subside into a delightful calm."

"But what are we to do in the meantime? We shall be murdered!"

"A mere trifle, my dear Doctor;—a mere re-modification of matter."

"A re-modification of the devil: I don't at all like this."

"It's a d—d aristocratical church-and-king mob,"[145] cried Frederick. "I have been to talk to them, but they are deaf to the voice of reason: they are increased by a number of market-women, who vow vengeance against Stupeo for his three wives, and the Doctor for his kept mistress. This is no republican mob, inspired with the divine frenzy of liberty and equality."

"Oh! curse it," cried Doctor Alogos, "they seem to have liberty enough; they are treading down my fine flower garden like a herd of swine: there go all my exotic shrubs!—I believe they are a troop of Goths and Vandals, who pay no regard to science."

"There is your whole congregation!" cried Laura, weeping. "My dear uncle, they are all gone mad; they are talking about rights and liberties, and destroying every thing before them."

"Let us defend ourselves," cried Frederick, running to the front window. "Citizens!" cried he, "is it thus you abuse your friends?"

"Friends!" shouted a countryman, "there be no such thing as friendship. Equality for ever!—and down with the Doctor!" Frederick immediately fired a fowling-piece, loaded with small shot. A volley of stones was returned, which broke half the windows in front, and dashed out one of the orator's teeth. Stupeo instantly advanced, with a blunderbuss, which he fired, and checked the fury of the mob for an instant; but the soldiers leading the attack, swore they would murder man, woman, and child, and burn the house to the ground.

Not a moment was to be lost in this case of extreme necessity; and Frederick even debated whether the resulting good did not require him to join the mob, and aid them in the destruction of property. All the Doctor's cabinet of natural history was destroyed; his fine library made a bon-fire, and his elegant mansion was reduced to ashes, amidst the shouts of liberty and equality.[146]

The fugitives found shelter in the house of a neighbouring gentleman, who saved them from the madness of the mob.— "For me," cried Frederick, "I am determined not to remain another week in this vile island, where there is not a single spark of liberty and national spirit remaining."

"What do you call this?" demanded the Doctor: "I think it's liberty sufficient to burn a man's house about his ears."

"But that must have been a mob hired by the government," said Stupeo: "had it been a republican mob, it would have been a different thing; we should then have had a fine display of rational principles."

"All mobs," said the gentleman, "are alike, whatever name you may give them. Mischief is their only desire—plunder the only object. To their leaders they are a subject of perpetual dread. For my part, I would rather live under a Turkish bashaw, or in a country under martial law, than in a revolutionary country governed by mobs."

"For the reason," said Stupeo, "you are a man of *property*, but, for a man without any property, the latter is preferable, as it renders, in a summary way, the accumulations of wealth."

"But then," answered the gentleman, "you are not one moment sure of your plunder—a stronger man may tear it from you, and, like a worm caught by a chicken, the whole flock will in turn catch it from each other, till it is either pulled in pieces, or gulphed down by some one at the hazard of choaking."

"But that has nothing to do with liberty," cried Frederick. "All riches, and especially hereditary riches, are to be considered as the salary of a sinecure office, where the labourer and the manufacturer perform the duties, and the principal spends the income in luxury and idleness. Hereditary wealth is in reality a premium paid to idleness, an immense annuity expended to retain mankind in *brutality* and ignorance, by the want of leisure (or time to be idle). The *rich* are furnished indeed with the means of cultivation and literature, but they are paid for being dissipated and indolent. The most powerful means that malignity could have invented, are employed to prevent them from improving their talents, and becoming useful to the public."*

"You have made a very long speech," said the gentleman, "on a very short subject; all you have said amounting to this, that the poor are ignorant, because they have not leisure to be idle, and the rich are ignorant, because they are paid to be idle; so that, in fact, all real knowledge centres in yourself; and I have very little doubt, but, in your eyes, all the rest of mankind are little more than ideas, or at best machines."

"I will prove it by a demonstrable argument," cried Stupeo.

"They are very destructive ideas then," said Doctor Alogos.

---

* Godwin's Political Justice, page 804. [Editor's note: *All riches ... to the public*: an almost verbatim citation from Godwin's *Political Justice*, Book VIII, Chap. ii ("Benefits Arising from the Genuine System of Property"), 429 (the passage is actually on pp. 804-5 in the original).]

"To say the truth, I am become quite sick of society, and all human nature together. I will go and bury myself in the wilderness of America, where no mob will burn my house and destroy my library."

"Oh!" cried Frederick, "there the people are free;—there the spirit of truth fought with irresistable energy: republicans always fight with double ardour."

"Enthusiasm," said the gentleman, "is no proof of either truth or justice; but it is certain to inspire a desperate spirit in those who feel it, let the cause be liberty, religion, rebellion, revenge, plunder, or what not; though it is very well to ascribe to the justice of the cause what in fact is only due to the intoxicating enthusiasm of attaining a point. Revenge in general inspires revolutions. The people feel the evils they suffer under; they forget that a change most probably will be for the worse; and to be revenged on one set of men, they become slaves of another. I believe there never yet happened a revolution, where the then living generation did not feel accumulated ill, and the benefit to the next is very doubtful. Time and the natural improvement of the human mind gradually introduces reform, and in our own constitution we find always some trifle to improve; and it is well known, that at this moment we enjoy more *real liberty than any of our ancestors*; for in the days, called the golden days of good Queen Bess, did not she grant so many monopolising patents, that a gentleman demanded, in the House, if there was going to be a patent for selling bread."[147]

The next day the Doctor began to arrange his plans of emigration, procuring all the information he could of that delectable country, where poor people live better than the rich; where provisions are so plentiful, you have money to take them away; where more is paid to mechanics for their labour than the articles sell for; where there are no taxes, and where the travellers *bundle* with[148] the daughters of the family.

Frederick felt his enthusiasm rise at this description, and determined to accompany the Doctor to Philadelphia, one of the finest and most regular cities in the world.—"It is there," said he, "we shall begin to breathe on the broad basis of truth and reason; there all the puerile distinctions of religion and country are unknown, and man is respected for his good qualities."

Laura raised many objections to the scheme, and Susan absolutely refused to trust herself in a foreign country without being married. Thus the Doctor was under a philosophical necessity of complying with a superstitious custom; and he could not refrain from observing, that if he would have submitted to matrimony before, he might have married a lady of education and fortune, and not an ignorant pert baggage, who assumed the airs of a lady, without the qualifications.

The estate and ruins of the mansion being sold, the Doctor determined to set out without putting in his claim to the damages he could demand from the county.

Frederick for a while suspended his designs upon Laura, fore-seeing, that when they should be settled in a wilderness, she must of necessity be either his or Stupeo's, and he had no doubt but she would prefer the greater good.

CHAPTER V.

REFLECTIONS IN A STORM—THE DELIGHTS OF PHILADELPHIA—THE DOCTOR PURCHASES A LARGE ESTATE IN KENTUCKY.

A pleasant gale wafted these adventurers from the detestable island, where every thing was conducted in the worst manner possible, and where law and religion influenced the majority of men. Their hopes were high, and they discoursed and disputed with true metaphysical ardour. The rest of the passengers were mechanics and countrymen, going over to make their fortunes, and the praises of America bounded from one mouth to another.

"I am astonished," said a man who had sold a very good trade to emigrate, "I am astonished that any man remains in Europe, when all the blessings of life await him in America. I am going to purchase some lots of ground in the great city of Washington,[149] which will shortly be the most magnificent in the world. All the houses will be polished free-stone, the most narrow streets will be as wide as Portland Place in London. Ships already arrive there, and the city will be the emporium of commerce: I understand that it already makes a noble appearance."

"A very noble appearance indeed," said the Captain: "the streets are all laid out in right angles, upon paper. The number of workmen and mechanics employed in building this magnificent city is truly astonishing, they amount to nearly one hundred and fifty. But the chief advantage attending this city is, that it is contiguous to the estates of the President."

"You speak," said the passenger, "as if you were an Englishman, and wished to discourage new settlers. I suppose you are jealous of others partaking in the pleasures of your country."

"Very far from it," said the Captain. "I am amused with the golden dreams of emigrants, who expect to find silver crows in America; and I can assure you what I tell you of Washington is literally true, and more than that, it never will be finished, on account of the local and multiplied inconveniences around it."[150]

"But how comes it," said the other, "that such advertisements are inserted in the newspapers?"[151]

"How comes it," said the Captain, "you puff off any article you wish to dispose of?—Do you think it is natural for a man who has discovered a treasure, to call all the world to share it with him? This very reason ought to deter people, if they were not mad: they might be certain, if America was that happy land held out to them by designing men, all the vagabonds in Europe would not be invited to its bowers."

After they had sailed many days before a fair wind, the heavens became suddenly obscured; black clouds embattled over the deep, which hissed in rising breakers against the ship's side. Sudden squalls furrowed the dark bosom of the ocean, and threatened to tear the sails from the yards. All hands were ordered to work; the sails were furled, the yards struck, the pumps cleared, and every preparation made for a storm.

"My dear Doctor," said Frederick, in the cabin, "now we shall behold a grand display of magnificent scenery; we shall see Nature in a rage, and admire the terrific features of her countenance."

"I hope not," said the Doctor; "I have no curiosity to behold the bottom of the terrible sea, to be hacked in pieces by the sword-fish, smothered in the embraces of polypusses, or devoured by aligators."

"A true philosopher," cried Stupeo, "will behold the combustion of elements with tranquillity; he would not tremble were all the human race scattered round his feet with a blaze of lightning; though the clouds were to become ignited and flame around his head; though the concave vault of the heavens was to become red-hot; though the earth was to dissolve with fulminations beneath his feet, and parting nature to mix in chaotic confusion, yet would he stand firm and undismayed:—such are the effects of real philosophy."

At that moment a loud crash of thunder burst over them, and rattled to a distance in various directions.

"The devil take it," cried Stupeo, "that's a horrid smash; the wind howls like an hundred wolves in a forest hung with snow. The sea thumps against the vessel as if it would break in the timbers. After all, men are very foolish to trust themselves so far from land in an egg-shell."

"It is nothing but an idea," said Laura. "What, are you frightened at your own ideas?"

"I am fearful," said the Doctor, "that even Mr. Hume must allow this storm to be something more than idea."

"I shall go on deck," said Frederick. "I am like an Englishmen so far, that I am only afraid when I don't see the danger."

"I will go with you," said Laura; "the ship trembles so much I cannot sit."

It was with difficulty they could preserve themselves from falling, by grasping the hatchway; but the scene that presented was the most terrible sublime. One universal canopy of black clouds seemed to unite the ocean with the heavens, and the rain poured down in such torrents, that they might be said to be overwhelmed in water; through this the vivid flashes of lightning played at leisure, dancing on the mountainous billows, and giving to the ridges of rolling waves, which tumbled over each other as if contending in a race, the momentary appearance of melting gold. The thunder was so near, that it appeared rather surrounding than above them, and the whole was a promiscuous confusion of fire and water, the waves reflecting and refracting the variegated lightnings in every direction.

"Oh! great Creator of the universe," said Laura, a tear of piety starting from her eye; "Oh! that man would acknowledge thy power, for what prevents that thou shouldst at this moment destroy the whole earth, and expunge it from thy presence for the crimes of its people!"

"Surely," said Frederick, "this is more than an idea:—there must be an omnipotent Being, notwithstanding Mr. Hume and Stupeo. Were this storm the production of chance, it might continue, it *naturally* would continue for ever, and overwhelm creation."

"Chance!" repeated Laura: "How has it happened that this whole globe has never deviated from its orb? Why do not the planets leave their harmonic circles and dash each other to pieces?—Harmony is not an attribute of chance, for the very word chance implies confusion. Surely, had not some infinite Being, whom we should tremble to name, given them their motions, they never could have continued within their orbit. But man, weak and silly man, denies Providence and miracles, because Providence is not every day working miracles to provide him a dinner."

"That peal of thunder seemed to me to shake the foundations of the universe," said Frederick:—"but you look quite composed, Laura—are you not frightened?"

"I am indeed," said she, "very much frightened, but I am not dismayed. 'Tis true I am a weak woman, but I look beyond these heavy and sulphurous clouds, to a Deity who knows the weakness of his creatures, and can, in his omnipotence, as well protect me as a world."

"But do you think," said Frederick, "that he regards at all the actions of human beings? If he did, why in the shipwreck of a vessel shall perhaps every man be drowned, except the most execrable villain amongst them?"

"Because that the good and the bad are so connected, that a storm cannot fall upon one without touching the other, and to a good man drowning is a very trifling evil."

"How so? You speak now like a philosopher. Is it a trifle to be annihilated to self-consciousness, to lose all the pleasures of life, and become no more than the stone or vegetating shrub?"

"Indeed," answered Laura, "if such are your sentiments, death is to you the most tremendous of evils—you must shudder at

the idea, and to secure yourself some paultry, transient gratifications, perpetrate unnumbered crimes. But, amidst this storm,
when the next moment may whelm us beneath the deep, see
how calm a woman can be, whose mind is acted upon by the
cheering hopes of religion, and who expects hereafter to live to
a beatified eternity."

"But I have no ideas of such a state, and we know that the
vulgar notion of an heaven above us cannot physically be true."

"And why not?" said Laura:—"you will tell me perhaps, that
beyond our system there are other systems, and beyond these
others, reaching to distances surpassing comprehension. But, is
space bounded by our imagination, or is all space filled with
systems? Beyond all these systems may there not be a surrounding space, where every idea of heaven may be realised, where
new regions of inconceivable formation and glory may exist, for
who shall limit the Supreme? Even suppose all space to be filled
with systems and worlds, may not these stars be so many different paradises, fitting the disposition of different spirits?"

"These things," said Frederick, "may not be impossible; but
they are very contrary to the doctrine of the great Stupeo. What
a grand scene is he losing!—I will go and call him."

The storm now raged with such violence, that the ship was
given to the winds, driving between the furrows of the rushing
waves. The great Stupeo laid upon the cabin floor, uttering the
most horrid execrations—swearing that all hell was broke loose,
and that the black demons of the air were running the ship into
the clouds.

"That is a very sublime idea," said Frederick, "but I hope not
literal, for if there be an hell, what will become of us?"

"O God!" cried Doctor Alogos, "I do acknowledge thy power;
I was a fool ever to doubt it."

Laura endeavoured to comfort poor Susan and the rest of the
passengers in the cabin; and the better to prevent reflection, she
desired them to sing some psalms, setting the example by beginning the 104th.[152] The novelty of such an action in so despairing
a situation gained their attention, and many joining in, the terror
of the danger was damped, and they felt a something of conscious
satisfaction, which is unknown to any but those who have been

in some similar situation, or have felt the tranquillity of a quiet conscience—Even Stupeo himself changed his execrations into groans, and Frederick hung down his head in silent reflection.

The storm gradually subsiding, by degrees the several characters of the company returned, with this difference, that Stupeo maintained with more obstinacy than ever his doctrine of chance and scepticism. Frederick wavered in his mind according to the impulse of his passions; and Doctor Alogos became convinced that there was more in religion and *common-place* maxims of good and evil than the great Stupeo would allow.

In this disposition they arrived at Philadelphia, and rejoiced at the prospect of having reached a place where truth and justice had erected the standard of reason. Frederick was surprised to find the renowned city not so large as that part of Mary-le-Bone which is built;[153] but consoled himself with the loss of one of the finest cities in the world, as he could look over the ground where it *was* to stand.

As they passed along the streets, they were hooted at by the children, and called vagabond English, with other opprobious names.—"This is very strange," said Frederick: "I thought the Americans made no distinctions of country; but we are only strangers yet—they will respect us when they know us better."

They procured lodgings at an extravagant rate, and calling for refreshment, received some very coarse cakes, wretched butter, and salt meat, for in summer no *fresh* meat will keep a day; and for this they paid more than the best articles would have cost in London.

"Things are not quite as they should be even here," said the Doctor.

"What do you mean by that?" said an American *waiter*. "Do you mean to stigmatise Congress?"

"Heaven forbid," replied the Doctor: "I should like to speak to your master about my baggage."

"My master! I don't know such a man. Do you think I am a slave?—I am a republican, free-born American. But who are you? Some lousy, beggarly emigré,[154] come here to cut wood and hew stone for us."

Doctor Alogos looked in silent amazement. Frederick was rising to kick the republican down stairs; but Stupeo observed that this was the genuine blunt spirit of freedom: that, like Spartans, the Americans took perfect liberty of speech.[155]

"But they do not seem to allow it to others," said Laura.

The heat was extremely intense, so much so, that the whole company confined themselves within doors, deliberating on the mode they should adopt in promoting their pastoral scheme. Laura amused herself at the windows: to her it had an air of novelty to see every third person a black; but she was astonished to see the people labouring notwithstanding the violent heat, which was almost suffocating to those who remained inactive; and the swarms of muscatoes were to Englishmen a perfect plague.

"These labourers," said a waiting-maid, "are Scotch, Irish, and German emigrants, who earn *eleven shillings* a day currency."

"Eleven shillings a day!" exclaimed Frederick; "it is more than our peasants in England earn in a week: they must live like noblemen. But what do you call currency?"

"Why it's about six and sixpence English; but they are very badly off for all that, for every thing is so dear they can hardly live upon it, and one half of them soon die of fevers and agues."

The landlord's daughter was a prettyish girl, and night coming on, Frederick requested her to *bundle* with him.—"If you insult me," said she, "our Matthew shall bundle you into the Delaware."

Frederick was astonished at this frankness.—It is very different here, said he to himself, but I don't know whether it is all for the better.

In the night Frederick was disturbed by the rumbling of carts:— it is very strange, thought he, that so many night-men are at work at once in such a little city, or perhaps they all come through this street. The Americans surely don't go in carts to balls.—In the morning he inquired, and was informed it was only the *dead carts* that carried away those who died in the course of the day.

"That's strange," said he; "I counted near twenty, and this city is of very narrow extent."—"It is a very magnificent city, and the largest in all the union," said the landlord; "but the yellow fever carries off some dozens in a day:[156] however, we don't mind these things since we have got our independence."

"Very true," replied the Doctor; "liberty sweetens every thing, and it is a glorious epoch in the annals of man, that property ceases in this great western Continent to influence the actions of men."

The landlord gazed with surprise.—"Property," said he, "is the only stimulus to commerce—commerce is the support of arts and sciences, and no man will be above trade: we have no honest gentlemen here—no idle hands—if a man will not work, he may starve."

"That's a detestable system," said Stupeo; "the ancient Spartans never degraded themselves with work.[157] Man in a state of nature does not work, he has few wants, and these the waters or the woods supply."

"That may be, friend; but our motto is *Endure, but hope*, and that of all new-comers is *Work, or starve*. I see you are a green-one yet, and unseasoned; all you people from the old world think money is made for nothing here—but it is all a farce."

"Where in the world," said the Doctor, "shall we find the genuine principles of liberty and equality?"

"As to liberty," said the American, "every man has liberty to follow any trade he pleases, and to vote for the Congress if he is a naturalized citizen; and as to equality, we have no titles except 'squire, but for equality of property, as some of our own people would like it, it's a mere fire-fly of a dark evening."

The idea of the yellow fever had damped the spirits of the whole company, and it was resolved to quit the city of Philadelphia with all convenient speed. This matter was under consideration when a thin man entered the room.

"My good friends," said he, "I understand you intend settling upon an agricultural plan. Agriculture is the most noble pursuit of independent man, and a sure source of wealth."—"How did you know our intention?" said the Doctor; "we have not yet been twenty-four hours in the city."

"My desire to serve all mankind," replied he, "and to prevent the schemes of impostors, who, taking advantage of their local knowledge, often deceive and cheat strangers, has led me to intrude upon you."

"Indeed," said Alogos, "I thought all the people of the new world had been disinterested and benevolent towards all mankind, who fly from the old world to be free of its crimes."

"Human nature, Sir, is not yet arrived at perfection: 'tis true we are advancing rapidly forward—witness the great public roads and canals which intersect the country."

"Why are these roads?" said Frederick: "You ought to throw every impediment in the way of commerce—it is thence arises all our evils."

"That is very true, Sir, but in this country to talk disrespectfully of commerce is high treason: we are a commercial people. By means of these roads and canals, we have peopled the great wilderness, and planted settlements where only rattlesnakes used to bask.—To what part of the Continent do you intend journeying?"

"That we are undetermined upon," said the Doctor; "we would be as far from society as we can, and in a country where we can enjoy the advantages of nature."

"Then Kentucky is your object; it is the most delectable spot on the face of the earth; it is a second Arcadia, a continued scene of romantic delight and picturesque prospects. An author of *undoubted* veracity has given an history of that heavenly region. Sympathy, says he, *is* regarded as the essence of the human soul, participating of celestial matter, and as a spark engendered to warm our benevolence, and lead to the raptures of love and rational felicity.

'With such sentiments our amusements flow from the interchange of civilities, and a reciprocal desire of pleasing. That sameness may not cloy and make us dull, we vary the scene as the nature or circumstances will permit.—The opening spring brings with it the prospect of our summer's labour, and the brilliant sun actively warms into life the vegetable world, which blooms and yields a profusion of aromatic odours. A creation of beauty is now a feast of joy, and to look for amusement beyond this genial torrent of sweets would be a perversion of nature, and a sacrilege against heaven.

The season of sugar-making occupies the women, whose mornings are cheered by the modulated buffoonery of the mocking-bird, the tuneful song of the thrush, and the gaudy plumage of the parroquet. Festive mirth crowns the evening. The business of the day being over, the men join the women in the *sugar-groves*, where enchantment seems to dwell. The lofty trees wave their spreading branches over a green turf, on whose soft down the mildness of the evening invites the neighbouring youth to sportive play, while our rural Nestors, with calculating minds, contemplate the boyish gambols of a growing progeny; they recount the exploits of their early age, and in their enthusiasm, forget there are such things as decripitude and misery. Perhaps a convivial song, or a pleasant narration closes the scene.'"*

"Or perhaps," said Laura, with a smile, "the fairy strikes with her silver wand, and the whole vanishes, leaving behind an uncultivated wilderness."

"It's every word true," said Citizen Common: "I have not told you half what Mr. Im—y says of it. I am a surveyor, and can point you out the most eligible situations, which, out of my respect for your characters, I will do without reward. Here are plans of eight different estates, from one hundred acres to five thousand. There are three qualities of land, but I suppose you would prefer the best, which will be parted with prodigiously cheap—twelve guineas for the hundred acres."

"Twelve guineas for the hundred acres!" exclaimed the Doctor: "why you mistake, you are giving the land away. Ah! if all the poor vagabonds in the old world knew that here they could have a portion of earth for almost nothing, they would beg, borrow, or steal, to procure a passage to this land of milk and honey."

"There are thousands every year," said the stranger, "who benefit by our hospitality. If I might advise, this plat of ground, situated on the north fork of the Elkhorn,[158] is the most eligible for a first settlement."

"Well," said the Doctor, "if you bring me the title deeds and witnesses, I will purchase that: a thousand acres is just an hundred and eight guineas, and that's a mere song."

"Indeed," said Common, with a stare, "you shall have the deeds drawn out and registered with precision."—This being settled, he observed that at such a distance, they would require to take with them various implements of husbandry,[159] and articles of necessity, every thing being tripled in expence beyond the Allegany mountains.

---

* See Imley's *Romantic* Account of Kentucky. [Editor's note: *Sympathy .... closes the scene*: an almost verbatim citation from Gilbert Imlay's *A Topographical Description of the Western Territory of North America* (London, 1792), 138-39. For more information on Gilbert Imlay, here lampooned as "Citizen Common," see Introduction.]

"But why," said Frederick, "should we encumber ourselves with articles of luxury? We intend to quit society, and will not load ourselves with its inconveniences."

"My dear Sir," said Common, "you advance beyond the mark: so much do we depend upon each other, that we can neither begin nor proceed without the co-operations of our fellows: for instance, how will you cultivate the earth? Will you tear down the trees with your bodily prowess? or will you turn the sod with your nails? You must have spades and ploughs, and a variety of other articles."

"We are obliged to have all these in England," said Frederick: "I do not see that labour is less or more easy in the new world than the old."

"Infinitely so," cried Common; "farmers here work for themselves, wages are so high that they cannot afford to hire men, and land is so cheap that servants soon become masters."

"That is as it should be," said Stupeo, "that is something like equality; in our country, a farmer with a few hundred acres does little more than overlook his servants."

Under the directions of Common, near a thousand pounds were expended in articles necessary for a settlement.—The patent was made out at the regular office, and four waggons waited the pleasure of these great men, who quitted the haunts of luxury in search of virtue and liberty in an howling wilderness.

Every article as they passed along the road was exorbitantly dear, seventeen dollars being charged for a common dinner for themselves and their horses: but what more astonished them, was the impertinence of the inn-keepers, who being all agricultural men, did not altogether depend on their inns, and conceived travellers to be the obliged parties.

"This is very singular hospitality," said the Doctor: "I have read a book which informed me it was customary to travel from farm-house to farm-house, and from New England to Maryland, almost free of expence."

"Republicans," said Stupeo, "are independent people, they do now cringe and fawn upon you for a shilling like your traders in Europe, they possess a conscious manly dignity."

"The dignity of an inn-keeper is certainly very great," said

Laura; "but I prefer the slavish European, where people seem obliged to you at least."

As they advanced over the mountains to Fort Pit, they were charmed with the scenery and the majestic river Ohio, down which they sailed,[160] between extensive savannahs and high-towering forests, where scarcely the beams of day, much less the foot of man, ever penetrated.

Stupeo, who as a man of profound reflection, was frequently subject to melancholy, to dissipate which, he had recourse to peach brandy and American rum, (indeed these mingled with water are the common drink); but though he was no milksop, he was soon seized with a dysentery, which to his comfort he found was very usual to new comers.

Being arrived at Lexington,[161] the metropolis of the finest country in the world, they were a little surprised at sight of about thirty ill-looking wooden houses, but they had seen so many wonders in the new world, that they were not altogether confounded, and Stupeo declared that he was delighted at the prospect of coming nearer a state of nature than they had even hoped or expected.

Their large train of baggage was a sufficient sign of importance to procure them several visitors: by this means the place of their intended settlement was quickly known, and a great deal of unnecessary trouble avoided, there being already a family at Lexington, come from Virginia, with a grant for the same land, which they were unable to settle, it being already in the possession of another holder.

"This is inconceivable," said Doctor Alogos; "one had need possess a share of *suffering* philosophy to endure this: but how am I to be righted?"

"You may go to law," replied the informant. "I am an attorney, and will do you justice; for though the other purchaser has been at law this twelve-month, and has lost his cause, that was because he did not employ me."

"Go to law!" cried the Doctor with horror; "what are there laws and lawyers in a wilderness? I expected to have found nothing worse than rattle-snakes and tigers."

"The world could not exist without law," said the lawyer.

"Why, it is almost impossible to purchase a lot of land here without a law-suit entailed, for at the office they grant patent upon patent, so that any man may choose what part he prefers of the whole country, and when he is here he cannot easily return."[162]

"That is right," cried Stupeo, "that is exactly my system of argument, the greatest resulting good is the first to be defined; the wilderness must be peopled, and the human race expanded over the surface of the earth."

"But can we have no land?" said Frederick; "surely this prodigious country is not all monopolised?"

"You may have thousands of acres," replied the lawyer; "but, if you would be safe, you must purchase at second-hand—that is, a lot from the great farmers. You may have good uncultivated land at six guineas the hundred acres.—Mr. Common imposed upon you more than one half, but I am an honest man."

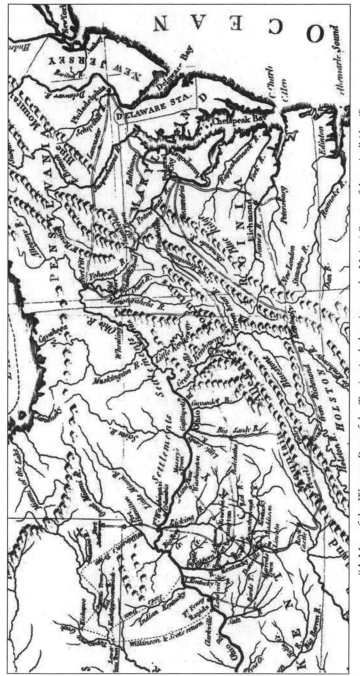

"A Map of the Western Part of the Territories belonging to the United States of America" (detail).
From Gilbert Imlay, *A Topographical Description of the Western Territory of North America* (London, 1795).

CHAPTER VI.

THE PLEASURES OF BENDING NATURE TO THE RULES OF ART—STUPEO AND SUSAN DETERMINE TO PEOPLE THE WILDERNESS—THE SUPERIORITY OF SAVAGE LIFE EXEMPLIFIED.

Having made a purchase of three hundred acres, about one hundred and fifty miles from Lexington, nearer the Ohio, containing two fine mill seats, with water carriage for timber, they began their march through the wilderness. Every ten or twelve miles along the road a little plantation was begun. Laura looked in vain for the blooming orchards and sugar-groves, with fine lawns beneath them; she saw indeed some clusters of sugar-mapple trees at intervals in the woods, where *Nature* had planted them; but as to the velvet meadows, nothing of that sort appeared, the native grass being several feet high, matted so as to be almost impassable, and too rank for any use. The weather was insufferably hot— millions of insects tormented them night and day—snakes curled along the tracts (called roads) and prodigious large frogs and toads wallowed in every little tank of stagnate water, which the impenetrable forest prevented the sun from evaporating.

Neither milk nor butter were procureable at any price, and they were under the necessity of drinking spirits and water, which threw them all into slight fevers, and added strength to the disease of Stupeo.

Being arrived at the place where they were to settle, they were a little surprised to find it covered with prodigious large trees, which seemed to bid defiance to human labour. A thick cane brake over-ran half the surface, and was so matted and entangled with the trees, that they could not even clear a path through. The ground, which was not thus covered, was apparently so barren, that the black heaths of England were a sort of comparative garden.

"It is plain to me," said Stupeo, "that cultivating the ground is a deviation from the state of nature. Has she not spread her wide extended branches to shelter us from heat and from rain? Has she not scattered various fruits and shrubs within our reach, and what do we want more? When we shall have spent our strength in destroying these trees, and laboured to raise the rotten sods into life, shall we not set some value on the earth? We shall become proud, selfish, and tyrannical—we shall not readily yield it to another, and thus we give birth to all the horrors of civil life."

"It is too late now to retract," said Laura; "surely the resources of philosophy are not exhausted, reason and truth have now full power to expand unchecked, in the desart wild."

"To be perfectly free," said Stupeo, "we should become like the roaming Indians; let us give to mankind a great and glorious example; let us cast aside our clothes, they are an incumbrance beneath the dignity of virtue, let us live like the wild Indians."

"You may if you like," said Laura, laughing, "but I fear you will not easily do without brandy, and that's a forbidden article in the big book of Nature."

"For my part," said Frederick, "I will try the inconveniences of a detached life before I wholly enter into a state of savagism; we have contracted so many unnatural wants, which reason knows to be useless, that it requires time to root out our habits and prejudices."

In about a week's time, an uncomfortable hovel was erected, with the help of some neighbours; but those philosophers had so little resolution in encountering great difficulties, that these three men were another week before they had cut off the lower boughs of a few trees, where they had planned a kitchen garden.

Stupeo was thrown off his legs with the little exertion he had made, the heat and the bad provisions, no meat keeping without salt. No physician was within many miles, and that one, an ignorant quack, whose whole knowledge was drawn from a Salmon's Dispensatory,[163] and the London Compleat Art of Healing.[164]

Stupeo pretended he rejoiced that nature would have her course; but she soon so reduced him, that it was evident the great man would quit the world without having caused one revolution; and the Doctor dispatched a messenger for the surgeon, who, on his arrival, prescribed some common medicines, which greatly relieved the patient.

Doctor Alogos lamented the want of books, though he had very little time to read: what leisure he had was spent in idle repining, and cursing the day he ever set his foot on the new world, which to his eyes appeared only half formed. He had another subject of disquiet in Susan, who was every day reproaching him with having carried her out of the world to die in a desart. Laura was the only one any way contented, for the sweetness of her disposition, and her affection to her uncle, over-looked many difficulties.—Surely, thought the Doctor, there is something at least very pleasant in the attachment of kindred, and though she may love me as an individual, contrary to the new philosophy, I do not perceive any great evil in it.

The progress they made in cultivation, served only to shew them the futility of their undertaking, and a whole family happening to die of a fever occasioned by over labour, they purchased the farm, which had been brought into some degree of cultivation. The ground, which had never been turned up to the air, being composed of rotten vegetable substance, was loaded with febrile[165] particles and noxious vapour, the effects of which are frequently seen in the deaths of new-comers; nor did the Doctor and Frederick escape without a severe fit of the ague, which disabled them from labour.

The great Stupeo seemed here buried in unworthy obscurity: he saw his genius and talents unemployed, and mankind unben-efitted by his labours. He had fruitlessly attempted to injure the innocence of Laura, who detested him even more than Frederick; and he resolved no longer to suffer the unjust monopoly which Doctor Alogos practised in the person of Susan. The latter was heartily tired of the Doctor, who was not so young as Stupeo, and having imbibed the real principles of equality, she made very little difficulty of aiding to people this wilderness, where, it must be confessed, there was a little too much of solitude.

The Doctor beheld as a singular phenomenon, the change of Susan's shape, which neither reason nor argument could account for, though it was evident there must have been a cause superior to chance.

"It may be nothing more than an idea," said Stupeo; "but at any rate it does not signify who is the parent of the child—the result-ing good is equal: it is of no consequence to the child, because under the protection of philosophy, its mind will gradually expand to the genial beams of truth. I am of opinion, that children should be brought up indifferently by the male or female, as it may happen. Why, I would ask, in the name of common sense, are not men as well calculated for nurses as women?"

"Because," said Laura, "they are not so domestic, and because Providence has provided the female with a nutriment adapted to the tenderness of infancy."

"That arises from mere repletion," said the great philosopher, "and is the source of all our diseases—we draw in corruption at the breast, and if we would one day become immortal, I am of opinion we should be educated independent from the birth, and fed upon something more natural than milk, which is of all substances soonest corrupted."

"Of course upon brandy," said Laura; "brandy is one of the least corruptible of fluids."

Susan, in due course, brought a man child into the world; but no physician or person of skill being within reach, an ignorant old woman officiated, and the poor wretch expired in agony.

"Such," cried Stupeo, "are the consequences of being neither in nor out of society:—here we are in a desart, abandoned by our species, with all the habits we contracted in society, and no means to satisfy them:—if we had been in a state of nature, nature would have accomplished every thing."

The Doctor was shocked at the event, though satisfied she had not been constant to himself; and he more than ever began to doubt the reality and practicability of the sublime doctrines of the new philosophy. Stupeo undertook the education of the boy, whom he insisted should enjoy perfect freedom, and be allowed to crawl about the house like any other animal.

"He shall not be thwarted in any thing," said he: "the great Rousseau tells us that we only implant vices into children by pretending to teach them justice, and destroy the temper by checking the sallies of imagination." Unfortunately for the enlightened system of education, this grand experiment proved abortive. The tender infant sickened, and died of a consumption.

Frederick, however, maintained that it was the kindness of Laura which killed it; and Stupeo discovered that it was stung to death by muscatoes, its body being delicate, and not plaistered over with ungents of grease, like the infants of the Indians; and the Doctor swore that Stupeo had poisoned it with brandy. Thus these three great men could not agree upon so insignificant a thing as the death of a child under a grand philosophical experiment: where then is the wonder that men are daily cutting each others throats for a difference of political opinion?

One day when these three philosophers were labouring in the field, sometimes uttering execrations, and sometimes disputing, not a little to the prejudice of *immutable* truth, which often appeared in different shapes, a troop of Miama Indians[166] crossed the Ohio in their punts, and carried off all the portable articles at the little farm, which they had dignified with the name of Clarens.[167] Poor Laura shared the fate of the rest of the stock, and it was not known to the philosophers till their return home.

"Black for ever be the day!" exclaimed the Doctor, "when I left England with all its evils—there, persons and property enjoyed some protection. Alas! my dear Laura, my beloved child is murdered and scalped!"

"Nothing more natural," said Stupeo, coolly: "savages do not make those childish distinctions we do between beauty and ugliness—revenge is all they seek, for the unjust usurpation of the Europeans:—are we not driving them from their ancient possessions, and daily narrowing their bounds and power to live?"

"What have they done," said the Doctor, "in the course of some thousand years? The utmost extent of their knowledge in agriculture, is the planting of a few slips of maize and tobacco."

"But they enjoy perfect liberty," said Frederick; "they have few vices and few wants—they roam at will over the face of the creation:—I feel myself enamoured of savage life."*

---

* It is the practice of the new school to exalt every thing savage. An Indian is with them the most virtuous of human beings; and they make him utter sentiments he never heard, and perform actions which never were witnessed. Why is all this but to loosen men from their reciprocal bonds of society, and to sap the foundations of human governments. So far indeed are the Indians removed from these *sentimental phantoms*, that they are totally the contrary; though the emancipation of the negroes and the inhumanity of Christians, is an excellent stalking horse, for those who pretend to finer feelings than the rest of mankind. The following note will illustrate the tenderness of the emancipated negroes, and the *fine feelings* of their *deliverers*. See the note in Playfair's History of Jacobinism, page 341.

"I see plainly," returned the Doctor, "that very few men can exist in a savage state: I see we must have made a progress in arts and sciences before we can pretend to civil life. Thus arts and sciences, with all their defects, tend to increase the numbers of mankind.—Indeed, I begin to perceive philosophy has not every claim I supposed to universal acceptance."

"The new philosophy is immutable," cried Stupeo; "and notwithstanding every check from selfishness, it will in time sap all society, and depopulate those hot-houses of vice and disease—large cities."

"My life," cried Alogos, "is a burden in this wilderness:—I have no books to amuse and instruct me—no intercourse of polished friendship, all is rugged and rude. There is *no market* for commodities that might stimulate avarice. I feel a thousand wants I cannot gratify, and even common necessaries I cannot procure.—Affection, which I once thought a blind partiality, I now find like a balm amidst the evils of life; and as I have lost my Laura, I am completely wretched. I am not now equal to the task of cultivating the ground; and I might have procured more comforts, conveniences, and luxuries in England, as a day-labourer, than in this wild with all its freedom."

"I must grant," said Frederick, "that we have too much labour: this is not a state congenial to human nature—this is solitude without its concomitants, plenty, liberty, and ease. What signifies my being at liberty to wander in a forest and shoot deer, when I must till the ground or starve: this is not genuine equality, and I am determined to seek it in a savage state."

"The insurrections, massacres, and cruelties of St. Domingo, would make a large volume, were they to be detailed. The Abbé Gregoire and Brissot were two of the most active instigators of the revolt of the negroes and mulattoes. Gregoire, who was member of the Assembly, when he heard of a terrible massacre, in which the negroes had for their bloody standard a *white infant*, impaled on a spear, declared it was the *plus beau jour de sa vie*. This philosophic cannibal was at supper when the news was brought, and he and his friends finished the evening with mutual congratulations and joy, on the success of their plans."

[Editor's note: A verbatim citation of part of a footnote in Playfair's *History of Jacobinism* (1:341 n.). The reference in the second paragraph is to the St. Domingo slave insurrection of 1791, when slaves attacked their masters and ransacked the plantations on the Caribbean island. The event sent shock-waves of horror through Britain and other slave-owning nations.]

"For me," said the Doctor, "I am so completely wretched, that I will seek no farther for a bauble—I will die here."

"The great moralist, Rousseau," said Stupeo, "has said, *by rendering life insupportable, God orders one to quit it.*[168] Now you believe in a Deity, and surely you may trust his mercy."

"I will not provoke his anger, thou fiend of darkness," said Doctor Alogos, with more energy than he usually displayed: "do I suffer one single inconvenience I have not brought upon myself, and you would have me close the account with murder. The Deity does not act by evils, nor are the consequences of our head-strong passions, our follies, and our crimes, to be laid to his charge. Rousseau was a fool, with all his rants and declamations, and many of his followers shew their long ears."

A black slave, whom these advocates for universal freedom had *purchased,* his labour being cheaper than an hired servant, now entered the hut, with the tidings that Laura had been seen crossing the Ohio with the Indians, in a western direction.[169]

Doctor Alogos, at this intelligence, roused himself to action, and the two philosophers proposed to accompany him, more from an expectance of novelty than any desire to recover Laura, who would never attend to the lectures of these great men.

They set out on horseback well armed, pursuing the track pointed out to them. For four days they followed the Indians, till their provisions were exhausted, and their horses nearly jaded out. They subsisted upon the wild berries and fruit in the forests, still continuing their rout, and having plenty of powder, the birds supplied them a frequent repast.

By degrees they lost all knowledge of the direction of the country. Their horses fell beneath them, and the underwood became almost impenetrable. A council of war was called, in which Frederick pleaded streniously that they should join the first band of Indians they might meet, and cast away every trace of society; he even proposed that they should abandon their arms and clothes, and trust wholly to chance.

This he was prevailed upon to give up, by the observance that the Indians were not so divested of all art as to be without arms, these being necessary in a roaming life to procure themselves food.

Doctor Alogos, who had no wish to return without his niece, complied with the sublime whims of these great men; and though he was far from being in perfect health, he attended them through the dreary labyrinths of an almost impassable forest, where hunger and thirst were their constant companions.

For near ten days they did not see a single human being except themselves. They had fallen in with a drove of buffaloes, on one of which they made a plentiful repast. Their shoes were already worn out, and the green hide bound with thongs supplied the place; though they now ran considerable hazard from the swarms of snakes which basked in the sun, or hung from the trees like caterpillars in an English hedge. Frederick being the tallest, had received several severe contusions from the boughs of the trees, and the infinite swarms of muscatoes which seemed to fill the air, goaded the whole party incessantly.

Some Indians they accidentally fell in with, ran away from them in terror.—In the woods they found several skeletons, which, from their mutilated state, appeared to have been killed in battle.

"It is very singular," said Frederick, "that even these savages, who are very little more advanced in civil life than ouran-outangs, should delight so much in war."

"War," replied Stupeo, "is congenial to human nature:—what, are all the civilised states that now exist immersed in volup-tuousness and sloath?—All the manly virtues are lost, when arts and sciences are cultivated. Look back to the ancients—the Celtæ, the Danes, the Goths, the Scytheans,[170] and all those hardy tribes who lived only in war, we shall there find all the heroic virtues, the contempt of danger, the bravery of seasons, the generosity of friendship, and the gallantry to the fair, so peculiar to the times of chivalry—all these are the children of a state of perpetual war."

"I thought," said the Doctor, "you held gallantry in contempt, as a pusilanimous trifling, unworthy a great mind; and that partic-ular friendships are an outrage against political justice."

"So I do," cried Stupeo; "and who ever knew me retract what I once advanced?"

"But how do you reconcile the contradiction?"

"A philosopher can reconcile every thing. The new philoso-phy is founded upon the broad expanded basis of universal truth;

it establishes principles not all the powers of kings and priests shall overthrow, much less a few contradictions."

This warm debate was interrupted by some female screams. The Doctor cocked his rifle piece, and the whole company moved towards the place, where, in a little retreat, they saw an Indian severely beating two women with a cane.

"This is very astonishing gallantry," said Doctor Alogos, "this is a warlike people; but let us inquire what is the reason of this usage."

Their black servant, Mungo, who understood the dialect of the five nations,[171] inquired the meaning of the chastisement.

"Because I choose it," said the Indian: "I have a great mind to shoot them both with my arrow."

"Well, but you have some cause for your anger," said the Doctor, through the medium of Mungo.—"To be sure I have:—I ordered them to shoot some plovers for my dinner, while I was painting myself with this delightful blue, and they return to tell me they can find none."

"I suppose," said the Doctor, "you are related to them?"—"They are my wives."—"One of them is very young."—"She is my daughter."*—

---

*   See Byron's Narrative, Cook's Voyages, Loss of the Grosvenor, &c. [Editor's note: *Byron's Narrative*: John Byron (1723-86), *The Narrative of the Honourable John Byron (Commodore in a late expedition round the world) containing an account of the great distresses suffered by himself and his companions on the coast of Patagonia, from the year 1740, till their arrival in England, 1746: with a description of St. Jago de Chili, and the manners and customs of the inhabitants: also a relation of the loss of the Wager man of war, one of Admiral Anson's squadron* (London, 1768); *Cook's Voyages*: Thomas Cook (1728-79), *Captain Cook's voyages round the world. the first performed in the years 1768, 1769, 1770, 1771; the second in 1772, 1773, 1774, 1775; the third and last in 1776, 1777, 1778, 1779, and 1780; for making discoveries in the northern and southern hemispheres, by order of His present Majesty; containing a relation of all the interesting transactions which occurred in the course of the voyages; including Captain Furneaux's journal of his proceedings during the separation of the ships. With a narrative of Commodore Phipps's voyage to the North Pole and an abridgment of Foster's introduction to his History of northern discoveries on the progress of navigation. To which is added, Governor Phillip's voyage to Botany-Bay; with an account of the establishment of the colonies of Port Jackson and Norfolk Island, &c. &c.* (Newcastle, 1790); *Loss of the Grosvenor*: the Grosvenor was an East India Company ship which was sunk in August 1782 off the coast of South Africa, having run aground in shallow waters, allegedly because the captain was busy eating dinner. It was bound for England from Ceylon, and was rumored to be carrying a treasure of gems, gold and money. Among the accounts of the loss of the Grosvenor that Walker may have seen, are: Alexander Dalrymple's *An Account of the Loss of the Grosvenor Indiaman, commanded by Capt. John Coxon, on the 4th August, 1782-inferred from the Portuguese description of the coast of Africa*

"What, do you use your daughter as a wife?"—"To be sure I do—have not I the most right to my own? Does not Nature and the great Manetaw[172] of the lakes tell us to do so?"

"We must acknowledge," said the Doctor, "this is very strange: —the women appear universally to be slaves to the men; but, alas! what a mere brute is man, when some greater law than his own will does not curb his passions. If this be liberty, bind me for ever to a galley oar."

"I find nothing strange in all this," said Stupeo. "These men are ignorant of the sublime doctrines of philosophy—they do things without seeing their fitness, and therefore may err a little in promoting universal good; for instance, what is there unnatural in this revultion of kindred; is it not a common practice with animals."

"What horrid principles," said Alogos: "how would it be possible to rear brothers and sisters to maturity?"

"That's none of my business," replied Stupeo; "I do not concern myself with trifles."

Doctor Alogos felt the truth of this reply; and having witnessed the brilliant virtues of a warlike nation in the savage state, he concluded that the whole human species was under some dreadful curse, for insanity seemed to influence all their actions.

The following day they crossed a large savannah, where they could not procure the smallest sustenance; and in the evening tired and exhausted, they arrived at a little settlement of Indians.

"Now," cried Frederick in rapture, "we shall behold genuine hospitality; we shall see pure nature, unsophisticated by the vices of society?"

They requested of an Indian, in an humble tone, some hoecake,[173] but received for an answer, that they had scarcely sufficient for themselves, and a demand of some of their arms.

This was very unexpected to these philosophers, who, notwithstanding their knowledge of human nature, often made egregious mistakes, and finding pity and hospitality alike unknown, they

---

to have happened between 20.° and 29.° S.—with a relation of the events which befel those survivors who have reached England ... (London, 1783) and George Carter's A narrative of the loss of the Grosvenor East Indiaman. which was unfortunately wrecked upon the coast of Caffraria, somewhere between the 27th and 32d degrees of southern latitude, on the 4th of August, 1782. compiled from the examination of John Hynes (London, 1791).]

bargained for a supply of provisions, in exchange for a brace of pistols and some shot.

"These men," said Stupeo, "must have been contaminated by trading with Europeans, at least they possess the virtues of sacred friendship; with them the security of oaths is unnecessary."

"Sacred friendship!" said Doctor Alogos; "you are a profound philosopher—you can acknowledge what you stand in need of:—you deny and affirm just as it suits your then convenience."

"And what is the use of words," returned the other, "if we are not to turn them to our own advantage?"

Having with difficulty procured leave to repose in one of the wigwams, they made many inquiries into the situation of the country, but received no satisfactory answer, and from the tone of their dialect, they appeared to be a tribe beyond any that had immediate connection with Europeans. They lay down upon some long grass; their weariness caused them to sleep particularly sound, and they were not a little amazed to find in the morning most of their clothes stolen, with two of their fowling pieces.

"So much for savage honesty and justice," said Alogos: "they are a parcel of rascally thieves, and where is their sacred hospitality in leaving us here to perish in a wild, without arms or clothes; for we have saved nothing but what we kept on our backs, or concealed beneath the grass at the request of Mungo."

"In the first place," said Stupeo, "we have no right to complain, they have not taken our lives, which, from our imprudence, was in their power: and in the second, we mistake terms. In society, I grant this would be called a robbery, but, amongst the children of nature, it is only taking from another what they want to use themselves: they have not our ideas of particular property."

"It seems to me however," said Frederick, "that they were conscious of injustice, or they would not all have departed in this sneaking way. I begin to think the savage state of man is not conducted on philosophical principles."

"That is what I have been saying all the time," cried Stupeo. "Listen while I explain to you the progress of human nature, from gross darkness to superstition; from superstition to the great light of truth; and from thence to philosophical ignorance, which is the genuine state of real felicity."

"You might as well talk of the light darkness of the full noon of night," cried the Doctor in a rage.—"I'll demonstrate it," cried Stupeo.—"You contradict yourself," said Frederick; "I'll prove that philosophy——"

"You may prove the devil," said Stupeo, "if you will, but you shan't overturn my argument, which is founded on the broad basis of truth and universal man."

"What, will you have eatee masses?" said Mungo:—and the three great philosophers arose to provide themselves breakfast from a neighbouring brook, where they gathered some herbs.

CHAPTER VII.

THE VAGABONDS ARRIVE AT A PERFECT REPUBLIC, ON THE PRINCIPLES OF EQUALITY AND POLITICAL JUSTICE.

Our troop of philosophical vagabonds set out, they knew not whither, and had not gone far before they found, exposed beneath a tree, an Indian child, puny, weak, and almost expiring.

"Behold!" cried Alogos, "the humanity of savages! this, I suppose, is parental care. This poor wretch is so ill-formed, that it will take too much trouble to rear; and savages have too many wants to supply, and are too ignorant of physic to encumber themselves with a sickly child."

"It is a glorious practice," exclaimed Stupeo; "and shews them to be, in fact, more human than ourselves. Of what value is life with an unhealthy or deformed person? We are, in such a case, a burden to ourselves and to others."

"But how many great heroes and philosophers have had very little persons," said Doctor Alogos. "I do not apprehend the human mind to be in admeasurement to the prowess of the body—so far from it, that men of brilliant genius, have most frequently been of weak constitutions; the hardy and robust being too full of animal spirits to be contented with speculations, and why may we not find, in this very custom, the reason that Indians remain in a stationary state, as they deprive themselves of these persons of intellect?"

"It explains to me," said Frederick, "what I attributed to their manner of life and want of luxuries. It is easy to have none but people of strength and vigour, if all that are otherwise be destroyed in infancy."

"Experience," replied Alogos, with a deep sigh, "is the best school, but the mischief is, that those who are yet well, will not take warning by example, till they suffer themselves."

For forty days they continued to wander, more than once encountering a few straggling Indians, who attempted to convince them, that in a state of nature, *force* was the only law, and passion the only standard of right. They came at length to a great chain of mountains, extremely barren, and placed in such confusion, that they appeared scattered by the hand of tempest.

They had continued their journey, merely from the restless spirit of rambling, and the dread they felt of returning to their delightful farm of Clarens. They now debated whether they should climb the summit, or take some other route; but the expectation of beholding an entire new country, invited them to labour at the steep. They were by this time so accustomed to hardship, that a trifle could not intimidate them, and in three days they gained the elevation of the mountains.

They gazed upon the prospect beneath them, which was much superior to their expectation. A fine level country, interspersed with gentle swellings, and intersected with limpid streams, watering extended groves, presented itself. Amongst the groves appeared high spires and lofty domes, evidently the workmanship of ingenious artists.

The philosophers were enraptured, and wearied themselves in conjectures of what region they could be advanced to. They waited impatiently for the morning, when they began to unravel the mazes which wound down from the mountains, and it was the ensuing day before they reached the base.

They then refreshed themselves with some fine fruit, which seemed to grow neglected, and proceeded forward towards the great piles of buildings which they had seen from far. They overtook a man who was slowly walking, with his eyes bent upon the ground, as if in deep study, and totally naked. Our philosophers were therefore not put out of countenance by their own ragged appearance.

Doctor Alogos accosted him in various languages, but without being understood, when the man inquired in Hebrew what they were, and how they came into that country.—"Why do you walk naked?" said the Doctor.

"Because we have nobody to make clothes."—"How do you employ yourselves?"—"I am studying the public good."

"Studying the public good!" repeated the Doctor: "you are then a legislator of the country?"—"No, I am a private individual; but it is the place of every man to study to promote the public good."

Having passed this politician, who seemed unwilling to speak much, our vagabonds disputed with themselves on the nature of the country, which they thought very strange, especially as they met several persons employed studying the public good. A man striking a tree sometimes with his fist, and then with his head, induced the Doctor to inquire the meaning of so singular an action.—"What are you doing?" said the Doctor.—"I am endeavouring to drive this *idea* out of my path."—"That is not an idea," said the Doctor, "that is a reality."—"All things are ideas," replied the man: "every thing which appears to exist, is merely an idea: we cannot prove that there is reality, body, substance, extension, or any such quality."

"Very good," said the Doctor: "I fancy before you have beat that idea in form of a tree, out of your way, you will have an idea of a fractured skull."*

As they advanced along the high road, the hedges of which were fallen into decay, they overtook a troop of people, who were moving a tree by means of a machine; the greater part stood idle, while five or six furthered the work. Doctor Alogos enquired of

---

* It is astonishing how ridiculous and even irrational the new doctrines appear, when taken from the page of metaphysics, and contrasted with practice. [Editor's note: An allusion to the idealist philosophy of George Berkeley and David Hume (see above), who denied the existence of matter and instead maintained that nothing exists unless it perceives or is perceived; that material objects are ideas in our mind, with no independent existence.]

the nearest what was the name of the country. The man paused for some time, at length replied, "I do not think it for the public good to answer you—I will reflect upon it."—While he stood reflecting, he was called by his comrades;—the first gang of labourers retiring for another to take their places.

The travellers proceeded onwards towards the great city. They perceived some builders repairing an house, which, from its singular construction, engaged their attention. While they stood admiring, all the labourers gave over work. A man, who was half-way up a ladder, fixed his burden on an hook, which seemed there on purpose. Some men winding up a crane, fixed the pulley upon a catch, and left the beam hanging in the air. The whole party sauntered away different ways, and a new set advancing, began to labour. The travellers reflected on this incident, remaining stationary for some time. In half an hour this new set of builders retired like the former, and another troop advanced.

"This is a curious mode of building," said the Doctor.—"It seems an equal division of labour," said Stupeo; "I dare say we are arrived at last in a country of philosophers."[174]

"But at this rate an house will not be finished in ten years:— the public good does not seem much promoted by this means."

They proceeded on, and saw on one side of the road a smith's shop. They paused to see if labour was here equally divided. Some iron in the fire was heated to a proper heat, taken out, and laid upon the anvil, when the man who was working left it there and marched away. Another took his place, but the welding heat was lost, and the iron was returned again to the fire.

A man drew near them in deep thought, and the Doctor ventured to inquire the subject of his reflection.—"I am debating," replied he, "whether it will be most to the public good, that I should help half an hour at getting in the harvest, or labour half an hour at building the new granary; I have spent all the morning in considering, and cannot determine."

"Then is it necessary to do one?"—"Yes, it has been proved in a volumnious book of political justice; that, in the old system of things, the labour which was performed by a certain number of the lower people, could be done in half an hour's labour, for each individual per diem.* But I don't know how it is, since we are all equal, and all labourers, and all studying the public good, our country is going rapidly to decay. An house that used to be built in three months, is not now done in as many years; and as to works of genius, it was found utterly impossible for different sets of workmen to paint a picture, write a book, or finish a device."

"At least," observed the Doctor, "you might provide yourselves clothes."

"We do manufacture some coarse canvass, but it is a matter of prodigious difficulty, for no man will work more than half an hour; and the hands wanted from the sowing of the seed, till it is finished in the web and fashioned to the body, is astonishing, for it is strange how stupid the people grow since one man knows every thing."

"That is an excellent remark," said the Doctor: "more good is produced in society, by the diversity of genius, than if each individual were endowed with a small but equal proportion."

A stately personage, with a small piece of coarse canvass round his waist, advanced, and seeing the travellers, courteously inquired whence they came, and whither they were going.

"We have a curiosity," said the Doctor, "to visit that great city which rises before us—we are strangers, and not a little surprised at the customs of your country."

"You see then," said the stranger, whose name was Parecho, "the utmost limits of human perfection: you see a people who had arrived at the height of various arts and sciences, so much so, that scarcely a peasant who laboured in the field, but could read the divine books of our ancestors: we were surrounded with mountains, which prevented the invasions of an hostile foe, but still we were not happy. It was thought that the rich lived in voluptuous

---

* Godwin's Political Justice, 8vo. edition, chap. VI. also Enquirer, page 163. [Editor's note: *Political Justice, 8vo. edition*: Walker is referring to a passage from the third edition of Godwin's *Political Justice*, Book VIII, Chap. vi (Book VIII, Chap. iv in the first edition of the text; see Appendix A.6.ii). *Enquirer*, page 163: Godwin argues a similar point about the division of labor in *The Enquirer*: "The injustice I suffer, is not in the actual labour, but in the quantity of that labour. If no man were absolutely compelled to perform a greater share of labour than, multiplied by the number of members in the community, he would have no right to complain on that account. But the labour then required, would be diminished to a tenth, perhaps a twentieth part of the labour now imposed upon the husbandman and the artificer" (163).]

idleness on the labours of the poor, and that we should never be happy till the most perfect equality was established.

It would be endless to enumerate the devices of a set of madmen and knaves, who stunned the peoples' ears perpetually with systems so impracticable, that mankind must have been remodelled to suit them; and indeed several treatises were written, and several experiments tried to change the very constitution of the human nature. It was proved that no man could die if fear and *prejudice* had not prepared his mind for death; and consequently it followed, that to divest our minds of this prejudice was to become immortal.

It was proved clearly, by some systemisers, that the people ought, without exception, to have a right of voting and sending delegates to our Council of the Elders, and that new representatives should be chosen every year. Not to say any thing of the riots, debauchery, and excess, which disgraced the whole nation at those periods, it was soon found that scarce any man of real worth and learning was returned to the Council. Those who were most extravagant, and could tickle the rude humours of a mob, were chosen representatives. The lower orders likewise took pleasure in sending some of their own class, and persons of the meanest description were elected in a drunken frolic. These representatives would, however, have been cyphers, if any proportion had been preserved, and would very ably have represented their constituents:—but the great mischief arose from the middle class of society, who, in point of numbers were nearly equal, and in point of influence more than equal; for, if a man had any domestics or journeymen, these were necessiated to vote with their master, and then masters were universally influenced by the powers of oratory. Any man who could rant and declaim was certain of their support, and our great Council became like the forum of the ancients, where a demagogue could work the people into passion, and lead them to any preposterous scheme he fancied.

The influence of the crown was soon overturned:—the people were deluded with the ostensible prospect of liberty, which none of them could describe; and their leaders throwing off the mask, a civil war ensued, in which near a million of people perished. The royal family was destroyed; the aristocracy nearly annihilated, for the nobles adhered to the crown, from which their honours were derived; and the rich were compelled to divide their property, or were *proscribed*, and the most shocking excesses took place; during which, all men of any property were in danger of destruction.* Equality in every sense of the word was to be established, and all laws, sacred and civil, were abrogated. All things valuable and curious lost their worth, because there was no longer a market. If a man worked, or if he remained idle, food and raiment was all he had to expect; and genius in one hour seemed blasted from the land.

No man would work for his neighbours, because the reward destroyed the just balance of equality. It was found that no work could be done without having some subordinate class, like the Helots,[175] who did the drudgery of the Spartans. This in our country not being practicable, and the women having declared themselves no longer dependents on the men, but equal in every point, it was resolved to subject them by force to the labour necessary for providing food, raiment, and shelter for the community, while the men should be employed in studying the public good.

The female sex soon drooped under this usage, and entreated to be reinstated in the ancient slavery, for they found the rough

---

* For the information of the reader, I will translate a picture of the domiciliary visits at Paris, from Mr. Peltier's *Dernier*, Tableaux de Paris, printed in London. "At ten o'clock at night groups of soldiers, placed at angles of all the streets, arrested whoever was yet found straying about.—Two hours had not yet been sufficient for those who sought a place of secrecy and surety against the formidable inquisition. The husband fled from his wife, and the father from his children, whom he pressed to his bosom, thinking it was for the last time. Every one thinks himself accused: every one fears that amongst their visitors will be found an enemy or a spy, or a servant who will discover his place of refuge. One flies to the most distant quarter of the city, here one is received, there one is repulsed, and the fatal moment which approaches doubles the inquietude and anxiety. Decency is in a degree violated by friendship:—here the brother shares the bed of his sister, and there chastity and virtue implores an asylum from vice; and many whose lives had been without a stain, seek security under the curtains of prostitution. Every where persons and property are concealed, every where the interrupted sounds of the muffled hammer are heard striking with a slow and fearful stroke." [Editor's note: In fact, this is not Walker's own translation; he is merely lifting the "translation" from a footnote in Playfair's *History of Jacobinism*, 2:485–86 n. In the footnote Playfair translates a passage from Jean Gabriel Peltier (1760–1825), *Dernier Tableau de Paris, ou récit historique de la Révolution du 10 Août, des causes qui l'ont produite, des événemens* [sic] *qui l'ont précédée et des crimes qui l'ont suivi*, 2 vols. (London, 1793). The original is on 1:220.]

employments not only spoil their features, and render them object of indifference, but they were incapable of building houses, and other laborious exertions. The whole labour of the nation was now at a stand, till a prodigious great philosopher observed, that were all men necessiated to work, the labour would scarcely be felt by any.

It was computed, that under the old regime, one twentieth of the people had been employed in agriculture. If then this were divided, it would amount to half an hour a day: no one would shrink from this—nothing could be fairer—but, how was this to be enforced? For it had been proved by this same great man, in a very elaborate and verbose book of political justice, that *no people could represent or be represented*;* that no man could give his vote away by delegation, and the people believed him."

"I have no doubt of it," said Doctor Alogos. "My companions are very great philosophers, and made me believe wonderful impractibilities."

"Well," continued Parecho, "anarchy and massacre would have been the consequence, if a few men had not seized themselves the helm of business, and declared themselves censors general. This was by no means difficult, for they had only to talk more about the public good, and profess principles more hyperbolical than the philosophers, to lead people any way.

It might naturally have been supposed, that genius would have roused itself from the torpor of an equality with dullness; but there remained no stimulant, no man being allowed to enjoy greater conveniences or luxuries than another, and therefore labours of ingenuity lost their reward. Every species of trade was crushed at once, because it is the nature of *trade to amass*, and the nature of *equality to destroy*.

Our metropolis, to which we are advancing, is daily sinking into decay. Nothing new is projected—all our arts are falling into oblivion, as children are not allowed to employ their attention

---

* What will the advocates for a representative government say to this doctrine of Mr. Godwin? [Editor's note: Walker is alluding to a passage in Godwin's *Political Justice*, Book III, Chap. ii: "If the people, or the individuals of whom the people is constituted, cannot delegate their authority to a representative; neither can any individual delegate his authority to a majority, in an assembly of which he is himself a member" (86).]

on any one thing in particular, but to be provided at five-and-twenty, well regulated, active, and *prepared* to learn;* thus while they pretend to learn every thing, they learn nothing, for the human mind is of narrow extent, and the next generation will be within a shade of actual savagism."

During this discourse they had reached the precincts of a large and venerable city, but evidently under a rapid decay. The most disgusting filth covered the streets, emitting a shocking and mephetic vapour.[176] The people were all naked, marked with extreme dejection, and half the houses were shut up.†

"What is the reason of this?" said the Doctor; "we generally impute the decrease of population to the pernicious effects of sedentary and mechanical employ."

"It is disease," replied Parecho: "our physicians have forgot their skill, and no new students can be reared from the want of ostensible reward, and some distinction to talent."

"But common humanity, one would suppose, should stimulate them to promote the public good," said the Doctor.

"Very likely," answered Parecho, "but common humanity will not teach men skill, there must be a laborious exertion of mind, and that cannot be the case when we have so many other demands, and the man of genius is lost in the promiscuous crowd. We were told indeed that genius was to be the only claim to distinction; but it was soon found, that where all was equal, there could be no distinction, and genious had no means of expanding."

"I begin to think," said the Doctor, "that at least there must be

---

* Godwin's Enquirer, page 5. [Editor's note: The passage in *The Enquirer* that Walker is alluding to reads: "Many things that, in the dark and unapprehensive period of youth, are attained with infinite labour, may, by a ripe and judicious understanding, be acquired with an effort inexpressibly inferior. He who should affirm, that the true object of juvenile education was to teach no one thing in particular, but to provide against the age of five and twenty a mind well regulated, active, and prepared to learn, would certainly not obtrude upon us the absurdest of paradoxes" (5).]

† The reader is referred to Dr. Meyer's *Fragmens sur Paris* translated into French by Dumourier, where he will find a true but wretched description of a country labouring under the practice of the new philosophy. [Editor's note: A reference to Friedrich Johann Lorenz von Meyer (1760–1844), *Fragmente aus Paris im IVten Jahr der Französischen Republik*, 2 vols. (Hamburg, 1798), which appeared in a French translation by Charles François Du Périer Dumouriez (1739–1823), *Fragments sur Paris, trad. De l'Allemand par le général Dumouriez*, 2 vols. (Hamburg, 1798).]

two orders in society, those who project, and those who execute; for no man will project when he must execute himself, and where no reward is to be gained superior to food and raiment."

"But if you allow rewards," said Parecho, "equality is sapped to the foundation; you introduce luxury, and property rises to its old standard. Beside, how many fools would share it with the men of genius, without any merit of their own."

"Surely," replied Alogos, "have I not a right to do what I will with the wealth I have honestly acquired? May not the chief stimulus to my actions have been this very privilege of rendering a foolish thick-brained son my heir?—It strikes me that your present system cannot possibly continue—your people will not be sufficient to the task of gathering in a plentiful harvest."

"Indolence in the extreme," replied Parecho, "possesses every man, so much so, that the very cares of connubial affection are become burthensome, and I have actually heard a man debate with his wife, whether half an hour was not too much labour for the human œconomy."

"My companions," said the Doctor, "are two very great philosophers, and not quite so sublime in their ideas.—Their system of equality goes to a right of possessing any of the sex, and I dare say they will not object to the custom of your country, in labouring half an hour for the public good."

By this time they arrived in a great square, it was about noon, and our travellers began to be hungry at sight of some large piles of loaves, cakes, and fruits.—"We do not eat in common," said Parecho, "because we are not obliged to be hungry at the same time, but each comes to this repository, and takes what he wants."

"Some may eat double to others," observed the Doctor; "how do you manage that?"

"At first there were many debates, but it being urged that the labour of all being equal, those who eat little could not be injured, as they could do nothing with their superfluous earnings."

"It's very singular," said Stupeo, (the Doctor interpreting) "that such an admirable institution should have such a strange effect. Is your government patriarchial, monarchial, tyrannical, aristo-cratical, oligarchial, or republican?"

"It is republican," replied Parecho.—"Then I will maintain," said

Stupeo, "that it is the best possible form; every thing is for and by the people themselves, and they are not taxed to provide for others,"

"Taxes," replied Parecho, "if within moderation, and not sent out of the country, are like the returning moisture of the dews. Titles, wealth, and honours, are incentives to exertion, like prizes amongst school-boys;—and, to speak a truth, the mass of mankind are only grown-up children."

"And why?" cried Stupeo, in triumph; "because they are held in profound ignorance."

"I will maintain," said Frederick, "that men are more happy ignorant than half learned: they will then follow the pursuits of real life, and are satisfied with the comforts within their reach. I am almost tired of speculation."

"It is true," said Parecho, with a languid smile, "that your greatest sticklers for freedom, if they see their folly, become as great champions for slavery, always in extremes. Under our former government, which was a limited monarchy, we had every gradation in society. It was observed, that the very rich, and the very poor ranks rarely produced great men. It was from the various shades of middle life these arose, and to judge of our real liberty, I will observe to you the general routine of property. A man of talents, in humble life, generally raised himself to independence; his son continuing his track, or pursuing his maxims, became rich; his grandson claimed titles and honours, and blazed in the zenith of power; but his great grand-son generally squandered the estates, and the family again sunk, to rise after two or three generations."

"That is exactly as it is in Great Britain," said Doctor Alogos.

"But truth," cried Stupeo, "is omnipotent. It is self-demonstrated that that government which is instituted by and for the people, is for the benefit of the people, and equality* is as necessary to genuine liberty as air is to life."

---

* I know many of the new school will say that I misrepresent the meaning of equality, that they do not mean equality of property, but equality of rights: the truth is, they mean *both*, though the fairest pretence is held out, Are not titles and distinctions property? But that is not where they would stop, as every man of common intelligence knows. [Editor's note: Walker appears to be alluding here to a Jacobin pamphlet, "An Explanation of the Word Equality," in which the anonymous author argues exactly this point, viz. "the equality insisted on by the friends of Reform, is an Equality of Rights," *not* "an equality of wealth and possessions" ([London], [1795?], 1).

"But here," said the Doctor, "is an example."—"Examples have nothing to do with rational principles and metaphysical arguments."

"Do the people always prefer their own good?" inquired Parecho. "Do they not cut each others throats to-day, for what they despise to-morrow? Are they ever constant to one point? Is it possible then that such a mass of contradiction should govern itself? Look at this wretched half-peopled city, abandoned to idleness and vice, for it is necessary the human mind should be employed, and when it is not in good, it is in evil. It is only indolence prevents this people cutting each others throats; as it is, there scarcely passes a day without some violent atrocity, and two or three suicides."

"But is there no means to stimulate them to some great action?" said the Doctor; "and again introducing aristocracy, for to me aristocracy appears the universal government; for, most certainly the select possessors of the greatest power and connection, govern the monarch by their strength and advice, or the people by their influence and intrigues."

"A government," replied Parecho, "to be invulnerable against the attacks of time, and for the benefit of every individual, must be like a pyramid, rising from a broad base to a point. The greatest portion of mankind will of necessity be mean; these are at the base, and every advance higher is to the benefit of the class or structure, till we rise to a solitary point, which finishes the work. We may indeed make our forms of structure, but no one without a base: if it is all base, all equality, there can be no building, and of all buildings, the pyramidical is found to resist longest the destruction of the elements. Had Nature designed men to be equal, (in exception to all other productions,) she would have endowed them with equal stature, prowess, and intellect."

Turning the corner of the street, they saw a man standing on a tub, declaiming to a concourse of naked people.—"This," said Parecho, "is one of our philosophers—we will hear him a moment."

"Citizens!" said the rhetorician, "let us never forget the glorious day of our emancipation from slavery, when a new era, a new

Interestingly, from a hand-written note on a copy of this pamphlet held by the British Library (Shelf mark 8135.b.6[2]) it appears that Walker sold this pamphlet in his shop on Great Portland Street ("Sold at Walker's—Bookseller Portland St.").]

epoch, ever to be celebrated in the annals of man, began; when a great people set aside at once every species of government, allotted each individual his share in the terrestial globe, and set their feet upon the necks of trade and commerce. These two monsters are happily strangled, and exulting men heard their expiring groans. Now, citizens, no man labours for others, it is all for himself, and he may enjoy the fruits of it beneath his own vine, and under his own fig-tree. The sun of science has arisen, and darkness flies before her to the borders of the universe. Where shall we stop? Who shall set bounds to our pursuits? Yes, you will wonder at the discoveries of the intellect. This earth upon which we stand, is proved to be no bigger in reality than an apricot, so wonderful are the deceptions of our senses. What is matter composed of but particles *ad infinitum?* And these are united by attraction, so that attraction is, in fact, the only cause of bulk or extension. But, have we not magnifying glasses, which make an insect *appear* as big as a cart-horse? And what are our eyes but magnifying glasses, which so deceive us, that what we take for men six feet high, and forests rising to the clouds, are nothing more than imperceptible animals upon a peach, to whom the down appears in their eyes, large trees? Who after this will give credit to their senses? Who will not doubt every thing?—Citizens, I have an amazing improvement to offer your reflection—it requires your assistance, as the artist will not be able to complete it in less than a thousand days, with six changes of twenty hands per day, which will only be one hundred and twenty, a number that will do little more than plant an acre of garlic. This grand invention is a plough, which will work by itself, ploughs three acres of ground in ten minutes, reaps it at the same time, and thrashes it out into bins. Thus, citizens, we see the effects of the human mind when untrammelled by tyrants, and thus shall mind overcome matter, insomuch, that I will venture to pronounce a solemn fact, that we shall shortly be able to make automatons, to do every act of labour the human species are now necessiated to perform."

"Is it possible," said the Doctor, "the orator believes himself?"

"The people must be fools to believe him," said Frederick: "he will persuade them next he will thrash the corn before it grows."

"And I should not wonder if they gave him credit," answered

Parecho. "This man was an apothecary before he commenced orator, but his eloquence gaining him applause, he left the rattle of the pestle, for the clatter of his own tongue, and he is now so great a favourite, that any thing he utters is received with applause. Have you no men in your country who are heard with delight while they speak nonsense?"

"Yes," replied the Doctor mournfully, "we have too many: I fear our country will one day be like yours, or even worse, for my countrymen are of so restless a disposition, that, were they equal to-day, like your citizens, to-morrow they would be plunged in anarchy."

"I hope," said Parecho, "they will not quit the reality of felicity with some natural evils, for the shade with every possible ill."

CHAPTER VIII.

MORAL VIRTUES, THEORY AND PRACTICE—STUPEO IS CONVINCED THERE ARE OTHER EXISTENCES BESIDES HIS OWN IDEAS, BY A TREMENDOUS PHENOMENON IN NATURE.

Our philosophers were invited to the house of their guide, which had once been extremely magnificent, and yet bore the vestages of fading grandeur; it contained some rich furniture, which time had not devoured, for as to any thing new, it was impossible to be procured.

"What you see here," said Parecho, "is only the fragments of what I once possessed—my whole property is divided, and of this house I only could claim two rooms, a chimney-sweeper, and several other equally important personages possessing the others; but since the mortality in the city, I am allowed my whole house— I had a library of ancient Syriac and Egyptian manuscripts, containing an account of the most early ages, together with thirteen thousand modern productions. But these enlighteners of the human race, during their struggle for liberty, and the promotion of general knowledge, being in want of cases for their fire-powder and ball, condemned all the libraries to that purpose."*

"How is it possible," said the Doctor, "you should be acquainted with gun-powder, which is a very modern invention, and only a few hundred years introduced into America."

Parecho smiled.—"My friend," said he, "as our great ancestor said, there is nothing new under the sun.—This art we learnt from a people of India, calling Oxydracæ: Alexander the Great feared to march against this people, and pretended it was on account of religion, but had he passed the Hyphasis, he might doubtless have made himself master of the country all round them; but their cities

---

* At Narbonne the books have been sent to the arsenal; and at Fontaine le Dijon, the library of the Fuillants has been thrown aside as waste, in the hall of old papers Horace and Virgil have been condemned not only for acknowledging tyrants, but for having been often printed for the use of tyrants, and by the permission of tyrants. The *meridian circles* made by Butterfield, for the globes of Coronelli, and the *medals* which are at the national library, were calculated to amount to half a little cannon. At Lyons, Cassenet threw into the crucible 800 antique medals of gold. Notes at the end of Playfair's History, where the new philosopher will find a catalogue of *glorious* exploits of a similar nature. [Editor's note: *At Narbonne .... medals of gold*: Walker has gleaned this information verbatim from Playfair's *History of Jacobinism*, Appendix T, 2:806, 809-10; *the Fuillants*: during the French Revolution, the *Club des Feuillants* was a conservative club which was formed in 1791 when a number of deputies to the Assembly left the more radical Jacobin Club in opposition to a petition calling for the replacement of King Louis XVI. They named themselves after the religious order of the Feuillants (Reformed Cistercians), in whose former monastery near the Tuilleries, in Paris, they met. After the insurrection of 10 August 1792, when the Jacobins overthrew the monarchy and went on the rampage against political enemies, killing thousands, the Feuillant Club ceased to exist, its members targeted by murderous Jacobin gangs, and its papers destroyed; *Horace*: full Latin name Quintus Horatius Flaccus (65-8 BC), Roman lyric poet and satirist; *Virgil*: full Latin name Publius Vergilius Maro (70-19 BC), Roman poet; *meridian circles*: astronomical instrument consisting of a telescope carrying a large graduated circle, by which the right ascension and declination of a star may be determined (*OED*); *Butterfield*: Michael Butterfield, English instrument maker who worked in Paris, where he made the horizontal circles for Coronelli's globes, in consultation with the mathematician Philippe de la Hire; *globes of Coronelli*:Vincenzo Maria Coronelli (1650-1718), renowned Italian cosmographer and geographer, and maker of maps and globes. He was invited to come to France by Cardinal César d'Estrées, Ambassador Extraordinary of the French king Louis XIV in the Court of Rome, to make two large and beautifully ornamented globes (a celestial and a terrestial). The globes were presented to Louis XIV in 1683. Measuring fifteen feet in diameter, Coronelli's globes were the largest ever made to that date. They were put on display in the Chateau of Marly, and later in the Bibliothèque Nationale, and became one of the sights of Paris, bringing their maker much fame; *Cassenet*: not identified.]

he could never have taken, though he had led a thousand as brave as Achilles, or three thousand such as Ajax to the assault. For they came not into the field to fight those who attacked them: but these holy men, beloved by the gods, overthrew their enemies with tempests, thunder-bolts, and lightning from the walls."*

"It is very singular, indeed," replied the Doctor, "but by no means surprising: but pray of what race of people are you, since you seem acquainted with the old world?"

"We are part of the tribes of Abraham," [177] said Parecho; "we crossed the great deserts of Tartary and China, travelling those regions of desolation and eternal ice which unite the Continents, and in about one hundred years wandering discovered this valley, where we were as happy as it is possible for the transient and perishable existence of man to be."

"Have you no religion?" inquired the Doctor.

"To-morrow," answered their host, "you shall visit our temple, it is sabbath."

The philosophers retired to their room, where some clean straw was laid upon the floor, the beds having been sequestered for the public purposes.

"It must be owned," said Frederick, "these people are a whimsical set, and do not seem much better for their liberty."

"This is a philosophical republic," said Alogos; "the ancient republics were fighting republics;—the Americans and the Hollanders are trading republics, but men seemed neither better satisfied, better governed, or better fed in any of them; nor in fact, do they enjoy so many benefits as in a limited monarchy."

"But I insist upon it," said Stupeo, "monarchy is unnatural. It

---

* See this extraordinary passage in the life of Apollonius Tyanaus, by Philostratus, Lib. ii. Cap. 14. [Editor's note: *Apollonius Tyanaus*: a wandering Pythagorean philosopher and mystic (b. c. 4 BC), who attained so great a fame by his wonder-working powers that divine honors were paid to him. He wrote a life of Pythagoras and other works, of which hardly anything has survived. His own life was written by Philostratus Sophista (second and third centuries AD). *This art we learn ... from the walls*: Parecho's story of Alexander's campaign in Asia is closely based on a passage in Philostratus's *Vita Apollonii* (2,33). *Oxydracæ*: one of the Indian hill peoples that resisted the Macedonians during their Asian campaign; *Hyphasis*: present-day Beas, a river in northern India; *Achilles*: the hero of Homer's *Iliad*, he took part in the Trojan War on the side of the Greeks as their most illustrious warrior; *Ajax*: the most famous hero of the Trojan War after Achilles.]

is one tyrant usurping the privileges of the whole people, contrary to the sacred majesty of the body politic."

"But how came that body politic into being?" said the Doctor. "The roaming families of men," replied the great politician, "found the need of mutual assistance and defence, and they united into nations."

"No;" replied the Doctor, "you talk absurd; it is contrary to the nature of man—Man is a rapacious animal, and is perpetually (if not curbed by laws and subordination) seeking objects of rapine and violence.—Let us look back to the origin of any people, to the remote annals of *heroic ages*, and we shall find an herd of robbers gathering together for the sake of plunder. The boldest becomes their leader and chief; the weak tribes submit and join them, till their power is irresistable, and they found extensive empires. Conquest is at first the only compact, and the people, little better than an herd of murderers directed by a chief. The ambition of this chief to excel in splendor, introduces luxury and softens the ferocious habits of his followers; the arts of peace follow a court.—The fermentation subsides, or is let off by continual wars, while the peaceable remain at home, and this is the history of man in reality. To talk of a people assembling from the woods, and forming general laws and social compacts, is as absurd as it is false. In all established governments, the origin was the same, whether they were republican or monarchical; though, for a thousand reasons, a limited monarchy seems to me the best calculated for man, as diffusing the most general good, and, in fact, the greatest proportion of real freedom."

"I am still convinced," cried Stupeo, "that a state of nature is the more eligible.—It signifies nothing that the human species may be multiplied in society. The happiness, and not the numbers of mankind is to be considered; and the greatest possible good would be, to let *one* family reside upon a thousand acres, in the most perfect freedom and happiness, rather than have a family upon every acre, with the present consequences of society."

"You talk strange contradictions," said the Doctor.—"You are never consistent in your opinions: do you not know, that in society we must *barter* some privileges for a portion of *social happiness.*"[178]

"But truth, eternal truth," cried Stupeo, "is——"

"What we have heard an hundred times," said Frederick, "in as many different definitions; for my part, I am disgusted with every thing." These philosophers were here interrupted by the snoring of Mungo, who had quietly laid down upon the straw, untroubled with the nature of truth or metaphysical disquisitions; and the three great men concluded, that ignorance was in some measure necessary to happiness. The next morning, Parecho attended his guests to a large hall, where they found a great number of people sitting upon benches; in the midst of the hall was a square platform, railed round, similar to a small stage. There was no ornament to fix the eye, nor any music to catch the ear, a profound silence remained.

"Why," said Alogos to Parecho, "is the place painted black.— Have you no priests,—no music?"

"There was once very fine paintings," said Parecho, "representing the miracles in Egypt and the Wilderness;[179] but it was feared by the philosophers that these symbols would recal to mind the God of their fathers, which they wished to expunge from the human soul.—We used to have fine music; but the musicians could not be paid, and the whole art fell rapidly into decay, for who would or could attend to the acquirement of skill, when all their reward was a bare existence. As to the old priests, they were deemed to have enslaved the people, by darkening their minds with superstition, and indulging themselves in licentiousness; so that they were most of them destroyed, and the rest mingled with the people."

A person now moved from the crowd, and mounting the stage, made an oration for half an hour upon morality, political justice, and the great book of Nature, where he asserted every thing was to be learnt that was worth knowing: he concluded with declaring against the power of revealed religion,[180] to check the crimes of men, asserting, that morality was every thing, and the light of nature the real standard of virtue.

The people then waited some time; and no one else coming forward, they dispersed to walk in the fields, the day being an holiday.

Our philosophers likewise quitted the city, following at a distance the orator, who had harangued about morality.—They entered a grove of trees where they sat down, conversing on politics. A young woman was walking in the grove, to whom the moralist advanced, and seemed to press her to something she objected. He was proceeding to violence, when a young man sprung upon him; they both fell to the ground, but the orator being the strongest, rose, and with a long knife stabbed the youth to the heart, and ran away.

"Horrid!" cried Doctor Alogos, "is there no means of punishing the monster?"

"This man," said Parecho indignantly, "is a reformer of the people, and such the consequence of his doctrine. If you destroy in the minds of men the belief of an avenging and infinite Power, you give loose to every passion in the corrupted heart of man.— It is not possible to bring this wretch to justice, because *no individual* has the power of life and death, unless it is done in a private manner, by way of retaliation:—beside, it is contrary to political justice, that any *past* offence should be punished by coercion."[181]

"Very true," said Stupeo, "that I taught the people of England.— But he might be fined—no man, or body of men, can have a right to punish with death."

"But how will you fine a man who has no property, and where all are equal—and what could be done with the fine? You would soon destroy equality."

"But you might imprison him," said Frederick, "to prevent his doing the same again."

"Impossible," replied Parecho.—"My dear Sir, hear the opinions of our great philosophers. The body is perpetually changing—the soul of man becomes every moment a different being: so that were we to put this man in prison, to-morrow we should be confining a totally different being, wholly innocent of the crime."

"Very good," replied Doctor Alogos, "the fashionable Mr. Hume has made most of the *young* men converts to these very doctrines in my country. So that, nothwithstanding I can recollect a friend or a wife for twenty years back, they are not the same persons. I and they are changed, transformed, and renewed, nobody knows how often: and Mr. Hume, who finished the essays, was not the Mr. Hume who wrote the treatise on Human Nature.[182] So Alexander the Great, who was the son of Philip of Macedon, was not the Alexander the Great who subdued Greece by his flatteries, nor him who overthrew the Persians."[183]

"Such being the case," said Parecho, "it is plain, that there can be no punishments without they are corporeal, nor any corporeal punishments without infringing political justice: you cannot restore the injury done to society, by committing an outrage in the article of punishment."

"Then crime may be done with impunity," said Doctor Alogos.

"What a delightful country," cried Stupeo. "I will never quit it. The human mind is here in perfect freedom. At length, my dear Frederick, we have found the place where our principles are practicable, where truth and philosophy shines with beams of eradiating splendour, and the dignity of human nature is unsophisticated in its pursuits."

"Would that I were once more in England with my dear Laura, if the children of nature have not murdered her," said the Doctor, with a deep sigh.

Frederick knew not what to think; his senses frequently contradicted the profound Stupeo, and often led him to think his tutor in the wrong; but the philosophical disquisitions, the grand doctrines of the greatest good, and the elegant Romance of Political Justice,[184] inclined him again to the new philosophy.

Our vagabonds returned to the city, when they became hungry.—Stupeo grumbled very much to find only coarse bread and fruits, with clear water.—"Have you no fermented liquors," said he, "no spirits?"

"No," answered Parecho: "spirits could not be the universal drink, independent of the labour to procure them: they are, therefore, unallowable in a state of equality. At first, when they were distributed according to every one's pleasure, the streets were filled with drunkards. Nature never designed men to drink liquid fire."

"At least," said Frederick, "I should think animal food would give variety to your table."

"What!" replied Parecho, "rear animal on purpose to destroy them. Nature never tells us any such thing—we used formerly to have excellent oxen, but since labour has been equally divided, no body will undertake to breed them; and the species is become almost extinct; beside, no one would take the unpleasant office of butcher, where there was no reward."

"Human life," said the Doctor, "is not worth enjoying, when we thus limit our pursuits—the very peasants in my country enjoy infinitely more advantages: and what does any government signify, if in reality men are not benefited, the intellects expanded, and their gratifications increased?"

"It is a false taste," said Stupeo, "which has introduced animal food: and if we do indulge in it, why not eat it raw?—Nature, had she intended we should feed upon dressed dishes, would have produced animal ready roasted and boiled."

"And why not," said Parecho, "have loaves and cakes ready baked, grow upon stalks in the field: all this is a deviation from nature, and very absurd in great philosophers to follow. But seriously, what is this jargon about nature—What is nature?"

"Why, nature," answered Stupeo, "is that which every man sees with his eyes—it is visible at first view to all understandings—it is the influence of rational principles impinging upon men, actions palpable to every comprehension:—It is derived from the single letter N.—Take the Latin words nascor, natus, natura, and the French né, for *born*, analyse them, and you will find that

Ascor being but a frequentive,
Atus a common idiomatic expression,
Atura the same,
é the same,

reduces all these words to the single letter N, which offers no sense; restore the eliptic syllable *ge*, cut off by the usual tendency of languages to contraction, or to euphony, you have geN-ascor, geN-atus, geN-atura, geN-é; in which *gen.* the radical of *generative*, of *kind*, of *beginning*, and of hundreds more, gives a clear sense, and consequently are derived from Γεν ναω* thus nature signifies beginning, or begetting, so that to act according to nature, it to begin, to beget, to produce, which is according to the light of reason and nature."[185]

"But what is the light of nature?" cried Doctor Alogos:—"We know the genuine meaning of the word, but you apply to nature

---

* Etymological Dictionary. [Editor's note: Γεν νάω: to beget, to engender.]

a *personality*: you make a mere *action* an *active being*: such are the consequences of applying terms, when the real meaning of the word is not understood; and thus we go to deny a Creator, and place in his stead not a power, not a being, but an absolute *action*, called a beginning or a begetting. Thus to express ourselves clearly, we should say, *The act of beginning* teaches us to prefer good for evil. The *act of beginning* has produced all things. Thus we should avoid the absurdity of confounding an act with the person of the actor, for even a new philosopher would startle, if, in place of saying man can be no longer happy than while he lives according to nature, we were to say—man can be no longer happy than while he lives according to the *act of beginning*. Let the worshippers of the *act of beginning, or nature*, remember the advice of Mr. Lock,[186] to be perfectly acquainted with the *meaning* of words they begin to dispute about, and not overthrow society with a cant jargon of equivocal expression. But we are now plunging into the profound and muddy abyss of metaphysics, and shall lose ourselves in the darkness."

"How do you marry in this country of equality?" said Frederick: "Is it a civil or a religious ceremony?"

"It cannot well be called either," replied Parecho. "At the first establishment of equality, every man gave a full sway to his passions, and in one week there was scarcely a maid above fourteen. The labour of the females, as I informed you before, rendered them very indifferent objects to the young men, and it was judged a deviation from equality, that one man should have a pretty wife, and another an ordinary one. It was proposed that all young people, arrived at the age of marriage, should once a year assemble, and the *nearest of stature* divided into parcels, each casting lots for his partner:—they are then deemed married, and if they have children cannot be disunited; but if they have not, they may, by mutual consent, change every year, because the numbers of the people are the strength of the republic; thus we attempt to increase population, while we smother the principles of vitality."

"Have you any mode of punishing adultery?" inquired Stupeo.

"No; the will of the sex is free, and were it not a matter of policy, no man would marry."

"That is as it should be," said Stupeo: "if the rich of the old world knew of this blessed spot, you would have no reason to complain of the decay of your people."

"No grass grows in our highways," said Parecho: "licentiousness and debauchery will never increase or improve the human species; the people must have a taste for domestic enjoyments; a hope must be excited of reward for the rearing of an offspring, or natural affection will do very little."

"You shall go with me to England," said Doctor Alogos; "you shall see there the remains of conjugal affection, and the virtues which still linger in Europe; you shall tell the people the effects of this horrid and impracticable system of equality."

"Impossible," said Parecho; "a man who is really a patriot, will not abandon his country when it is in danger. The hour may come when the people will awake, and they will need some one to direct their rising hopes."

"I will return," cried the Doctor, "that I may at least set my example before them, and would to God they could see the precipice to which they are blindly straying, and open their eyes to the private views and interests of those miscreants who are shaking the torch of sedition in their face, while they seek only an opportunity of picking their pockets."

Stupeo made a long oration against leaving the country, where the new philosophy completely triumphed, protesting if they had but a little brandy, he would prefer it to any spot on the earth; and Frederick, who was nearly ashamed of his former opinions, consented to follow the Doctor.

Having taken leave of Parecho, they returned by the way they came, not a little amused with those naked philosophers, who were studying the public good, and working in ratio for the support of equality.

"It seems to me," said the Doctor, "that to study private good would be more advantageous: it is impossible the public good can be established upon private evils."

They clambered the rugged mountains with difficulty, descending again to the forests of America. The day was extremely sultry, not a breath of air whispered amongst the trees, and a strong sulphurous smell exhaled around them. A thick haze overspread the face of the heavens, through which the sun appeared one moment purple, and the next violet.

"Oh horrible!" cried Stupeo: "what do I see? The phenomenæ of nature are changing—the desolation of all things is at hand."

"What desolation?" said the Doctor calmly; "are you frightened at your own ideas? or do you think this terene habitation will dissolve? Do you believe in the revelations and prophecy?"

"Is this a moment to talk of such things?" said Stupeo, "when an instant may swallow us alive into the gulph of hell? Do you not feel the ground tremble beneath you?"

"The ground tremble!" said the Doctor; "what, have you an idea in your head of the ground being in convulsions?"

"An idea!" cried Stupeo; "can any man in his senses call this an idea? Look at the dreadful appearance of the sun, and say if that's an idea: see how the trees bend—the earth moves like the waves of the ocean:—O God! what will become of us!"

At these words Stupeo cast himself upon the ground, which was agitated by an earthquake, and exhibited a scene tremendously grand. The mountains, over which they had just passed, split with dreadful chasms, and tumbling fragments of rocks broke from their beds, and rushed into the plains, tearing all before them. The earth undulated like a moving lake—at the intervals of a few minutes, yawning with a frightful rent, and closing with a dreadful concussion; a large savannah sunk at a distance, and a body of water overwhelmed it for ever.

"Oh! omnipotent Being," cried Doctor Alogos, falling on his knees, "protect us from the surrounding ruin—if such, O Preserver of mankind, be the consequence of some trifling disorder in nature, what would this world be if governed alone by chance?—It depends upon thee for ever for its existence, and, if thy power be withdrawn, every atom will disunite, and the wind bear them like chaff through the regions of space."

"I acknowledge," said Frederick, his eye gazing upon the dun face of the heavens; "I acknowledge there is a great and ETERNAL POWER. The phenomenæ of nature must convince us if we are not fools, but it is easy in a calm region, where the seasons are scarcely ruffled by a storm, to doubt the existence of a God, as men frequently doubt in their own minds, whether they shall die before they arrive at an hundred while health floats in their veins."

"It is not sufficient," said Doctor Alogos, "that we behold the wonders of nature, these can only inspire our minds with the sublime and the terrific; we must be taught first by revelation, the great truths of religion, and then shall we find a confirmation in every particle of matter."

For half an hour the shocks of the earth continued, and the profoundest silence sealed the lips of these philosophers. Horror chilled their veins, and they expected that the hour of final vengeance was come, when the most High should judge the world. By degrees the undulations became fainter; the starting rocks remained in their beds, and the philosophers found sufficient courage to seat themselves upon a fragment.

"At this moment," said Frederick, "a solemn awe, a strange sensation trembles through my frame—I feel that I am re-assured, and I do not fear this scene of desolation:—I would at this moment that I could believe in the immortality of the soul; but we are told in the eighteenth century, that it is a modern invention of Christianity."

"Like many other falsehoods which are delivered dogmatically," said the Doctor; "there are none greater than this. There is scarcely a nation or people under the heavens who have not believed in it, though some of their *ignorant young* men have pretended to set it aside, merely because it did not agree with the excess of their passions. Those people we call heathens, in the Elysian fields, plainly testify their belief, which is as ancient as record can refer to.—Homer was no philosopher of the eighteenth century—but we might go higher than Homer, we might travel to the ages immediately succeeding the deluge when the Noahchidæ settled in the Median mountains, when the Cushites hued out the mountains of Thebes into caverns, which exist to this day, an everlasting memorial of that great devastation. In these caverns, safe, as they hoped, from another flood, and before they dared venture into the plains (where they built the city of Thebes) they invented the mysteries of hyrogliphics to convey the sacred doctrines of their religion, which, doubtless they received by traditions prior to the deluge.* In these hyrogliphics the Thebaic beetle had principal part, and was the emblem of immortality for two reasons: the first, because after the waters of the Nile subside, and leave the mud behind; this insect is the first which appears, and is thence emblematic of the resurrection; and the second, because the beetle is the longest lived of any insect known, far exceeding the age of man. From these people descended the Egyptians, the fathers of science. A colony also spread eastward, and were the founders of the Hindoo nations, professing the religion of Buddha or Boodh, who was the Hermes, or Mercury of the western, and the Woden, Odin, or Gwoden of the northern world.† It is remarkable that all the primitive mythologies agree in every grand point, as the existence of a great Supreme, the creation, the immortality of the soul, and future rewards and punishments. The Δρυιδαι or Druids, who, according to Pliny, took their name from δρυς an oak, though inhabiting the regions of the North, yet agree in these points of religion with the people of the torrid zone. Were I to enter into the astonishing discussion, which, of itself must strike the mind with amazement, we should perceive that the first inhabitants of the earth had a pure religion, unmixed with fable, and that it is *time* which has introduced amongst them so many fictitious deities: but, to prove to you what I have said, I will repeat to you part of a passage relative to a future heaven, which is taken from the Icelandic, and was the tradition of the ancient Celtæ, Danes, Scytheans, &c. from whom the nations of Europe are descended.[187]

Speaking of the destruction of the world:—*The fire consumes every thing, and the flame reaches up to heaven; but presently after, a new earth springs up from the bosom of the waves, adorned with green meadows; the fields there bring forth, without culture; calamities are there*

---

* Bruce's Travels. [Editor's note: James Bruce (1730-94), *Travels to Discover the Source of the Nile, in the Years 1768, 1769, 1770, 1771, 1772, and 1773* (London, 1790).]

† See Maurice's very curious work of Indian Antiquities. [Editor's note: Thomas Maurice (1754-1824), *Indian Antiquities; or, Dissertations, relative to the ancient geographical divisions, the pure system of primeval theology, the grand code of civil laws, the original form of government, and the various and profound literature of Hindoostan: compared, throughout, with the religion, laws, government, and literature of Persia, Egypt, and Greece; the whole intended as introductory to, and illustrative of, the history of Hindoostan* (London, [1792?]-1800).]

unknown; a palace is there raised more shining than the sun, all covered with gold: this is the place that the just inhabit, and enjoy delights for ever more. Then the powerful, the valiant, He who governs all things, comes forth from his lofty abodes to render divine justice—He pronounces decrees—He establishes the sacred destinies which shall endure for ever. *

Such is the doctrine of those men we call heathens, whom we are told only invented deities through fear. But let us one moment now, when the earth ceases its concussions ask, if the point-blank assertion of the new philosophers be true, when they tell us that the immortality of the soul cannot be traced from the Old Testament."

"Prove that it can," said Stupeo;—"prove that, and I will believe any thing."

"What do you say of Saul and the Witch of Endor?"[188] said the Doctor. "The very identical spirit of Samuel was supposed to appear, which could not have been, if they believed the soul either a bundle of transient ideas with Hume, or mere matter. What do you say of the charmers and dealers with similar spirits? or in the Ecclesiastes, chap. 3, v. 21, where Solomon asks, who knoweth the *spirit* of a *man* that goeth *upward*, and the *spirit* of a beast that goeth *downward* to the earth? But even more plain than all this, we read in the twelfth chapter of Daniel, *Many of them that sleep in the dust of the earth shall awake, some to everlasting life, and some to shame, and everlasting contempt.*—In the 4th chapter of Job, he says, Then a *spirit* passed before my face, and the hair of my head stood up."†

"But why," said Stupeo, "is not the Old Testament as full in this point as the New? And why did not Moses' law declare future rewards and punishments?"

---

* See this passage, amongst many very singular remains of antiquity, in Mallet's Northern Antiquities. [Editor's note: Paul Henri Mallet (1730-1807), *Northern Antiquities; or, A description of the manners, customs, religion and laws of the ancient Danes, and other northern nations; including those of our own Saxon ancestors. With a translation of the Edda, or system of Runic mythology, and other pieces, from the ancient Icelandic tongue,* trans. Thomas Percy, 2 vols. (London, 1770). The passage that Walker here cites (with some changes in punctuation) can be found on 1:115-16.]

† The book of Job is reckoned one of the most ancient by canonists. [Editor's note: Job 4:15 actually reads in the Authorized Version: "Then a spirit passed before my face; / The hair of my flesh stood up." The tendency among recent scholars is to put the book of Job not earlier than the fifth century BC; internal evidence suggests that it dates from the fourth century BC].

"The Old Testament," answered the Doctor, "contains only the civil code of the Jews, holding up to them a deity who held sin in so much abhorrence, that its effects were entailed to the fourth generation. The sublime doctrines of Christianity were reserved for a greater than Moses to promulgate; though it was evident the Jews, as well as other nations, believed the immortality of the soul."

"Why," said Frederick, "could you ever doubt, when you seem so capable of removing the doubts of others?"

"Because," answered Doctor Alogos, "the human mind is charmed with novelty, and loses solid reason in the glare of plausible Hypothesis. It requires reflection to perceive that the philosophers of the present day are supremely ignorant, and to cover which, they pretend to deny and discredit every relic of antiquity, by which they would plunge the world again into ignorance. What are the dead languages is a common cry—they teach us nothing—we should be studying man: but, how pray are we to study man; —man, who is a creature of experience, when we destroy the experience of ages? I have actually heard a public character,[189] a man of the literary world maintain, that all the classics were mere forgeries of the fifth century, and that he did not believe there ever existed such persons as Homer, Demosthenes, &c."

The face of the sky by degrees became serene, and the vagabonds bent their course by the altitude of the sun. Stupeo supported his principles with more vehemence than ever, and ridiculing his late trepidation, he asserted that it was a mere accidental impulsion of the animal œconomy, arising from the action of the air in its perturbed state, and had nothing in common with his rational faculties, and the grand principles of truth and reason, and universal man.

Frederick resolved in silence the words of Doctor Alogos— he shuddered at the remembrance of his former actions, and would have openly derelicted from his professions, had he not been ashamed of the reproaches of Stupeo, who perpetually declaimed against that imbecility of mind, which, having once felt the force of reason, and the grand light of truth, returned again to superstition and ignorance.

To these taunts Doctor Alogos steadily replied, *that, to say he had changed his opinion, was only to say he was wiser to day than he was yesterday.*

CHAPTER IX.

STUPEO QUITS THE WORLD IN A BLAZING IDEA— AN UNEXPECTED MEETING, AND THE CONCLUSION OF WHAT IS NOT CONCLUDED.

During many days, these philosophers wandered in the woods, till their ammunition was expended, and their spirits exhausted.—They had no means of making a fire, and had for some time devoured all their game raw, to the no small prejudice of a state of nature—for even Stupeo himself allowed, that the idea of provisions dressed, was better than the idea of them raw.—Their bodies were worn out with fatigue and want: and they were so miserable, as to desire death as a relief.

For three days they tasted nothing but water, and a few berries which grew wild.—Their cloaths were partly worn from their backs, and the remnants were animated with living multitudes:— a severe fever burnt in the veins of Frederick, and but for the steady encouragement of the Doctor, he would have sunk by the way:— their beards were grown to a philosophical length, and take them all in all, they appeared truly the vagabond children of nature.

In this forlorn condition, Stupeo uttered curses with volubility, arraigning the conduct of Providence, if such there really were.

Doctor Alogos endeavoured to inspire him with patience, observing, that Providence was not to blame, as themselves had wilfully plunged into the wilderness in search of an *ignus fatuus*. [190]

When they were all nearly at the last exertion, they were overtaken by a tribe of Indians returning from an expedition against another tribe; and as they could make no defence, they became prisoners without a struggle. These men of nature having fed them with a paste of pounded Indian corn, tied their hands behind them, and, notwithstanding they were every moment at the point of fainting, urged them forward in a rapid march— poor Mungo fell down and expired, with the over-exertion; but his fate did not move with *false pity*, the callous bosoms of these children of nature.

Stupeo was almost distracted at his condition, though he obstinately insisted, that pity was a false feeling of weakness in the human heart. Frederick now remembered, that Rousseau had said, "That *pity* was a natural sentiment, which moderates in each individual the activity of self-love, concurring to the mutual preservation of all the species."[191] So wonderfully do great philosophers contradict each other in the grand affair of immutable truth.

On the following day they reached a little Indian village.—On setting up the war-hoop, a number of women and children came out to meet them, with screams and yells, surpassing in variety and sublimity of tone, a chorus of an hundred cats howling by moonlight.

"This is the music of a natural ear," said the Doctor—but Stupeo was too much absorbed in his execrations, to reply. These great men were confined in a little hut, and had a plentiful repast of bruised Indian wheat and water.—"After all," said Stupeo, "these savages are better than men in civilized life: this hut or prison is wholesome and clean, we are not confined in a loathsome dungeon—the light of nature is always pure, and the actions of simple men cannot fail to be just. We only become monsters when we condemn each other to eternal flames for a bug-bear, or drag each other to stakes for the sake of religion. I am more than ever a sceptic: all existence is to my eyes a farce, a folly, an idea. Pain, pleasure, life, death, every thing is an idea, or Hume must be wrong."

While he thus spoke to his silent companions, an hideous howl and continued roar of joy advanced towards them. It was night, and the Indians drew near, dancing in rude figures, with torches of pitch-pine, blazing in the air.

"These are very singular ideas," said the Doctor; "if your ideas and my perceptions are alike, we shall have a comfortable idea of roasting."

"I maintain," said Stupeo:—the door of the hut at that instant was opened, and several black children of reason dragged out the miserable philosopher, and bore him triumphantly to a green, in the centre of the village. There they fastened him to a stake, and sticking his body full of pine-knots, set fire to the whole, which consumed the miserable wretch with the most agonizing tortures, while the sons of nature danced around him, mocking his cries, and encouraging their children to dart at him little pointed arrows.*

Such was the termination of that enlightened great man, who, while he lived, endeavoured to kindle the world, and set society in a flame, but expired himself in the midst of a blaze.

"Alas!" cried Frederick, in extreme agitation, "What is man? A being influenced by cruelty and rapine:—he is worse than the savage hyena of the desert, or the untamed tyger of the burning sands. I see with bitter conviction, that coercion and laws are necessary to restrain the arm of destruction and violence: in the imperfect nature of all terrene existences, no law can be made to deter the wicked, without being a restraint, or in some instances a grievance, to some who are innocent. I see that society, with all its drawbacks, possesses the greatest portion of real happiness; and that half our miseries we bring on ourselves, by endeavouring to raise human nature superior to itself."

"I am afraid," said the Doctor, "it will be our turn next. These wretches are ignorant of the *laws of nations*; and they have not sufficient *religion* to teach them the duties of man to man."

Thus these two vagabonds, turn-coats, unworthy the great name, or glorious martyrdom of the immortal Stupeo, who perished in the heat of his own ideas, bewailed the accident of a gentle roasting.—But the Indians had no sooner perfectly reduced the great philosopher, metaphysician, and politician to the idea of a few cinders, than they advanced to the cottage, and dragged out the two prisoners to renew their pastime.

As they approached the stakes, they were buffetted on every

---

* Note from Playfair's History of Jacobinism, page 496. "Amongst these prisoners (*i.e.* 200 whom the new philosophers murdered at the grand Chatelet) was a woman who formerly sold flowers, and who in a fit of jealousy, had mutilated her lover, one of the French guards, in a very barbarous and shameful manner. She had been condemned, but obtained a respite for some time.—The rage of the murderers was redoubled on seeing the woman who had thus murdered one of their companions:— she was tied to a stake, her feet nailed to the ground, her breasts cut off with a sabre, and then tortured with lighted torches and pointed instruments, in a more cruel and brutal manner than it would be fit to describe." The learned may infer that savages are much alike, all over the world. [Editor's note: Walker's footnote reprints most of a footnote in Playfair's *History of Jacobinism* (2:496–97 n.), but he adds the bracketed text, and truncates Playfair's last sentence, which continues: "or than any of the North American Indians treat their prisoners" (2:497 n.).]

side by severe blows from the delicate fists of the ladies, who, out of spite at the fair skin of the dirty, lousy Frederick, bit and pinched him with a very agreeable and sportive air.—Indeed, if one might judge by their cries, they were even more delighted than the tender European ladies who crowd to see some poor wretches extended on a gibbet, or run screaming to contemplate an house in flames; or, than the fair daughters of France, who danced the Carmagnole round the guillotine.[192]

While they were tying these victims to the stake, and dancing round with their blazing torches, the report of a gun struck them with consternation, and a loud yell bespoke their despair:—a second fire which sent a bullet whistling amongst them, urged them to flight, and our heroes remained exposed to whatever might ensue—a large fire gleamed on one side of them, by the light of which they perceived several persons advancing, dressed in frocks, like American hunters.

They drew near with their rifles in their hands, and seemed to start with astonishment when they saw two white men naked, and covered with dirt.—"Whoever are you?" said Frederick, in a doleful voice, "have *pity* upon our situation, and release us before these monsters return."

"Who are you?" said one of the strangers, whose hat was adorned with a feather—"Surely, I am no stranger to your voice."

"My name is Frederick Fenton."

"Frederick Fenton!" exclaimed the stranger: "O! eternal Providence, what mysteries involve us finite beings?—Hast thou brought into the wilderness of America the man I had most reason to abhor, and made me the instrument of his preservation.—Me, whom he so cruelly injured in the person of my Amelia?"

"What," cried Frederick, "are you Vernon? Point your rifle at me, and finish at once the days of a miscreant."

"No," replied Vernon: "it is not for me to wrest vengeance to myself; but how are you in this situation? *Gratitude* to your father makes me almost rejoice that I have saved his son."

"Gratitude," sighed Frederick.—"Ah, Vernon! had I but felt it more early; had I listened to the common claims of nature and society, I might have been a worthy member.[193]—But the new sophisticated jargon of philosophy and impracticable liberty, had rendered me insane. I have, however, been the pupil of experience,[194] and have seen the ashes of Stupeo scattered by the wind."

"I will return to society," said Vernon: "it was the loss of a woman which embittered it to me, and drove me a forlorn wanderer in these woods; where I have fortunately found another to supply her loss, and lead me again into the world.—I fancy, Frederick, she is not unknown to you; and if I may judge right, this is Doctor Alogos, her uncle."

"Can it be," cried the enraptured man, "that my dear Laura yet lives—is it possible she has escaped from these horrid savages?"

"She now, I hope, waits us at your plantation," replied Vernon, "where I left her to search for you, in company with these my friends; though I confess with very little expectation of finding you."

"Thou art too good: O Providence!" cried Alogos, shedding tears, "what is man, that thou art mindful of him?"

"I am glad," said Frederick:—"I feel at this moment more satisfaction than I have felt for years—surely, there is something in virtue not to be described—you will be happy Vernon, with Laura—she is formed for you, and I rejoice that I did not succeed in debasing her purity. I am tired with philosophy; I detest politics; and I perceive, that, an *equality*, the most exact and perfect in respect of every moral and social obligation, springs from *inequality* itself."

"Have you heard lately from Europe?" inquired Doctor Alogos. "Yes," replied Vernon: "I have news, that in Frederick's present sentiments, will increase his satisfaction.—His mother yet lives; she recovered with much difficulty from her wound—but she mourns with her husband the deviation of their son."

"I will fly," cried Frederick—"I will cast myself at their feet, and implore them to pardon me."

In less than a month, they arrived again in Kentucky, where they found population increasing with the numerous emigrations, but unhappiness and discontent prevailed:[195] for though the grounds which were cultivated were productive, there was no channel for trade—and it signifies nothing to a farmer, that his harvest is plentiful, if he has no market to meet his commodities.

Taxes increased, and every man was obliged to learn the military exercise, and keep in check the predatory Indians.

Doctor Alogos remarked, that the people of America were equally dissatisfied with the people of England; and saw clearly, that no government would be universally approved, which was not to the exact model and interest of *every* private individual.

At Philadelphia he settled his accounts, and drew his money from the bank.—Laura gave her hand to Vernon; and Frederick could not but feel a wish, that he had some amiable maid to unite her destiny with his—and by mutual good offices, smooth the rugged road of life. He felt at that moment, that the endearing and tender smile of a modest woman, has more real pleasure than the most wanton blandishments of promiscuous intercourse.

The wind favoured their return to the land of genuine liberty, where there is not *one* man so obscure as not to possess a right, not *one* man so high, as not to be subject to the laws.

Where the noble and the peasant are upon *equality* in the *penal* code, and no man can suffer for his crimes, but with the consent of twelve of his equals,—a right unknown to every government heretofore existing—a right which checks at once the arm of power, bribery, or malice.

Doctor Alogos threw himself upon the beach, while tears of pleasure gushed from his eyes.—"Happy, happy shores," exclaimed he, "How few comparative evils do you know? Unvisited by savage war—insulated from a treacherous and rapacious foe—untainted by pestilence, and at a distance from the climes, where earthquakes and tornados in one moment swallow up, or sweep away the exertions of a century.—Thy lands are never parched with the beams of a torrid sun, or gelid with the frosts of the polar circles: thou never feelest the blaze of perpetual day, or the stillness of constant twilight.—Thy fields never fail in their produce, and half the world brings the tributes of commerce to thy shores—though the *smallest* nation on earth in local territory, thy situation and the valor of thy *genuine* children, render thee impregnable.—Nor is there a spot upon the universal globe, so favoured by Nature, and so blessed by Heaven.

May then thy fair face never be blasted by the insidious attacks of self-interested and ignorant *empirics*;[196] may the mania of impracticable political dreams be dispersed by the surges of thy rocky shores; and may thy fair daughters know, that modesty and maternal feelings are the chief ornaments of a celestial mind. Experience has qualified me to judge of learning, whose researches have taught me the paucity of the human mind; taught me, that in this age of reason, in the eighteenth century, I may exclaim with the learned and polished Socrates—"*'All that I know is, that I know nothing.'"*[197]

THE END

Notes

1   *Bishop of Landaff*] Richard Watson (1737-1816), professor of chemistry, later divinity, at Cambridge, before becoming Bishop of Llandaff (1782-1816). Initially a Whig in politics and a liberal in thought, Watson was an inspiration for many Romantic radicals; upon becoming Bishop, however, he developed a more orthodox view on religious and political matters, and was subsequently vilified by reformers, including Samuel Coleridge. His *Apology for the Bible* (1796), an attack on Thomas Paine, went through many editions.

2   *Plutarch*] Greek biographer (c. 46–c. 120). The citation occurs in *Quaestiones Convivales* 719b10, and reads more accurately, τὸ δίκαιον ἴσον, ἀλλὰ μὴ τὸ ἴσον δεῖν ποιεῖσθαι δίκαιον, or, "you must consider whatever is just, equal, but not whatever is equal, just."

3   *The Pursuits of Literature*] An anti-Jacobin verse satire (1794-97) by the satirist Thomas James Mathias (?1754-1835), in which the author unleashes vicious attacks on writers of Whig, liberal or radical persuasion, including the radical philosopher William Godwin and the novelist Matthew Lewis. Walker's motto is a condensed citation from the "Introductory Letter to a Friend, on the general Subject of the following Poem on the Pursuits of Literature," which was first prefixed to the fifth edition of the text (published in January 1798). The full text reads: "The wayward nature of the time, and the paramount necessity of securing to this kingdom her political and religious existence, and the rights of society, have urged and stimulated me, as you well know, to offer *this endeavour* to preserve them, by a solemn, laborious, and disinterested appeal to my countrymen" (*The Pursuits of Literature: A Satirical Poem in Four Dialogues*, 10th ed. [London, 1799], 5).

4   *late Lord Orford … to be true*] Horace Walpole, 4th Earl of Orford (1717-97), author, prolific letter-writer, antiquarian and politician. Chiefly celebrated as the author of *The Castle of Otranto* (1764), the first Gothic novel published in England. Walpole is known to have made observations on the relative nature of history and romance similar to the one here alluded to by Walker on various occasions in his life; one version occurs in Walpole's letter to Dr. Henry of 15 March 1783, in which he claims that "History in general is a Romance that is believed, and … Romance is a History that is not believed" (Edwine M. Martz *et al.*, eds., *Horace Walpole's Correspondence*, Vol. 15, ed. W.S. Lewis [New Haven: Yale University Press, 1951], 173; see also 173, n. 28).

5   *Mr. Godwin's Political Justice, 4to. Edition*] The quarto edition of *Enquiry Concerning Political Justice* by William Godwin (1756-1836) was the first edition, which appeared in 1793 in two volumes. The second and third editions, which appeared in 1796 and 1798 respectively (both in octavo), made substantial changes to the text of the first edition. Unless indicated otherwise, references to Godwin's *Enquiry Concerning Political Justice* in all editorial matter in this edition are to the first (1793) edition, edited by Mark Philp (see Select Bibliography).

6   *the doctrines of Godwin, Hume, Rousseau*] For general remarks on the doctrines of William Godwin, David Hume (1711-76) and Jean-Jacques Rousseau (1712-78), see the Introduction; for extracts from their writings, see Appendix A.

7   *Mr. Pain*] Thomas Paine (1737-1809), British pamphleteer and political radical, who in *The Rights of Man, Part I* (1791), remarks, "we may fairly conclude that though it has been so much talked about, no such thing as a constitution exists, or ever did exist, and consequently the people have yet a constitution to form" (93-94).

8   *Let those men … are despised*] Jean Louis de Lolme (1740-1806), Swiss jurist and constitutional writer. Forced to leave his native Geneva after publishing a critical pamphlet, De Lolme settled in England, where he studied British constitutional law, the result of which he published in his *Constitution de l'Angleterre* (Amsterdam, 1771). Comparing English constitutional law favorably with the constitutions of other countries, De Lolme's book excited much interest and was republished in English many times, as well as appearing in translations throughout Europe.

9   *Mr. Playfair*] William Playfair (1759-1823), one of Britain's most outspoken anti-Jacobin writers. The citation is from Playfair's influential *History of Jacobinism, Its Crimes, Cruelties, and Perfidies, from the Commencement of the French Revolution, to the Death of Robespierre…*, 2 vols. (London: 1795), 1:108-9. Walker's cites Playfair's text almost verbatim (Playfair has "he produced none" for "it produced none" and "in his place" for "in the place"). However, the concluding rhetorical question ("Let the rich ask … those who do not?") is not in Playfair's text and was added by Walker. Playfair's remark about the success of the radical press is in reference to a popular pamphlet by the Paris deputy to the States General, the Abbé Seyeyes. "What is the Third State?," which Playfair regards as containing "the foundation of the whole Jacobin creed" (104), was lavishly sponsored by the Duke of Orléans. Playfair estimates that more than five hundred thousand copies of the pamphlet were circulated.

10 *Circulating Libraries … Rights of Man*] From the mid-eighteenth century onward, the proliferation of commercial circulating libraries had given many who could not afford to buy books access to a wide variety of writings, in particular novels. Though the bulk of the population was still excluded from reading, circulating libraries certainly had a democratizing impact on readership, the distribution of knowledge, and public debate. The reference to Paine's *Rights of Man* is probably to the author's campaign in the summer of 1792 to spread his radical ideas among as many people as possible and as quickly as possible by publishing cheap, six-penny, nonprofit editions "for the benefit and information of the POOR" (qtd. in Keane, *Tom Paine*, 342). Thus, the passage from Playfair's *History of Jacobinism* Walker cites above is footnoted by a reference to the astonishing popular success of Tom Paine's *Rights of Man*.

11 *Two Editions … six months*] See, however, A Note on the Text.

12 *But if they … dispute about*] Playfair, *History of Jacobinism*, 1:271.

13 *Volunteers*] In 1794 the Pitt government founded a volunteer force, ostensibly to create a body of able men with rudimentary military training, who might eventually form a kind of armed national reserve. In reality, however, the volunteer force was an integral part of the government's campaign to break up Whig opposition against the war with France, build an effective conservative coalition, and harrass reformists by violent attacks and hate campaigns. The loyalist Volunteer corps was thus a crucial weapon in the government's efforts to prevent the Jacobins from establishing a bridgehead in Britain in advance of what they feared was an inevitable French invasion.

14 *Barrere*] Bertrand Barère de Vieuzac (1755-1841), French lawyer, politician, journalist and orator, and one of the most notorious members of the French National Convention. Unscrupulous, devoid of a conscience, and without any guiding principle other than self-interest and influence, Barère was a member of the States General for the constitutional party before joining the republican party when it became clear that it would be victorious in its dispute with the king. A prominent member of the infamous Committee of Public Safety (the de facto government of Jacobin France between 1793 and 1795), Barère became deeply involved in France's foreign affairs, as well as in the Reign of Terror, during which the radical Jacobin party eliminated its political enemies in a ruthless and bloody campaign. The reference to London as

a "selfish and shop-keeping city" has not been identified, but is certainly typical of Barère's style of oratory, known for its telling phrases and memorable witticisms.

15   *All property ... your pocket*] Walker is ridiculing Godwin's principles of the "greater good" (see Appendix A.6.i) and the "monopoly of property" (see Appendix A.6.ii).

16   *John Doe and Richard Roe*] Names used to indicate a party to legal proceedings whose true name is unknown. In his *Political Justice* Godwin argued that an assassin "is propelled to act by necessary causes and irresistible motives.... The assassin cannot help the murder he commits, any more than the dagger" (368, 369).

17   *reform of the individual*] Cf. Godwin's assertion in *Political Justice* that "punishment, unless for reform, is peculiarly absurd" (369).

18   *William the Third*] William of Orange (1650-1702), replaced his son-in-law James II in 1688, and during the "Glorious Revolution" that followed introduced constitutional changes that established parliamentary monarchy in Britain. See Introduction for the significance of the Glorious Revolution for Walker's novel.

19   *Go ... to your parish ... poor's rates*] The poor-rate was a rate or assessment, for the relief or support of the poor. In Britain, parish districts—at first identical with an original parish, but later often having quite different limits—were constituted for various purposes of civil government. Thus, parishes were designated for the administration of the Poor-law, and were for that reason sometimes distinguished as "poor-law parishes," legally defined as places "for which a separate poor-rate is or can be made, or for which a separate overseer is or can be appointed." Hence the phrase "kept by the parish" meant "in receipt of parochial relief"; similarly, "on the parish," "to be brought up by the parish," "buried by the parish" and so on (*OED*).

20   *immortal truth*] Stupeo is a satirical portrait of William Godwin, whose ideas he generally reflects in the novel—though he also propagates the philosophies and doctrines of Hume, Rousseau and Priestley. Here he echoes Godwin's adage, "Truth is omnipotent" (*Political Justice*, 3rd ed. [1798], 140).

21   *starting*] "That starts, in various senses of the verb: leaping, bounding, hence full of energy; making sudden movements; suffering displacement or disintegration, etc." (*OED*).

22   *Voltaire*] Pseudonym of François Marie Arouet (1694-1778), French satirist, philosopher, historian, dramatist and poet. A formidable Enlightenment thinker, Voltaire notoriously aimed his merciless satire and ruthless critical analysis at organized religion, social injustice, intolerance and superstition, causing him to be the scourge of political and religious authorities of his time.

23   *War ... fight about*] These views on war are expressed in Paine's *Rights of Man, Part I*, "Conclusion," 167-68.

24   *Aristotle*] Renowned Greek philosopher (384-322 BC); *Grotius*] Latinized form of Hugo de Groot (1583-1645), Dutch jurist and statesman, founder of the science of international law; *Puffendorf*] Samuel Pufendorf (1632-94), German jurist and historian, best known for his defense of the concept of natural law, *On the Law of Nature and Nations* (1672), and widely read in the eighteenth century; *Locke*] John Locke (1632-1704), influential English empiricist philosopher, whose *An Essay Concerning Human Understanding* (1690) and *Two Treatises on Government* (1690) were among the founding texts of Enlightenment thought.

25   *I send word to a merchant*] Walker lifts the example of meeting a merchant at the 'Change, or Royal Exchange, from Godwin's *Political Justice* (90). The Royal Exchange was not a stock exchange but the place (on the Thames, opposite the Bank of England) where London merchants transacted their business.

26   *But it may only exist in your idea*] Walker is here ridiculing the philosophical skepticism of Hume, who restricted knowledge to the experience of ideas or impressions,

maintaining that the mind consists only of accumulated perceptions. Hume described his own *Treatise on Human Nature* (1739) as "very skeptical," observing, "Almost all reasoning is there reduced to experience; and the belief, which attends experience, is explained to be nothing but a peculiar sentiment, or lively conception produced by habit" (see Appendix A.1).

27   *That must be ... Westminster Hall*] That is, if one did not keep one's "philanthropy"—or marital infidelity, as Walker would see it—a secret, one might find oneself entangled in a divorce suit. A divorce was a long and costly affair mainly because obtaining a divorce required an Act of Parliament (hence the reference to Westminster Hall, the home of the British Parliament). Moreover, the damages awarded in divorce cases involving adultery (or "criminal conduct," as it was called) were often so much beyond the defendant's means that the verdict was tantamount to a sentence to life imprisonment for debt.

28   *Your existence will terminate ... in like manner*] The reference here is to the doctrine of philosophical materialism, as propagated by Joseph Priestley and many others (including several French *philosophes*). Materialists believed that man exists solely in Nature, and is "mechanically" submitted to the laws of nature, from which he will never be able to extract himself. Hence materialists deny the mind and the soul an immaterial existence independent of the body (though granting it may be "concealed"). Or, as Priestley puts it, "man is wholly material," and hence "the human mind is nothing more than a modification of [man's material existence]" and "no man has a soul distinct from his body" (see the extract from Priestley's *Disquisitions Relating to Matter and Spirit* in Appendix A.3).

29   *necessity*] Philosophical necessity is another doctrine central to the "new philosophy"; in fact, the doctrine of necessity is a direct inference from the doctrine of materialism. Necessitarianism starts from the premise that all human action is determined, or necessitated, by a physical reality outside of man—Nature—which is itself governed by "laws of nature" that are "necessary" and "constant." The most fundamental of these laws is the law of cause and effect. Necessitarians like Priestley argued that there could be no effect without a cause, and that the same cause would always have the same effect. Every aspect of man's physical *and* mental existence was subject to this fundamental principle. Not surprisingly, this had far-reaching consequences for man's volition or free will. According to Necessitarians, man had no "philosophical liberty" and hence no absolute free will—everything, even man's mind and motives, being the result of an infinite string of causes and effects and thus far beyond man's control. However, this did not mean that man had no *practical* autonomy over his actions; unlike under Calvinist predestination, Necessitarianism allowed for the possibility of changing man's motives, and therefore the choices he made in everyday life, by changing man's social conditions. This is ultimately why the doctrine appealed to so many reformists at the time. First fully formulated by the British physician and theologian David Hartley (1705-57) in his *Observations on Man* (1749), Necessitarianism was disseminated by Joseph Priestley, with poets like Samuel Coleridge (1772-1834) and William Wordsworth (1770-1850) among his early converts.

30   *like the children ... in the mud*] In Greek mythology, Deucalion, son of Prometheus and Clymene, was the king of Phthia, in Thessaly. When Zeus sent a deluge, Deucalion built a ship, and he and his wife, Pyrrha, were the only mortals to survive. According to one version, he and his wife landed on Mount Parnassus. Inquiring how to renew the human race, they were ordered to cast behind them the bones of their mother. The couple correctly interpreted this to mean they should throw behind them the stones of the hillside. Those stones thrown by Deucalion became men; those thrown by Pyrrha became women. Also in Greek mythology, Cadmus was a son of Agenor and

Telephassa. He founded the city of Thebes in Boeotia. Killing the dragon that guarded the sacred spring of Ares at Thebes, Cadmus sowed its teeth, and from the ground where they fell armed men sprang up, called "Sparti" in Greek, or "sown men."

31   *first cause*] The original cause or Creator of the Universe (*OED*).

32   *like so many dragons guarding the Hesperian fruit*] In Greek mythology, three sisters guarded the golden apples that the goddess Hera had received as a marriage gift. They were assisted by the dragon Ladon. The place where the golden apples grew is often referred to as the garden of Hesperides.

33   *Rights of Man*] A political treatise by Thomas Paine (published in two parts, in 1791 and 1792), in which he argues that a man's "civil rights" (such as the right to protection against violence) should never make inroads on or replace his "natural rights" (such as the right to liberty), that civil government can only exist through a "contract" with the majority of the people, and that all of this should be contained in a written constitution. See Introduction and Appendix A.4.

34   *the old times of chivalry*] The concept of chivalry—which comprised such values as "honor," "reputation" and "duty"—was regarded by many reformers as belonging to a superseded, "aristocratic" moral economy governed by "self-love," paternalism, and a fundamentally unequal distribution of power in society (see, for instance, Godwin, *Political Justice*, Book IV, Chap. viii, "Of the Principle of Virtue").

35   *gratitude*] Cf. Godwin's provocative claim, "Gratitude   , a principle which has so often been the theme of the moralist and the poet, is no part either of justice or virtue" (*Political Justice*, Book II, Chap. ii, 51; see Appendix A.6.i).

36   *placemen*] A placeman is someone who holds an appointment in the service of the sovereign or the state from motives of interest, without regard to fitness (*OED*); a political appointee to a public office.

37   *Persian plenipotence*] A generic phrase denoting eastern despotism.

38   *Morality ... priestcraft*] Cf. Godwin's assertion that "Morality is that system of conduct which is determined by a consideration of the greatest general good: he is entitled to the highest moral approbation whose conduct is, in the greatest number of instances, governed by views of benevolence, and made subservient to public utility.... The foundation of morality is justice" (*Political Justice: Variants*, Book II, Chap. i, 60; Book III, Chap. iii, 91).

39   *the great book of Nature*] A reference to the idea that all that is useful or important for man to know, is contained in God's creation—as revealed in Nature—from which it can be gleaned, or read, by man using the faculties of reason and understanding. An advocate of revealed religion, as opposed to natural religion (see Introduction), Walker is critical of the idea that mankind could ever discover the will of God by studying His creation.

40   *swinish multitude*] A phrase used by Edmund Burke (1729-97), Irish-born English statesman and author, known for his orations in the House of Commons and his writings on politics and society, notably his treatise *Reflections on the Revolution in France* (1790), in which he attacks the leaders and principles of the French Revolution. His remark in the *Reflections* that "Along with its natural protectors and guardians, learning will be cast into the mire and trodden down under the hoofs of a swinish multitude" was often misconstrued to mean that he actually thought the people to be no better than swine (78).

41   *To one half . . . means of detection*] This quotation has not been identified.

42   *John the painter*] a painter by profession (hence his alias), James Hill—also known as James Hinde (or Hind), James Actzen and James (also John) Aitken—was tried and sentenced to death in March 1777 for having set fire to the rope-house in his majesty's

dock-yard at Portsmouth in December of the year before. The case attracted much attention at the time, with the prosecution successfully persuading the jury that Hill had acted on direct orders from the American Continental Congress, and that his crime was in fact an act of sabotage aimed at crippling Great Britain's navy deploy-ability during the first months of the armed struggle between the British and the Americans. However, accounts from the trial suggest that the British authorities used the incident as part of the diplomatic warfare between Britain and the rebellious colony, and that John the Painter was but an innocent pawn in this game. The anti-American bias associated with the trial of James Hill became relevant again in the 1790s' Revolutionary Debate, and it is therefore no coincidence that in a novel intended to disparage emigration to America, Walker should have Frederick fancy himself "as great as the immortal John the Painter" (see page 113); *Massanielo*] an abbreviation of Tommaso Aniello (1622-47), an Amalfi fisherman who became leader of the popular revolt against Spanish rule and fiscal oppression in Naples in 1647, and whose eventful life and violent death subsequently became the subject of several poems and operas; *Alexander*] Alexander III of Macedon, or Alexander the Great (356-323 BC), famous Greek statesman and military leader, son of Philip of Macedon. He was appointed to his father's position as leader of the Greek confederation and, having done away with his rivals to the throne, began the invasion and conquest of Asia. He defeated Darius III, King of Persia, and marched through Syria, Egypt, Babylon, Susa and Persepolis. On their way through India, his exhausted troops rebelled, and Alexander was forced to begin his retreat to Macedon. However, he fell ill of a fever and died shortly afterwards, aged thirty-three.

43   *I am speaking as if I was in Rome*] An allusion to a strategy adopted by the radical polit-ical orator John Thelwall (1764-1834), who, after the "Gagging Acts" of 1795 had outlawed political lecturing, continued his lecturing activities under the guise of talks on Roman history, particularly on the abuses of monarchy and aristocracy in ancient Rome (for more information on Thelwall, see Introduction). In the course of 1793 Thelwall grew increasingly paranoid over government spies infiltrating and disrupt-ing meetings he addressed, but not without good reason. Eager to arrest Thelwall for sedition, the authorities had begun to shadow his movements and had informers in every hall he spoke. Gangs of loyalist thugs followed him through the streets, and mobs armed with bludgeons, often accompanied by police officers, were always ready to start riots—only to have a pretext to disrupt meetings.

44   *philippic*] Tirade.

45   *Citizen Ego*] A satirical reference to John Thelwall. Arthur Young once described Thelwall as "one of the boldest political writers, speakers, and lecturers of his time" (*The Example of France A Warning to Britain* [London, 1793]), and it was his immense popular appeal among reformists, who often came to his lectures more for the man himself than for the content of his radical message, that made anti-Jacobins like Walker represent Thelwall as a vain and conceited megalomaniac. Thus, Thelwall appears in Isaac Disraeli's anti-Jacobin novel *Vaurien; or, Sketches of the Times* (London, 1797) as "Mr. Rant," orator to the masses. *Aldermon Cromwell*] a reference to Oliver Cromwell (1599-1658), English Puritan leader who, as commander of a famous cavalry regiment called the Ironsides, contributed significantly to the ultimate victory of the Parliamentary party against the Royalists during the second phase of the English Civil War (1648-52).

46   *ninny-hammer*] A simpleton (*OED*).

47   *the stocks*] "An obsolete instrument of punishment, consisting of two planks set edge-wise one over the other (usually framed between posts), the upper plank being capable

of sliding up and down. The person to be punished was placed in a sitting posture with his ankles confined between the two planks, the edges of which were furnished with holes to receive them. Sometimes there were added similar contrivances for securing the wrists" (*OED*).

48   *Citizen Pepper ... scald your fingers*] This sentence is in the first (and "second") but not in the third edition of the novel.

49   *counterscarp*] In a fortification, the outer wall or slope of the ditch, which supports the covered way; sometimes extended to include the covered way and glacis (*OED*).

50   *the rioters in St. George's Field*] A reference to the Gordon Riots (see Introduction). St. George's Fields was an undrained tract of land between Westminster Bridge and Blackfriars Bridge in London, on the Surrey side of the Thames. On 2 June 1780, more than 60,000 people assembled in the Fields to attend a meeting convened by the Protestant Association in protest against the partial emancipation of Roman Catholics. After a speech by the Association's President, Lord George Gordon, the huge crowd spilled back into London, where rioting broke out almost immediately. The "Gordon Riots" would last for over a week, causing more damage to property in London than the French Revolution did in Paris.

51   *the glorious dawn ... America*] An allusion to the American War of Independence, which had begun in 1775 and was only to be formally concluded with the Peace of Paris in 1783—three years after the Gordon Riots.

52   *Hudson's Bay factory*] that is, the Hudson's Bay Company, a joint stock company chartered in 1670 by Charles II for the purpose of buying furs from the Indians. At the end of the eighteenth century, the Hudson's Bay Territory covered much of what is now Canada. *Newfoundland fishery*] a reference to the rich fishing grounds off the island of Newfoundland, contested for that reason by various European seafaring nations since the seventeenth century.

53   *Johnson's Dictionary*] Samuel Johnson (1709-84), English lexicographer, essayist, poet and moralist. His monumental *Dictionary of the English Language* (1755), though faulty and quirky, made his reputation and was the standard dictionary of English during the eighteenth century.

54   *Rollin*] Charles Rollin (1661-1741), French historian and educationist, and author of *Histoire ancienne des Egyptiens, des Carthaginois, des Assyriens, des Babyloniens, des Mèdes, et des Perses, des Macédoniens, des Grecs*, 13 vols. (Paris, 1730-38).

55   *draymen*] A man who drives a dray, a low cart without sides used for carrying heavy loads.

56   *I employ a workman ... go without*] Walker is parodying Godwin's concept of justice as expressed in *Political Justice*, Book II, Chap. ii ("Of Justice"), 53.

57   *The fashionable Hume ... existed*] An allusion to Hume, *Treatise of Human Nature*, Book I ("Of the Understanding"), Sections vi ("Of Personal Identity") and vii (conclusion to Book I). Walker may have been thinking in particular of the episode toward the end of Section vii in which Hume finds he has reasoned himself into such a state of "philosophical melancholy and delirium" that he doubts his very existence: "Where am I, or what? From what causes do I derive my existence, and to what condition shall I return? Whose favour shall I court, and whose anger must I dread? What beings surround me? and on whom have I any influence, or who have any influence on me? I am confounded with all these questions, and begin to fancy myself in the most deplorable condition imaginable, inviron'd with the deepest darkness, and utterly depriv'd of the use of every member and faculty" (269).

58   *Cogitas ergo sum*] That is, *Cogito ergo sum* (I think, therefore I am), famous observation by René Descartes (1596-1650), French philosopher and mathematician (*Le Discours de la Méthode* [1637], Part IV). Descartes' skepticist philosophy begins with universal doubt.

But there is one thing that cannot be doubted: doubt itself. The very attempt to doubt one's own existence is self-defeating, since any such effort *is* an occurrence of thought; in turn, the occurrence of thought requires a thinker—to think, therefore, is to exist.

59 *Berkely*] George Berkeley (1685-1753), Irish-born English bishop and philosopher. One of the most influential thinkers of the philosophic school of idealism, Berkeley developed his "immaterialist hypothesis," denying the existence of matter. Positing that to be is to be perceived (*esse est percepi*), Berkeley maintained that material objects are only ideas in our minds.

60 *No Popery*] Popular slogan used by protestant protesters against the partial emancipation of Roman Catholics following the Relief Act of 1778. See the Introduction for an account of the background of the anti-Catholic protests and their culmination in the Gordon Riots of June 1780 (the historical basis for the riot is described in this and the following chapter).

61 *gammon*] humbug (*OED*); *grub*] food (*OED*).

62 *the pugilistic science of Athens and Sparta*] Pugilism or boxing was held in high esteem by the Greeks and the Romans alike. Although fist-fighting was supposed by the Greeks of the classic period to have been a feature of the mythological games at Olympia, it was not actually introduced into the historical Olympic contests until the 23rd Olympiad after the re-establishment of the famous games by Iphitus (about 880 BC).

63 *Whoever has read ... boxing*] An allusion to Thomas Holcroft (1745-1809), English man of many trades (including shoemaker and strolling player) before becoming a professional playwright, actor (at Drury Lane Theatre), novelist, translator and journalist. A prominent Jacobin radical, Holcroft was indicted for treason during the notorious Treason Trials of 1794, but was later released without charge (see Introduction). See also Walker's footnote on p. 106-7.

64 *a large cockade of blue ribbon*] An allusion to the Protestant Association meeting in St. George's Fields in June 1780, the overture to the Gordon Riots (see note 50), when each person was provided with a blue cockade, knot or rosette for hat decoration.

65 *Lord George Gordon*] After a brief career in the Navy, Gordon (1751-93) entered the House of Commons in 1774, aged twenty-three. A volatile and resolute politician, Gordon was president of the Protestant Association, a London-based organization campaigning for the repeal of pro-Catholic legislation in England. See note 50 above and the Introduction for more details.

66 *Newgate*] Notorious London prison, scene of many bloody executions. The newly rebuilt prison was ransacked and burnt to the ground by the rioters on 6 June 1780, releasing all the inmates. *Snow-hill*] street near Newgate Prison where several residences were attacked.

67 *Lycurgus*] Legendary legislator of Sparta (ancient capital of Laconia), about whom nothing certain is known, not even when he lived. He is said to be the founder of the Spartan constitution and the social and military systems, and so of the eunomia, "good order," the name generally applied to these.

68 *pallisadoes*] That is, palisado or palisade, a fence made of pales or stakes fixed in the ground, forming an enclosure or defence. Here, one of those stakes (made of iron).

69 *press-yard*] "Name of a yard or court of old Newgate Prison, in which the torture of *peine forte et dure* is supposed to have originally been carried out; and from which, at a later period, capitally convicted prisoners started for the place of execution." *Peine forte et dure* ("severe and hard punishment") was a form of punishment, formerly inflicted on persons arraigned for felony who refused to plead, in which the prisoner's body was pressed with heavy weights until he pleaded or died (*OED*).

70   *Langdale's … in Holborn*] A reference to Thomas Langdale & Co., a large distillers in Holborn (see note 80, below).

71   *Clerkenwell*] Clerkenwell Bridewell prison, which was attacked by the rioters after they had sacked Newgate earlier that day (6 June). Bridewell was spared but the inmates were released after the rioters had hacked their way in through the gates. The keepers at New Prison, adjacent to Bridewell, saved their building by opening the doors to the mob, after which the inmates were released from their cells and spilled out into the street.

72   *Lord Mansfield*] William Murray (1705-93), English judge and politician. For over thirty years Lord Chief Justice of the King's Bench (the principal common law court in England), Lord Mansfield was the preeminent judge of his day, widely respected for his legal knowledge and liberal ideas (which included a ruling in 1772 emancipating slaves on British soil). It was his support for Catholic relief that inspired the angry Protestant mob to attack and burn Lord Mansfield's town residence at the north-east corner of Bloomsbury Square during the Gordon Riots on 6 June.

73   *John the Painter*] See note 42.

74   *The New-river water*] The New River Head, London's water supply at the time. During the Gordon Riots soldiers were posted at the New River Head to keep the rabble at bay.

75   *The Museum*] The British Museum, which had been opened in Montagu House in Great Russell Street, Bloomsbury, in 1759 (demolished in 1852 when the present, larger building was built on the site).

76   *East-India warehouses*] headquarters and warehouses of the East Indian Company on Leadenhall Street; *Custom-house*] situated on the north shore of the Thames. Both buildings were placed under protection by armed soldiers.

77   *The Tower*] The Tower of London, famous London prison for political prisoners on the Thames; *the Bank*] The Bank of England, which came under serious attack from the mob on 7 June—a militia in the nick of time preventing the nation's assets from being plundered.

78   *the Borough*] A reference to the London borough of Southwark, south of the Thames, site of St. George's Fields, from where the riot spread to the rest of town. The burning of the tollhouses on the bridge is an allusion to the mob's robbing and torching of the tollhouses on Blackfriars Bridge on 7 June. The half-penny toll charged to all who crossed Blackfriar's Bridge had long been a source of grievance to the populace.

79   *platoon*] "A number of shots fired simultaneously by a platoon or body of men; a volley" (*OED*).

80   *link*] A torch made of tow and pitch, formerly much in use for lighting people along the streets (*OED*).

81   *Torrents of spirits … the flames*] Walker's description is historically accurate. Langdale's had recently stock-piled enormous quantities of alcohol in its two sites to avoid the imposition of new duties. When the drunken mob set fire to the premises, columns of flames erupted from the cellars, which were visible for thirty miles around London. Dozens of rioters, too intoxicated to escape, perished in the flames. When the fire began to threaten the entire neighborhood, the rioters allowed two fire-engines to operate. Unknown to the firemen, however, the wells had by then begun to yield spirits instead of water, so that the firemen found themselves trying to extinguish the flames with jets of alcohol. For days after, water pumps in the neighborhood of Langdale's would yield pure gin.

82   *half rectified*] To rectify alcohol is to purify it by repeated distillation.

83   *Fleet Prison, King's Bench, Toll-houses on Blackfriar's bridge*] Fleet Prison and King's Bench prisons were sacked and torched by the rioters on 7 June, on the same day that Langdale's and the tollhouses on Blackfriars Bridge were burnt.

84 *the immortal Brutus*] Marcus Junius Brutus (c. 85-42 BC), Roman politician and general, who joined a plot to murder his friend and protector Caesar (100-44 BC), thinking that this would restore the ideals of the republic, which had been trampled under Caesar's dictatorship.

85 *Cybelle*] Cybele, an ancient Asian goddess identified by the Greeks with Rhea. Originally a bisexual earth goddess, Cybele was made a female by the gods. When she fell in love with Attis, who was about to marry a nymph, she drove him to madness out of jealousy. Attis ultimately castrated himself and committed suicide. Cybele became the object of a mystery cult, and was celebrated in orgiastic rites by eunuch priests.

86 *Massienello*] See note 42; *William Tell*] Wilhelm Tell, legendary national hero of Switzerland, who, according to legend, led the popular revolt against Austrian rule in the fourteenth century; *Oliver Cromwell*] see note 45; *Cato*: Marcus Porcius Cato, known as Cato the Younger (95-46 BC), Roman statesman and adversary of Caesar; *Leonidas*] a legendary Spartan king (early fifth century), who resisted a superior Persian army at Thermopylae and perished with all of his men defending the pass; *Jaffier*] not further identified; *Judas Maccabæus*] leader of the Jews (d. c. 161 BC) in their revolt against the Seleucid King of Syria, and succeeded in recovering Jerusalem, dedicating the Temple anew, and protecting Judaism from Hellenization.

87 *emetics*] Agents that induce vomiting.

88 *I read over the Essays of the fashionable Hume ... no crime at all*] The reference is to Hume's *Essays and Treatises on Several Subject* (London and Edinburgh, 1767), which had originally been published under the title *Essays, Moral and Political* (Edinburgh, 1741). However, no literal—or even approximate—parallel of what Walker is here claiming to be Hume's view on adultery occurs on page 406 of vol. 2 of the 1767 edition of the *Essays*, though Walker may have had in mind Hume's observation on page 410: "Instances of licence, daily multiplying, will weaken the scandal with the one sex, and teach the other, by degrees, to adopt the famous maxim of LA FONTAINE, with regard to female infidelity, *that if one knows it, it is but a small matter; if one knows it not, it is nothing*★'" (the note ★ reads: "Quand on le sçait, c'est peu de chose: Quand on ne le sçait pas, ce n'est rien").

89 *Is there any sex in soul ... Rights of Women*] This passage is in part loosely based on Wollstonecraft's *Vindication*, Chap. II.

90 *oviparous*] Producing eggs that that develop and hatch outside the maternal body.

91 *bashaw*] Haughty, imperious (see note 105).

92 *Bethlem Hospital*] Commonly known as Bedlam, the popular name for the Hospital of St. Mary of Bethlehem, a public London insane asylum, infamous for the cruel treatment of its inmates, and as a popular attraction for domestic tourists.

93 *they had not been inoculated*] Smallpox inoculation has long been used by physicians in Asia and Africa by deliberately attempting to give people a mild smallpox infection. The technique became known in Europe in the eighteenth century. In 1717 Lady Montague arrived with her husband, the British ambassador, at the court of the Ottoman Empire. There she noted that the local practice of deliberately stimulating a mild form of the disease through inoculation conferred immunity. She had the procedure performed on both her children. The European medical establishment accepted the practice after Dr. Edward Jenner developed a safer technique of vaccination in 1798. This used the less dangerous cowpox rather than smallpox.

94 *proving that girls ... ought to be exploded*] The ideas expressed in this paragraph are loosely based on Mary Wollstonecraft's *Vindication of the Rights of Woman*, Chap. XII ("On National Education").

95 *six-penny debating societies*] Sixpence was the usual entrance fee charged at meetings of debating clubs and corresponding societies.

96 *masked battery*] A military phrase, denoting a battery concealed from the view of the enemy.

97 *beau*] "A man who gives particular, or excessive, attention to dress, mien, and social etiquette; an exquisite, a fop, a dandy" (*OED*).

98 *Cicero*] Marcus Tullius Cicero (106-43 BC), Roman orator, statesman, and man of letters. Renowned for his rhetorical prose style, and its uncommonly persuasive qualities.

99 *as Æschines said of Demosthenes*] Aeschines (c. 397-c. 322 BC), Athenian orator and great rival of Demosthenes (c. 383-322 BC), Athenian orator and writer, much revered for his style of writing. They were both part of an embassy sent to negotiate peace terms with Philip II of Macedon, in the process of which Aeschines and Demosthenes got involved in a bitter feud, in which they attacked each other in pointed speeches. There is no direct correspondence between Walker's text and anything in Aeschines' speeches.

100 *Il retourne chez ses Egaux*] Walker is citing the caption for the frontispiece of the first edition of Jean-Jacques Rousseau's *Discours sur l'origine et les fondements de l'inégalité parmi les hommes* (Amsterdam, 1755). The text ("He returns to his own") is a paraphrase of footnote 13 in the main body of the essay. See frontispiece to the present edition.

101 *as some writer has said ... all voyages and travels*] Not identified. Walker does not have his hero set off randomly for the North-West of England, for it is in the direction of the town of Birmingham, home of Dr. Joseph Priestley (see Introduction), whom Frederick is about to meet in the character of Dr. Alogos.

102 *The proper study of mankind is man*] Alexander Pope (1688-1744), *An Essay on Man* (1733), Epistle II, l. 2. The complete couplet reads: "Know then thyself, presume not God to scan; / The proper study of mankind is Man" (ll. 1-2).

103 *enclosures ... common right*] The process by which common land was converted into enclosed fields in order to increase yields and farming efficiency. The process had been going on since medieval times, but was stepped up markedly between 1793 and 1815. Although enclosure contributed toward the increase of England's economic growth generally, and its agricultural output in particular, it benefited large farmers and landowners much more than tenant farmers. The real victims were the landless, who stood to lose their traditional access to grazing, firewood and gaming. For that reason, enclosure came under fierce attack from radicals, including John Thelwall (see, for instance, his lecture "On the causes of the present dearness and scarcity of provisions," delivered on 1 May 1795, published in *The Tribune* XVII).

104 *truth is omnipotent*] This ultimate tribute to truth's unlimited potential occurs verbatim in Godwin, *Political Justice*, 3rd ed. (1798), 140.

105 *Bashaw*] Earlier form of the Turkish title *pasha*, formerly borne by officers of high rank, as military commanders or governors of provinces (*OED*).

106 *apophthegms*] Terse, pointed sayings, embodying important truths in few words.

107 *Principles of Penal Law*] A study of criminal law in Great Britain by William Eden, Baron Auckland (1744-1814), published in London in 1771 (the estimated number of one hundred executions annually is mentioned on page 199).

108 *Cæsar*] Julius Caesar (100-44 BC), Roman general and statesman, assassinated by a group of conspirators under Brutus and Cassius.

109 *Charles the Twelfth*] Karl XII (1682-1718), King of Sweden from 1697 to his death. Not long after his succession, Charles XII took on the combined forces of Denmark, Poland-Saxony and Russia, finally suffering a decisive defeat during an expedition into Russia.

110 *whins*] Gorse.

111 *Would Rome ... name of a friend*] Lucius Junius Brutus was one of the first two consuls in Rome's history, and is known as the founder of the Roman Republic; *the second*

Brutus is Marcus Junius Brutus (c. 85-42 BC), who betrayed Caesar's trust and friendship by joining the plot to murder him.

112 *Annual Register … people*] *The Annual Register, or a View of the History, Politics, and Literature* was an annual review of events of the past year, founded in 1758. Under the heading "Natural History" (part of the section on "Characters"), the issue for the year 1789 (London, 1792) printed "A Table containing an authentic Statement of the Population of China, divided into Provinces; made in the 27th Year of the Reign of Kien-Long, i.e. in 1761—From the Translation of Abbé Grosier's Description of China." In the accompanying text we read that China "contains at present two hundred millions of inhabitants" (48).

113 *a pudding of marble flour*] A cake made of light and dark sponge, having a mottled appearance suggestive of marble (*OED*).

114 *Jupiter … Juno … Venus*] In Roman mythology Jupiter, also known as Jove, the supreme deity; Juno was the wife of Jupiter, and the queen of gods; Venus was the goddess of beauty and love

115 *hasty-pudding*] A pudding made of flour (sometimes oatmeal) stirred in boiling milk or water to the consistency of a thick batter (*OED*).

116 *pension-list*] Regular payment made to one who is not a professed servant or employee, to retain his alliance, good will, secret service, assistance when needed, etc. (*OED*).

117 *Rousseau's Teresa*] Thérèse Levasseur, Rousseau's companion (see footnote on Rousseau's *Confessions* in Vol. I, p. 83).

118 *Corn had been dear … transported*] Failed harvests due to bad weather conditions and the growing impact of the *laissez faire* economics had led to food shortages and soaring prices in Britain in the 1790s, particularly in 1795; as a result, food riots erupted in various parts of the country, with some of rioters ending up being hanged or transported.

119 *And are men not … demonstration*] Walker may well have been thinking of such a statement by Rousseau as: "Behold then the human race divided into herds of cattle, each with its chief, who preserves it in order to devour it" (*Social Contract*, 47).

120 *The management … public*] A verbatim compilation from Chapter VI of Wollstonecraft's *A Vindication of the Rights of Woman* (68).

121 το καλον] That is, τὸ καλόν (Greek) the beautiful.

122 *Emilius*] Short English title (in full, in one version, *Emilius and Sophia; or, A New System of Education*) of *Émile, ou L'Éducation* (1762), an educational romance by Jean-Jacques Rousseau. It describes the bringing up of the boy Émile according to what Rousseau called the principles of nature (learning by experience, physical exercise, learning useful trades, and hard work). Chapter V deals with the education of Sophie, a young woman intended to become Émile's wife. She is educated to please men, and to be charming, modest, virtuous, and submissive.

123 *Eloisa*] Short English title (in full, in one version, *Eloisa, or, A Series of Original Letters*) of *Julie, ou la Nouvelle Héloïse* (1761), an immensely popular epistolary novel by Rousseau. It tells the story of Julie d'Etanges, who is beset by her former lover and tutor, Saint-Preux (a character based on Rousseau himself). Her husband, M. de Wolmar, invites him to live with them. When the situation becomes unbearable, Saint-Preux leaves, but is later recalled by the dying Julie. He promises her that he will educate her children after her death.

124 *Beware … eternal sleep*] Walker is citing from St. Paul's Epistle to the Colossians, which reads in full: "Beware lest any man spoil you through philosophy and vain deceit, after the tradition of men, after the rudiments of the world, and not after Christ" (*The Holy Bible, King James Version*, Colossians 2:8).

125 *glims*] Candles, or dark lanterns, used in housebreaking (*Dictionary of the Vulgar*

Tongue); *quiz*] an odd or eccentric person, in character or appearance (*OED*).
126 *gab*] Prattle, twaddle.
127 *possibles*] Necessaries, means, supplies (slang, *OED*).
128 *Dr Paley*] William Paley (1743-1805), English theologian and moral philosopher, remembered mainly for his contributions to natural theology. Among his most influential publications are *Principles of Moral and Political Philosophy* (1785) and *A View of the Evidences of Christianity* (1794). Chapter fifteen of the first volume of the *Principles* deals with the nature of lies, defining a lie as "a breach of promise: for whoever seriously addresses his discourse to another, tacitly promises to speak the truth, because he knows that the truth is expected" (1:183). Paley does not mention "equivocation," but Walker may have been thinking of Paley's remarks on "prevarication," which he defines as a lie "without literal or direct falsehood" (1:188). Interestingly, according to Paley's *Principles*, Frederick would *not* have been guilty of lying had he equivocated about where Alogos kept his money, for to mislead "a robber, to conceal your property," says Paley, is a "falsehood" that does not constitute a lie (1:185).
129 *Reading a great book ... do mention*] This passage appears to be based on Godwin's observations on "the absurdity of coercion" in Book VII, Chapter iv ("Of the Application of Coercion") in *Political Justice*: "What we want to ascertain is not the intention of the offender, but the chance of his offending again. For this purpose we reasonably enquire first into his intention. But, when we have found this, our task is but begun. This is one of our materials, to enable us to calculate the probability of his repeating his offence, or being imitated by others. Was this an habitual state of his mind, or was it a crisis in his history likely to remain an unique? What effect has experience produced on him; or what likelihood is there that the uneasiness and suffering that attend the perpetration of eminent wrong may have worked a salutary change in his mind? Will he hereafter be placed in circumstances that shall impel him to the same enormity? Precaution is, in its own nature, a step in a high degree precarious. Precaution that consists in inflicting injury on another will at all times be odious to an equitable mind. Meanwhile, be it observed that all which has been said upon the uncertainty of crime tends to aggravate the injustice of punishment for the sake of example. Since the crime upon which I animadvert in one man can never be the same as the crime of another, it is as if I should award a grievous penalty against persons with one eye, to prevent any man in future from putting out his eyes by design" (387).
130 *Chatterton*] Thomas Chatterton (1752-70), English poet, best known for his Rowley poems, fabrications couched in elaborately archaic spelling which he claimed to be the work of a fifteenth-century monk named Thomas Rowley. With James MacPherson's Ossian poems, Chatterton's Rowley poems are among the most important literary forgeries of the age, reflecting a growing interest from the 1770s onward in the antique in poetry. Finding it hard to get his poems published (for one reason, because an increasing number of people began to doubt their authenticity), Chatterton died in poverty of an arsenic overdose, within four months after arriving in London. When the Rowley poems were finally published in 1777, they provoked a controversy which lasted into the 1780s and beyond. Chatterton's dramatic death at the age of seventeen was regarded by many Romantic poets as the untimely demise of a neglected and misunderstood genius; Chatterton thus became a literary role model for poets like William Wordsworth and John Keats, and the garret where he died became a tourist attraction. Whether he committed suicide or not, many modern literary historians doubt whether Chatterton was really as poor and desperate when he died as Romantic literary legend has it.

131 *What with emigration … follow its beams*] See Introduction for more information on the radical transatlantic emigration movement referred to here.

132 *Stuff*] Made of woollen fabric.

133 *Helvetius says … in the universe*] Claude Adrien Helvétius (1715-71), French materialist philosopher and encyclopedist. In his most influential work, *De l'esprit* (1758), Helvétius asserts that the human mind is at birth like a clean slate, and that man's moral being is shaped by the social conditions in which he grows up, by education, society's institutions and laws. According to Helvétius, religion is no longer relevant because it has failed to provide a framework for morality—the only true basis for morality and the law being public interest, i.e., the greatest good for the greatest number.

134 *If you do not believe … no longer*] Unlike what the quotation marks suggest, this does not appear to be a verbatim citation from Hume, though it may be based on the following passage from Hume's *Treatise*, Book I, Part iv, Section 6: "If any one upon serious and unprejudic'd reflexion thinks he has a different notion of *himself*, I must confess I can reason no longer with him" (252).

135 *vacuo*] Not listed in *OED* as a noun, hence belonging to Stupeo's new philosophical jargon.

136 *Jack Ketch*] John Ketch (d. 1686), English hangman and executioner, notorious for his barbarity. Ketch worked in London's equally notorious Newgate Prison (see above, notes 66 and 69).

137 *felo de se*] Self-murder, suicide.

138 *Monro's anatomical comparisons*] Alexander Monro (1697-1767), Scottish physician and author of many authoritative treatises on medical topics, including *Anatomical Lectures, or, The Anatomy of the Human Bones, Nerves, and Lacteal Sac and Duct: Containing not only the mere descriptive or proper anatomical part of osteology, but also observations on the structure and morbid phaenomena of bones* (London, 1775).

139 *scoræ*] That is, scoriæ, rough clinker-like masses formed by the cooling of the surface of molten lava upon exposure to the air, and distended by the expansion of imprisoned gases (*OED*).

140 *Our earth … ouran-outang*] In the last decades of the eighteenth century, geology became an exciting and fashionable new discipline. Focusing on the make-up and history of the earth, geology grafted itself on a number of earlier traditions, from exegesis of the Bible to speculative cosmology, and from mineral collecting to travel literature. Especially in the wake of the French Revolution, science began to push out theology in geological accounts of the history of the earth and the creation of life on earth. Enlightenment thinkers like the natural philosopher James Hutton (1726-97) and the physician Erasmus Darwin (1731-1802) had proposed a cyclical vision of the earth's geological history that introduced a time-scale far beyond the few thousand years associated with that process in the Biblical tradition. In fact what was emerging in this period was a conflict between the older school of Creationism and the early stirrings of evolutionism. In *The Vagabond*, Walker unconditionally sides with the Creationists, and associates evolutionists like Stupeo consistently with an ideological and political position that is both atheist and anti-British.

141 *Peace … exultation*] The Peace of Paris of 1783 formally put an end to the Revolutionary War between the American colonies and Britain, which had started in April 1775, when the first armed skirmishes erupted at Concord and Lexington, Massachusetts.

142 *Milton's devils … violation*] John Milton (1608-74), English poet and prose writer, whose epic poem *Paradise Lost* (1667) is considered to be one of the greatest epic poems in the English language. It tells the story of Adam and Eve's rebellion against God's commands, their Fall from Paradise, and the resulting misery for humanity.

143 *crab cudgel*] A stick or cudgel made of the wood of the crab-tree; a crab-stick (*OED*).
144 *this many-headed monster*] A common phrase for a mob.
145 *aristocratical church-and-king mob ... liberty and equality*] Fighting either on behalf of external, "aristocratic" interests or themselves, church-and-king mobs defended the pillars of the British political and social establishment, i.e., royalty, the Constitution, and the Church of England; Republican mobs fought for social and constitutional reform. During actual riots, however, socio-political principles often quickly gave way to the temptations of pillaging and the settling of old scores.
146 The attack on Doctor Alogos's house and library is closely modeled on the attack on Dr. Priestley's property during the Birmingham Riots of 1791, which made him decide to emigrate to America (see Introduction).
147 *for in the days ... selling bread*] Licenses, patents and monopolies were Queen Elizabeth's usual means of rewarding her favorites, but they were hated by merchants, manufacturers and consumers alike because they interfered with the market and made products more expensive, especially when the recipients of the "monopolis-ing patents" exploited them harshly. The "gentleman" referred to by Walker has not been identified.
148 *bundle with*] To sleep in one's clothes on the same bed or couch, as was formerly customary with persons of opposite sexes, in Wales and New England (*OED*); by extension, to have sex with.
149 *the great city of Washington*] During the War of Independence, Philadelphia had been the principal seat of the Continental Congress, but after it was driven from there by mutinous soldiers in 1783, jealousy among the states prevented a permanent site to be found for the national capital for seven years. The 1787 Constitution provided for the establishment of a seat of government, and when Virginia and Maryland ceded the land to the nation for such a purpose, a bill was passed and plans were made for establishing the capital on the Potomac river.
150 The captain's sarcastic comments about Washington are justified. When, in 1800, the government was moved to Washington, it was described as a "backwoods settle-ment in the wilderness." One wing of the Capitol and the President's House were nearly completed, but the town existed principally on paper, with much of the surroundings of the Capitol still marshland, and with no streets to speak of. For many years to come, Washington was known as "Wilderness City," "Capital of Miserable Huts," and "City of Streets without Houses."
151 *But how comes it ... newspapers?*] Especially in the first half of the 1790s the streets and taverns of London were awash with pamphlets, plans and newspaper advertise-ments in which both British and American land-jobbers, speculators, con-men, as well as some radical reformers, were frantically trying to persuade people to buy land in America, for settlement or speculation. The decision to build a permanent seat of the government of America at the junction of the Potomac and the Eastern Branch in the District of Columbia, was a golden opportunity for London land-jobbers to make their case. See, for instance, "A Description of the Situation and Plan of the City of Washington, Now Building for the Metropolis of America, and Established as the Permanent Residence of Congress after the Year 1800," which appeared on 12 March 1793, and copies of which were available at the York Hotel, Bridge Street, Blackfriars.
152 *she desired them ... the 104th*] The opening lines of Psalm 104 in the King James version of the Bible read: "Bless the LORD, O my soul. O LORD my God, thou art very great; thou art clothed with honour and majesty./Who coverest thyself with light as with a garment: who stretchest out the heavens like a curtain:/Who layeth

the beams of his chambers in the waters: who maketh the clouds his chariot: who walketh upon the wings of the wind:/Who maketh his angels spirits; his ministers a flaming fire:/Who laid the foundations of the earth, that it should not be removed for ever"(1-5).

153 *Mary-le-Bone*] Now a neighborhood of the City of Westminster, London (located to the south and west of Regent's Park and north of Mayfair), Marylebone was still a rural parish during much of the eighteenth century. Rapid population growth in later decades of the eighteenth century led to a sharp increase of building activity in the area, with terraced houses being characteristic of development at that time.

154 *emigré*] Originally one of those Royalists who fled at the French Revolution; by extension, an emigrant of any nationality, especially a political exile (*OED*).

155 *like Spartans ... liberty of speech*] Probably a reference to the Spartan reputation for terseness of expression. Sparta was the capital of Laconia, a state in ancient Greece in the south-east of the Peloponnese; Laconia gave the English language the word "laconic," for terseness of speech. Thus, when Philip of Macedon wrote to them, "If I invade Laconia I shall turn you out," they wrote back, "If."

156 *yellow fever ... in a day*] Epidemics of yellow fever were not unknown to colonial America. Endemic to the West Indies, the plague frequently visited ports on the East coast, notably Philadelphia, which, as a leading center of trade and the nation's capital, attracted many visitors and migrants from the West Indies. The terrible outbreak of the plague in the summer of 1793 killed almost 2,500 people in Philadelphia; the outbreak of 1797 was almost as bad. The ravages of the plague and the constant coming and going of the "dead carts" had been widely covered in European newspapers.

157 *the ancient Spartans ... with work*] Probably an allusion to the custom of the Spartans to reduce the people living on the lands they conquered to dependents or even serfs, who were made to work the land for their Spartan masters. Relieved of tending the land themselves, the Spartans were able to spend much of their time training as soldiers.

158 *Elkhorn*] A small river which empties itself into the Kentucky River just north of Frankfort, KT.

159 *husbandry*] Agriculture, farming.

160 *As they advanced ... down which they sailed*] Walker is here describing the usual route settlers would take to get from Philadelphia to Kentucky—a route described in much detail in Imlay's *Topographical Description*: by wagon across the Allegheny Mountains to Fort Pitt (present-day Pittsburgh), and then on barges down the Ohio River all the way into Kentucky.

161 *Being arrived at Lexington*] Walker's geography is not quite accurate; Lexington is not on the Ohio River (unlike Louisville, which is where Imlay directs his emigrants to go): it is actually situated between the north and south forks of the Elkhorn.

162 *It is almost impossible ... patent upon patent*] Buying land in the western territory was a notoriously risky affair, and buying land in Kentucky, then a frontier state, was more risky than anywhere else. Land-jobbers like Imlay would frequently sell inferior, or even non-existing lots to unsuspecting emigrants, or would sell the same lot several times over. To make things worse, the records that were kept of land deals were badly administered, and various land offices would issue their own deeds independently.

163 *Salmon's Dispensatory*] William Salmon (1644-1713), *Pharmacopoeia Londinensis or, The new London dispensatory in six books: translated into English for the Pharmacopoeia Londinensis publick good and fitted to the whole art of healing: illustrated with the preparations, virtues and uses of all simple medicaments, vegitable, animal and mineral, of all the compounds both internal and external, and of all the chymical preparations now in use: together*

with several choise medicines added by the author: as also the praxis of chymistry as it's now exercised, fitted to the meanest capacity (London, 1678).

164 *the London Compleat Art of Healing*] No publication of this title has been identified, but Walker may have been alluding to a number of medical treatises, including Charles Gabriel Le Clerc, *The Compleat Surgeon, or, The whole art of surgery explain'd in a most familiar method ... To which is added, a surgical dispensatory; shewing the manner how to prepare all such medicines as are most necessary for a surgeon, etc.* (London, 1696).

165 *febrile*] Feverish.

166 *a troop of ... the Ohio*] An important tribe of Algonquian stock formerly claiming prior dominion over the whole of what is now Indiana and western Ohio, including the territories drained by the Wabash, St. Joseph, Maumee, and Miami rivers.

167 *dignified with the name of Clarens*] The settlers significantly name their new wilderness home after the country home of Julie, the heroine in Rousseau's novel *Julie ou la Nouvelle Héloïse* (1761), and the setting of Julie's complex triangular relationship with her former lover, Saint-Preux, and husband, M. de Wolmar. See note 123.

168 *by rendering life ... quit it*] A translation of a passage from Rousseau's novel *Julie, ou la Nouvelle Héloïse* (1761), Part Three, Letter xxi, 311.

169 The episode in this chapter involving Laura's kidnapping by hostile Indians is modeled after a similar captivity interlude in Gilbert Imlay's novel *The Emigrants* (192 ff.).

170 *Scytheans*] The Scythians, an ancient nomadic people inhabiting a region extending over a large part of European and Asiatic Russia, notorious for their cruelty, who threatened in turn both the Assyrian and Persian empires.

171 *five nations*] Also called Iroquois League, the Five Nations was a confederation of five North American Indian tribes across upper New York state, which joined in confederacy c. 1570 by the efforts of the Huron prophet Deganawida and his disciple Hiawatha. Speaking the Iroquoian languages, the five Iroquois nations were the Mohawk, Oneida, Onondaga, Cayuga, and Seneca. After the Tuscarora joined in 1722, the confederacy became known to the English as the Six Nations and was recognized as such at Albany, New York (1722). During the seventeenth and eighteenth centuries the Five (Six) Nations played a strategic role in the struggle between the French and British for mastery of North America. However, divisions in the confederacy occasioned by conflicting support of the various contestants in the War of American Independence saw the rapid decline of the Six Nations in the late eighteenth century, with half the League (i.e., the Cayugas, Mohawks, and Seneca) migrating north to Canada, where they accepted grants of land as allies of the defeated Loyalists and where they still continue to live. Traditional Iroquois society revolved around matrilineal residential and social organization.

172 *The great Manetaw of the lakes*] Manitou (also manitu and manito), a supernatural force that according to an Algonquian conception pervades the natural world (*Britannica*).

173 *hoe-cake*] Coarse bread, made of Indian meal, water, and salt, and usually in the form of a thin cake (*OED*).

174 *an equal division of labour ... philosophers*] Walker is ridiculing Godwin's theory of the division of labor "in a state of equality"—i.e., in an egalitarian, utopian society (see *Political Justice*, Book VIII, Chap. iv and Appendix A.6.ii).

175 *the Helots ... Spartans*] Descendants of the original inhabitants of Laconia, the helots were serfs in the state of Sparta, who were assigned to individual Spartans for agricultural and domestic work. The helot system relieved the Spartans of the need of tending the land themselves, thus enabling them to spend much of their time in military training.

176 *mephetic*] That is, mephitic, offensive to the smell, foul-smelling; noxious, poisonous, pestilential (*OED*).

177 *the tribes of Abraham*] In the Old Testament, Abraham was the founder and first patriarch of the Hebrew people. Chosen by Jehovah to establish a new nation, Abraham
emigrated with his wife Sarah to Canaan. Later, Jehovah and Abraham made a
covenant, according to which Jehovah promised that He would be God to Abraham
and his children, and that Abraham should be "the father of many nations" (Genesis
17:6-8). Parecho apparently traces his ancestry back all the way to Abraham.

178 *in society ... social happiness*] An allusion to a key issue in the reformist/conservative
controversy of the 1790s, i.e., the question of what constituted an individual's "civil
rights," as opposed to his "natural rights." Civil rights, in Thomas Paine's definition,
are those rights "which appertain to man in right of his being a member of society," such as the right to security and protection; natural rights are those "which
always appertain to man in right of his existence," and include "all the intellectual
rights, or rights of the mind, and also all those rights of acting as an individual for
his own comfort and happiness" (*Rights of Man*, Part I, 90). Conservative commentators such as Edmund Burke argued that an individual had to surrender some of
his natural rights in order to gain his civil rights (society *grants* an individual his civil
rights). Reformers such as Paine, however, argued that man's natural rights were
inalienable and could never be surrendered; in order to gain his civil rights, the individual had to "deposit" or invest some of his natural rights "in the common stock
of society," and could then "draw on the capital as a matter of right" (an individual's natural rights were therefore "the foundation" of his civil rights [ibid.]).

179 *miracles ... Wilderness*] A reference to the Ten Plagues in the Old Testament (Exodus
7-12). The plagues were called down upon Egypt by Jehovah through Moses to
persuade the Pharaoh to release the Jews from bondage so that they could serve
Him "in the wilderness." Although most of the plagues were natural phenomena,
they were so extreme and occurred in such rapid succession that the Pharaoh was
convinced they were miraculous works of God. Among the plagues were the plague
of frogs, the plague of hail, the plague of locusts, and the plague of darkness.

180 *revealed religion*] See Introduction.

181 *it is contrary to ... coercion*] An allusion to a passage in Godwin's *Political Justice*, Book
VII, Chap. i ("Limitations of the Doctrine of Punishment which Result from the
Principles of Morality"): "It is right that I should inflict suffering, in every case
where it can be clearly shown that such infliction will produce an overbalance of
good. But this infliction bears no reference to the mere innocence or guilt of the
person upon whom it is made. An innocent man is the proper subject of it, if it tend
to good. A guilty man is the proper subject of it under no other point of view. To
punish him, upon any hypothesis, for what is past and irrecoverable and for the
consideration of that only, must be ranked among the most pernicious exhibitions
of an untutored barbarism. Every man upon whom discipline is administered, is to
be considered as to the rationale of this discipline as innocent" (370). The 1798
edition of *Political Justice* adds at this point: "The only sense of the word punishment
that can be supposed to be compatible with the principles of the present work is
that of pain inflicted on a person convicted of past injurious action, for the purpose
of preventing future mischief" (635).

182 *The body is perpetually changing ... on Human Nature*] An allusion to Hume's assertion in his *Treatise on Human Nature* that like sense perceptions, the soul and the self
(or personal identity) are in a perpetual flux and movement: "But setting aside some
metaphysicians of this kind, I may venture to affirm of the rest of mankind, that they
are nothing but a bundle or collection of different perceptions, which succeed each
other with an inconceivable rapidity, and are in a perpetual flux and movement. Our

eyes cannot turn in their sockets without varying our perceptions. Our thought is still more variable than our sight; and all our other senses and faculties contribute to this change; nor is there any single power of the soul, which remains unalterably the same, perhaps for one moment. The mind is a kind of theatre, where several perceptions successively make their appearance; pass, re-pass, glide away, and mingle in an infinite variety of postures and situations" (Book I, Section vi, 252-53).

183   *Alexander the Great ... Persians*] See note 42 above.

184   *elegant Romance of Political Justice*] This may be a sarcastic allusion to Godwin's *Political Justice*, or, more likely, a reference to Godwin's influential Jacobin novel *Things As They Are; Or the Adventures of Caleb Williams* (London, 1794), in which he expounds his principles of political justice in the format of a fictional and highly exciting narrative.

185   *It is derived from ... reason and nature*] Whilst not entirely irrelevant in some of its detail, the bizarre etymology of the word "nature" that Stupeo offers here is by and large nonsense and clearly intended to expose him as a charlatan and a crank; thus, the forms "geN-ascor," "geN-atus," and "geN-atura" do not exist in classical Latin, and are not derived from the Greek, either, but more likely from an Indo-European stem (-gn-).

186   *remember the advice ... equivocal expression*] John Locke (1632-1704), English philosopher. Locke's most famous philosophical treatise is *An Essay Concern Human Understanding* (1690), an inquiry into the nature of knowledge. In the work, Locke rejects the notion of "innate ideas"; instead, he argues, the human mind begins as a *tabula rasa* ("blank slate"), and acquires knowledge through sense perception and a process of reflection. In Book III, "Of Words," Locke argues that since words stand for nothing but ideas in the mind of the person that uses them, words can easily be abused: "Besides the Imperfection that is naturally in Language, and the obscurity and confusion that is hard to be avoided in the Use of Words, there are several *wilful Faults and Neglects*, which Men are guilty of, in this way of Communication, whereby they render these signs less clear and distinct in their signification, than naturally they need to be" (Chap. X, "Of the Abuse of Words," 490). Walker is likely to have applauded Locke's bitter condemnation of the "learned Disputants, these all-knowing Doctors," who fill "their Discourse with abundance of empty unintelligible noise and jargon," which "can be imputed to nothing but great Folly, or greater dishonesty" (495, 492, 492-93).

187   *Elysian fields*] The Paradise or Happy Land of the Greek poets ("Elysium," abode of the blessed); *Homer:* Ionian poet, assumed author of the epic poems the *Iliad* and *Odyssey* (ninth century BC); *Noahchidæ*] descendants of Noah, the Old Testamental patriarch whom God chose to spare from the Flood that covered the face of the earth (Genesis 6-9); *Median mountains*] mountainous plateau in present-day northwestern Iran, inhabited in ancient times by the Medes; *Cushites*] descendants of Cush (eldest son of Ham, who was one of the three sons of Noah), who settled in Upper Egypt; *Thebes*] the Greek name of the ancient capital of Upper Egypt, on the Nile (present-day Luxor), where, during the reign of the Pharaohs, extensive tombs were carved out in the rocks, which were decorated with religious scenes and hieroglyphic texts; *Thebaic beetle*] a reference to the scarab beetle or scarabæid beetle, a large dung beetle (*Scarabaeus sacer*), reverenced by the ancient Egyptians and associated with ideas of spontaneous generation and renewal of life (also carved as a gem in the form of a scarab beetle, engraved with hieroglyphs on the flat underside); *Buddha or Boodh*] the Sanskrit word buddha means "enlightened," "awakened," and is the past participle of *budh*, to awake, know, perceive (*OED*). *Boodh* and *booddha* are variant spellings; *Hermes ... Mercury*] Hermes was an ancient Arcadian deity, often

regarded as the god of flocks, of roads, and of trading, identified by the Romans as Mercury, their god of tradesmen; *Woden, Odin, Gwoden*] Woden was a deity of the Anglo-Saxons, the name being the Anglo-Saxon counterpart of the Scandinavian Odin, their chief deity, identified by the Romans with Mercury ("Wednesday," or "Woden's day," being the Romans' translation of *dies Mercurii*); *Druids*] members of a pre-Christian Celtic class of priests, religious teachers, and sorcerers; *Pliny ... oak*] Pliny the Elder, or Caius Plinius Secundus (AD 23-79), Latin author who, in his *Naturalis Historiae*, refers to the possible Greek origin of the word "druid" (16.249), though he does not actually mention the word δρῦς.

188   *Saul and the Witch of Endor*] According to the biblical narrative, the Witch of Endor called up the prophet Samuel from the dead to answer King Saul's questions concerning the fateful battle in which he would meet his death. Samuel is a judge and prophet, a religious and political reformer of early Israel, who lends his name to two books of the Old Testament.

189   *a public man of character ... Demosthenes, &c.*] Not further identified.

190   *ignus fatuus*] A delusive guiding principle, hope, aim (*OED*).

191   *Rousseau ... species*] Walker is citing a passage from a translation of Rousseau's *Discours sur l'origine et les fondements de l'inégalité parmi les hommes*, which reads: "Il est donc bien certain que la pitié est un sentiment naturel, qui, modérant dans chaque individu l'activité de l'amour de soi-même, concourt à la conservation mutuelle de toute l'espèce" (*Discourse on the Origin of Inequality*, Part I, 47).

192   *tender european ladies ... guillotine*] Perhaps the worst shock to the British establishment's sense of morality, decency and decorum was the fact that *women* played a part in the Reign of Terror and were actually involved in some of the executions and other acts of aggression and violence by the Jacobins against the royalists and other "enemies" of the Revolution. The behavior of these "daughters of the Revolution" was often associated in the conservative press with the bloody scalpings by North American Indians (see, for instance, Burke, *Reflections on the Revolution in France*, 67). *Carmagnole*] name of a lively song and dance, popular among the French revolutionists in 1793 (*OED*).

193   *Gratitude*] An allusion to Godwin's dismissal of gratitude as being "no part either of justice or virtue" (see note 35 above).

194   *the pupil of experience*] Probably an allusion to *Berkeley Hall; or, The Pupil of Experience*, an anti-Jacobin novel published anonymously in London in 1796. The anti-Jacobins frequently offered "experience" as the practical, common-sensical *British* alternative to impractical, Jacobin and *French* "philosophy" or "system."

195   *Kentucky ... numerous emigrations*] Even though at the time he was writing *The Vagabond* migration to Kentucky from Europe and from other parts of America was declining, Walker's observation is historically correct, for during the time the events in this part of the novel are set (c. 1784), migration to the western territories of America increased sharply, following the Peace of Paris (1783) and the end of hostilities between Britain and the American colonies.

196   *empirics*] Imposters, charlatans.

197   *All that I know is, that I know nothing*] Although conventionally attributed to the Greek teacher of wisdom Socrates (c. 470-399 BC), the actual source of the saying is the Greek philosopher and writer Plato (c. 427-c. 348 BC). Socrates left no writings, but Plato reports him saying something resembling Walker's text in his *Apology* (an account of Socrates' defense at his impiety trial) on two occasions, *Apology* 21b and *Apology* 22c.

A Note on the Appendices

The extracted texts included in Appendices A and B are intended
to assist the reader in better understanding the numerous political,
historical and philosophical sources and allusions that form the raw
materials from which Walker constructed his tale. *The Vagabond* is
exceptionally encyclopedic, even for an explicitly satirical anti-
Jacobin novel, and only a substantive selection from his sources
would do any kind of justice to the extraordinary degree of inter-
textuality of Walker's novel. The editor's Introduction provides a full
historical and intellectual context for the authors and texts included
in Appendices A and B, which for that reason have been annotated
only sparingly. Further background information on the extracts can
be found in the endnotes to the text of the novel, and in the editor's
annotations of Walker's own footnotes. Appendix A contains texts
representing the Jacobin side of the Revolutionary Debate in
Britain in the 1790s; Appendix B contains texts representing the
anti-Jacobin side of that debate. Appendix C, finally, offers extracts
from contemporary reviews of *The Vagabond*.

Appendix A: Sources and Contexts: The Jacobin Side of the Revolutionary Debate

1. From David Hume, "An Abstract of a Book Lately Published, Entitled *A Treatise of Human Nature, &c.*" (1740), 5–7; 8–9; 10–20; 21–22; 24

[One of the leading figures in the Scottish Enlightenment, the philosopher David Hume is known for his philosophical skepticism. Ironically describing his key text, *A Treatise on Human Nature* (1739), as "very skeptical," Hume restricted knowledge to the experience of ideas or impressions, and maintained that the mind consists only of accumulated perceptions. Arguing that there was no existence beyond the visible, materialist world, Hume believed that man had no soul, and ruled out the possibility of an afterlife. Though preceding the Jacobins by several decades, Hume was regarded by many conservatives in the 1790s with the Jacobins, as being part of the same, general onslaught on orthodox Christian morality and ethics. Writing in the third person, Hume wrote his "Abstract" to render the ideas expressed in his *Treatise* more accessible to the general reading public. Introducing his well-known analogy of the billiard balls, Hume attempts to demonstrate that all human knowledge and action is determined (or "necessitated") by the law of cause and effect, thus ruling out the existence of an irrational beyond.]

This book seems to be wrote upon the same plan with several other works that have had a great vogue of late years in *England*. The philosophical spirit, which has been so much improved all over *Europe* within these last fourscore years, has been carried to as great a length in this kingdom as in any other. Our writers seem even to have started a new kind of philosophy, which promises more both to the entertainment and advantage of mankind, than any other with which the world has been yet acquainted. Most of the philosophers of antiquity, who treated of human nature, have shewn more of a delicacy of sentiment, a just sense of morals, or a greatness of soul, than a depth of reasoning and reflection. They content themselves with representing the common sense of mankind in the strongest lights, and with the best turn of thought and expression, without following out steadily a chain of propositions, or forming the several truths into a regular science. But 'tis at least worth while to try if the science of *man* will not admit of the same accuracy which several parts of natural philosophy are found susceptible of. There seems to be all the reason in the world to imagine that it may be carried to the greatest degree of exactness. If, in examining several phenomena, we find that they resolve themselves into one common principle, and can trace this principle into another, we may at last arrive at those few simple principles, on which all the rest depend. And tho' we can never arrive at the ultimate principles, 'tis a satisfaction to go as far as our faculties will allow us....

Beside the satisfaction of being acquainted with what most nearly concerns us, it may be safely affirmed, that almost all the sciences are comprehended in the science of human nature, and are dependent on it. *The sole end of* logic *is to explain the principles and* Operations *of our reasoning faculty, and the nature of our ideas*; morals and criticism *regard our tastes and sentiments; and* politics *consider men as united in society, and dependent on each other.* This treatise therefore of human nature seems intended for a system of the sciences. The author has finished what regards logic, and has laid the foundation of the other parts in his account of the passions....

As his book [Hume's *Treatise*] contains a great number of speculations very new and remarkable, it will be impossible to give the reader a just notion of the whole. We shall therefore chiefly confine ourselves to his explication of our reasonings from cause and effect. If we can make this intelligible to the reader, it may serve as a specimen of the whole.

Our author begins with some definitions. He calls a *perception* whatever can be present to the mind, whether we employ our senses, or are actuated with passion, or exercise our thought and reflection. He divides our perceptions into two kinds, *viz. impressions* and *ideas*. When we feel a passion or emotion of any kind, or have the images of external objects conveyed by our senses; the perception of the mind is what he calls an *impression*, which is a word that he employs in a new sense. When we reflect on a passion or an object which is not present, this perception is an *idea*. *Impressions*, therefore, are our lively and strong perceptions; *ideas* are the fainter and weaker. This distinction is evident; as evident as that betwixt feeling and thinking.

The first proposition he advances, is, that all our ideas, or weak perceptions, are derived from our impressions, or strong perceptions, and that we can never think of any thing which we have not seen without us, or felt in our own minds. This proposition seems to be equivalent to that which Mr. *Locke* has taken such pains to establish, *viz. that no ideas are innate.* Only it may be observed, as an inaccuracy of that famous philosopher, that he comprehends all our perceptions under the term of idea, in which sense it is false, that we have no innate ideas. For it is evident our stronger perceptions or impressions are innate, and that natural affection, love of virtue, resentment, and all the other passions, arise immediately from nature....

Our author thinks, "that no discovery could have been made more happily for deciding all controversies concerning ideas than this, that impressions always take the precedency of them, and that every idea with which the imagination is furnished, first makes its appearance in a correspondent impression. These latter perceptions are all so clear and evident, that they admit of no controversy; tho' many of our ideas are so obscure, that 'tis almost impossible even for the mind, which forms them, to tell exactly their nature and composition." Accordingly, wherever any idea is ambiguous, he has always recourse to the impression, which must render it clear and precise. And when he suspects that any philosophical term has no idea annexed to it (as is too common) he always asks *from what impression that idea is derived?* And if no impression can be produced, he concludes that the term is altogether insignificant. 'Tis after this manner he examines our idea of *substance* and *essence*; and it were to be wished, that this rigorous method were more practiced in all philosophical debates.

'Tis evident, that all reasonings concerning *matter of fact* are founded on the relation of cause and effect, and that we can never infer the existence of one object from another, unless they be connected together, either mediately or immediately. In order, therefore to understand these reasonings, we must be perfectly acquainted with the idea of a cause; and in order to that, must look about us to find something that is the cause of another.

Here is a billiard-ball lying on the table, and another ball moving towards it with rapidity. They strike; and the ball, which was formerly at rest, now acquires a motion. This is as perfect an instance of the relation of cause and effect as any which we know, either by sensation or reflection. Let us therefore examine it. 'Tis evident, that the two balls touched one another before the motion was communicated, and that there was no interval betwixt the shock and the motion. *Contiguity* in time and place is therefore a requisite circumstance to the operation of all causes. 'Tis evident likewise, that the motion, which was the cause, is prior to the motion, which was the effect. *Priority* in time, is therefore another requisite circumstance in every cause. But this is not all. Let us try any other balls of the same kind in a like situation, and we shall always find, that the impulse of the one produces motion in the other. Here therefore is a *third* circumstance, *viz.* that of a *constant conjunction* between the cause and effect. Every object like the cause, produces always some object like the effect. Beyond these three circumstances of contiguity, priority, and constant conjunction, I can discover nothing in this cause. The first ball is in motion; touches the second; immediately the second is in motion; and when I try the experiment with the same or like balls, in the same or like circumstances, I find, that upon the motion and touch of the one ball, motion always follows in the other. In whatever shape I turn this matter, and however I examine it, I can find nothing farther.

This is the case when both the cause and effect are present to the senses. Let us now see upon what our inference is founded, when we conclude from the one that the other has existed or will exist. Suppose I see a ball moving in a straight line towards another, I immediately conclude, that they will shock, and that the second will be in motion. This is the inference from cause to effect; and of this nature are all our reasonings in the conduct of life: on this is founded all our belief in history: and from hence is derived all philosophy, excepting only geometry and arithmetic. If we can explain the inference from the shock of two balls, we shall be able to account for this operation of the mind in all instances.

Were a man, such as *Adam*, created in the full vigour of understanding, without experience, he would never be able to infer motion in the second ball from the motion and impulse of the first. It is not any thing that reason sees in the cause, which make us *infer* the effect. Such an inference, were it possible, would amount to a demonstration, as being founded merely on the comparison of ideas. But no inference from cause to effect amounts to a demonstration, as being founded merely on the comparison of ideas. Of which there is this evident proof. The mind can always *conceive* any effect to follow from any cause, and indeed any event to follow upon another: whatever we *conceive* is possible, at least in a metaphysical sense: but wherever a demonstration takes place, the contrary is impossible, and implies a contradiction. There is no demonstration, therefore, for any conjunction of cause and effect. And this is a principle which is generally allowed by philosophers.

It would have been necessary, therefore, for *Adam* (if he was not inspired) to have had *experience* of the effect, which followed upon the impulse of these two balls. He must have seen, in several instances, that when the one ball struck upon the other, the second always acquired motion. If he had seen a sufficient number of instances of this kind, whenever he saw the one ball moving towards the other, he would always conclude without hesitation, that the second would acquire motion. His understanding would anticipate his sight, and form a conclusion suitable to his past experience.

It follows, then, that all reasonings concerning cause and effect, are founded on experience, and that all reasonings from experience are founded on the supposition, that the course of nature will continue uniformly the same. We conclude, that like causes, in like circumstances, will always produce like effects. It may now be worth while to consider, what determines us to form a conclusion of such infinite consequence.

'Tis evident, that *Adam* with all his science, would never have been able to *demonstrate*, that the course of nature must continue uniformly the same, and that the future must be conformable to the past. What is possible can never be demonstrated to be false; and 'tis possible the course of nature may change, since we can conceive such a change. Nay, I will go further, and assert, that he could not so much as prove by any *probable* arguments, that the future must be conformable to the past. All probable arguments are built on the supposition, that there is this conformity betwixt the future and the past, and therefore can never prove it. This conformity is a *matter of fact*, and if it must be proved, will admit of no proof but from experience. But our experience in the past can be a proof of nothing for the future, but upon a supposition, that there is a resemblance betwixt them. This therefore is a point, which can admit of no proof at all, and which we take for granted without any proof.

We are determined by CUSTOM alone to suppose the future conformable to the past. When I see a billiard-ball moving towards another, my mind is immediately carry'd by habit to the usual effect, and anticipates my sight by conceiving the second ball in motion. There is nothing in these objects, abstractly considered, and independent of experience, which leads me to form any such conclusion: and even after I have had experience of many repeated effects of this kind, there is no argument, which determines me to suppose that the effect will be conformable to past experience. The powers, by which bodies operate, are entirely unknown. We perceive only their sensible qualities: and what *reason* have we to think, that the same powers will always be conjoined with the same sensible qualities?

'Tis not, therefore, reason, which is the guide of life, but custom. That alone determines the mind, in all instances, to suppose the future conformable to the past. However easy this step may seem, reason would never, to all eternity, be able to make it.

This is a very curious discovery, but leads us to others, that are still more curious. *When I see a billiard ball moving towards another, my mind is immediately carried by habit to the usual effect, and anticipate my sight by conceiving the second ball in motion.* But is this all? Do I nothing but CONCEIVE the motion of the second ball? No surely. I also BELIEVE that it will move. What then is this *belief*? And how does it differ from the simple conception of any thing? Here is a new question unthought of by philosophers.

When a demonstration convinces me of any proposition, it not only makes me conceive the proposition, but also makes me sensible, that 'tis impossible to conceive any thing contrary. What is demonstratively false implies a contradiction; and what implies a contradiction cannot be conceived. But with regard to any matter of fact, however strong the proof may be from experience, I can always conceive the contrary, tho' I cannot always believe it. The belief, therefore, makes some difference betwixt the conception to which we assent, and that to which we do not assent.

To account for this, there are only two hypotheses. It may be said, that belief joins some new idea to those which we may conceive without assenting to them. But this hypothesis is false. For *first*, no such idea can be produced. When we simply conceive an object, we conceive it in all its parts. We conceive it as it might exist, tho' we do not believe it to exist. Our belief of it would discover no new qualities. We may paint out the entire object in imagination without believing it. We may set it, in a manner, before our eyes, with every circumstance of time and place. 'Tis the very object conceived as it might exist; and when we believe it, we can do no more.

Secondly, the mind has a faculty of joining all ideas together, which involve not a contradiction; and therefore if belief consisted in some idea, which we add to the simple conception, it would be in a man's power, by adding this idea to it, to believe any thing, which he can conceive.

Since therefore belief implies a conception, and yet is something more; and since it adds no new idea to the conception; it follows, that it is a different MANNER of conceiving an object; *something* that is distinguishable to the feeling, and depends not upon our will, as all our ideas do. My mind runs by habit from the visible object of one ball moving towards another, to the usual effect of motion in the second ball. It not only conceives that motion, but *feels* something different in the conception of it from a mere reverie of the imagination. The presence of this visible object, and the constant conjunction of that particular effect, render the idea different to the *feeling* from those loose ideas, which come into the mind without any introduction. This conclusion seems a little surprizing; but we are led into it by a chain of propositions which admit of no doubt. To ease the reader's memory I shall briefly resume them. No matter of fact can be proved but from its cause or its effect. Nothing can be known to be the cause of another but by experience. We can give no reason for extending to the future our experience in the past; but are entirely determined by custom, when we conceive an effect to follow from its usual cause. But we also believe an effect to follow, as well as conceive it. This belief joins no new idea to the conception. It only varies the manner of conceiving, and makes a difference to the feeling or sentiment. Belief, therefore, in all matters of fact arises only from custom, and is an idea conceived in a peculiar *manner*.

Our author proceeds to explain the manner or feeling, which renders belief different from a loose conception. He seems sensible, that 'tis impossible by words to describe this feeling, which every one must be conscious of in his own breast. He calls it sometimes a *stronger* conception, sometimes a more *lively*, a more *vivid*, a *firmer*, or a more *intense* conception. And indeed, whatever name we may give to this feeling, which constitutes belief, our author thinks it evident, that it has a more forcible effect on the mind than fiction and mere conception. This he proves by its influence on the passions and on the imagination; which are only moved by truth or what is taken for such....

We have confin'd ourselves in this whole reasoning to the relation of cause and effect, as discovered in the motions and operations of matter. But the same reasoning extends to the operations of the mind.

Whether we consider the influence of the will in moving our body, or in governing our thought, it may safely be affirmed, that we could never foretel the effect, merely from the consideration of the cause, without experience. And even after we have experience of these facts, 'tis custom alone, not reason, which determines us to make it the standard of our future judgements. When the cause is presented, the mind, from habit, immediately passes to the conception and belief of the usual effect. This belief is something different from the conception. It does not, however, join any new idea to it. It only makes it be felt differently, and renders it stronger and more lively....

By all that has been said the reader will easily perceive, that the philosophy contain'd in this book is very sceptical, and tends to give us a notion of the imperfections and narrow limits of human understanding. Almost all reasoning is there reduced to experience; and the belief, which attends experience, is explained to be nothing but a peculiar sentiment, or lively conception produced by habit. Nor is this all, when we believe anything of *external* existence, or suppose an object to exist a moment after it is no longer perceived, this belief is nothing but a sentiment of the same kind. Our author insists upon several other sceptical topics; and upon the whole concludes, that we assent to our faculties, and employ our reason only because we cannot help it....

2. From John James Rousseau [Jean-Jacques Rousseau], *An Inquiry into the Nature of the Social Contract; or, Principles of Political Right* (1762), translated from the French of John James Rousseau (London, 1791), iii; 33–41 (Preface, and Book I, Chapter vi)

[The concept of the social contract was one of the most hotly debated issues throughout the second half of the eighteenth century. In the wake of the French Revolution, it became a site of contestation in Britain where the ideological doctrines of the radicals and the conservatives met in head-on confrontation (which accounts for this new 1791 translation of Rousseau's treatise originally published in 1762). As Rousseau explains in the extract that follows, the fundamental idea of the social compact is that "each person gives himself to ALL, but not to any INDIVIDUAL." This ostensibly simple idea had far-reaching consequences for the organization of society. It not only introduced the notion of a *people* consisting of equal *citizens* (thus doing away with social hierarchy), but it also ushered in the concept of the state or sovereign power as a *body politic*, from which individuals were chosen to govern the people on behalf of the people.]

PREFACE

The high honours which have been recently paid to the memory of Rousseau, by the National Assembly of France; avowedly from a persuasion that a treatise of his, entitled *Du Contrat Social*, had prepared the way for the Revolution which has lately taken place in that country, must naturally excite a desire in the minds of Englishmen, to be acquainted with a work, which could lay the foundation of so important an event. A translation is therefore offered to the public; in which care has been taken to give the sense of the author, in the plainest language; that all who choose to trace, in this treatise, the principles of the new system of French government, may do so, without that difficulty which is sometimes found in reading translations of philosophical works....

Book the First
Chap. VI

Of the Social Compact.

We will suppose that men in a state of nature are arrived at that crisis, when the strength of each individual is insufficient to defend him from the attacks he is subject to. This primitive state can therefore subsist no longer; and the human race must perish, unless they change their manner of life.

As men cannot create for themselves new forces, but merely unite and direct those which already exist, the only means they can employ for their preservation is to form by aggregation an assemblage of forces that may be able to resist all assaults, to be put in motion as one body, and act in concert upon all occasions.

This assemblage of forces must be produced by the concurrence of many: and as the force and the liberty of a man are the chief instruments of his preservation, how can he engage them without danger, and without neglecting the care which is due to himself? This doubt, which leads directly to my subject, may be expressed in these words:

"Where shall we find a form of association which will defend and protect with the whole aggregate force the person and the property of each individual; and by which every person, while united with ALL, shall obey only HIMSELF, and remain as free as before the union?" Such is the fundamental problem, of which the Social Contract gives the solution.

The articles of this contract are so unalterably fixed by the nature of the act, that the least modification renders them vain and of no effect. They are the same every where, and are every where understood and admitted, even though they may never have been formally announced: so that, when once the social pact is violated in any instance, all the obligations it created cease; and each individual is restored to his original rights, and resumes his native liberty, as the consequence of losing that conventional liberty for which he exchanged them.

All the articles of the social contract will, when clearly understood, be found reducible to this single point—THE TOTAL ALIENATION OF EACH ASSOCIATE, AND ALL HIS RIGHTS, TO THE WHOLE COMMUNITY. For every individual gives himself up entirely—the condition of every person is alike; and being so, it would not be the interest of any one to render himself offensive to others.

Nay, more than this—the alienation is made without any reserve; the union is as complete as it can be, and no associate has a claim to any thing: for if any individual were to retain rights not enjoyed in general by all, as there would be no common superior to decide between him and the public, each person being in some points his own proper judge, would soon pretend to be so in every thing; and thus would the state of nature be revived, and the association become tyrannical or be annihilated.

In fine, each person gives himself to ALL, but not to any INDIVIDUAL: and as there is no associate over whom the same right is not acquired which is ceded to him by others, each gains an equivalent for what he loses, and finds his force increased for preserving that which he possesses.

If, therefore, we exclude from the social compact all that is not essentially necessary, we shall find it reduced to the following terms:

"We each of us place, in common, his person, and all his power, under the supreme direction of the general will; and we receive into the body each member as an individual part of the whole."

From that moment, instead of so many separate persons as there are contractors, this act of association produces a moral collective body, composed of as many members as there are voices in the assembly; which from this act receives its unity, its common self, its life, and its will. This public person, which is thus formed by the union of all the private persons, took formerly the name of *city*,[1] and now takes that of *republic* or *body politic*. It is called by its members *state* when it is passive, and *sovereign* when in activity: and whenever it is spoken of with other bodies of a similar kind, it is denominated *power*. The associates take collectively the name of *people*, and separately that of *citizens*, as participating the sovereign authority: they are also styled *subjects*, because they are subjected to the laws. But these terms are frequently confounded, and used one for the other; and a man must understand them well to distinguish when they are properly employed.

3. From Joseph Priestley, *Disquisitions Relating to Matter and Spirit, To which is added the history of the philosophical doctrine concerning the origin of the soul, and the nature of matter; with its influence on Christianity, especially with respect to the doctrine of the pre-existence of Christ* (1777), 2nd ed., 2 vols. (Birmingham/London, 1782), I:i–iv; 72–76

[Central to the work of the British philosopher and scientist Dr. Joseph Priestley was the doctrine of philosophical materialism. Materialists believed that man exists solely in Nature, and is "mechanically" submitted to the laws of nature, from which he will never be able to extract himself. Hence materialists denied the mind and the soul an immaterial existence independent of the body (though granting it may be "concealed"). Or, as Priestley puts it in his *Disquisitions Relating to Matter and Spirit*, "man is wholly material," and hence "the human mind is nothing more than a modification of [man's material existence]" and "no man has a soul distinct from his body." Dr. Priestley appears in *The Vagabond* as Doctor Alogos, whose thoughts on matter and spirit are a parody of the original ideas reflected in the following extract from Priestley's *Disquisitions*.]

---

[1]   The true sense of this word is almost entirely lost amongst the moderns. The name of *city* is now generally used to signify a corporate town, and that of *citizen* applied to a burgess of such a corporation. Men do not seem to know that *houses* make a *town*, and *citizens* a *city* ... [Rousseau's note].

INTRODUCTION

LEST any person should hastily misapprehend the *nature*, or *importance*, of the questions discussed in this treatise, or the manner in which I have decided for myself with respect to them, I shall here state the several subjects of inquiry as concisely, and with as much distinctness, as I can, and also inform the reader what my opinions concerning them really are.

It has generally been supposed that there are *two distinct kinds of substance* in human nature, and they have been distinguished by the terms *matter* and *spirit*. The former of these has been said to be possessed of the property of *extension*, viz. of length, breadth and thickness, and also of *solidity* or *impenetrability*, but it is said to be naturally destitute of all powers whatever. The latter has of late been defined to be a substance entirely *destitute of all extension*, or *relation to space*, so as to have no property in common with matter; and therefore to be properly *immaterial*, but to be possessed of the powers of *perception, intelligence* and *self-motion*.

Matter, is that kind of substance of which our *bodies* are composed, whereas the principle of perception and thought belonging to us is said to reside in a *spirit*, or immaterial principle, intimately united to the body; while the higher orders of intelligent beings, and especially the Divine Being, are said to be purely immaterial.

It is maintained in this treatise, that neither *matter* nor *spirit* (meaning by the latter the subject of sense and thought) correspond to the definitions above-mentioned. For, that matter is not that *inert* substance that it has been supposed to be; that *powers of attraction* or *repulsion* are necessary to its very being, and that no part of it appears to be *impenetrable* to other parts. I therefore define it to be a substance possessed of the property of *extension*, and of *powers of attraction* or *repulsion*. And since it has never yet been asserted, that the powers of *sensation* and *thought* are incompatible with these, (*solidity*, or *impenetrability* only, having been thought to be repugnant to them,) I therefore maintain, that we have no reason to suppose that there are in man two substances so distinct from each other as have been represented.

It is likewise maintained in this treatise, that the notion of two substances that have no *common property*, and yet are capable of *intimate connexion* and *mutual action*, is both absurd and *modern*; a substance without extension or relation to place being unknown both in the

Scriptures, and to all antiquity; the human mind, for example, having till lately been thought to have a proper *presence in the body*, and a *proper motion* together with it; and the Divine Mind having always been represented as being, truly and properly *omnipresent*.

It is maintained, however, in the SEQUEL of this treatise, that such a distinction as the ancient philosophers *did* make between *matter* and *spirit*, though it was by no means such a distinction as was defined above (which does not admit of their having any common property), but a distinction which made the Supreme Mind the author of all good, and *matter* the source of all evil; that all inferior intelligences are *emanations from the Supreme Mind*, or made out of its substance, and that matter was reduced to its present form not by the Supreme Mind itself, but by *another intelligence*, a peculiar emanation from it, has been the real source of the greatest corruptions of true religion in all ages, many of which remain to this very day. It is here maintained, that this *system of philosophy*, and the *true system of revelation*, have always been diametrically opposite, and hostile to each other; and that the latter can never be firmly established but upon the ruins of the former.

To promote this firm establishment of the system *of pure revelation*, in opposition to that of a vain and absurd *philosophy*, here shewn to be so, is the true object of this work; in the perusal of which I beg the candour and patient attention of the judicious and philosophical reader.

It may not be unuseful to observe, that a distinction ought to be made with respect to the *relative importance* and *mutual subordination of the different positions* contended for in this treatise. The principal object is, to prove the uniform composition of man, or that what we call *mind*, or the principle of perception and thought, is not a substance distinct from the body, but the result of corporeal organization; and what I have advanced preliminary to this, concerning the *nature of matter*, though subservient to this argument, is by no means essential to it: for, whatever matter be, I think I have sufficiently proved that the human mind is nothing more than a modification of it.

Again, that man is wholly material is eminently subservient to the doctrine of the *proper*, or *mere humanity* of Christ. For, if no man has a soul distinct from his body, Christ, who, in all other respects, appeared as a man, could not have had a soul which had existed before his body; and the whole doctrine of the *pre-existence of souls* (of which the opinion of the pre-existence of Christ was a branch) will be effectually overturned. But I apprehend that, should I have failed in the proof of the materiality of man, arguments enough remain, independent of this, to prove the non-pre-existence of Christ, and of this doctrine having been introduced into Christianity from the system of Oriental philosophy.

Lastly, the doctrine *of necessity*, maintained in the Appendix, is the immediate result of the doctrine of the materiality of man; for mechanism is the undoubted consequence of materialism. But, whether man be wholly material or not, I apprehend that proof enough is advanced that every human volition is subject to certain fixed laws, and that the pretended *self-determining power* is altogether imaginary and impossible.

In short, it is my firm persuasion, that the three doctrines *of materialism*, of that which is commonly called *Socinianism*, and of philosophical *necessity*, are equally parts of *one system*, being equally founded on just observations of nature, and fair deductions from the Scriptures; and that whoever shall duly consider their *connexion*, and *dependence on one another*, will find no sufficient consistency in any general scheme of principles, that does not comprehend them all. At the same time, each of these doctrines stands on its own independent foundation, and is capable of such separate demonstration, as subjects of a moral nature require or admit.

I have advanced what has occurred to me in support of all the three parts of this system; confident that, in due time, the truth will bear down before it every opposing prejudice, how inveterate soever, and gain a firm establishment in the minds of all men....

SECTION VII

Considerations more immediately relating to IMMATERIAL SUBSTANCES, *and especially to the* CONNEXION OF THE SOUL AND BODY.

PART I.
Of the PRESENCE *of the Soul with the Body.*

THE idea of an *immaterial substance*, as it is defined by metaphysicians, is entirely a modern thing, and is still unknown to the vulgar. The original, and still prevailing idea concerning a *soul* or *spirit*, is that of a kind of attenuated aerial substance, of a more subtle nature than gross bodies, which have weight, and make a sensible resistance when they are pushed against, or struck at. The *form* of it may be variable, but it is capable, in certain circumstances, of becoming the object of sight. Thus when our Lord appeared to his disciples walking on the sea, and also after his resurrection, they thought it had been a *spirit*; and, therefore, to convince them of their mistake on the latter of these occasions, he bade them handle him; for that a spirit had not flesh and bones, as they might be convinced that he had. He did not observe to them, that a spirit could not be the object of *sight*, any more than of *touch*. Also, whatever expressions might casually drop from any of the ancient philosophers, it is evident to all who consider the whole of their doctrine, that their idea of a spirit was widely different from that which is now contended for.

That a spirit is, strictly speaking, *indivisible*, which is essential to the modern idea of it, is absolutely incompatible with the notion that is known to have run through almost all the systems of the ancients, derived originally from the *East, viz.* that all human souls, and all finite intelligences, were originally *portions of the great soul of the universe*; and though detached from it for a time, are finally to be absorbed into it again; when the separate consciousness belonging at present to each of them will be for ever lost. How the idea of a spirit came to be refined into the very *attenuated state* in which we now find it, I shall endeavour to investigate in its proper place; and, in the mean time, shall bestow a few observations upon it, as it appears in the writings of the latest and most celebrated metaphysicians.

A spirit, then, or an *immaterial substance*, in the modern strict use of the term, signifies a substance that has no *extension* of any kind, nor any thing of the *vis inertia*; that belongs to matter. It has neither *length*, *breadth*, nor *thickness*, so that it occupies no portion of space; on which account, the most, rigorous metaphysicians say, that it bears no sort of relation to space, any more than sound does to the eye, or light to the ear. In fact, therefore, *spirit* and *space* have nothing to do with one another, and it is even improper to say, that an immaterial being *exists in space*, or that it *resides* in one place more than in another; for, properly speaking, it is *no where*, but has a mode of existence that cannot be expressed by any phraseology appropriated to the modes in which matter exists. Even these spiritual and intellectual beings themselves have no idea of the manner in which they exist, at least while they are confined by gross matter.

It follows also from this view of the subject, that the *Divine mind* can only be said to be *omnipresent* by way of figure; for, strictly speaking, this term implies *extension*, of which all immaterial substances are utterly incapable. By the omnipresence of the Deity, therefore, they mean his power of *acting every where*, though he *exists no where*. The mind of any particular person, also, they suppose not to be confined within the body of that person; but that though itself bears no relation whatever to space or place, its exertions and affections are, by the sovereign appointment of his Creator, confined to a particular system of organized matter, wherever that happens to be, and continues so limited in its operations as long as the organization subsists; but, that being dissolved, the immaterial principle has no more to do with the matter that had been thus organized, than with any other matter in the universe. It can neither affect it, nor be affected by it.

Others, however, I believe, considering that, though *mathematical points* occupy no real portion of space, they are yet capable of bearing some relation to it, by being fixed in this or that place, at certain distances from each other, are willing to allow that spirits also may be said to be in one place in preference to another; and, consequently, that they are capable of changing place, and of moving hither and thither, together with the body to which they belong. But this is not the opinion that seems to prevail in general; since it supposes spirit to have, at least, one property in common with matter, whereas a being strictly *immaterial* (which, in terms, implies a negation of all the properties of matter) ought not to have any thing in common with it.

Besides, a mathematical point is, in fact, no *substance* at all, being the mere *limit*, or termination of a body, or the *place* in void space where a body is terminated, or may be supposed to be so. Mere points, mere *lines*, or mere *surfaces*, are alike the mere *boundaries of material substances*, and may not improperly be called their *properties*, necessarily entering into the definition of particular bodies, and consequently bear no sort of relation to what is immaterial. And therefore, the *consistent immaterialist* has justly disclaimed this idea.

Indeed, it is evident, that if nothing but immaterial substances, or pure intelligences, had existed, the very idea of *place*, or *space*, could not have occurred to us. And an idea, that an immaterial being could never have acquired without having an idea of body, or matter, cannot belong to *itself*, but to matter only. Consequently, according to the strict and only consistent system of immateriality, a spirit is properly *no where*, and altogether incapable of *local motion*, though it has an arbitrary connexion with a body that is confined to a particular place, and is capable of moving from one place to another. This, therefore, being the only consistent notion of an immaterial substance, and every thing short of it being mere materialism, it is to the consideration of this idea that I shall confine myself.

4. From Thomas Paine, *Rights of Man: Being an Answer to Mr. Burke's Attack on the French Revolution* (1791; London, 1792), 74; 76–78 (Part One, "Conclusion")

[Thomas Paine's *Rights of Man* was probably the most widely disseminated text in the 1790s representing the Jacobin position in the Revolutionary Debates. Whereas Edmund Burke had argued that in order to gain civil rights an individual had to give up some of his natural rights, Paine staunchly defended man's natural rights as unalienable—to be invested in part in the "common stock" of society, but never to be given up. Since all individuals share the same natural rights ("liberty, property, security, and resistance of oppression"), the only rational form of government for Paine is a representative government, which is bound by the will of the people, whose natural rights it must protect and defend.]

CONCLUSION

REASON and Ignorance, the opposites of each other, influence the great bulk of mankind. If either of these can be rendered sufficiently extensive in a country, the machinery of Government goes easily on. Reason obeys itself; and Ignorance submits to whatever is dictated to it.

The two modes of Government which prevail in the world, are, *first*, Government by election and representation: *Secondly*, Government by hereditary succession. The former is generally known by the name of republic; the latter by that of monarchy and aristocracy.

Those two distinct and opposite forms, erect themselves on the two distinct and opposite bases of Reason and Ignorance.—As the exercise of Government requires talents and abilities, and as talents and abilities cannot have hereditary descent, it is evident that hereditary succession requires a belief from man, to which his reason cannot subscribe, and which can only be established upon his ignorance; and the more ignorant any country is, the better it is fitted for this species of Government.

On the contrary, Government in a well-constituted republic, requires no belief from man beyond what his reason can give. He sees the *rationale* of the whole system, its origin and its operation; and as it is best supported when best understood, the human faculties act with boldness, and acquire, under this form of Government, a gigantic manliness....

From the Revolutions of America and France, and the symptoms that have appeared in other countries, it is evident that the opinion of the world is changed with respect to systems of Government, and that revolutions are not within the compass of political calculations. The progress of time and circumstances, which men assign to the accomplishment of great changes, is too mechanical to measure the force of the mind, and the rapidity of reflection, by which revolutions are generated: All the old Governments have received a shock from those that already appear, and which were once more improbable, and are a greater subject of wonder, than a general revolution in Europe would be now.

When we survey the wretched condition of man under the monarchical and hereditary systems of Government, dragged from his home by one power, or driven by another, and impoverished by taxes more than by enemies, it becomes evident that those systems are bad, and that a general revolution in the principle and construction of Governments is necessary.

What is government more than the management of the affairs of a Nation? It is not, and from its nature cannot be, the property of any particular man or family, but of the whole community, at whose expense it is supported; and though by force or contrivance it has been usurped into an inheritance, the usurpation cannot alter the right of things. Sovereignty, as a matter of right, appertains to the Nation only, and not to any individual; and a Nation has at all times an inherent indefeasible right to abolish any form of Government it finds inconvenient, and establish such as accords with its interest, disposition, and happiness. The romantic and barbarous distinction of men into Kings and subjects, though it may suit the condition of courtiers, cannot that of citizens; and is exploded by the principle upon which Governments are now founded. Every citizen is a member of the Sovereignty, and, as such, can acknowledge no personal subjection; and his obedience can be only to the laws.

When men think of what Government is, they must necessarily suppose it to possess a knowledge of all the objects and France, operates to embrace the whole of a Nation; and the knowledge necessary to the interest of all the parts, is to be found in the centre, which the parts by representation form: But the old Governments are on a construction that excludes knowledge as well as happiness; Government by monks, who know nothing of the world beyond the walls of a convent, is as consistent as government by Kings.

What were formerly called Revolutions, were little more than a change of persons, or an alteration of local circumstances. They rose and fell like things of course, and had nothing in their existence or their fate that could influence beyond the spot that produced them. But what we now see in the world, from the Revolutions of America and France, are a renovation of the natural order of things, a system of principles as universal as truth and the existence of man, and combining moral with political happiness and national prosperity.

"I. *Men are born and always continue free, and equal in respect of their rights. Civil distinctions, therefore, can be founded only on public utility.*
II. *The end of all political associations is the preservation of the natural and imprescriptible rights of man; and these rights are liberty, property, security, and resistance of oppression.*
II. *The Nation is essentially the source of all Sovereignty; nor can any* INDIVIDUAL, *or* ANY BODY OF MEN, *be entitled to any authority which is not expressly derived from it.*"

In these principles, there is nothing to throw a Nation into confusion by inflaming ambition. They are calculated to call forth wisdom and abilities, and to exercise them for the public good, and not for the emolument or aggrandizement of particular descriptions of men or families. Monarchical sovereignty, the enemy of mankind, and the source of misery, is abolished; and sovereignty itself is restored to its natural and original place, the Nation. Were this the case throughout Europe, the cause of wars would be taken away.

It is attributable to Henry the Fourth of France, a man of an enlarged and benevolent heart, that he proposed, about the year 1610, a plan for abolishing war in Europe. The plan consisted in constituting an European Congress, or as the French Authors style it, a Pacific Republic; by appointing delegates from the several Nations, who were to act as a Court of arbitration in any disputes that might arise between nation and nation.

Had such a plan been adopted at the time it was proposed, the taxes of England and France, as two of the parties, would have been at least ten millions sterling annually to each Nation less than they were at the commencement of the French Revolution.

To conceive a cause why such a plan has not been adopted, (and that instead of a Congress for the purpose of *preventing* war, it has been called only to *terminate* a war, after a fruitless expense of several years), it will be necessary to consider the interest of Governments as a distinct interest to that of Nations.

Whatever is the cause of taxes to a Nation, becomes also the means of revenue to a Government. Every war terminates with an addition of taxes, and consequently with an addition of revenue; and in any event of war, in the manner they are now commenced and concluded, the power and interest of Governments are increased. War, therefore, from its productiveness, as it easily furnishes the pretence of necessity for taxes and appointments to places and offices, becomes a principal part of the system of old Governments; and to establish any mode to abolish war, however advantageous it might be to Nations, would be to take from such Government the most lucrative of its branches. The frivolous matters upon which war is made, show the disposition and avidity of Governments to uphold the system of war, and betray the motives upon which they act.

Why are not Republics plunged into war, but because the nature of their Government does not admit of an interest distinct from that of the Nation? Even Holland, though an ill-constructed Republic, and with a commerce extending over the world, existed nearly a century without war: and the instant the form of Government was changed in France, the republican principles of peace and domestic prosperity and economy arose with the new Government; and the same consequences would follow the same causes in other Nations.

As war is the system of Government on the old construction, the animosity which Nations reciprocally entertain, is nothing more than what the policy of their Governments excites, to keep up the spirit of the system. Each Government accuses the other of perfidy, intrigue, and ambition, as a means of heating the imagination of their respective Nations, and incensing them to hostilities. Man is not the enemy of man, but through the medium of a false system of Government. Instead, therefore, of exclaiming against the ambition of Kings, the exclamation should be directed against the principle of such Governments; and instead of seeking to reform the individual, the wisdom of a Nation should apply itself to reform the system.

Whether the forms and maxims of Governments which are still

in practice, were adapted to the condition of the world at the period they were established, is not in this case the question. The older they are, the less correspondence can they have with the present state of things. Time, and change of circumstances and opinions, have the same progressive effect in rendering modes of Government obsolete, as they have upon customs and manners.—Agriculture, commerce, manufactures, and the tranquil arts, by which the prosperity of Nations is best promoted, require a different system of Government, and a different species of knowledge to direct its operations, than what might have been required in the former condition of the world.

As it is not difficult to perceive, from the enlightened state of mankind, that hereditary Governments are verging to their decline, and that Revolutions on the broad basis of national sovereignty, and Government by representation, are making their way in Europe, it would be an act of wisdom to anticipate their approach, and produce Revolutions by reason and accommodation, rather than commit them to the issue of convulsions.

From what we now see, nothing of reform in the political world ought to be held improbable. It is an age of Revolutions, in which everything may be looked for. The intrigue of Courts, by which the system of war is kept up, may provoke a confederation of Nations to abolish it: and an European Congress, to patronize the progress of free Government, and promote the civilization of Nations with each other, is an event nearer in probability, than once were the Revolutions and Alliance of France and America.

5. From Mary Wollstonecraft, *A Vindication of the Rights of Woman* (1792), in *The Works of Mary Wollstonecraft*, gen. eds. Janet Todd and Marilyn Butler, 7 vols. (London: Pickering, 1989), 5:74–77 ("Introduction")

[Mary Wollstonecraft is often described as the founding mother of modern feminism, and her treatise *A Vindication of the Rights of Woman* as the founding text. While there were many others, and many other texts that provided arguments for the emancipation of women at the end of the eighteenth century, the *Vindication* became an icon for equal rights for women and for a radical overhaul of the social, political, and economical structures that had effectively turned women into second-rate citizens. Growing out of the idea of a perfectible society, Wollstonecraft placed much emphasis in her text on education and parenting. If girls and women were often "weak, artificial creatures," she argues in the following passage, this was because they had been raised and educated to be such; raise and educate them as rational beings, and they will become such. Wollstonecraft is lampooned in *The Vagabond* in the figure of Frederick Fenton's mistress "Mary."]

Yet, because I am a woman, I would not lead my readers to suppose that I mean violently to agitate the contested question respecting the equality or inferiority of the sex; but as the subject lies in my way, and I cannot pass it over without subjecting the main tendency of my reasoning to misconstruction, I shall stop a moment to deliver, in a few words, my opinion.—In the government of the physical world it is observable that the female in point of strength is, in general, inferior to the male. This is the law of nature; and it does not appear to be suspended or abrogated in favour of woman. A degree of physical superiority cannot, therefore, be denied—and it is a noble prerogative! But not content with this natural pre-eminence, men endeavour to sink us still lower, merely to render us alluring objects for a moment; and women, intoxicated by the adoration which men, under the influence of their senses, pay them, do not seek to obtain a durable interest in their hearts, or to become the friends of the fellow creatures who find amusement in their society.

I am aware of an obvious inference:—from every quarter have I heard exclamations against masculine women; but where are they to be found? If by this appellation men mean to inveigh against their ardour in hunting, shooting, and gaming, I shall most cordially join in the cry; but if it be against the imitation of manly virtues, or, more properly speaking, the attainment of those talents and virtues, the exercise of which ennobles the human character, and which raise females in the scale of animal being, when they are comprehensively termed mankind;—all those who view them with a philosophic eye must, I should think, wish with me, that they may every day grow more and more masculine.

This discussion naturally divides the subject. I shall first consider women in the grand light of human creatures, who, in common with men, are placed on this earth to unfold their faculties; and afterwards I shall more particularly point out their peculiar designation.

I wish also to steer clear of an error which many respectable writers have fallen into; for the instruction which has hitherto been addressed to women, has rather been applicable to *ladies*, if the little indirect advice, that is scattered through Sandford and Merton, be excepted; but, addressing my sex in a firmer tone, I pay particular attention to those in the middle class, because they appear to be in the most natural state. Perhaps the seeds of false-refinement, immorality, and vanity, have ever been shed by the great. Weak, artificial beings, raised above the common wants and affections of their race, in a premature unnatural manner, undermine the very foundation of virtue, and spread corruption through the whole mass of society! As a class of mankind they have the strongest claim to pity; the education of the rich tends to render them vain and helpless, and the unfolding mind is not strengthened by the practice of those duties which dignify the human character.—They only live to amuse themselves, and by the same law which in nature invariably produces certain effects, they soon only afford barren amusement.

But as I purpose taking a separate view of the different ranks of society, and of the moral character of women, in each, this hint is, for the present, sufficient; and I have only alluded to the subject, because it appears to me to be the very essence of an introduction to give a cursory account of the contents of the work it introduces.

My own sex, I hope, will excuse me, if I treat them like rational creatures, instead of flattering their *fascinating* graces, and viewing them as if they were in a state of perpetual childhood, unable to stand alone. I earnestly wish to point out in what true dignity and human happiness consists—I wish to persuade women to endeavour to acquire strength, both of mind and body, and to convince them that the soft phrases, susceptibility of heart, delicacy of sentiment, and refinement of taste, are almost synonymous with epithets of weakness, and that those beings who are only the objects of pity and that kind of love, which has been termed its sister, will soon become objects of contempt.

Dismissing then those pretty feminine phrases, which the men condescendingly use to soften our slavish dependence, and despising that weak elegancy of mind, exquisite sensibility, and sweet docility of manners, supposed to be the sexual characteristics of the weaker vessel, I wish to shew that elegance is inferior to virtue, that the first object of laudable ambition is to obtain a character as a human being, regardless of the distinction of sex; and that secondary views should be brought to this simple touchstone....

Women are, in fact, so much degraded by mistaken notions of

female excellence, that I do not mean to add a paradox when I assert, that this artificial weakness produces a propensity to tyrannize, and gives birth to cunning, the natural opponent of strength, which leads them to play off those contemptible infantine airs that undermine esteem even whilst they excite desire. Let men become more chaste and modest, and if women do not grow wiser in the same ratio, it will be clear that they have weaker understandings. It seems scarcely necessary to say, that I now speak of the sex in general. Many individuals have more sense than their male relatives; and, as nothing preponderates where there is a constant struggle for an equilibrium, without it has naturally more gravity, some women govern their husbands without degrading themselves, because intellect will always govern.

6. From William Godwin, *An Enquiry Concerning Political Justice, and Its Influence on General Virtue and Happiness* (1793), *Political and Philosophical Writings of William Godwin*, gen. ed. Mark Philp, 7 vols. (London: Pickering and Chatto, 1993), 3:49–51, 52–54 (Book II, Chapter II); 437–40 (Book VIII, Chapter IV); 449–55 (Book VIII, Chapter VI)

[If there is one text that made the Revolutionary Debate of the 1790s in Britain it is William Godwin's *Political Justice*. Godwin's incisive analysis of the evils of modern society, and his radical proposals to amend them, fired the minds of those dreaming of a just and equitable society, but shocked the British establishment. Not surprisingly, Godwin (or "Stupeo") and his *Political Justice* are the main butts of Walker's vitriolic venom in *The Vagabond*. The following extracts from Godwin's treatise reflect those ideas and concepts most vehemently attacked and most viciously parodied by Walker in his novel. These include: the notion of political justice; the nature of gratitude; of duty; the general good; (equality of) property; and marriage and cohabitation].

i. Book II, "Principles of Society"; Chapter II, "Of Justice" (49–51; 52–54)

From what has been said it appears, that the subject of the present enquiry is strictly speaking a department of the science of morals. Morality is the source from which its fundamental axioms must be drawn, and they will be made somewhat clearer in the present instance, if we assume the term justice as a general appellation for all moral duty.

That this appellation is sufficiently expressive of the subject will appear, if we consider for a moment mercy, gratitude, temperance, or any of those duties which in looser speaking are contradistinguished from justice. Why should I pardon this criminal, remunerate this favour, abstain from this indulgence? If it partake of the nature of morality, it must be either right or wrong, just or unjust. It must tend to the benefit of the individual, either without intrenching upon, or with actual advantage to the mass of individuals. Either way it benefits the whole, because individuals are part of the whole. Therefore to do it is just, and to forbear it is unjust. If justice have any meaning, it is just that I should contribute every thing in my power to the benefit of the whole.

Considerable light will probably be thrown upon our investigation, if, quitting for the present the political view, we examine justice merely as it exists among individuals. Justice is a rule of conduct originating in the connection of one percipient being with another. A comprehensive maxim which has been laid down upon the subject is, "that we should love our neighbour as ourselves." But this maxim, though possessing considerable merit as a popular principle, is not modelled with the strictness of philosophical accuracy.

In a loose and general view I and my neighbour are both of us men; and of consequence entitled to equal attention. But in reality it is probable that one of us is a being of more worth and importance than the other. A man is of more worth than a beast; because, being possessed of higher faculties, he is capable of a more refined and genuine happiness. In the same manner the illustrious archbishop of Cambray was of more worth than his chambermaid, and there are few of us that would hesitate to pronounce, if his palace were in flames, and the life of only one of them could be preserved, which of the two ought to be preferred.

But there is another ground of preference, beside the private consideration of one of them being farther removed from the state of a mere animal. We are not connected with one or two percipient beings, but with a society, a nation, and in some sense with the whole family of mankind. Of consequence that life ought to be preferred which will be most conducive to the general good. In saving the life of Fenelon, suppose at the moment when he was conceiving the project of his immortal Telemachus, I should be promoting the benefit of thousands, who have been cured by the perusal of it of some error, vice and consequent unhappiness. Nay, my benefit would extend farther than this, for every individual thus cured has become a better member of society, and has contributed in his turn to the happiness, the information and improvement of others.

Supposing I had been myself the chambermaid, I ought to have chosen to die, rather than that Fenelon should have died. The life of Fenelon was really preferable to that of the chambermaid. But understanding is the faculty that perceives the truth of this and similar propositions; and justice is the principle that regulates my conduct accordingly. It would have been just in the chambermaid to have preferred the archbishop to herself. To have done otherwise would have been a breach of justice.

Supposing the chambermaid had been my wife, my mother or my benefactor. This would not alter the truth of the proposition. The life of Fenelon would still be more valuable that that of the chambermaid; and justice, pure, unadulterated justice, would still have preferred that which was most valuable. Justice would have taught me to save the life of Fenelon at the expence of the other. What magic is there in the pronoun "my," to overturn the decisions of everlasting truth? My wife or my mother may be a fool or a prostitute, malicious, lying or dishonest. If they be, of what consequence is it that they are mine?

"But my mother endured for me the pains of child bearing, and nourished me in the helplessness of infancy." When she first subjected herself to the necessity of these cares, she was probably influenced by no particular motives of benevolence to her future offspring. Every voluntary benefit however entitles the bestower to some kindness and retribution. But why so? Because a voluntary benefit is an evidence of benevolent intention, that is, of virtue. It is the disposition of the mind, not the external action, that entitles to respect. But the merit of this disposition is equal, whether the benefit was conferred upon me or upon another. I and another man cannot both be right in preferring our own individual benefactor, for no man can be at the same time both better and worse than his neighbour. My benefactor ought to be esteemed, not because he bestowed a benefit upon me, but because he bestowed it upon a human being. His desert will be in exact proportion to the degree, in which that human being was worthy of the distinction conferred. Thus every view of the subject brings us back to the consideration of my neighbour's moral worth and his importance to the general weal, as the only standard to determine the treatment to which he is entitled. Gratitude therefore, a principle which has so often been the theme of the moralist and the poet, is no part either of justice or virtue. By gratitude I understand a sentiment, which would lead me to prefer one man to another, from some other consideration than that of his superior usefulness or worth: that is, which would make something true to me (for example this preferableness), which cannot be true to another man, and is not true in itself....*

Having considered the persons with whom justice is conversant, let us next enquire into the degree in which we are obliged to consult the good of others. And here I say, that it is just that I should do all the good in my power. Does any person in distress apply to me for relief? It is my duty to grant it, and I commit a breach of duty in refusing. If this principle be not of universal application, it is because, in conferring a benefit upon an individual, I may in some instances inflict an injury of superior magnitude upon myself or society. Now the same justice, that binds me to any individual of my fellow men, binds me to the whole. If, while I confer a benefit upon one man, it appears, in striking an equitable balance, that I am injuring the whole, my action ceases to be right and becomes absolutely wrong. But how much am I bound to do for the general weal, that is, for the benefit of the individuals of whom the whole is composed? Every thing in my power. What to the neglect of the means of my existence? No; for I am myself a part of the whole. Beside, it will rarely happen but that the project of doing for others every thing in my power, will demand for its execution the preservation of my own existence; or in other words, it will rarely happen but that I can do more good in twenty years than in one. If the extraordinary case should occur in which I can promote the general good by my death, more than by my life, justice requires that I should be content to die. In all other cases, it is just that I should be careful to maintain my body and my mind in the utmost vigour, and in the best condition for service.

I will suppose for example that it is right for one man to possess a greater portion of property than another, either as the fruit of his industry, or the inheritance of his ancestors. Justice obliges him to

---

* This argument respecting gratitude is stated with great clearness in an Essay on the Nature of True Virtue, by the Rev. Jonathan Edwards. 12mo. Dilly [Godwin's note].

regard this property as a trust, and calls upon him maturely to consider in what manner it may best be employed for the increase of liberty, knowledge and virtue. He has no right to dispose of a shilling of it at the will of his caprice. So far from being entitled to well earned applause for having employed some scanty pittance in the service of philanthropy, he is in the eye of justice a delinquent if he withhold any portion from that service. Nothing can be more incontrovertible. Could that portion have been better or more worthily employed? That it could is implied in the very terms of the proposition. Then it was just it should have been so employed.—In the same manner as my property, I hold my person as a trust in behalf of mankind. I am bound to employ my talents, my understanding, my strength and my time for the production of the greatest quantity of general good. Such are the declarations of justice, so great is the extent of my duty.

But justice is reciprocal. If it be just that I should confer a benefit, it is just that another man should receive it, and, if I withhold from him that to which he is entitled, he must justly complain. My neighbour is in want of ten pounds that I can spare. There is no law of political institution that has been made to reach this case, and to transfer this property from me to him. But in the eye of simple justice, unless it can be shewn that the money can be more beneficently employed, his claim is as complete, as if he had my bond in his possession, or had supplied me with goods to the amount.

To this it has sometimes been answered, "that there is more than one person, that stands in need of the money I have to spare, and of consequence I must be at liberty to bestow it as I please." I answer, if only one person offer himself to my knowledge or search, to me there is but one. Those others that I cannot find belong to other rich men to assist (rich men, I say, for every man is rich, who has more money than his just occasions demand), and not to me. If more than one person offer, I am obliged to balance their fitness, and conduct myself accordingly. It is scarcely possible to happen that two men shall be of exactly equal fitness, or that I shall be equally certain of the fitness of the one as of the other.

It is therefore impossible for me to confer upon any man a favour, I can only do him a right. What deviates from the law of justice, even I will suppose in the too much done in favour of some individual or some part of the general whole, is so much subtracted from the general stock, is so much of absolute injustice.

The inference most clearly afforded by the preceding reasonings, is the competence of justice as a principle of deduction in all cases of moral enquiry. The reasonings themselves are rather of the nature of illustration and example, and any error that may be imputed to them in particulars, will not invalidate the general conclusion, the propriety of applying moral justice as a criterion in the investigation of political truth.

Society is nothing more than an aggregation of individuals. Its claims and its duties must be the aggregate of their claims and duties, the one no more precarious and arbitrary than the other. What has the society a right to require from me? The question is already answered: every thing that it is my duty to do. Any thing more? Certainly not. Can they change eternal truth, or subvert the nature of men and their actions? Can they make it my duty to commit intemperance, to maltreat or assassinate my neighbour?—Again, What is it that the society is bound to do for its members? Every thing that can contribute to their welfare. But the nature of their welfare is defined by the nature of the mind. That will most contribute to it, which enlarges the understanding, supplies incitements to virtue, fills us with a generous consciousness of our independence, and carefully removes whatever can impede our exertions....

ii. BookVIII, "Of Property"; Chapter IV, "Objection to this System [of Equality] from the Allurements of Sloth," 437–40

Another objection which has been urged against the system which counteracts the accumulation of property, is, "that it would put an end to industry. We behold in commercial countries the miracles that are operated by the love of gain. Their inhabitants cover the seas with their fleets, astonish mankind by the refinement of their ingenuity, hold vast continents in subjection in distant parts of the world by their arms, are able to defy the most powerful confederacies, and, oppressed with taxes and debts, seem to acquire fresh prosperity under their accumulated burthens. Shall we lightly part with a system that seems pregnant with such inexhaustible motives? Shall we believe that men will cultivate assiduously what they have no assurance they shall be permitted to apply to their personal emolument? It will perhaps be found with agriculture as it is with commerce, which then flourishes best when subjected to no control, but, when placed under rigid restraints, languishes and expires. Once establish it as a principle in society that no man is to apply to his personal use more than his necessities require, and you will find every man become indifferent to those exertions which now call forth the energy of his faculties. Man is the creature of sensations; and, when we endeavour to restrain his intellect, and govern him by reason alone, we do but show our ignorance of his nature. Self love is the genuine source of our actions, and, if this should be found to bring vice and partiality along with it, yet the system that should endeavour to supersede it, would be at best no more than a beautiful romance. If each man found that, without being compelled to exert his own industry, he might lay claim to the superfluity of his neighbour, indolence would perpetually usurp his faculties, and such a society must either starve, or be obliged in its own defence to return to that system of injustice and sordid interest, which theoretical reasoners will for ever arraign to no purpose."

This is the principle objection that prevents men from yielding without resistance to the accumulated evidence that has already been adduced. In reply, it may be observed in the first place, that the equality for which we are pleading is an equality that would succeed to a state of great intellectual improvement. So bold a revolution cannot take place in human affairs, till the general mind has been highly cultivated. The present age of mankind is greatly enlightened; but it is to be feared is not yet enlightened enough. Hasty and undigested tumults may take place under the idea of an equalisation of property; but it is only a calm and clear conviction of justice, of justice mutually to be rendered and received, of happiness to be produced by the desertion of our most rooted habits, that can introduce an invariable system of this sort. Attempts without this preparation will be productive only of confusion. Their effect will be momentary, and a new and more barbarous inequality will succeed. Each man with an unaltered appetite will watch his opportunity to gratify his love of power or his love of distinction, by usurping on his inattentive neighbours.

Is it to be believed then that a state of so great intellectual improvement can be the forerunner of barbarism? Savages, it is true, are subject to the weakness of indolence. But civilised and refined states are the scene of peculiar activity. It is thought, acuteness of disquisition, and ardour of pursuit, that set the corporeal faculties at work. Thought begets thought. Nothing can put a stop to the progressive advances of mind, but oppression. But here, so far from being oppressed, every man is equal, every man independent and at his ease. It has been observed that the establishment of a republic is always attended with public enthusiasm and irresistible enterprise. Is it to be believed that equality, the true republicanism, will be less effectual? It is true that in republics this spirit sooner or later is found to languish. Republicanism is not a remedy that strikes at the root of the evil. Injustice, oppression and misery can find an abode in those seeming happy seats. But what shall stop the progress of ardour and improvement, where the monopoly of property is unknown?

This argument will be strengthened, if we reflect on the amount of labour that a state of equal property will require. What is this quantity of exertion from which we are supposing many members of the community to shrink? It is so light a burthen as rather to assume the appearance of agreeable relaxation and gentle exercise, than of labour. In this community scarcely any can be expected in consequence of their situation or avocations to consider themselves as exempted from manual industry. There will be no rich men to recline in indolence and fatten upon the labour of their fellows. The mathematician, the poet and the philosopher will derive a new stock of chearfulness and energy from the recurring labour that makes them feel they are men. There will be no persons employed in the manufacture of trinkets and luxuries; and none in directing the wheels of the complicated machine of government, tax-gatherers, beadles, excisemen, tide-waiters, clerks and secretaries. There will be neither fleets nor armies, neither courtiers nor footmen. It is the unnecessary employments that at present occupy the great mass of the inhabitants of every civilised nation, while the peasant labours incessantly to maintain them in a state more pernicious than idleness.

It has been computed that not more than one twentieth of the inhabitants of England are employed seriously and substantially in the labours of agriculture. Add to this, that the nature of agriculture is such, as necessarily to give full occupation in some parts of the year, and to leave others comparatively unemployed. We may consider these latter periods as equivalent to a labour which, under the direction of sufficient skill, might suffice in a simple state of society for the fabrication of tools, for weaving, and the occupation of taylors, bakers and butchers. The object in the present state of society is to multiply labour, in another state it will be to simplify it. A vast disproportion of the wealth of the community has been thrown into the hands of a few, and ingenuity has been continually upon the stretch to find out ways in which it may be expended. In the feudal times the great lord invited the poor to come and eat of the produce of his estate upon condition of their wearing his livery, and forming themselves in rank and file to do honour to his well born guests. Now that exchanges are more facilitated, we have quitted this inartificial mode, and oblige the men we maintain out of our incomes to exert their ingenuity and industry in return. Thus in the instance just mentioned, we pay the taylor to cut our clothes to pieces, that he may sew them together again, and to decorate them with stitching and various ornaments, without which experience would speedily show that they were in no respect less useful. We are imagining in the present case a state of the most rigid simplicity.

From the sketch which has been here given it seems by no means impossible, that the labour of every twentieth man in the community would be sufficient to maintain the rest in all the absolute necessaries of human life. If then this labour, instead of being performed by so small a number, were amicably divided among them all, it would occupy the twentieth part of every man's time. Let us compute that the industry of a labouring man engrosses ten hours in every day, which, when we have deduced his hours of rest, recreation and meals, seems an ample allowance. It follows that half an hour a day, seriously employed in manual labour by every member of the community, would sufficiently supply the whole with necessaries. Who is he that would shrink from this degree of industry? Who is there that sees the incessant industry exerted in this city and this island, and would believe that, with half an hour's industry *per diem*, we should be every way happier and better than we are at present? Is it possible to contemplate this fair and generous picture of independence and virtue, where every man would have ample leisure for the noble energies of mind, without feeling our very souls refreshed with admiration and hope...?

iii. Book VIII, "Of Property"; Chapter VI, "Of the Objection to this System [of Equality] from the Inflexibility of Its Restrictions," 449–55

An objection that has often been urged against a system of equal property, is, "that it is inconsistent with personal independence. Every man according to this scheme is a passive instrument in the hands of the community. He must eat and drink, and play and sleep at the bidding of others. He has no habitation, no period at which he can retreat into himself, and not ask another's leave. He has nothing that he can call his own, not even his time or his person. Under the appearance of a perfect freedom from oppression and tyranny, he is in reality subjected to the most unlimited slavery." But the truth is, that a system of equal property requires no restrictions or superintendence whatever. There is no need of common labour, common meals or common magazines. These are feeble and mistaken instruments for restraining the conduct without making conquest of the judgment. If you cannot bring over the hearts of the community to your party, expect no success from brute regulations. If you can, regulation is unnecessary. Such a system was well enough adapted to the military constitution of Sparta; but it is wholly unworthy of men who are enlisted in no cause but that of reason and justice. Beware of reducing men to the state of machines. Govern them through no medium but that of inclination and conviction.

Why should we have common meals? Am I obliged to be hungry at the same time that you are? Ought I to come at a certain hour, from the museum where I am working, the recess where I meditate, or the observatory where I remark the phenomena of nature, to a certain hall appropriated to the office of eating; instead of eating, as reason bids me, at the time and place most suited to my avocations? Why have common magazines? For the purpose of carrying our provisions a certain distance, that we may afterwards bring them back again? Or is this precaution really necessary, after all that has been said in praise of equal society and the omnipotence of reason, to guard us against the knavery and covetousness of our associates? If it be, for God's sake let us discard the parade of political justice, and go over to the standard of those reasoners who say, that man and the practice of justice are incompatible with each other.

Once more let us be on our guard against reducing men to the condition of brute machines. The objectors of the last chapter were partly in the right when they spoke of the endless variety of mind. It would be absurd to say that we are not capable of truth, of evidence and agreement. In these respects, so far as mind is in a state of progressive improvement, we are perpetually coming nearer to each other. But there are subjects about which we shall continually differ, and ought to differ. The ideas, the associations and the circumstances of each man are properly his own; and it is a pernicious system that would lead us to require all men, however different their circumstances, to act in many of the common affairs of life by a precise general rule. Add to this, that, by the doctrine of progressive improvement, we shall always be erroneous, though we shall every day become less erroneous. The proper method for hastening the decay of error, is not, by brute force, or by regulation which is one of the classes of force, to endeavour to reduce men to intellectual uniformity; but on the contrary by teaching every man to think for himself.

From these principles it appears that every thing that is usually understood by the term cooperation, is in some degree an evil. A man in his solitude, is obliged to sacrifice or postpone the execution of his best thoughts to his own convenience. How many admirable designs have perished in the conception by means of this circumstance? The true remedy is for men to reduce their wants to the fewest possible, and as much as possible to simplify the mode of supplying them. It is still worse when a man is also obliged to consult the convenience of others. If I be expected to eat or work in conjunction with my neighbour, it must either be at a time most convenient to me, or to him, or to neither of us. We cannot be reduced to a clock-work uniformity.

Hence it follows that all supererogatory cooperation is carefully to be avoided, common labour and common meals. "But what shall we say to cooperation that seems to be dictated by the work to be performed?" It ought to be diminished. At present it is unreasonable to doubt, that the consideration of the evil of cooperation is in certain urgent cases to be postponed to that urgency. Whether by the nature of things cooperation of some sort will always be necessary, is a question that we are scarcely competent to decide. At present, to pull down a tree, to cut a canal, to navigate a vessel, requires the labour of many. Will it always require the labour of many? When we look at the complicated machines of human contrivance, various sorts of mills, of weaving engines, of steam engines, are we not astonished at the compendium of labour they produce? Who shall say where this species of improvement must stop? At present such inventions alarm the labouring part of the community; and they may be productive of temporary distress, though they conduce in the sequel to the most important interests of the multitude. But in a state of equal labour their utility will be liable to no dispute. Hereafter it is by no means clear that the most extensive operations will not be brought within the reach of one man; or, to make use of a familiar instance, that a plough may not be turned into a field, and perform its office without superintendence. It was in this sense that the celebrated Franklin conjectured, that 'mind would one day become omnipotent over matter'....

Another article which belongs to the subject of cooperation is cohabitation. A very simple process will lead us to a right decision in this instance. Science is most effectually cultivated, when the greatest number of minds are employed in the pursuit of it. If an hundred men spontaneously engage the whole energy of their faculties upon the solution of a given question, the chance of success will be greater, than if only ten men were so employed. By the same reason the chance will be also increased, in proportion as the intellectual operations of these men are individual, in proportion as their conclusions are directed by the reason of the thing, uninfluenced by the force either of compulsion or sympathy. All attachments to individuals, except in proportion to their merits, are plainly unjust. It is therefore desirable, that we should be the friends of man rather than of particular men, and that we should pursue the chain of our own reflexions, with no other interruption than information or philanthropy requires.

This subject of cohabitation is particularly interesting, as it includes in it the subject of marriage. It will therefore be proper to extend our enquiries somewhat further upon this head. Cohabitation is not only an evil as it checks the independent progress of mind; it is also inconsistent with the imperfections and propensities of man. It is absurd to expect that the inclinations of two human beings should coincide through any long period of time. To oblige them to act and live together, is to subject them to some inevitable portion of thwarting, bickering and unhappiness. This cannot be otherwise, so long as man has failed to reach the standard of absolute perfection. The supposition that I must have a companion for life, is the result of a complication of vices. It is the dictate of cowardice, and not of fortitude. It flows from the desire of being loved and esteemed for something that is not desert.

But the evil of marriage as it is practised in European countries lies deeper than this. The habit is, for a thoughtless and romantic youth of each sex to come together, to see each other for a few times and under circumstances full of delusion, and then to vow to each other eternal attachment. What is the consequence of this? In almost every instance they find themselves deceived. They are reduced to make the best of an irretrievable mistake. They are presented with the strongest imaginable temptation to become the dupes of falshood. They are led to conceive it their wisest policy to shut their eyes upon realities, happy if by any perversion of intellect they can persuade themselves that they were right in their first crude opinion of their companion. The institution of marriage is a system of fraud; and men who carefully mislead their judgments in the daily affair of their life, must always have a crippled judgment in every other concern. We ought to dismiss our mistake as soon as it is detected; but we are taught to cherish it. We ought to be incessant in our search after virtue and worth; but we are taught to check our enquiry, and shut our eyes upon the most attractive and admirable objects. Marriage is law, and the worst of all laws. Whatever our understandings may tell us of the person from whose connexion we should derive the greatest improvement, of the worth of one woman and the demerits of another, we are obliged to consider what is law, and not what is justice.

Add to this, that marriage is an affair of property, and the worst of all properties. So long as two human beings are forbidden by positive institution to follow the dictates of their own mind, prejudice is alive and vigorous. So long as I seek to engross one woman to myself, and to prohibit my neighbour from proving his superior desert and reaping the fruits of it, I am guilty of the most odious of all monopolies. Over this imaginary prize men watch with perpetual jealousy, and one man will find his desires and his capacity to circumvent as much excited, as the other is excited to traverse his projects and frustrate his hopes. As long as this state of society continues, philanthropy will be crossed and checked in a thousand ways, and the still augmenting stream of abuse will continue to flow.

The abolition of marriage will be attended with no evils. We are apt to represent it to ourselves as the harbinger of brutal lust and depravity. But it really happens in this as in other cases, that the positive laws which are made to restrain our vices, irritate and multiply them. Not to say, that the same sentiments of justice and happiness which in a state of equal property would destroy the relish for luxury, would decrease our inordinate appetites of every kind, and lead us universally to prefer the pleasures of intellect to the pleasures of sense.

The intercourse of the sexes will in such a state fall under the same system as any other species of friendship. Exclusively of all groundless and obstinate attachments, it will be impossible for me to live in the world without finding one man of a worth superior to that of any other whom I have an opportunity of observing. To this man I shall feel a kindness in exact proportion to my apprehension of his worth. The case will be precisely the same with respect to the female sex. I shall assiduously cultivate the intercourse of that woman whose accomplishments shall strike me in the most powerful manner. "But it may happen that other men will feel for her the same preference that I do." This will create no difficulty. We may all enjoy her conversation; and we shall all be wise enough to consider the sensual intercourse as a very trivial object. This, like every other affair in which two persons are concerned, must be regulated in each successive instance by the unforced consent of either party. It is a mark of the extreme depravity of our present habits, that we are inclined to suppose the sensual intercourse any wise material to the advantages arising from the purest affection. Reasonable men now eat and drink, not from the love of pleasure, but because eating and drinking are essential to our healthful existence. Reasonable men then will propagate their species, not because a certain sensible pleasure is annexed to this action, but because it is right the species should be propagated; and the manner in which they exercise this function will be regulated by the dictates of reason and duty.

Such are some of the considerations that will probably regulate the commerce of the sexes. It cannot be definitively affirmed whether it be known in such a state of society who is the father of each individual child. But it may be affirmed that such knowledge will be of no importance. It is aristocracy, self love and family pride that teach us to set a value upon it at present. I ought to prefer no human being to another, because that being is my father, my wife or my son, but because, for reasons which equally appeal to all understandings, that being is entitled to preference. One among the measures which will successively be dictated by the spirit of democracy, and that probably at no great distance, is the abolition of surnames....

7. From Gilbert Imlay, _The Emigrants, &c.; or, The History of an Expatriated Family_ (1793), ed. W.M. Verhoeven and Amanda Gilroy (New York: Penguin Books, 1998), 232–36 (Letter LXVII), 245–48 (Letter LXX)

[Set around the middle of the 1780s, the plot of the novel turns on the fate of an English family that emigrates to America. After a surprisingly effortless journey across the Allegheny Mountains and down the Ohio River, the T—ns settle down in the pristine wilderness of what is now Kentucky, near Louisville. The T—ns have been escorted there by Mr. Il—ray and his friend Captain Arl—ton, a Revolutionary War veteran. In the first passage Arl—ton, now married to the heroine, Caroline T—n, describes to his friend the wilderness utopia ("Bellefont") that he has begun to lay out on the banks of the Ohio; in the second passage Caroline, now Mrs. Arl—ton, adds her description in a letter to her sister, Mrs. F——. Also mentioned is Mr. P——, Caroline's uncle.]

LETTER LXVII

CAPT. ARL——TON TO MR. IL——RAY.

Louisville, March.

We can scarcely cast our eyes upon a page of history which is not stained with the relation of some bloody transaction—the sacrifice of innocence—the proscription of the virtuous, or the triumph of a villain; which is sufficient to convince every unprejudiced man, that the greater part of the world has hitherto been governed by barbarians: and which must prove to all men of sentiment and humanity, that it is high time to inquire into the cause which has so often destroyed the repose of the world, and stained the annals of mankind with indelible disgrace. Such were the considerations, you know my friend, that first induced me to turn my thoughts towards the western territory of this continent, as its infancy affords an opportunity to its citizens of establishing a system conformable to reason and humanity, and thereby extend the blessings of civilization to all orders of men.—And if a circumstance that at first distracted my brain, and debarred me from thinking of living in a country that contained the most lovely woman in the world, but which now affords me such undescribable joy, for a time frustrated my object, and induced me to determine to leave the country; I now assure you that I am more than ever attached to an object interesting to every human being.

I have not the vanity to suppose my exertions will materially tend to effect this important end;—but I have the satisfaction to know I shall be entitled to the reputation of a good, if not a very useful citizen; an honour, in my opinion, that has more real splendour annexed to it than all the inflated eulogiums which have been lavished upon vain and inhuman conquerors, or intriguing and unprincipled ministers of state.

As the government of this district is not organized, it is my intention to form in epitome the model of a society which I conceive ought to form part of the polity of every civilized commonwealth;—for which purpose I have purchased a tract of country lying upon the Ohio from the rapids of Louisville, and extending above Diamond island to a point sixteen miles from its beginning, and running back an equal distance, which will constitute an area of two hundred and fifty-six square miles, or nearly, making an allowance for the bends of the river.

This tract I have laid out into two hundred and fifty-six parcels, upon which I am settling men who served in the late war, giving to each a fee-simple in the soil he occupies, who shall be eligible to a seat in a house of representatives consisting of twenty members, who are to assemble every Sunday in the year, to take into consideration the measures necessary to promote the encouragements of agriculture and all useful arts, as well to discuss upon the science of government and jurisprudence.

Every male being of the age of twenty-one, and sound in his reason, is intitled to a vote in the nomination of a member to represent them, and every member is intitled to the rewards and honours which the institution may think proper to bestow. And in order that their debates shall be perfectly free and uncontrouled, the right of electing their president is invested in them also, every member being eligible to the office; but not to the dignity for more than one year; and he must then remain out of office for seven years before he can be eligible again; by which means all unwarrantable views will be frustrated, and the object of every member will be limited to the ambition of meriting the thanks of his country: and thus by the fundamental laws of the society, every expectation of aggrandizement will fall to the ground, and love, and harmony, must consequently be productive of every generous advantage; and the respectability of every citizen be established upon that broad basis—the dignity of man.

Mr. P—— thinks the object is laudable, and he has promised to lend his assistance in framing the particular instructions immediately necessary to give order and motion to the machine; and he has moreover promised, if they will do him the honour to elect him president, to serve the first year, and give them every information in his power.

He has also offered to build a house for the assembly with

galleries large and capacious enough to contain all the inhabitants of the district; for he says, every thing of this sort ought to have the greatest publicity—and by that means the people will be edified by hearing what passes, and will also be prevented from listening to those itinerant preachers who travel about the country under a pretence of propagating the pure Christian religion, but who are, in truth, the disturbers of domestic felicity,—the harbingers of hypocrisy, and whose incoherent sermons are a cloud of ignorance that too often spreads a gloom over the understanding of the uninformed, which nothing but the rays of reason can dispel, and which have too long darkened the intellect of mankind, and produced an obscurity of ideas that is truly lamentable.

The plan I am determined shall not be merely theoretical, for it is in great part already carried into execution.—The land is not only purchased and parcelled out, but there is upwards of one hundred families settled, and Mr. P—— is making preparations for the public building. Therefore you see, my friend, if I have been folded in the arms of love, I have not been idle as to what ought to be the object of every human being, i.e. promoting the good of his fellow creatures.

Caroline has not either been unemployed for she has paid constant visits to the wives of these brave men, my fellow soldiers, and brothers, and has instructed them in various and useful employments, which must tend not a little to promote their comfort.

Such, you see, is my prospect of happiness after a tempestuous and dangerous conflict that was so near destroying my happiness for ever: and which I have the greater pleasure of repeating as it is a tribute I owe to your unparalleled worth and philanthrophy.

You are too well convinced, I am certain, of the advantages this sort of system will produce, to make it necessary for me to be elaborate upon the subject:—but if you will forgive me, I shall observe that while the embellishment of manners, and the science of politics, have been engrossed by the higher orders of society, the bulk of mankind have been the mere machines of states;—and they have acted with a blind zeal for the promotion of the objects of tyrants, which has often desolated empires, while the once laughing vineyards have been changed into scenes of butchery; and the honest and industrious husbandmen, those supporters of all our wealth and all our comfort, have mourned for the sad havock of their cruel depradations.

The intercourse of men and nations has tended, not a little, to accelerate the advancement of civilization, and I am convinced the only cause why philanthropy is so uncommon a virtue, is owing to the want of a just knowledge of the human heart.

Small societies of this kind established throughout a great community would help to soften the manners of the vulgar, correct their idle and vicious habits—extend their knowledge—ameliorate their judgement—and afford an opportunity to every genius or man of sense of becoming useful to his country, who often lie obscured, uncultivated, unknown, and their talents unappropiated while the state has suffered: and at the time tyrants would be effectually prevented from trampling upon the laws of reason and humanity....

God bless you my friend, Adieu!

J. ARL——TON.

LETTER LXX

MRS. ARL——TON TO MRS. F——.

Bellefont, June.

The Ohio has been celebrated by geographers for its beauty, and its country for fertility, but this delightful spot has a combination of charms, that renders it altogether enchanting.

Capt. Arl——ton has purchased a tract of country, sixteen miles square, adjoining to the rapids, which form a stupendous cataract.

This tract is bounded by the Ohio to the west; and here the expansive river displays in varied pride the transparent sheet, that gushing, shoots impetuous over its rocky bed; which, as if in a rebellious hour had risen to oppose its genial current, presents a huge, but divided barrier; and while nature seems to scorn its feeble power, the repercussive thunder proclaims her triumph, and the ethereal hills on the adjacent shore give lustre to the rising moisture, which creeping through the vistas of the groves, the country round, high illumined, in blushing charms its sweets diffuse, and nature shines effulgent to the joyous sight.

The winding river here presents itself in two directions, and on either hand the eye dwells with peculiar delight upon its fair bosom; and while the whispering breezes curl its limpid waters, the azure veins seem to swell, as if they were enraptured with the soft dalliance of their fragrant sweets.

A small island lies in the center of the river immediately in our front, in the shape of a diamond, overspread with sycamore and acar saccharinum, or sugar tree, and with their umbrageous branches, which impend over the river banks, give a deeper hue to the passing waters.

The country gently rises from the banks of the river, for nearly six furlongs, and presents a ridge, that runs parallel with it for several leagues; which elevated prospect affords the expanded beauties of the country a long distance back, and at this genial season, the earth, where Pomona reigns, yields bounteous plenty to all, and every being shares the golden stores that gild the variegated plains.

The country on the opposite shore, over hung with woods, is not less rich in variety; but as it remains yet uninhabited, we have the charms of cultivation contrasted by the beauties of wildness.

This body of land, Arl——ton has parcelled out into a number of lots, which are in part settled, and the remainder are settling, he having reserved six for himself and those friends who may in future wish to join us.

Nearly in the center of one of these lots, is a fountain, I have called *Bellefont*, from whence the name of our seat is taken.

It is in every respect entitled to the distinction; for nothing of the sort can possibly be more beautiful. It gushes from a rock; and when its different pliant rills have joined at its base, they form an oval bason, about three hundred feet diameter, which float over a bed of chrystals, that eradiates its surface, and gives to it a polish more transparent than a mirror of glass.

The water steals off in several directions, and in their meandering course moistens the flowery banks, which, as if to return the loan, spread their blooming sweets on every side, and the soft gales gather their odours as they pass; and while they perfume the ambient air, the wanton hours dancing to the gentle harmony of sweet sounds, which the feathered songsters warble in modulated strains, love seems to have gained absolute and unbounded empire, and here in the couch of elegance and desire, to dally in all the charms of its various joys; to say with the poet,

—"*And young eyed health exalts,*
The whole creation round."—

Arl——ton's mornings are occupied in laying out his grounds, and planting the several fruits, and other things necessary to the comfort and pleasure of living. He not only attends to this business, but he does great part of it with his own hands, which gives him that exercise so necessary to invigorate the constitution, and to give zest to the hours of relaxation. And when he returns, which is generally at eleven o'clock, he takes some refreshment, and then devotes the remainder of the day to different employments; and after dinner, which is between five and six, we walk into the sugar groves, wherein the gaiety and festivity of our neighbours, who dancing to the rude music of the country seem to have forgotten all their troubles, we pass a few hours perfectly congenial to my sentiments of happiness.

Andrew, a faithful servant and friend of Arl——ton's, and the mountaineer to whom I am equally obliged for his care of me the day I was rescued from the Indians, are generally the promoters of these pleasing entertainments: for most of the settlers are old soldiers, that served under Arl——ton, and whom he regards as his best friends, and the comrades of Andrew.

Their happiness adds not a little to ours, and our uncle seems delighted with our plan of life; for he appears to take peculiar satis-faction in teaching them appropriate knowledge; and it is thus he says, my dear sister, the benefits of society may be extended equally to every description of men.

These are not our only pleasures, for we have a great number of neighbours, independent of our select society, who are sensible and intelligent, and possess all the social virtues in an eminent degree; so that our amusements have all the variety that a rational being can wish. Indeed we seldom dine alone, or at home; for such is the hospitality of the country, and the plenty which every where prevails, that there is no such thing as want.

To a mind formed like yours, replete with sentiment, it is im-possible for it not to experience in this way of living, every degree of felicity it could wish.

And it is one of the most singular pleasures of my life, to have it in my power to accompany my wishes with assurances, that your happiness must be compleat, when you shall have joined us. We all shall embrace you with one heart, and will love you with one soul; and you will be protected by the same generous hand from insult, and that tyranny which the caprices of men in the European hemi-sphere inflict upon unprotected women.

God bless you my dear and fond Eliza. Put yourself under the protection of Mr. Il——ray, and fly immediately from bondage to a land of freedom and love; and here in the bosom of peaceful affection, let the effusions of our hearts drown in oblivion the recollection of former distresses. Fly upon the pinions of the wind, for your uncle and Arl——ton, will be made as happy as myself to receive you; and that the gales which ruffle the ocean that now separates us, may prove propitious to your passage, and waft you safe to its western shores, shall be the constant prayers of,

Your affectionate
CAROLINE

8. Writings on "Pantisocracy"

i. From Samuel Coleridge, *Collected Letters of Samuel Taylor Coleridge*, ed. Earl Leslie Griggs, 4 vols. (Oxford: Clarendon Press, 1956–59), 1:83–84 (6 July 1794); 96–97 (29 August 1794); 99 (1 September 1794); 103 (18 September 1794); 115 (21 October 1794); 150 (19 January 1795)

[Frustrated with the lack of any fundamental social and political change in Britain, many progressive poets and thinkers in the 1790s contemplated at various times emigrating to the pristine wilderness of America to found agrarian utopian communities. The best-known of these emigration schemes was the one set up in 1794 by two Cambridge undergraduates, the Romantic poets Samuel Coleridge and his friend Robert Southey. Their utopian society, or "Pantisocracy" as they called it, was to be founded on the picturesque banks of the Susquehanna River in Pennsylvania (a place they picked off a map, because they liked the sound of the name "Susquehanna"). It was to be governed by the Godwinian doctrine of perfectibility and political justice, and would be run on the principle of sharing property, labor, and self-government equally among all of its adult members, both men and women. The following extracts from the correspondence between Coleridge and Southey document the birth and ultimate demise of their ill-fated scheme (partly because of lack of funds, but mainly because Southey began to have second thoughts). Thomas Poole's letter provides the most detailed contemporary description of the "Pantisocracy." The two poems Coleridge wrote about their pet scheme reflect some of the spirit of hope and boundless optimism that characterized radical circles during the early and mid 1790s in Britain.]

July 6th—[1794.] Sunday Morn. Gloucester

S.T. Coleridge to R. Southey—Health & Republicanism!

When you write, direct to me to be left at the Post Office, Wrexham, Denbighshire N. Wales. I mention this circumstance *now*, lest carried away by a flood of confluent ideas I should forget it....

Our Journeying has been intolerably fatiguing from the heat and whiteness of the Roads—and the un*hedged* country presents nothing but *stone-fences* dreary to the Eye and scorching to the touch— But we shall soon be in Wales....

My companion is a Man of cultivated, tho' not vigorous, understanding—his feelings are all on the side of humanity yet such are the unfeeling Remarks, which the lingering Remains of Aristocracy occasionally prompt. When the pure System of Pantocracy [sic] shall have aspheterized the Bounties of Nature, these things will not be so—I trust, you admire the word "aspheterized" from α non, σφέτερος proprius! We really *wanted* such a word—instead of travelling along the circuitous, dusty, beaten high-Road of Diction you thus cut across the soft, green pathless Field of Novelty!...

[To Charles Heath]

Jesus College, Cambridge. 29th August, 1794

Sir,
Your brother has introduced my name to you; I shall therefore offer no apology for this letter. A small but liberalized party have formed a scheme of emigration on the principles of an abolition of individual property. Of their political creed, and the arguments by which they support and elucidate it, they are preparing a few copies—not as meaning to publish them, but for private distribution. In this work they will have endeavoured to prove the exclusive justice of the system and its practicability; nor will they have omitted to sketch out the code of contracts necessary for the internal regulation of the society; all of which will of course be submitted to the improvements and approbation of each component member. As soon as the work is printed, one or more copies shall be transmitted to you. Of the characters of the individuals who

compose the party, I find it embarrassing to speak; yet, vanity apart, I may assert with truth, that they have each a sufficient strength of head to make the virtues of the heart respectable; and that they are all highly charged with that enthusiasm which results from strong perceptions of moral rectitude, called into life and action by ardent feelings. With regard to pecuniary matters it is found necessary, if twelve men with their families emigrate on this system, that 2000£ should be the aggregate of their contributions; but infer not from hence that each man's quota is to be settled with the littleness of arithmetical accuracy. No; *all* will strain *every* nerve, and then I trust the surplus money of some will supply the deficiencies of others. The minutiae of topographical information we are daily endeavouring to acquire; at present our plan is, to settle at a distance, but at a convenient distance, from Cooper's Town on the banks of the Susquehannah. This, however, will be the object of future investigation. For the time of emigration we have fixed on next March. In the course of the winter those of us whose bodies, from habits of sedentary study or academic indolence, have not acquired their full tone and strength, intend to learn the theory and practice of agriculture and carpentry, according as situation and circumstances make one or the other convenient.

Your fellow Citizen,
S. T. Coleridge.

[To Robert Southey]

Monday Morning. [1 September 1794]

Every night since my arrival I have spent at an Ale-house by courtesy called "a Coffee House"—The "Salutation & Cat," in Newgate Street—We have a comfortable Room to ourselves—& drink Porter & *Punch* round a good Fire.—My motive for all this is that every night I meet a most intelligent young Man who has spent the last 5 years of his Life in America—and is lately come from thence as An Agent to sell Land. He was of our School—I had been kind to him—he remembers it—& comes regularly every Evening to "benefit by conversation" he says—He says, two thousand Pound will do—that he doubts not, we can contract for our Passage under

400£.—that we shall buy the Land a great deal cheaper when we arrive at America—than we could do in England—or why (adds he) am I sent over here? That 12 men may *easily* clear *three hundred* Acres in 4, or 5 months—and that for 600 hundred Dollars a Thousand Acres may be cleared, and houses built upon them—He recommends the Susqusannah [sic] from it's excessive Beauty, & it's security from hostile Indians—Every possible assistance will be given us—We may get credit for the Land for 10 years or more as we settle upon it—That literary Characters make *money* there—that &c &c—He never saw a *Byson* in his Life—but has heard of them—They are quite backwards.—The Musquitos are not so bad as our Gnats—and after you have been there a little while, they don't trouble you much. He says, the Women's *teeth are* bad there—but not the men's—at least—not nearly so much—attributes it to neglect—to particular foods—is by no means convinced, it is the necessary Effect of Climate....

[To Robert Southey]

Sept—18th—[1794] 10 o clock Thursday Morning

Well, my dear Southey! I am at last arrived at Jesus [College]. My God! how tumultuous are the movements of my Heart—Since I quitted this room what and how important Events have been evolved! America! Southey I Miss Flicker!—Yes—Southey—you are right—Even Love is the creature of strong Motive—I certainly love her. I think of her incessantly & with unspeakable tenderness—with that inward melting away of Soul that symptomatizes it.

Pantisocracy—O I shall have such a scheme of it! My head, my heart are all alive—I have drawn up my arguments in battle array....

[To Robert Southey]

Jes[us] Coll[ege] Cambridge. Oct. 21st [1794]

What have been your feelings concerning the War with America, which is now inevitable? To go from Hamburgh will not only be an heavy additional expence—but dangerous & uncertain—as

Nations at War are in the habit of examining Neutral Vessels to prevent the Importation of Arms and seize subjects of the hostile Governments. It is said, that one cause of the Ministers' being so cool on this business is that it will prevent Emigration, which it seems would be treasonable, to an hostile Country—Tell me all you think on these subjects.—

What think you of the difference in the Prices of Land as stated by Cowper from those given by the American Agents? By all means read & ponder on Cowper—and when I hear your thoughts, I will give you the Result of my own....

[To Robert Southey]

Monday Morning. [19 January 1795]

Southey! I must tell you, that you appear to me to write as a man who is aweary of a world, because it accords not with his ideas of perfection—your sentiments look like the sickly offspring of disgusted Pride. *Love* is an active and humble Principle—It flies not away from the Couches of Imperfection, because the Patients are fretful or loathsome.

Why, my dear very dear Southey! do you wrap yourself up in the Mantle of self-centering *Resolve*—and refuse to us your bounden Quota of Intellect? Why do you say, I—I—I—will do so and so—instead of saying as you were wont to do—It is all *our Duty* to do so and so—for such & such Reasons—

For God'[s] sake—my dear Fellow—tell me what we are to gain by taking a Welsh Farm? Remember the principles & proposed Consequences of Pantisocracy—and reflect in what degree they are attainable by Coleridge, Southey, Lovell, Burnet & Co—some 5 men *going partners* together? In the next place—supposing that we had proved the preponderating Utility of our aspheterizing in Wales—let us by our speedy & united enquiries discover the sum of money necessary—whether such a farm with so very large a house is to be procured without launching our frail & unpiloted Bark on a rough Sea of Anxieties?—How much money will be necessary for *furnishing* so large a house? How much necessary for the maintenance of so large a family—18 people—for a year at least?...

ii. From a letter by Thomas Poole to Mr. Hoskins (22 September 1794), in Mrs. Henry Sandford, *Thomas Poole and His Friends*, 2 vols. (London: Macmillan and Co, 1888), 1:97–98

Twelve gentlemen of good education and liberal principles are to embark with twelve ladies in April next. Previous to their leaving this country they are to have as much intercourse as possible, in order to ascertain each other's dispositions, and firmly to settle every regulation for the government of their future conduct. Their opinion was that they should fix themselves at—I do not recollect the place, but somewhere in a delightful part of the new back settlements; that each man should labour two or three hours in a day, the produce of which labour would, they imagine, be more than sufficient to support the colony. As Adam Smith observes that there is not above one productive man in twenty, they argue that if each laboured the twentieth part of time, it would produce enough to satisfy their wants. The produce of their industry is to be laid up in common for the use of all; and a good library of books is to be collected, and their leisure hours to be spent in study, liberal discussions, and the education of their children.... The regulations relating to the females strike them as the most difficult; whether the marriage contract shall be dissolved if *agreeable* to one or both parties, and many other circumstances, are not yet determined. The employments of the women are to be the care of infant children, and other occupations suited to their strength; at the same time the greatest attention is to be paid to the cultivation of their minds. Every one is to enjoy his own religious and political opinions, provided they do not encroach upon the rules previously made, which rules, it is unnecessary to add, must in some measure be regulated by the laws of the state which includes the district in which they settle. They calculate that each gentleman providing £125 will be sufficient to carry the scheme into execution. Finally, every individual is at liberty, whenever he pleases, to withdraw from the society....

iii. Two poems by Samuel Taylor Coleridge

a. "Pantisocracy" (1794)

PANTISOCRACY

No more my visionary soul shall dwell
On joys that were; no more endure to weigh
The shame and anguish of the evil day,
Wisely forgetful! O'er the ocean swell
Sublime of Hope, I seek the cottag'd dell
Where Virtue calm with careless step may stray,
And dancing to the moonlight roundelay,
The wizard Passions weave an holy spell.
Eyes that have ach'd with Sorrow! Ye shall weep
Tears of doubt-mingled joy, like theirs who start
From Precipices of distemper'd sleep,
On which the fierce-eyed Fiends their revels keep,
And see the rising Sun, and feel it dart
New rays of pleasance trembling to the heart.

1794.

b. "On the Prospect of Establishing a Pantisocracy in
America" (1794)

ON THE PROSPECT OF ESTABLISHING
A PANTISOCRACY IN AMERICA

WHILST pale Anxiety, corrosive Care,
The tear of Woe, the gloom of sad Despair,
And deepen'd Anguish generous bosoms rend;—
Whilst patriot souls their country's fate lament;
Whilst mad with rage demoniac, foul intent,
Embattled legions Despots vainly send
To arrest the immortal mind's expanding ray
Of, everlasting Truth;—I other climes
Where dawns, with hope serene, a brighter day
Than e'er saw Albion in her happiest times,
With mental eye exulting now explore,

And soon with kindred minds shall haste to enjoy
(Free from the ills which here our peace destroy)
Content and Bliss on Transatlantic shore.

1794.

9. From John Thelwall, "A Warning Voice to the Violent of
All Parties; with Reflections on the Events of the First Day
of the Present Session of Parliament; and an Enquiry
whether Conciliatory or Coercive Measures are best calculated to allay Popular Ferments. Delivered Friday, Nov. 6,
1795," *The Tribune*, No. XLVII, in *The Politics of English
Jacobinism: Writings of John Thelwall*, ed. and intro. Gregory
Claeys (University Park: Pennsylvania State University
Press, 1995), 314–316; 320–322; 323–327

[A pamphleteer, journalist, playwright, and lecturer, Thelwall was a
close friend of the poet Samuel Coleridge, and was no mean poet
himself. Initially a dedicated follower of Godwin, Thelwall led the
London Corresponding Society away from Godwin's political utopia
of perfectibility to a more practical agenda, especially seeking ways
to improve the socio-economic conditions of the working man.
Lampooned in *The Vagabond* as "Citizen Ego," Thelwall was a gifted
orator who could incite audiences to a frenzy with his energizing
rhetoric—a talent he displayed to great effect at the many political
meetings he organized. The speech extracted below was delivered
three weeks after Thelwall addressed a crowd at Copenhagen Fields
of nearly 150,000 people. During the "tumult" that erupted in the
wake of the meeting, the King's carriage was beleaguered by an
excited mob, triggering the introduction a month later of two
repressive laws known as the "Gagging Acts." Thelwall published his
speeches and other writings in his magazine, *The Tribune*.]

THE TRIBUNE. No. XLVII.
A WARNING VOICE TO THE VIOLENT OF ALL PARTIES;
with Reflections on the Events of the FIRST DAY
of the present SESSION *of* PARLIAMENT;
and an Enquiry whether CONCILIATORY *or* COERCIVE MEASURES
are best calculated to allay POPULAR FERMENTS.
Delivered Friday, Nov. 6, 1795.

CITIZENS,

THE war-hoop of faction once more resounds through this distracted country; and persecution is about to rage, perhaps, with more ferocity than ever. No sort of toleration it seems is to be allowed by persons of one class to those of another. Those, in particular, who are in power, and possess the offices of magistracy, seem to be infected with a baleful anxiety who shall be foremost in singling out the stigmatized reformer for destruction; and in exercising the new authority which they seem to think may be created by those *edicts of the cabinet, called royal proclamations.* With so little moderation is this power exercised—with so little discretion, that even the man who lifts his voice in behalf of moderation, and wishes to allay the furious passions of the times is singled out as an object of indignation; and even to talk of warning "the violent of all parties," of the danger of their furious prejudices is regarded as a crime not to be endured. The poor bill sticker who stuck the bills of this day, has been seized by the merciless hand of power, and thrown into prison.

Still, however, unmoved by resentments, uninfluenced by any sentiment but that love of mankind which inspires in the enlightened breast an ardent enthusiasm for liberty, once more I step forward to warn you with the voice of reason and candour to allay the furious tempests of passion which seem to threaten the total dissolution of all social virtue: and chiefly on you, my fellow Citizens, embarked in the great cause of liberty—on you I call with confidence: by you at least I expect, that the voice of warning will not be heard in vain. Let reason, I pray you, be your sole guide in that pursuit of parliamentary reform which I trust you will never abandon but with your lives. Believe me, Citizens, in all the situations in which man can be placed, in all circumstances of society, moderation, well understood, is the first of virtues. The exercise of this virtue dignifies the character of man, and lifts him from that brutal state to which ignorance and aristocratic fury would degrade him.

But, Citizens, however useful this moderation in all the circumstances of society, it is particularly necessary at a time when persecuting fury endeavours to deprive us at once of our rights and faculties, and to provoke us by every species of irritation and insult into excesses and tumults which might furnish pretences for the usurpations of a corrupt and vicious administration.

When I speak of moderation, however, understand, I pray you, the sense in which I use the word. Properly understood it describes one of the greatest virtues that adorn humanity: but it has frequently been abused to the most corrupt and vicious purposes. The hypocrite, or the coward, who dares not look any principle in the face, and pursue it through all its moral consequences, or a part of whose system of politics it is, to confound for party purposes, all distinctions between right and wrong, talks of moderation and abandons truth. This is not the sort of moderation I wish you to adopt: this is a moderation I abhor: I would rather be at once the prostituted pander of corruption, than the sneaking half-way *moderé* who bawls for liberty and yet shrinks from the manly investigation of rights and principles....

Citizens, I have professed to treat this evening particularly upon the events of the first day of the present session of parliament. There are two parts of these proceedings which might be dwelt upon, to illustrate the necessity of that candour I have endeavoured to inculcate. I have already said something upon what passed in the inside of the House of Commons. I shall dwell more particularly on what passed without those walls. Upon this subject, as upon all others, there are two statements, made by the opposite parties. The aristocrat affirms, that the tumults of Thursday originated in these lectures, and in the popular societies; and particularly the meeting at Copenhagen House. The democrat, or reformer, affirms, on the contrary, that the tumults of Thursday arose from the bad conduct of the administration: from the present corrupt and profligate war, and that system of measures equally unconstitutional and unwise, which have plunged this country from misery to misery, into the abyss of ruin, till, at last, to close the great climax of human affliction, famine begins to stare us in the face; and our only way to remedy the scarcity of bread is to do without it. The aristocrat says, if you permit political discussion, treasonable lectures (as they are called) and seditious societies, where people enquire into their rights, and wrongs, the consequence will be tumult and disorder. The friend of liberty says:—if you oppress the people they will be tumultuous; if you ruin trade, you will turn numbers of families out of employment, and overwhelm the people with distress; and, in consequence, poor beings who know nothing but their distresses—no principle but the stimulus of want, will commit depredations upon society.

Now let us fairly investigate these two statements. Remember, Citizens, that the aristocrats have yet brought forward no argument whatever, to shew the connexion between political investigation and these disturbances. Perhaps they think assertion and authority better than argument, especially when they come from a man who wears a great wig in Westminster Hall or Lincoln's Inn. We have heard of a great number of persons being apprehended; and the magistrates, I conclude, would have been anxious enough to find it out, if it had been the case, and yet it does not appear that any of them were members of the popular associations. What is the conclusion? Why that political associations have prevented the outrage, since those only have been outrageous who were no members of them; and that, therefore, if every man had been in the habits of political enquiry no outrage would have happened. Political enquiry and association shew a better way of redress. Tumult only gives fresh handle to the minister for adopting measures of worse oppression. It is true that a proclamation insinuates, and that a great and learned authority of the law absolutely asserts that there was a connection between the meeting at Copenhagen-house and the tumult which took place four days afterwards. The learned Lord, indeed, to whom I allude, makes a little mistake in order to support his statement; and says that the meeting was called the day before the meeting of Parliament: whereas the meeting took place on Monday, and it was not till Thursday that the tumult happened. Now, Citizens, what idea must we form of the inflammatory proceedings of a meeting that could keep the public mind without sleeping three whole days and nights till the opportunity should come to throw mud and stones against the gilt coach of majesty, and thus insult the sacred person and institution of royalty. Citizens, a part of these proceedings was a speech of an hour long on the necessity of using nothing but reason in the pursuit of reform, and a demonstration that every act of violence would only give the minister an opportunity to increase the chains and fetters of the people.

But what are the arguments by which the democrat and reformer support this side of the question. The arguments are of two kinds, the deductions of abstract reason, and the experience of all ages, from the first period of history to the present hour. These will shew, that the persons fondest of violence are those who are most ignorant. Violence always begins either with those oppressors who wish to destroy all knowledge but their own, or among those who, though they can feel the oppression, can neither write nor read—among poor, harassed, and degraded beings who have neither opportunities nor inclination for enquiry....

The tumult arose, not in consequence of reason and enquiry, but from the misery in which the people are plunged. How great and aggravated this misery has been is proved from documents collected not for any purposes of party; by documents collected even by persons of aristocratic principles. Remember I have proved to you that a man now gets but a fourth part of those necessaries of life, by a day's labour, which he got 3 or 400 years ago by less labour. Remember I have proved to you that a man bought as much corn, as much beer, as much meat, as much cloathing for one day's labour, when he got but 2d for that day's labour, as now, when he gets 14d. Nay, the disproportion is still greater; for this was calculated from the state of facts in the year 1787: the necessaries of life are since increased two-fold; and, in many instances, a man must now labour 6 or 8 days to procure the necessaries that formerly he could procure for one day's labour. The result is, that the great body of the people are slaves; that they toil for arbitrary masters from morn to night; and almost from night to morn again; and get not even the common necessaries of life; but are obliged to go, with suppliant voice, to beg for that to which they are entitled as the reward of useful labour. Thus men having no longer the means of getting even a scanty subsistence, fly into tumult. But are these members of political societies? Where should they find even the small pittance that should keep up those societies, or pay for admission to these lectures? Oh! that I could extend my voice to those poor individuals whose necessities preclude them from attendance. I have no doubt that, if I could have an opportunity of collecting these lower and despised orders of society around me, from all the nations of the earth, that I should be able to persuade them to lay all dispositions to violence aside.

I am convinced that the arguments I could bring forward would be irresistible to minds uncorrupted by the arrogance and selfishness, which debilitates and exhausts the understanding of the higher orders. I am convinced that I could bring the conviction of truth to their minds; and that the tyrants of the earth would no longer be able to get military slaves to commit fresh murders to promote their ambition.

Regarding even this slight, hasty and imperfect sketch of the arguments on our side, it is obvious that it is not in consequence of political association—not in consequence of the investigation of the principles of truth and justice—not from pursuing parliamentary reform, that tumults and violence have taken place: but that they are to be attributed to that misery which renders enquiry impossible, because it takes from man the means of purchasing the knowledge which could illuminate his understanding. This misery, while it checks information, diffuses irritation: and the minister, to allay this irritation, aggravates the cause. A wise physician would, perhaps, apply palliatives—not provocatives. But palliatives are not in favour with our state quacks. In their whole political pharmacopoeia there is not a nostrum of this description.

The ministerial papers tell you that they foresaw the late disturbances;— that they saw inflammatory hand-bills about town, exciting to these excesses. If they did, why did not they send forth answers? Why did they not exhort the people to come peaceably and quietly, or to send their delegates peaceably and quietly to represent their grievances? that if they had wrongs justice might be done? But no—mark the only use they made of the foreknowledge; and then see which is most precious in the eyes of certain *supposed loyal persons*—the life of the monarch, or of the minister! A brave, honest and virtuous minister, aware that the indignation of the people were roused, would have asked his own heart, who roused that indignation? His own conscience must have convinced him that he was the man. If, therefore, there was any danger, and if he had any loyalty, he would have been the first to brave the tempest, that its fury having been spent his royal master might have passed in safety. But did he do so? Did the minister, whom the "*True Briton*" and all the ministerial papers tell you, knew of the tumult that was to happen—did he go first and expose himself as a brave man would have done, and have said, "Citizens—deluded Citizens—or, if he liked it better, deluded swinish multitude—why are you tumultuous? If any crime of government has caused your miseries, the guilt lies on me, not on that royal master whom I serve, and whom it is my duty to protect."

This candour, generosity, honour, and fortitude would have dictated; and that very honour, generosity and fortitude, would have disarmed resentment. But instead of this, he sends his royal master to the House, and stays behind himself, till he knows that the tumult is over; and then he sneaks to the House of Commons in a *hackney coach*! Is this the conduct of a man conscious of his own integrity? or is his zeal for royalty like his attachment to the constitution, which while he extols in verbose panegyrics, he is stabbing to the vitals—or his care for the protection of liberty and property, for the security of which he encourages *loyal associations* in every parish, while he himself is destroying the one to gratify his ambition, and plundering the other to carry on a mad and ruinous war?

Citizens, I shall dwell no longer upon this subject at present: but before I dismiss you, I shall say a few words on the crisis to which we are arrived. I feel the solemnity of the situation in which I stand. I feel the solemnity of the situation of my country. My heart grows too big for the breast that contains it. I feel it impossible even to restrain my voice or my feelings within that compass necessary for the preservation of my health—perhaps of my life. For the prolongation of my exertions, I wish I could command a moderation of feeling, as well as that candour and humanity I am endeavouring to inculcate. Fain would I discover the secret, by which, without losing one atom of the energy, I might restrain and moderate the strong emotions of my heart, that I might imprint the same truths upon your understandings, without doing any injury to my own frame. But if the two things cannot be united together—if this zeal and this energy cannot be exercised without this wreck of health and constitution, take what remains of this poor life; for I will not relax my exertions till uncontroulable force prevents their continuance.

The crisis approaches—the hour of trial comes, persecution and calumny usher it in; and however the storm may end, I must brave its fury. Rage and resentment I know are launched against me by the violent of both parties. While ministerial hirelings post me about the streets as a miscreant, and that scandalous and profligate paper called the "Times," accuses me with hiring the mob that committed the tumults of Thursday, I am informed that the poor, infatuated, deluded people, at the east end of the town, who in the present hour of distress throng about the shops to buy for themselves the garbage and offal formerly consigned to dogs, and pay 4d a pound for bullock's liver, will turn sometimes indignantly away, and after first cursing the wicked administration that brought them into such miseries, will accuse me of preventing them, by my pacific doctrines, from redressing their grievances.

I know the danger of the situation in which I stand. I know that those whose designs are not honest, and those whose knowledge is not accurate upon the causes of our grievances, and the means of redress, will be indignant against the man who endeavours to arrest the uplifted arm of violence, or calls on kindling vengeance to forbear.

For my part, however, my object is the peace, happiness, and welfare of society: I wish for the emancipation of the human race.

I wish for equal rights, equal laws, and universal peace and fraternity, the branches and members of genuine liberty. In proportion, therefore, as the fury of the storm increases, as far as I am able, I will increase my efforts; and as I find in different parts of the town, the arm of authority is stretched forth to prevent political discussion, I will increase the frequency of discussion in this place as long as I have strength, and no absolute and determinate law forbids.

I shall, therefore, henceforward, continue my Lectures on Mondays, Wednesdays, and Fridays, and may the spirit of enthusiasm that glows in my breast spread through every audience, and by them be diffused through wider circles, till liberty, equality and justice become the wish of every heart, and the theme of every tongue.

10. From William Godwin, *Memoirs of the Author of a Vindication of the Rights of Woman* (1798), in *The Collected Novels and Memoirs of William Godwin*, gen. ed. Mark Philp, 8 vols. (London: Pickering and Chatto, 1992), 1:114–116; 118–120 (Chapter VII)

[In her *Vindication of the Rights of Woman* (1792) Mary Wollstonecraft had put the case for feminist social reform firmly on the radical political agenda, much to the chagrin of the conservative side of British society. However, it was Godwin's intimate portrayal of Wollstonecraft's life and passions that triggered the vicious response from large sections of the press that still reverberates through Walker's novel. Notably Godwin's candid account of her love affairs and her suicide attempts were received with outrage both friends and critics alike. Walker's crude, even callous parody of Mary Wollstonecraft as Frederick's companion "Mary," is characteristic of the scorn and loathing that was heaped upon Wollstonecraft in the wake of Godwin's *Memoirs*.]

Chapter Seven 1792–1795

The original plan of Mary, respecting her residence in France, had no precise limits in the article of duration; the single purpose she had in view being that of an endeavour to heal her distempered mind. She did not proceed so far as even to discharge her lodging in London; and, to some friends who saw her immediately before her departure, she spoke merely of an absence of six weeks.

It is not to be wondered at, that her excursion did not originally seem to produce the effects she had expected from it. She was in a land of strangers; she had no acquaintance; she had even to acquire the power of receiving and communicating ideas with facility in the language of the country. Her first residence was in a spacious mansion to which she had been invited, but the master of which (monsieur Fillietaz) was absent at the time of her arrival.[1] At first therefore she found herself surrounded only with servants. The gloominess of her mind communicated its own colour to the objects she saw; and in this temper she began a series of *Letters on the Present Character of the French Nation*, one of which she forwarded to her publisher, and which appears in the collection of her posthumous works. This performance she soon after discontinued; and it is, as she justly remarks, tinged with the saturnine temper which at that time pervaded her mind.

Mary carried with her introductions to several agreeable families in Paris. She renewed her acquaintance with Paine. There also subsisted a very sincere friendship between her and Helen Maria Williams, author of a collection of poems of uncommon merit, who at that time resided in Paris.[2] Another person, whom Mary always spoke of in terms of ardent commendation, both for the excellence of his disposition and the force of his genius, was a count Slabrendorf, by birth, I believe, a Swede.[3] It is almost unnecessary to mention, that she was personally acquainted with the majority of the leaders in the French revolution.

But the house that, I believe, she principally frequented at this time, was that of Mr Thomas Christie, a person whose pursuits were mercantile, and who had written a volume on the French revolution. With Mrs Christie her acquaintance was more intimate than with her husband.[4]

It was about four months after her arrival at Paris in December 1792, that she entered into that species of connection for which her

---

[1]   Mr. Fillietaz was related to the mistress of the school in Putney where Mary Wollstonecraft's sisters worked.

[2]   Helen Maria Williams (1762–1827), English radical poet and novelist, who in a voluminous body of letters to her English readers provided an important and enthusiastic eye-witness account of the turbulent events surrounding the French Revolution.

[3]   Christophe Georg Gustav, Graf von Schlabrendorf (1750–1824) was a traveler and writer, and in fact not from Sweden but from Silesia.

[4]   Thomas Christie (1761–96), Scottish businessman, writer, and co-founder, with Joseph Johnson, of the *Analytical Review*, to which Mary Wollstonecraft was a contributor. Mary became close friends with Christie's wife, Rebecca.

heart secretly panted, and which had the effect of diffusing an immediate tranquillity and cheerfulness over her manners. The person with whom it was formed (for it would be an idle piece of delicacy to attempt to suppress a name, which is known to every one whom the reputation of Mary has reached), was Mr Gilbert Imlay, native of the United States of North America.

The place at which she first saw Mr Imlay was at the house of Mr Christie; and it perhaps deserves to be noticed, that the emotions he then excited in her mind, were, I am told, those of dislike, and that, for some time, she shunned all occasions of meeting him. This sentiment however speedily gave place to one of greater kindness.

Previously to the partiality she conceived for him, she had determined upon a journey to Switzerland, induced chiefly by motives of economy. But she had some difficulty in procuring a passport; and it was probably the intercourse that now originated between her and Mr Imlay, that changed her purpose, and led her to prefer a lodging at Neuilly, a village three miles from Paris. Her habitation here was a solitary house in the midst of a garden, with no other inhabitants than herself and the gardener, an old man, who performed for her many of the offices of a domestic, and would sometimes contend for the honour of making her bed. The gardener had a great veneration for his guest, and would set before her, when alone, some grapes of a particularly fine sort, which she could not without the greatest difficulty obtain when she had any person with her as a visitor. Here it was that she conceived, and for the most part executed, her *Historical and Moral View of the French Revolution*★ into which, as she observes, are incorporated most of the observations she had collected for her *Letters*, and which was written with more sobriety and cheerfulness than the tone in which they had been commenced. In the evening she was accustomed to refresh herself by a walk in a neighbouring wood, from which her old host in vain endeavoured to dissuade her, by recounting divers horrible robberies and murders that had been committed there.

The commencement of the attachment Mary now formed, had neither confidant nor adviser. She always conceived it to be a gross breach of delicacy to have any confidant in a matter of this sacred

---

★   No part of the proposed continuation of this work, has been found among the papers of the author [Godwin's note]. [Editor's note: In fact, one volume of *An Historical and Moral View of the Origin and Progress of the French Revolution, and the Effect It Has Produced in Europe* did appear, in London in 1794.]

nature, an affair of the heart. The origin of the connection was about the middle of April 1793, and it was carried on in a private manner for four months. At the expiration of that period a circumstance occurred that induced her to declare it. The French convention, exasperated at the conduct of the British government, particularly in the affair of Toulon, formed a decree against the citizens of this country, by one article of which the English, resident in France, were ordered into prison till the period of a general peace. Mary had objected to a marriage with Mr Imlay, who, at the time their connection was formed, had no property whatever; because she would not involve him in certain family embarrassments to which she conceived herself exposed, or make him answerable for the pecuniary demands that existed against her. She however considered their engagement as of the most sacred nature; and they had mutually formed the plan of emigrating to America, as soon as they should have realized a sum, enabling them to do it in the mode they desired. The decree however that I have just mentioned, made it necessary, not that a marriage should actually take place, but that Mary should take the name of Imlay, which, from the nature of their connection, she conceived herself entitled to do, and obtain a certificate from the American ambassador, as the wife of a native of that country.

Their engagement being thus avowed, they thought proper to reside under the same roof, and for that purpose removed to Paris....

Mary now reposed herself upon a person, of whose honour and principles she had the most exalted idea. She nourished an individual affection, which she saw no necessity of subjecting to restraint; and a heart like hers was not formed to nourish affection by halves. Her conception of Mr Imlay's "tenderness and worth had twisted him closely round her heart"; and she "indulged the thought, that she had thrown out some tendrils, to cling to the elm by which she wished to be supported." This was "talking a new language to her": but "conscious that she was not a parasite-plant," she was willing to encourage and foster the luxuriances of affection. Her confidence was entire; her love was unbounded. Now, for the first time in her life, she gave a loose to all the sensibilities of her nature.

Soon after the time I am now speaking of, her attachment to Mr Imlay gained a new link, by finding reason to suppose herself with child.

Their establishment at Paris, was however broken up almost as soon as formed, by the circumstance of Mr Imlay's entering into business, urged, as he said, by the prospect of a family, and this being a favourable crisis in French affairs for commercial speculations. The pursuits in which he was engaged, led him in the month of September to Havre de Grace, then called Havre Marat, probably to superintend the shipping of goods, in which he was jointly engaged with some other person or persons. Mary remained in the capital.

The solitude in which she was now left, proved an unexpected trial. Domestic affections constituted the object upon which her heart was fixed; and she early felt, with an inward grief, that Mr Imlay "did not attach those tender emotions round the idea of home, which, every time they recurred, dimmed her eyes with moisture." She had expected his return from week to week, and from month to month; but a succession of business still continued to detain him at Havre. At the same time the sanguinary character which the government of France began every day to assume, contributed to banish tranquillity from the first months of her pregnancy. Before she left Neuilly, she happened one day to enter Paris on foot (I believe, by the *Place de Louis Quinze*), when an execution, attended with some peculiar aggravations, had just taken place, and the blood of the guillotine appeared fresh upon the pavement. The emotions of her soul burst forth in indignant exclamations, while a prudent bystander warned her of her danger, and intreated her to hasten and hide her discontents. She described to me, more than once, the anguish she felt at hearing of the death of Brissot, Vergniaud, and the twenty deputies, as one of the most intolerable sensations she had ever experienced.

Finding the return of Mr Imlay continually postponed, she determined, in January 1794, to join him at Havre. One motive that influenced her, though, I believe, by no means the principal, was the growing cruelties of Robespierre, and the desire she felt to be in any other place, rather than the devoted city; in the midst of which they were perpetrated.

From January to September, Mr Imlay and Mary lived together, with great harmony, at Havre, where the child, with which she was pregnant, was born, on the fourteenth of May, and named Frances, in remembrance of the dear friend of her youth, whose image could never be erased from her memory.

In September, Mr Imlay took his departure from Havre for the port of London. As this step was said to be necessary in the way of business, he endeavoured to prevail upon Mary to quit Havre, and once more take up her abode at Paris. Robespierre was now no more; and, of consequence, the only objection she had to residing in the capital, was removed. Mr Imlay was already in London, before she undertook her journey, and it proved the most fatiguing journey she ever made; the carriage, in which she travelled, being overturned no less than four times between Havre and Paris.

This absence, like that of the preceding year in which Mr Imlay had removed to Havre, was represented as an absence that was to have a short duration. In two months he was once again to join her in Paris. It proved however the prelude to an eternal separation. The agonies of such a separation, or rather desertion, great as Mary would have found them upon every supposition, were vastly increased, by the lingering method in which it was effected, and the ambiguity that, for a long time, hung upon it. This circumstance produced the effect, of holding her mind, by force, as it were, to the most painful of all subjects, and not suffering her to derive the just advantage from the energy and elasticity of her character.

The procrastination of which I am speaking was however productive of one advantage. It put off the evil day. She did not suspect the calamities that awaited her, till the close of the year. She gained an additional three months of comparative happiness. But she purchased it at a very dear rate. Perhaps no human creature ever suffered greater misery, than dyed the whole year 1795, in the life of this incomparable woman. It was wasted in that son of despair, to the sense of which the mind is continually awakened, by a glimmering of fondly cherished, expiring hope.

Why did she thus obstinately cling to an ill-starred unhappy passion? Because it is of the very essence of affection, to seek to perpetuate itself. He does not love, who can resign this cherished sentiment, without suffering some of the sharpest struggles that our nature is capable of enduring. Add to this, Mary had fixed her heart upon this chosen friend; and one of the last impressions a worthy mind can submit to receive, is that of the worthlessness of the person upon whom it has fixed all its esteem. Mary had struggled to entertain a favourable opinion of human nature; she had unweariedly fought for a kindred mind, in whose integrity and fidelity to take up her rest. Mr Imlay undertook to prove, in his letters written immediately after their complete separation, that his conduct towards her was reconcilable to the strictest rectitude; but undoubtedly Mary was of a different opinion. Whatever the reader may decide in this respect, there is one sentiment that, I believe, he will unhesitatingly admit: that of pity for the mistake of the man, who, being in possession of such a friendship and attachment as those of Mary, could hold them at a trivial price, and, "like the base Indian, throw a pearl away, richer than all his tribe."*

11. From William Godwin, *Thoughts occasioned by the perusal of Dr. Parr's Spital Sermon, preached at Christ Church, April 15, 1800: being a reply to the attacks of Dr. Parr, Mr. Mackintosh, The Author of an Essay of Population, and others* (1801), *Political and Philosophical Writings of William Godwin*, gen. ed. Mark Philp, 7 vols. (London: Pickering and Chatto, 1993), 2:165–72; 177

[In this essay William Godwin presents a succinct but revealing survey of the rise and fall of the radical cause in the 1790s. He identifies 1797 as the turning point in the Revolutionary Debate, by which time the radical voice was all but silenced by an increasingly vociferous anti-Jacobin press. Yet to his surprise, Godwin observes in his essay, the anti-Jacobin fury against the now silent radicals only increased after 1797. What Godwin omits to note here is that it was his own memoirs of his deceased wife, published in 1798, that fueled much of the diatribe against him and his wife, and indirectly, against other one-time radicals.]

THOUGHTS
OCCASIONED, &C. [1]

I have now continued for some years a silent, not an inattentive, spectator of the flood of ribaldry, invective and intolerance which has been poured out against me and my writings. The work which has principally afforded a topic for the exercise of this malignity, has been the *Enquiry Concerning Political Justice*. This book made its appearance

---

* A person, from whose society at this time Mary derived particular gratification, "was Archibald Hamilton Rowan, who had lately become a fugitive from Ireland, in consequence of a political prosecution, and in whom she found those qualities which were always eminently engaging to her, great integrity of disposition, and great kindness of heart" [Godwin's note].

---

[1] Samuel Parr, *A Spital Sermon, preached at Christ Church, upon Easter Tuesday, April 15, 1800; to which are added Notes* (London, J. Mawman, 1801).

in February 1793; its reception with the public was favourable much beyond my conception of its merits; it was the specific and avowed occasion of procuring me the favour and countenance of many persons of the highest note in society and literature, of some of those who have lent themselves to increase the clamour, which personal views and the contagion of fashion have created against me. For more than four years, it remained before the public, without any man's having made the slightest attempt for its refutation; it was repeatedly said that it was invulnerable and unanswerable in its fundamental topics; high encomiums were passed on the supposed talents of the writer; and, so far as I have been able to learn, every man of the slightest impartiality was ready to give his verdict to the honest sentiments and integrity of spirit in which it was written.

If the temper and tone in which this publication has been treated have undergone a change, it has been only that I was destined to suffer a part, in the great revolution which has operated in nations, parties, political creeds, and the views and interests of ambitious men. I have fallen (if I have fallen) in one common grave with the cause and the love of liberty; and in this sense have been more honoured and illustrated in my decline from general favour, than I ever was in the highest tide of my success.

My book, as was announced by me in the preface, was the child of the French revolution. It is easy to understand what has been the operation of many men's minds on the subject of that great event. Almost every man entertains in his bosom some love for the public: there is, I suppose, no man that lives who has not some love for himself. Both these sentiments were extensively exercised, in the various European nations who were spectators of the French revolution. Where was the ingenuous heart which did not beat with exultation, at seeing a great and cultivated people shake off the chains of one of the most oppressive political systems in the world, the most replenished with abuses, the least mollified and relieved by any infusion of liberty? Thus far we were all of us disinterested and generous. But the reflex act of the mind is so essential a part of our nature, that it was impossible men should not, in the first interval of leisure, enquire how they would be affected by this event in their personal fortunes. The reasonings which guided the persons alluded to in this particular, are obvious. They believed that liberty could not be thus acquired by a most respected and considerable nation in the centre of Europe, without producing consequences favourable to liberty in every surrounding country. They inferred therefore that, while each man was indulging his enthusiasm and philanthropy, each man would find himself most effectually promoting his private interest. They worshipped the rising sun. They applauded their sagacity with long-sightedness, while they thus heaped up for themselves the merit of being the virtuous and early champions of infant, and as yet powerless liberty.

But these expectations and this sagacity have been miserably disappointed. The persons however who acted under their influence, were slow and unwilling in giving up their hopes. They had felt a real and honest passion for the French revolution: but honesty is a principle of an unaccomodating sort; and passion, once set in motion, will not be subdued in a moment. Beside, these persons, confiding in their sagacity, had declared themselves in a very peremptory and decisive manner. Shame therefore for a long time held them to their point. They saw that their retreat would come with a very ill grace; they would not retire upon the first symptoms of miscarriage; they cheered themselves and one another with assurances that these symptoms would speedily subside; they hoped to add to the praise of long-sightedness, the nobler praise of magnanimous perseverance in spite of adverse and discouraging appearances.

What was the consequence of this? Mr Burke published his celebrated book against the French revolution in 1790: they were unmoved. The powers of Europe began to concert hostile measures upon this subject in 1791: they were unmoved. Louis was deposed; monarchial government was proscribed in France: they were unmoved. In September 1792 scenes of execrable and unprecedented murder were perpetrated in the capital and many of the provinces: they scorned for the sake of a few private misdeeds to give up a great public principle. The head of Louis fell upon the scaffold: still they were consistent. The atrocious and inhuman reign of Robespierre commenced; it continued from May 1793 to July 1794; almost every day was marked with blood; almost all that was greatest and most venerable in France was immolated at the monster's shrine, the queen, madame Elizabeth, Vergniaud, Gensonné, Roland, madame Roland, Bailli, Lavoisier; it were endless to recollect a tithe of the bloody catalogue: still these advocates of the French revolution were consistent. Down to the spring of 1797, when petitions were sent up from so many parts of England for the removal of the king's ministers, scarcely one of those persons who had declared themselves ardently and affectionately interested for the success of the French, deserted their cause.

I am willing to yield to these men considerable praise for the constancy with which they persevered so long; as long perhaps as worldly prudence could in any degree countenance. But why, because I have not been so prudent as they, should I be made the object of their invective? I never went so far, in my partiality for the practical principles of the French revolution, as many of those men with whom I was accustomed to converse. I uniformly declared myself an enemy to revolutions. Many persons censured me for this lukewarmness; I willingly endured the censure. Several of those persons are now gone into the opposite extreme. They must excuse me; they have wandered wide of me on the one side and on the other; I did not follow them before; I cannot follow them now.

But, though I commend these persons for having persevered so long, I can be at no loss to assign the principal cause why they have persevered no longer. What has happened since the spring of 1797 to justify their revolt? Has any new system of disorganisation been adopted in France? Have the French embrued their hands in further massacres? Has another Robespierre risen, to fright the world with systematical, cool-blooded, never-satiated murder? No, none of these things. How then has it happened, that men who remained unaltered spite of these terrible events, now profess their conviction that the hope of melioration in human society must be given up; and, not contented with that, virulently abuse those by whom the hope is still cherished? To the government of Robespierre succeeded what was called an Executive Directory, a set of men whose principles and actions so nearly resembled those of the regular governments of Europe, that it is with an ill grace the advocates of those governments can pronounce a censure against them. Upon the dissolution of the Directory, we have seen an auspicious and beneficent genius arise, who without violence to the principles of the French revolution, has suspended their morbid activity, and given time for the fever which threatened to consume the human race, to subside. All the great points embraced by the revolution remain entire: hereditary government is gone; hereditary nobility is extinguished; the hierarchy of the Gallican church is no more; the feudal rights, the oppressive immunities of a mighty aristocracy, are banished never to return. Every thing promises that the future government of France will be popular, and her people free. It follows therefore, almost with the force of a demonstration, that it is nothing which has happened in France that has produced this general apostacy from the principles of her revolution.

But the persons for whose conduct I am accounting, while they have looked with less solicitude than before at what is passing in France, have looked very attentively at what is passing at home. Not that in our own country events have happened, to justify any better, in the way of argument, this transformation of their opinions, than the events in France. The revolutionary societies in this metropolis were once numerous; they had spread their ramifications through almost every county in England; revolutionary lectures were publicly read here and elsewhere with tumults of applause; almost every alehouse had its artisans haranguing in favour of republicanism and equality: at this time the persons of whom I am speaking conceived no alarm. The societies have perished, or, where they have not, have shrunk to a skeleton; the days of democratical declamation are no more; even the starving labourer in the alehouse is become a champion of aristocracy. Yet it is now that these persons come forth to sound the alarm; now they tread upon the neck of the monster whom they regard as expiring; now they hold it necessary to show themselves intemperate and incessant in their hostilities against the spirit of innovation....

I feel little resentment against those persons who, without any fresh reasons to justify their change, think it now necessary to plead for establishments, and express their horror at theories and innovation, though I recollect the time when they took an opposite part. But this I must say, that they act against all nature and reason when, instead of modestly confessing their frailty and the transformation of their sentiments, they rail at me because I have not equally changed. If I had expressed a certain degree of displeasure at their conduct, I should have had a very forcible excuse. But I was not prepared with a word of reproach: I would have been silent, if they would have permitted me to be so.

Down to about the middle of the year 1797, as I have said, the champions of the French revolution in England appeared to retain their position, and I remained unattacked. About that time a forlorn hope of two little skirmishing pamphlets began the war. But the writers of these pamphlets appear to have been uninstructed in the school of the new converts I have attempted to describe, and their productions were without scurrility. The next and grand attack was opened in Mr Mackintosh's Lectures. A book was published about the same time, professing to contain remarks upon some speculations of mine, entitled an Essay upon Population. Of this book and the spirit in which it is written I can never speak but with unfeigned respect. Soon after followed a much vaunted Sermon by Mr Hall of Cambridge, in which every notion of toleration or decorum was treated with infuriated contempt.[1] I disdain to dwell on the rabble of scurrilities which followed: the vulgar contumelies of the author of the Pursuits of Literature, novels of buffoonery and scandal to the amount of half a score, and British Critics, Anti-Jacobin Newspapers, and Anti-Jacobin Magazines without number.[2] Last of all, for the present at least, for I am not idle enough to flatter myself that the tide is gone by, Dr Parr, with his Spital Sermon before the Lord Mayor, brings up the rear of my assailants. I take occasion from this first avowed and respectable publication,* to offer the little I think it necessary to offer in my defence.

But, before I enter upon particulars, let me stop a moment to observe upon the singular and perverse destiny which has attended me on this occasion. I wrote my Enquiry Concerning Political Justice in the innocence of my heart. I sought no overt effects; I abhorred all tumult; I entered my protest against revolutions. Every impartial person who knows me, or has attentively considered my writings, will acknowledge that it is the fault of my character, rather to be too sceptical, than to incline too much to play the dogmatist. I was by no means assured of the truth of my own system. I wrote

---

* The main attack of the Essay on Population is not directed against the principles of my book, but its conclusions [Godwin's note].

1 James Mackintosh (1765–1832), A Discourse on the Study of the Law of Nature and Nations: Introductory to a Course of Lectures on that Science to be Commenced in Lincoln's Inn Hall, on Wednesday, Feb. 13, 1799 in Persuance of an Order of the Honourable Society of Lincoln's Inn (London, 1799); Thomas Robert Malthus (1766–1834), An Essay on the Principle of Population as It Affects the Future Improvement of Society: With Remarks on the Speculation of Mr. Godwin, M. Condorcet, and Other Writers (London, 1798); Robert Hall (1764–1831), Modern Infidelity Considered, with Respect to Its Influence on Society, in a Sermon Preached at the Baptist Meeting, Cambridge (Cambridge, 1800).

2 Thomas James Mathias, The Pursuits of Literature: A Satirical Poem in Four Dialogues, 5th ed. (London, 1798); the British Critic was an anti-Jacobin periodical (see Appendix C); the weekly newspaper The Anti-Jacobin; Or, Weekly Examiner was founded in 1797 specifically to curb the influence of the progressive Monthly Magazine and other Jacobin periodicals (it was replaced in July 1798 by The Anti-Jacobin Review and Magazine, which became one of the main platforms for conservative propaganda during the revolutionary period).

indeed with ardour; but I published with diffidence. I knew that my speculations had led me out of the beaten track; and I waited to be instructed by the comment of others as to the degree of value which should be stamped upon them. That comment in the first instance was highly flattering; yet I was not satisfied. I did not cease to revise, to reconsider, or to enquire.

I had learned indeed that enquiry was the pilot who might be expected to steer me into the haven of truth. I had heard a thousand times, and I believed, that whoever gave his speculations on general questions to the public with fairness and temper, was a public bene-factor: and I must add, that I have never yet heard the fairness or temper of my publication called into doubt. If my doctrines were formed to abide the test of scrutiny, it was well: if they were refuted, I should still have occasion to rejoice, in having procured to the public the benefit of that refutation, of so much additional disquisi-tion and knowledge. Unprophetic as I was, I rested in perfect tran-quillity, and suspected not that I should be dragged to public odium, and made an example to deter all future enquirers from the practice of unshackled speculation. I was no man of the world; I was a mere student, connected with no party, elected into no club, exempt from every imputation of political conspiracy or cabal. I therefore believed that, if my speculations were opposed, and if my opponent were a man of the least pretension to character and decorum, I should be at least opposed in that style of fairness and respect which is so eminently due from one literary enquirer to another....

All that I am now commenting upon, is the time which Dr Parr has chosen for this attack. There is nothing which I can perceive in the public situation of things that required it. Jacobinism was destroyed; its party, as a party, was extinguished; its tenets were involved in almost universal unpopularity and odium; they were deserted by almost every man, high or low, in the island of Great Britain. This is the time Dr Parr has chosen, to muster his troops, and sound the trumpet of war.

Thus stands the public view of the period. As to myself, after having for four years heard little else than the voice of commendation, I was at length attacked from every side, and in a style which defied all moderation and decency. No vehicle was too mean, no language too coarse and insulting, by which to convey the venom of my adversaries. The abuse was so often repeated, that at length the bystanders, and perhaps the parties themselves, began to believe what they had so vehemently asserted. The cry spread like a general infection, and I have been told that not even a petty novel for boarding-school misses now ventures to aspire to favour, unless it contain some expressions of dislike and abhorrence to the new philosophy, and its chief (or shall I say its most voluminous?) English adherent. I do then accuse Dr Parr that, instead of attempting to give the tone to his contemporaries, as his abilities well entitle him to do, he has condescended to join a cry, after it had already become loud and numerous.

Appendix B: Sources and Contexts: The Anti-Jacobin Side of the Revolutionary Debate

1. **From Edmund Burke, *Reflections on the Revolution in France, and on the Proceedings in Certain Societies in London, Relative to that Event. In a Letter Intended to Have Been Sent to a Gentleman in Paris* (1790), in *The Works of the Right Honourable Edmund Burke*, new ed., 8 vols. (London: Printed for F. and C. Rivington, 1801), 5:191–93; 198–203**

[If Godwin's *Enquiry Concerning Political Justice* was the unofficial manifesto for the Jacobin cause in Britain, Burke's *Reflections on the Revolution in France* was the same for the anti-Jacobin movement. Relying more on its superb rhetoric and evocative imagery than on any sustained philosophical argument, the *Reflections* inspired both sides of the Revolutionary Debate, leaving the conservatives thrilled and full of patriotic zeal, and the radicals infuriated and disgusted. The following extract, describing the attack of the Jacobin mob on the quarters of Louis VXI and Marie Antoinette in their palace at Versailles, is perhaps the most memorial passage in the *Reflections*. It is also considered to be one of the most exquisite pieces of English prose.]

Yielding to reasons at least as forcible as those which were so delicately urged in the compliment on the new year, the king of France will probably endeavour to forget these events, and that compliment. But History, who keeps a durable record of all our acts, and exercises her awful censure over the proceedings of all sorts of sovereigns, will not forget either those events or the æra of this liberal refinement in the intercourse of mankind. History will record, that on the morning of the 6th of October 1789, the king and queen of France, after a day of confusion, alarm, dismay, and slaughter, lay down, under the pledged security of public faith, to indulge nature in a few hours of respite, and troubled melancholy repose. From this sleep the queen was first startled by the voice of the centinel at her door, who cried out to her, to save herself by flight—that this was the last proof of fidelity he could give—that they were upon him, and he was dead. Instantly he was cut down. A band of cruel ruffians and assassins, reeking with his blood, rushed into the chamber of the queen, and pierced with an hundred strokes of bayonets and poniards the bed, from whence this persecuted woman had but just had time to fly almost naked, and through ways unknown to the murderers had escaped to seek refuge at the feet of a king and husband, not secure of his own life for a moment.

This king, to say no more of him, and this queen, and their infant children (who once would have been the pride and hope of a great and generous people) were then forced to abandon the sanctuary of the most splendid palace in the world, which they left swimming in blood, polluted by massacre, and strewed with scattered limbs and mutilated carcases. Thence they were conducted into the capital of their kingdom. Two had been selected from the unprovoked, unresisted, promiscuous slaughter, which was made of the gentlemen of birth and family who composed the king's body guard. These two gentlemen, with all the parade of an execution of justice, were cruelly and publickly dragged to the block, and beheaded in the great court of the palace. Their heads were stuck upon spears, and led the procession; whilst the royal captives who followed in the train were slowly moved along, amidst the horrid yells, and shrilling screams, and frantic dances, and infamous contumelies, and all the unutterable abominations of the furies of hell, in the abused shape of the vilest of women. After they had been made to taste, drop by drop, more than the bitterness of death, in the slow torture of a journey of twelve miles, protracted to six hours, they were, under a guard, composed of those very soldiers who had thus conducted them through this famous triumph, lodged in one of the old palaces of Paris, now converted into a Bastile for kings....

It is now sixteen or seventeen years since I saw the queen of France, then the dauphiness, at Versailles; and surely never lighted on this orb, which she hardly seemed to touch, a more delightful vision. I saw her just above the horizon, decorating and cheering the elevated sphere she just began to move in,—glittering like the morning-star, full of life, and splendour, and joy. Oh! what a revolution! and what an heart must I have, to contemplate without emotion that elevation and that fall! Little did I dream when she added titles of veneration to those of enthusiastick, distant, respectful love, that she should ever be obliged to carry the sharpe antidote against disgrace concealed in that bosom; little did I dream that I should have lived to see such disasters fallen upon her in a nation of gallant men, in a nation of men of honour and of cavaliers. I thought ten thousand swords must have leaped from their scabbards to avenge even a look that threatened her with insult. But the age of chivalry is gone. That of sophisters, œconomists, and calculators, has succeeded; and the glory of Europe is extinguished for ever. Never, never more, shall we behold that generous loyalty to rank and sex, that proud submission, that dignified obedience, that subordination of the heart, which kept alive, even in servitude itself, the spirit of an exalted freedom. The unbought grace of life, the cheap defence of nations, the nurse of manly sentiment and heroick enterprize is gone! It is gone, that sensibility of principle, that chastity of honour, which felt a stain like a wound, which inspired courage whilst it mitigated society, which ennobled whatever it touched, and under which vice itself lost half its evil, by losing all its grossness.

This mixed system of opinion and sentiment had its origin in antient chivalry; and the principle, though varied in its appearance by the varying state of human affairs, subsisted and influenced through a long succession of generations, even to the time we live in. If it should ever be totally extinguished, the loss I fear will be great. It is this which has given its character to modern Europe. It is this which has distinguished it to its advantage, from the states of Asia, and possibly from those states which flourished in the most brilliant periods of the antique world. It was this, which, without confounding ranks, had produced a noble quality, and handed it down through all the gradations of social life. It was this opinion which mitigated kings into companions, and raised private men to be fellows with kings. Without force, or opposition, it subdued the fierceness of pride and power; it obliged sovereigns to submit to the soft collar of social esteem, compelled stern authority to submit to elegance, and gave a domination vanquisher of laws, to be subdued by manners.

But now all is to be changed. All the pleasing illusions, which made power gentle, and obedience liberal, which harmonized the different shades of life, and which, by a bland assimilation, incorporated into politicks the sentiments which beautify and soften private society, are to be dissolved by this new conquering empire of light and reason. All the decent drapery of life is to be rudely torn off. All the superadded ideas, furnished from the wardrobe of moral imagination, which the heart owns, and the understanding ratifies, as necessary to cover the defects of our naked shivering nature, and to raise it to dignity in our own estimation, are to be exploded as a ridiculous, absurd, and antiquated fashion.

On this scheme of things, a king is but a man, a queen is but a woman; a woman is but an animal; and an animal not of the highest order. All homage paid to the sex in general as such, and without distinct views, is to be regarded as romance and folly. Regicide, and parricide, and sacrilege, are but fictions of superstition, corrupting jurisprudence by destroying its simplicity. The murder of a king, or a queen, or a bishop, or a father, are only common homicide; and if the people are by any chance, or in any way gainers by it, a sort of homicide much the most pardonable, and into which we ought not to make too severe a scrutiny.

On the scheme of this barbarous philosophy, which is the offspring of cold hearts and muddy understandings, and which is as void of solid wisdom, as it is destitute of all taste and elegance, laws are to be supported only by their own terrors, and by the concern, which each individual may find in them, from his own private speculations, or can spare to them from his own private interests. In the groves of *their* academy, at the end of every visto, you see nothing but the gallows. Nothing is left which engages the affections on the part of the commonwealth. On the principles of this mechanick philosophy, our institutions can never be embodied, if I may use the expression, in persons; so as to create in us love, veneration, admiration, or attachment. But that sort of reason which banishes the affections is incapable of filling their place, these publick affections, combined with manners, are required sometimes as supplements, sometimes as correctives, always as aids to the law. The precept given by a wise man, as well as a great critic, for the construction of poems, is equally true as to states. *Non satis est pulchra esse poemata, dulcia sunto.*[1] There ought to be a system of manners in every nation which a well-formed mind would be disposed to relish. To make us love our country, our country ought to be lovely.

But power, of some kind or other, will survive the shock in which manners and opinions perish; and it will find other and worse means for its support. The usurpation which, in order to subvert the antient institutions, has destroyed antient principles, will hold power by arts similar to those by which it has acquired it. When the old feudal and chivalrous spirit of *fealty*, which, by freeing kings from fear, freed both kings and subjects from the precautions of tyranny,

---

[1] "It is not enough for poems to be beautiful; they must also be sweet" (Horace, *De Arte Poetica*, 99–100).

shall be extinct in the minds of men, plots and assassinations will be anticipated by preventive murder and preventive confiscation, and that long roll of grim and bloody maxims, which form the political code of all power, not standing on its own honour, and the honour of those who are to obey it. Kings will be tyrants from policy when subjects are rebels from principle.

2. From Anon., "Proceedings of the Friends to the Abuse of the Liberty of the Press" (n.p., 1793), 6–12

[In the course of the 1790s hundreds of reform societies or "Jacobin clubs" sprang up all over England, some favoring moderate reform, others campaigning for annual parliaments, universal suffrage, electoral reform, or freedom of the press. To disseminate their views most societies held regular meetings and readings in taverns, and published scores of broadsides and pamphlets. Conservative writers and activists were quick to respond, and released a deluge of satirical counter-pamphlets, in which they ridiculed both the reform societies' objectives, and their tavern meetings and political speeching.]

SECOND MEETING.

ABUSE OF THE LIBERTY OF THE PRESS.
COUNSELLOR EGO in the Chair.

Crown and Anchor Tavern, Jan. 19, 1793.

MR. COUNSELLOR EGO said, that he did not care for calumny or misrepresentation, asfar as regarded himself (for he never thought about himself at all, as every one knew); yet, as far as regarded the public, it was material that the wickedness and folly of their meeting should not be made worse than it was, by misrepresentation; he should therefore read what he had to say, from a paper which he had written—He then read as follows:

"The impressions of Sensibility under which I rise to deliver my sentiments on this occasion, are no more than the natural feelings of a man who, unconscious of the little merit he may have, is anxious to collect, from every quarter, such testimonies of it as may preserve him from too timid a despondency. The flattering commendations with which, at our former Meeting, you honoured my poor endeavours *in our common cause*, and the applauses with which you received my Speech, lead me to hope that I shall not, on the present awful occasion, meet with less indulgence. I will confess to you, Gentlemen, that at the Trial which gave occasion to these Meetings, the hostile countenances of the Bench, the Jury, and the whole surrounding Auditory, had nearly overpowered my bashful mind. Accustomed to be heard, even on the wrong side, 'with the indulgence given to a child which lisps its prattle out of season,' I could ill encounter the formidable array of disapproving countenances, by which I found myself environed. My spirits sunk within me. Methought I heard them ask, at every period, what is this Man who dares to speak against the Sense, the Feelings, and the general Conviction of his country?—who pretends to love the Constitution, yet argues that it should be villified, and brought into contempt?—The idea of these reproaches; unjust as I might think them, oppressed me. I spoke as borne down by a heavy weight; and, however you might admire, which I am truly happy to be told you did, the fire and energy of my Oration, it was nothing, I assure you, to that which would have blazed upon the Audience, had I felt my Cause to be popular, or could I even have caught a single glance of approbation from the Court. It was to avoid, as much as possible, this painful situation, that I had previously determined to take up the only popular topic I could, by any art, connect with the defence of THOMAS PAINE—*The Freedom of the Press*—words so sacred to a British Mind—sounds in such harmony with every English ear, that I hoped they might have borne me through the business with applause at least, if not with triumph. I was severely disappointed. The stupid Jury seemed to be possessed invincibly with an idea that the Press might still be Free—though they should not suffer the Constitution in all its parts, the Revolution, and our Monarchs past and present, to be insulted with impunity. To draw them from this notion it was, that I studiously multiplied quotations on the general topic, omitting, as much as possible, the particular Case before us, and especially avoiding any mention of the *Bill of Rights*, being a *Bill of Wrongs and Insults*, which I knew to be a tender subject. It was all in vain: and if I had not found in you, Gentlemen, the support I there so fruitlessly attempted to obtain, my Speech might have continued unapplauded 'to the last syllable of recorded time,' to the utter ruin and destruction of my nerves.

Gentlemen, DR. JOHNSON, whom I frequently quote, would have said, perhaps, of our present efforts, as he said of those in favour of Liberty, in which the Poet THOMSON took a part, that they 'fill the Nation with clamours for the *Freedom of the Press*, of which no man felt the want, and with care for that *Freedom of the Press*, which never was in danger.' But Dr. JOHNSON, though a Writer of great weight, and therefore highly useful to a pleader who would prop his arguments by extraneous authority, is a Writer whose general sentiments I am not at all inclined to adopt. Would to Heaven, however, that we could realize one part of the Sentence I have quoted! Would we could 'fill the Nation with our clamours!' But, alas! Gentlemen—my modesty perhaps suggests the idea too strongly to me,—but I fear, indeed, the Nation disregards us. I fear like THOMSON, we shall 'call in vain upon the votaries of *a Free Press*, to read its praises, or *reward its encomiasts*. Its praises will be condemned to harbour spiders, and to gather dust.' I confess I feel this apprehension. Our Meetings are burlesqued, our Resolutions parodied, our Names nick-named, our Speeches anticipated; and these attacks upon us—I speak it with profound regret—the Public applauds. I have yet seen no fruit of my endeavours, except the title of *Counsellor Ego*; and even the worthy Chairman will meet, perhaps, no better recompense for his past and present labours, than the thanks of this Assembly, and the ever-adhering appellation of *Alexander the Coppersmith*.

These, Gentlemen, are melancholy topics: nor would I dwell upon them, but in hopes to raise your ardour in proportion to the difficulties you have to contend with, and to stimulate you to such noble, preserving efforts, as may command success. The Liberty of the Press, remember always, is a String, which, if with due perseverance harped upon, may yet at length produce the Music we desire to hear. It is a Nerve of such strong feeling in the Constitutions of the *English*, that the constant irritation of it may in time affect the brain. The Cause of PAINE may be perhaps irrelevant to it: but in the everlasting repetition of the general topic, the Cause may be forgotten; the tide of Favour may roll back, and buoy us up again; and they who now condemn us as seditious, may in the end regard us as true Patriots.

The Prosecutions of those Persons who have been apprehended for selling seditious Pamphlets, will continually afford us opportunities for renewing our complaints; and if any one among them be more contumacious than the rest, and the law fall therefore heavier upon him, this will raise compassion; and the cry of Tyranny, Oppression, Persecution, will gain us proselytes by means of the very impudence of the offender. Any money that can be raised for the defence of such delinquents, will be very wisely bestowed: and I doubt not that the same spirit which subscribed to maintain the cause of Paine, will persevere, in spite of disappointments, unfatigued, to aid all persons who may stand in any similarity of circumstances. Remember, that if one instance can be found, by great good fortune, of a Prosecution incautiously begun, or in any step imprudently pursued, we shall gain a triumph, and that triumph will give colour to our cause.

Gentlemen, though I most pointedly condemn Affectations to discourage offences, I do as heartily applaud all those which are or may be formed for the assistance of *persecuted* delinquents. The reason of this apparent inconsistency I shall not give. Congenial as your spirits are to mine, you must all know and feel it. Nor will I hazard the delivery of it to the world, or expose it to those comments and interpretations, which, though I should not choose to admit, I might find it rather difficult to refute. Suffice it to say, that I know we all agree, and understand each other.

Gentlemen, I shall soon begin to be exhausted; for though I have been used to speak for three, four, or five hours together, my person, as you see, is delicate, and it must be a very unfriendly hearer who will not believe that my strength is worn out rather than my arguments.

I have said *but little* of myself; but if in this moment of fatigue my powers will let me speak any subject, it must be on this. Mr. Burke, Gentlemen, has censured me as an Egotist. Alas! he little knows me! He mistakes me totally. I am only, as I think I hinted once before, nervously diffident. Approbation is necessary to me. I wish for every man's approbation. I wish even for that of Mr. Burke; and if I cannot either praise or censure him into admiration of me, what good will my life do me?

I have said, Gentlemen, on a former occasion, that the Parliament of this country is corrupt. I will give you as *Othello* calls it, 'Damning proof,'—proof that will extinguish every doubt. The House of Commons listens with delight to Mr. Burke. Even when he censures me, it listens—even when be ridicules me. Is this credible?—is it tolerable?—This same House, when I am on my legs, coughs, sneezes, talks, disperses, goes to dinner. Gentlemen, let me put it home to all of you; am I a Speaker to be heard without attention?—with disgust?—Am I a dinner-bell? the House must be corrupt, or this could never happen. To my mind this is absolute conviction: and a Reform of Parliament would, I think, be cheaply purchased, at any hazard, could it bring together a set of Representatives who would hear my Speeches with delight. Inattention destroys my powers. I cannot speak, surrounded with wet blankets.

I will impart to you Gentlemen, under the Seal of Confidence, a secret which I have never mentioned yet in any public Assembly. I was not originally educated for the Bar! I see you stare with wonder; but it is true. I was first in the Navy—then in the Army—and, after this was called late to the Profession of the Law; in which, arduous as it is, I have risen, notwithstanding every disadvantage to that eminence in which you see me. I have been the delight of Juries, and of all the Auditors that are assembled usually in Courts of Justice. Ought the Commons of Great Britain to be more refined than these? Where, then, is our Equality? If Members of Parliament can make distinctions that common Auditors cannot make, that is not such a Parliament as Britain ought to have. I repeat it, therefore, and I urge it strongly to your hearts and to your consciences, that, till a Parliament can be elected in which I can become a favoured Orator, there is no Freedom for this Country.

Gentlemen, I am, as I foresaw I should be, exhausted. But I have dwelt sufficiently on those topics which are nearest to my heart. Having so done, I shall conclude by recommending it to you, by all means to support such *Freedom in the Press* as may bring forward such a Parliament as I have now described;—a Parliament whose clamours may silence, in their turn those most tyrannic Speakers, Burke and Pitt; and put an end to that which they at present successfully maintain—a most unconditional and intolerably oppressive Aristocracy of Eloquence, Intellect and Integrity."

Having concluded amidst the plaudits and most unanimous approbation of his Auditors, *Mr. Damn'd Barebones*, after doing justice to the motives, to the zeal, and to the abilities of Mr. Counsellor Ego, and having stated the propriety of the Meeting's holding forth at once to the Public a pledge of the principles which influenced them; and upon which they meant to act, moved, "That the paper then read be adopted as the 'DECLARATION of the FRIENDS to the ABUSE of the FREEDOM of the PRESS'; which Motion was immediately carried without a dissenting voice; and in a short time the Declaration received above Five Hundred most respectable Signatures.

3. From William Playfair, *Peace with the Jacobins Impossible* (London, 1794), 3–13

[Playfair was one of the most uncompromising and rabid of anti-Jacobins, and is best-known for his *History of Jacobinism* (1795). The following extract, from the earlier, lesser-known pamphlet "Peace with the Jacobins Impossible," provides a sample of the xenophobic and jingoistic venom with which the anti-Jacobins responded to France's declaring war on Britain on 1 February 1793. Needless to say, any British subjects harboring only the slightest sympathy toward France or the French Revolution are villified by Playfair as "Jacobins" and traitors.]

Nothing can be more unjust than to represent the present war, carried on by the principal powers of Europe against France, as being a war of kings against liberty and the people; it is indeed represented as such by those men who wish to stir up anarchy and confusion, that they may themselves profit by the general wreck, and it is believed to be so by some few persons, who, without evil intentions themselves, believe with facility whatever is asserted with confidence.

The present contest is that of freedom and order, against anarchy and despotism; it is the contest of men who have something, against men who have nothing; and every proprietor and every honest man is engaged in it not only in England but all over Europe.

I do not hesitate to call the advocates of French principles JACOBINS, in whatever country they may be found, and of whatever rank they may be; and that I may not be misunderstood, I mean by Jacobins, all those persons who at the same time that they see without horror what passes in France, exclaim against those men who wish to preserve persons and property in other countries.

But it is to you honest and industrious citizens, to you fathers of families, and proprietors of all descriptions, that I address myself; to you who do not wish to see rape, murder, and plunder established, under the false name of patriotism and liberty: and I am happy to think, that in every country of Europe you make the most numerous class of inhabitants, and I shall endeavour, in as short a manner as possible, to prove the necessity of vigorous measures, in order to preserve yourselves from those evils, under which the oppressed and deluded French nation labours at this time—

"*The laws without execution; the constituted authorities impotent and disgraced; crimes unpunished; property of every kind attacked; personal safety violated; the morals of the people corrupted; no constitution; no government; no justice;—such are the features of French anarchy*," according to the very words of Brissot,* one of their leaders, at the time when the republic was declared, and the king dethroned: and who was a philosopher of the Jacobin sort, and one of the most violent chiefs in support of anarchy, until it turned against himself and his friends.

I do not think it necessary to prove, though I can do it whenever I think fit, that there are Jacobins in this country; because I take it for granted, that every man of plain common sense sees, that those men can be nothing else, who were the advocates of the French revolution three years ago, and continue to be so still.

When men complain against the rigour of English judges and juries, who punish with regret those who sow sedition and would overturn the present constitution, why do they wish us to copy the French, who punish a single unguarded word with the guillotine? Can such men be believed to be serious?

Can Doctor Priestley, for instance, be supposed really to prefer the French government to the English, while he submits to all the humiliation of persecution in England, as he pretends, to the honour of being a legislator in France? The fate of the too famous Thomas Paine shows that the doctor was right, when he refused the honour that was offered to him; and if his candour were but equal to his abilities, he would abandon openly a cause, which has led to the scaffold in one day twenty-one of his best philosophers, without any legal trials or crimes proved against them; for after having merited death fifty times for what they had done, they were condemned to die for the only public action in their lives that merited some praise; they had the audacity to wish to set bounds to that anarchy which they had themselves created, and of which they became at so early a period the victims.

The anarchists celebrated, by a salute of artillery, the triumph which they obtained over their former masters; and it was a real

---

* See Brissot's Address to his Constituents, translated from the French, with an incomparable and masterly preface. Printed for John Stockdale [Playfair's note].

triumph to all good citizens, when those men who had so lately commanded the massacres of September, and who had imbrued their hands in the blood of their virtuous sovereign, fell under the ax, which, with a cruel ingenuity, they had themselves constructed, and with an unrelenting fury, kept employed.

It was then that the excess of the evil seemed to begin to work a cure; and it is a matter of considerable consolation, that for several months past, the violence with which the party that ruled last winter has been pursued by the Jacobin club which they founded, is still greater than that with which they persecute their declared enemies; and it will be remembered to the latest posterity with pleasure, that when Brissot and his colleagues, but a few months before adored in Paris, were beheaded, it was applauded still louder than when they murdered their unfortunate queen, whom those same wretches had dragged from her palace to a dungeon: and it will appear evident, that even in their present degraded and ferocious state, the multitude makes (involuntarily perhaps) some distinction between vice and misfortune.

Can we believe that those persons, who wanted European powers to treat the ministers of last year, and thereby attempt to avoid a war, were sincere; when now that the rulers of France, with whom they would have treated, are almost all come to an untimely end, and yet they hold the same language?—No—it cannot be; they are certainly not sincere.

Of the six ministers who ruled under the faction of Brissot, at the time that the pretended friends of this country wished for a treaty, one alone is now in public favour, two are guillotined, and two have done justice upon themselves with their own hands: the sixth is saved by accident in a foreign dungeon, where the hand of despotism, as it is termed by the Jacobins, saves him from that death which would probably have been his lot had he stayed amongst his friends.

The enemies of this war (for of war in general every man ought to be an enemy) say, that wherever *we can fight we may treat*; but these gentlemen should remember, that although by fighting you certainly acknowledge the existence of your adversary, you do not acknowledge thereby his honour, his integrity, or your confidence in his word, and that is necessary to a treaty. Thus you fight with a robber, but you cannot take his word, and put yourself in his power.

That it was necessary to fight will never be doubted. Our allies were attacked abroad, and the basis of our government at home; to those who dispute this last, I can but answer that none are so deaf as those that will not hear, and it is only a matter of regret that those who undermine our government cannot be treated *à la Françoise,* since it is the French system that they have taken for their model.

Had England separated her cause from that of justice, and of the other European powers; had she made a treaty with men who trample under foot all laws human and divine, the probable consequence would have been as it was with Spain, that her offers would have been rejected with disdain by those mad republicans. But had they not been so, England in a general war, without one ally but the Brisotins themselves, would have been obliged to keep up an army, a navy, and a militia, at very nearly the same expence that the war now costs; and what is worse, she would have been obliged to permit the importation of French Jacobins and Jacobin principles into this country. In a word, the ax would have been laid to the root of the tree of our happy constitution; and if there had been no war, instead of seeing at this time Fisch Palmer, Muir, and Margarot sent to Botany Bay to cull simples and reflect on their imprudence, we would have seen a *permanent guillotine* in every town, and a *guillotine ambulante* for the use of villages. The water of the Thames, instead of carrying the ships of our merchants, would be stained with the blood of our merchants, and would deposit on its deserted banks their deformed carcases. The heads of our nobles would be laid low; and even those men, who now incite us to discontent, would, as in France, be the victims of their own system....

But what a picture do I draw! No, our country could never be in that state; all the horrors of ancient civil wars might be renewed, but the example of France, and the true patriotism of Englishmen, would make us unite. We might perish in the field, but never would Englishmen break the sacred doors of the prison house to search victims for the assassin's knife, Never would a strange land see the proprietors of English acres scattered on a foreign soil, they would die or live upon their own: No, ye searchers of discord, ye enemies of England, this island and its inhabitants are not suited for your principles; we may be loaded with debt, we may not always be successful in war, but we have a God whom we worship, a Constitution that we revere, and a King that we love; and we have not yet learned to make those fatal distinctions in *the origin of property* that subvert society, and render pillage and plunder acts of justice and of patriotism....

4. From Peter Porcupine [William Cobbett], *Observations on the Emigration of Dr. Joseph Priestley* (Philadelphia, 1794), 3–9; 27–32

[William Cobbett (1763–1835) was a British writer and political reformer. Born and raised on a Surrey farm, Cobbett enlisted in 1784, served in Nova Scotia, and was promoted sergeant-major. On returning to England in 1791 he tried unsuccessfully to expose financial corruption in the regiment, and had to flee to France and then to America. In Philadelphia (1792–99) Cobbett patriotically defended Great Britain, writing under the pseudonym of Peter Porcupine. When he returned to England in 1800, he was welcomed as a Tory supporter. However, he soon became disenchanted with what he called "The System" and from 1806 demanded parliamentary reform. Sentenced in 1810 to two years in Newgate gaol for seditious libel, Cobbett was henceforth regarded as a dangerous radical, and when Habeas Corpus was suspended in 1817 he fled to America. On his return home in 1819 he resumed farming and also wrote some of his finest pieces, published as *Rural Rides*.]

When the arrival of Doctor Priestley in the United States was first announced, I looked upon his emigration ... as no more than the effect of that weakness, that delusive caprice, that too often accompanies the decline of life; and which is apt, by a change of place, to flatter age with a renovation of faculties, and with the return of departed genius. Viewing him as a man that sought repose, my heart welcomed him to the shores of peace, and wished him, what he certainly ought to have wished himself, a quiet obscurity. But his Answers to the Address of the Democratic and other Societies at New-York, place him in quite a different light, and subject him to the animadversions of a public, among whom they have been industriously propagated.

No Man has a right to pry into his neighbours private concerns; and the opinions of every Man are his private concerns, while he keeps them so; that is to say, while they are confined to himself, his Family and particular Friends: But when he makes those opinions public; when he once attempts to make Converts, whether it be in Religion, Politics, or any thing else; when he once comes forward as a Candidate for public Admiration, Esteem, or Compassion, his Opinions, his Principles, his Motives, every Action of his life, public or private, become the fair Subject of public discussion. On this principle, which the Doctor ought to be the last among Mankind to controvert, it is easy to perceive that these observations need no apology.

His Answers to the Addresses of the New-York Societies are evidently calculated to mislead and deceive the People of the United States.[1] He there endeavours to impose himself on them for a Sufferer in the Cause of Liberty; and makes a canting profession of Moderation, in direct contraction to the Conduct of his whole Life.

He says, he hopes to find here, "that Protection from Violence, which Laws and Government promise in all Countries, but which he has not found in his own." He certainly must suppose that no European Intelligence ever reaches this side of the Atlantic, or that the Inhabitants of these countries are too dull to comprehend the sublime events that mark his life and character. Perhaps I shall show him, that it is not the people of England alone who know how to estimate the merit of Doctor Priestley.

Let us examine his claims to our compassion: Let us see whether his charge against the laws and government of his country be just, or not.

On the 14th of July, 1791, an unruly mob, assembled in the town of Birmingham, set fire to his house, and burnt it, together with all it contained. This is the subject of his complaint, and the pretended cause of his emigration. The fact is not denied; but in the relation of facts circumstances must not be forgotten. To judge of the Doctor's charge against his country, we must take a retrospective view of his conduct, and of the circumstances that led to the destruction of his property.

---

[1] Upon his arrival in the United States, a number of addresses to Priestley and his responses appeared in the press. "Address of the Democratic Society of New-York to Joseph Priestley," an article by James Nicholson, appeared in *General Advertiser* 1094 (Tuesday, 10 June 1794); Priestley's response, dated "New-York June 6th," followed this Address in the same issue with the caption title: "To the Members of the Democratic Society of New York." A letter by Henry Pope, "The Address of the Republican Natives of Great Britain and Ireland, Resident in the City of New York, to Doctor Priestley," appeared in *General Advertiser* 1101 (Wednesday, 18 June 1794); Priestley's response, dated 13 June 1794, followed the letter, with the caption title, "To the Republican Natives of Great Britain and Ireland, Resident in New York." John Carlton's "Address of the Medical Society of the State of New York, to Doctor Priestley" appeared in *General Advertiser* 1101 (Wednesday, 18 June 1794); Priestley's response, dated "New York, June 13, 1794," followed the Address, with the caption title, "To the Members of the Medical Society in New York."

It is about twelve years since he began to be distinguished among the Dissenters from established church of England. He preached up a kind of *deism*, which nobody understood, and which it was thought the Doctor understood full as well as his neighbours. This doctrine afterwards assumed the name of Unitarianism, and the *religious* of the order were called, or rather they called themselves, Unitarians. The sect never rose into consequence; and the founder had the mortification of seeing his darling Unitarianism growing quite out of date with himself, when the French Revolution came, and gave them both a short respite from eternal oblivion.

Those who know any thing of the English dissenters, know that they always introduce their political claims and projects under the masks of religion. The Doctor was one of those who entertained hopes of bringing about a Revolution in England upon the French plan; and for this purpose he found it would be very convenient for him to be at the head of a religious sect. Unitarianism was now revived, and the society held regular meetings at Birmingham. In the inflammatory discourses, called sermons, that were delivered at these meetings, the English constitution was first openly attacked; and doctrines were there held forth subversive of all civil and religious order. The press soon swarmed with publications expressive of these principles. The revolutionists began to form societies all over the kingdom, between which a mode of communication was established, in perfect conformity to that of the Jacobin clubs in France.

Nothing was neglected by this branch of the Parisian *Propagande* to excite the People to a general Insurrection. Inflammatory Handbills, Advertisements, Federation Dinners, Toasts, Sermons, Prayers; in short, every Trick that religious or political Duplicity could suggest, was played off to destroy a Constitution which has borne the Test, and attracted the admiration of ages; and to establish in its place a new system fabricated by themselves.

The fourteenth of July, 1791, was of too much note in the annals of modern Regeneration to be neglected by these regenerated politicians. A club of them, of which Doctor Priestley was a member, gave public notice of a feast, to be held at Birmingham, in which they intended to celebrate the French Revolution. Their endeavours had hitherto excited no other sentiments in what may be called the people of England than that of contempt. The people of Birmingham, however, felt, on this occasion, a convulsive moment. They were scandalised at this public notice for holding in their town a festival to celebrate events, which were in reality a subject of the deepest horror: and seeing in it at the same time an open and audacious attempt to destroy the Constitution of their Country, and with it their happiness, they thought their understandings and loyalty insulted, and prepared to avenge themselves by the chastisement of the English Revolutionists, in the midst of their scandalous orgies. The feast nevertheless took place; but the Doctor knowing himself to be the grand projector, and consequently the particular object of his townsmens' vengeance, prudently kept away. The cry of *Church and King* was the signal for the people to assemble, which they did to a considerable number, opposite the hotel where the convives were met. The club dispersed, and the mob proceeded to breaking the windows, and other acts of violence incident to such scenes; but let it be remembered that no personal violence was offered. Perhaps it would have been well if they had vented their anger on the persons of the Revolutionists, provided they had contented themselves with the ceremony of the horse-pond or blanket. Certain it is, that it would have been very fortunate if the riot had ended this way; but when that many-headed monster, a mob, is once roused and put in motion, who can stop its destructive steps!

From the *hotel of the federation*, the mob proceeded to Doctor Priestley's Meeting house, which they very nearly destroyed in a little time. Had they stopped here, all would yet have been well. The destruction of this temple of sedition and infidelity would have been of no great consequence; but, unhappily for them and the town of Birmingham, they could not be separated before they had destroyed the houses and property of many members of the club. Some of these houses, among which was Doctor Priestley's, were situated at the distance of some miles from town; the mob were in force to defy all the efforts of the civil power, and, unluckily none of the military could be brought to the place, until some days after the 14th of July. In the mean time many spacious and elegant houses were burnt, and much valuable property destroyed; but it is certainly worthy of remark, that during the whole of these unlawful proceedings, not a single person was killed or wounded, either wilfully or by accident, except some of the rioters themselves. At the end of four or five days, this riot, which seemed to threaten more serious consequences, was happily terminated by the arrival of a detachment of dragoons; and tranquillity was restored to the distressed town of Birmingham.

The magistrates used every exertion in their power to quell this riot in its very earliest stage, and continued so to do to the last. The Earl of Plymouth condescended to attend, and act as a justice of the peace: several clergymen of the church of England also attended in the same capacity, and they all were indefatigable in their endeavours to put a stop to the depredations, and to re-establish order and tranquillity. Every one knows that in such cases it is very difficult to discriminate, and that it is neither necessary nor just, if it be possible, to imprison, try, and execute the whole of a mob. Eleven of these rioters were, however, indicted; seven of them were acquitted, four found guilty, and of these four, two suffered death. These unfortunate men were, according to the law, prosecuted on the part of the king; and it has been allowed by the Doctor's own partizans, that the prosecution was carried on with every possible enforcement, and even rigour, by the judges and counsellors. The pretended lenity was laid to the charge of the jury! What a contradiction! They accuse the government of screening the rioters from the penalty due to their crimes, and at the same time they accuse the jury of their acquittal! It is the misfortune of Doctor Priestley, and all his adherents, ever to be inconsistent with themselves....

That a parliamentary reform was the handle by which the English revolutionists intended to effect the destruction of the constitution, need not be insisted on; at least if we believe their own repeated declarations. Paine, and some others, clearly expressed themselves on this head; the Doctor was more cautious while in England, but, safely arrived in his "asylum," he has been a little more undisguised. He says, the troubles in Europe are the natural offspring of the *"forms of government"* that exist there; and that the abuses spring from the *"artificial distinctions in society."* I must stop here a moment, to remark on the impudence of this assertion. Is it not notorious, that *changing* those forms of government, and *destroying* those distinctions in society, has introduced all the troubles in Europe? Had the form of government in France continued what it had been for twelve or thirteen hundred years, would those troubles ever have had an existence? To hazard an assertion like this, a man must be an idiot, or he must think his readers so.—It was then the *form* of the English government, and those artificial distinctions, that is to say, of king, prince, bishop, &c. that he wanted to destroy, in order to produce that *"other system of liberty,"* which he had been so long dreaming about. In his answer to the address of "the republican natives of Great Britain and Ireland, resident at New York," he says: "The wisdom and happiness of republican governments, and the evils resulting from hereditary monarchical ones, cannot appear in a stronger light to you than they do to me;" and yet this same man pretended an inviolable attachment to the *hereditary monarchical government* of Great Britain! Says he, by way of vindicating the principles of his club to the people of Birmingham: "The first toast that was drank, was, '*the king and constitution*'" What! does he make a merit in England of having *toasted* that which he abominates in America? Alas! Philosophers are but mere men.

It is clear that a parliamentary reform was not the object: an after-game was intended; which the vigilance of government, and the natural good sense of the people, happily prevented; and the Doctor, disappointed and chagrined, is come here to discharge his heart of the venom it has been long collecting against his country. He tells the Democratic society, that he cannot promise to be a better subject of this government than he has been of that of Great Britain. Let us hope, that he intends us an agreeable disappointment, if not, the sooner he emigrates back again the better.

System-mongers are an unreasonable species of mortals: time, place, climate, nature itself must give way. They must have the same government in every quarter of the globe; when perhaps there are not two countries which can possibly admit of the same form of government, at the same time. A thousand hidden causes, a thousand circumstances and unforeseen events conspire to the forming of a government. It is always done by little and little. When completed, it presents nothing like a system; nothing like a thing composed, and written in a book. It is curious to hear people cite the American government, as the summit of human perfection, while they decry the English; when it is absolutely nothing more than the government which the kings of England established here, with such little modifications as were necessary, on account of the state of society and local circumstances. If then the Doctor is come here for a change of government and laws, he is the most disappointed of mortals. He will have the mortification to find in his "*asylum*" the same laws as those from which he has fled, the same upright manner of administering them, the same punishment of the oppressor, and the same protection of the oppressed. In the courts of justice he will every day see precedents quoted from the English law-books; and (which to him may appear wonderful) we may venture to predict, that it will be very long before they will be supplanted by the bloody records of the revolutionary tribunal. Let him compare the government of these states, and the measures they have pursued, with what has passed under the boasted constitution that he wished to introduce into England, and see if he can find one single instance of the most distant resemblance. In the abolition of negro slavery, for example, the governments of the United States have not rushed headlong into the mad plan of the National Convention. With much more humane views, with a much more sincere desire of seeing all mankind free and happy, they have, in spite of clubs and societies, proceeded with caution and justice. In short, they have adopted, as nearly as possible, considering the circumstances and situation, the same measures as have been taken by the government which he abhors. He will have the further mortification to find, that the government here is not, any more than in England, influenced by the vociferations of fish women, or by the *toasts* and *resolutions* of popular societies. He will, however, have one consolation: here, as well as there, he will find, that the truly great, virtuous, and incorruptible man at the head of government, is branded for an *Aristocrat*, by those noisy gentry.

Happiness being the end of all good government, that which produces the most is consequently the best; and comparison being the only method of determining the relative value of things, it is easy to see which is preferable, the tyranny which the French formerly enjoyed, or the liberty and equality they at present labour under. If the Doctor had come about a year sooner, he might have had the satisfaction of being not only an ear, but an eye-witness also, of some of the blessed effects of this celebrated revolution. He might then have been regaled with that sight, so delectable to a modern philosopher—opulence reduced to misery.

The stale pretence, that the league against the French has been the cause of their inhuman conduct to each other, cannot by the most perverse sophistry, be applied to the Island of St. Domingo.[1] That fine rich colony was ruined; its superb capital and villas reduced to ashes; one half of its inhabitants massacred, and the other half reduced to beggary, before an enemy ever appeared on the

---

[1]   A reference to the St. Domingo slave insurrection of 1791, when slaves attacked their masters and ransacked the plantations on the Caribbean island. The event sent shock-waves of horror through Britain and other slave-owning nations.

coast. No: It is that system of anarchy and blood that was celebrated at Birmingham on the 14th of July, 1791, that has been the cause of all this murder and devastation.

5. From Anon., *Letters on Emigration. By a Gentleman, Lately Returned from America* (London, 1794), 61–71; 74–76 ("Letter V")

[Emigration to America, for idealistic or economic reasons, was a key battleground in the 1790s Jacobin/anti-Jacobin print war, with those in favor of emigration presenting America as the utopian alternative to the evils of British society, and those opposed to emigration presenting past and prospective emigrants as either traitors or fools, or both. Often this debate was conducted in the form of an exchange of "authentic" letters between (former) emigrants and their friends back home. The following is an extract of such an exchange.]

LETTER V.

DEAR SIR,

London, Sept. 1794.

The new inland state of Kentucky lies southwest of Pennsylvania, and is watered by the great river Ohio. From all the account I could receive in America (and I was inquisitive on the subject), I have reason to believe that it is superior in soil to every other of the States. But in speaking of it, we must consider it as a desart; its cultivation is so comparatively small. If a man can relinquish society, this State I should think would better suit the views of one who emigrates for agricultural purposes; its soil is said to be rich and deep, and its climate, tempered by local circumstances, to be peculiarly acceptable.

The Alleganny mountains, which the Americans term the *spinal bone* of America, borders on this country. But having mentioned the goodness of the soil, and the comparative temperature of its climate, it is to be remarked, that it labours under the same disadvantages, with respect to establishment, with the other States.—It is equally difficult to grub the trees here as elsewhere; labour is equally dear, and the same noxious vapours are to be dreaded wherever new earth is turned up. Its *peculiar* disadvantages are, its inland situation, which in a great measure excludes it from a market for its produce, and must prove, till a more extended population takes place, a perpetual barrier to any beneficial recompense for labour. Did the Ohio run eastward instead of southward, it would be otherwise. The next is, that the Indians are at war at this very period with the Americans, for the country bordering on the Ohio. Those who have hitherto inhabited Kentucky, are a hardy race of men, of the lower class of the Irish, rendered ferocious by the constant alarms they are subject to from the inroads of the Indians.

War is carried on, on both sides, with the most unrelenting animosity: the continual conflicts they sustain, in defence of their families and property, have rendered these people as savage as those they encounter; they neither give nor take quarter, nor is it unfrequent among them to make parties to hunt the Indians, and return exulting from a successful expedition, in which they have brought off scalps and other trophies, in the same manner as sportsmen with us after the fortunate run of a fox.

How far such friends, or such enemies, can be acceptable as neighbours, they can best determine, who think of establishing themselves in that country.

Among the paradoxes of the day, one of the most extraordinary to my apprehension is, that this should have been selected as a place of settlement, by some modern philosophers who have emigrated. The inroads of uncultivated savages can but ill accord with the calm pursuit of philosophers. Were I to form a conjecture on this subject, it would be, that after the edge of curiosity is somewhat blunted, and the inconveniences of an infant settlement experienced, these persons will first retreat to the cultivated States, and finally return to their native country. Those who cultivate science for the advantage of mankind, ought to have ease, leisure, and a favourable situation, none of which can be found in Kentucky; they can have no society but among themselves; and it is not always that philosophers make the best society to each other, not will it be long before they miss the conveniences to which they have been accustomed.

Though I do not admire the politics of those literary characters who cannot discover liberty in England, and who appear to have shaken off the restraints of civil society (which we voluntarily submit to, to increase our happiness), to return to a state of nature, I feel a respect for science, and its possessors even in the wilderness. Of one point I wish them to be sensible; that permanent admiration is no *trait* in the American character.

A new race of men have within these few years started up in America, distinguished by the name of *land-jobbers*. These persons, by themselves, or agents, purchase large tracts of land on speculation. Many have bought it at the rate of 4d. and 6d. an acre, what they have afterwards disposed of at the rate of a dollar. Large fortunes have been acquired in this manner; but it requires considerable judgement in land, and an accurate knowledge of a variety of circumstances, to make such purchases as will turn to account. Those who thus speculate, rely on the probable chance of quick population for emigration. One bad consequence immediately results from this to the United States, by rendering those lands in the neighbourhood of cultivated tracts, too dear for ordinary purchasers, who are from hence compelled to retire into the back country to make cheap purchases; a circumstance that prevents that close connected situation which would increase the general strength, at the same time that it would contribute to the more comfortable accommodation of individuals.

As many ingenious artisans and mechanics have left England, with the idea of rising quickly to affluence, I will treat briefly on the subject.

Most of those persons, on their arrival in America, are astonished that they do not get immediate employment; they have been taught to believe, that manufacturers and tradesmen would vie with each other to engage them.

Their want of success may be attributed to two causes; one, that there are but few manufactories in America, in general they depend on England for supply; the other, that in a country like England, where manufactures and mechanics have been brought to such a degree of perfection, there has in consequence ensued a *division* of *labour*, which renders a man only competent to one particular branch of a trade: wherever this is the case, the workman would not stand the smallest chance for employment in America, as a man must know every part of the trade, or he is useless....

Indeed, most of the workmen who have been so fortunate as to make a little money retire into the back countries, where they can have land cheap, preferring the activity of a farming life, to the sedentary employment of an artisan in a city. It is, besides, more reputable in an agricultural country, and holds out a better prospect of decent establishment for a family. Few ships return to England, Scotland, or Ireland, which do not carry back some of those unfortunate adventurers, who are many of them obliged to make up the expence of the passage, by disposing of the implements of their trade. The only workman that I know of who could be certain of employment is a carpenter; there is an universal demand for his labour in all parts.

As to those unhappy people called redemptioners, who stipulate to pay for their passage by years of servitude, it is to be regretted that the justice of nations should permit such iniquitous contracts. This class of people are treated worse than the negroes; the master knows that he has but a temporary property in them, and is therefore determined to extract the utmost profit from their labour while they are subject to him. Attention to his interest, secures better treatment to his negroes; should they die in consequence of hard usage, it is so much money lost.

The country people in America are ingenious at supplying their own wants; the same man can often act as carpenter, mason, and farrier, weave, make shoes, and even saddles and bridles—what we vulgarly term *a jack of all trades*, is the man for the people in the country. The great number of these renders workmen who are strangers unnecessary.

The disadvantage which a man who emigrates, and turns shop-keeper without connections in the country, labours under, is this, that by the time he comes to know who are persons of credit and responsibility, he has lost his property.

Whatever has been said as matter of advice to the gentleman who emigrates, will more or less apply to the little farmer. Such a man having made his little purchase, hurries into the woods with his family: to him society is but a secondary object; he toils incessantly till his labour is probably arrested by the ague; this disorder is very prevalent in America, and seldom fails to attack those who turn up new ground, or are in damp situations. Those who have been afflicted with this disorder, well know how enervating it is, and that it renders a man incapable of any kind of employment. Thus he probably languishes for months on a bed of sickness, incapable of any exertion, though his hopes of a harvest were dependent on it....

Again I address the country gentleman who plans to emigrate. I wish him to recollect, that without extraordinary exertions of industry, little can be expected from American culture; that many circumstances combine to impede it, and that the same exertion made at home would be more certain of its reward by an increase of property. Does a reduction of circumstances induce such a man to emigrate through a false pride? Let him consider that England is a large scene; that in no country can he so well arrange himself as in this; and that from the quantity of landed property always ready to be disposed of, it can never be more than the work of a few weeks to settle himself suitably—He can then begin life afresh, equally well as though he had passed over to a new world.—He can suit his society to his circumstances, and, in a new situation, commence his plan of œconomy without the pain of *being seen to descend*. Has he lived in the north, let him turn his face to the south—in the south, to the north.—That man is ill qualified for American society, whom pride induces to emigrate, when the commonest artisan would not hesitate to look him steadily in the face, and inform him that he was his equal. He who would emigrate from such a motive, might be compared to one who, endeavouring to avoid the sting of a wasp, would seek refuge among bee-hives. Let the man who seeks to avoid partial inconvenience by such a step, be impressed with one truth, namely, that mortification in *one* instance may preclude mortifications in others.

But, it may be asked, ought no description of persons to emigrate? The reply is obvious—The guilty *must*, and the very unfortunate *will*, though the prejudices of the natives are too apt to confound the latter with the former.

Believe me to be, &c.

THE END.

6. From Thomas Robert Malthus, *An Essay on the Principle of Population* (1798), ed. E.A. Wrigley and David Souden, in *The Works of Thomas Robert Malthus*, gen. ed. E.A. Wrigley and David Souden, 8 vols. (London: Pickering and Chatto, 1986), 1:5–7; 1:8–9 (Chapter I); 1:64–70 (Chapter X)

[Among the many responses that Godwin's *Political Justice* provoked, Malthus's *Essay* was one of the most rational and scientific. Malthus takes Godwin to task over the latter's principle of "perfectibility"— the idea that it is within the power of mankind to eradicate social evil by creating a society in which there is absolute equality among its members in terms of property, wealth, and subsistence. Malthus famously retorts by arguing that "the power of population is indefinitely greater than the power in the earth to produce subsistence for man." Stupeo's disastrous scheme in *The Vagabond* to "people the wilderness" of Kentucky, is meant to underscore this very point. Malthus's *Essay* is nowadays regarded as one of the earliest attempts to formulate a doctrine of sustainable development.]

CHAPTER I

Question stated—Little prospects of a determination of it, from the enmity of the opposing parties—The principal argument against the perfectibility of man and of society has never been fairly answered—Nature of the difficulty arising from population—Outline of the principal argument of the essay.

The great and unlooked-for discoveries that have taken place of late years in natural philosophy; the increasing diffusion of general knowledge from the extension of the art of printing; the ardent and unshackled spirit of inquiry that prevails throughout the lettered, and even unlettered world; the new and extraordinary lights that have been thrown on political subjects, which dazzle, and astonish the understanding; and particularly that tremendous phenomenon in the political horizon the French revolution, which, like a blazing comet, seems destined either to inspire with fresh life and vigour, or to scorch up and destroy the shrinking inhabitants of the earth, have all concurred to lead many able men into the opinion, that we were touching on a period big with the most important changes, changes that would in some measure be decisive of the future fate of mankind.

It has been said, that the great question is now at issue, whether man shall henceforth start forwards with accelerated velocity towards illimitable, and hitherto unconceived improvement; or be condemned to a perpetual oscillation between happiness and misery, and after every effort remain still at an immeasurable distance from the wished-for goal.

Yet, anxiously as every friend of mankind must look forwards to the termination of this painful suspense; and, eagerly as the inquiring mind would hail every ray of light that might assist its view into futurity, it is much to be lamented, that the writers on each side of this momentous question still keep far aloof from each other. Their mutual arguments do not meet with a candid examination. The question is not brought to rest on fewer points; and even in theory scarcely seems to be approaching to a decision.

The advocate for the present order of things, is apt to treat the sect of speculative philosophers, either as a set of artful and designing knaves, who preach up ardent benevolence, and draw captivating pictures of a happier state of society, only the better to enable them to destroy the present establishments, and to forward their own deep-laid schemes of ambition; or, as wild and mad-headed enthusiasts, whose silly speculations, and absurd paradoxes, are not worthy the attention of any reasonable man.

The advocate for the perfectibility of man, and of society, retorts on the defender of establishments a more than equal contempt. He brands him as the slave of the most miserable, and narrow prejudices; or, as the defender of the abuses of civil society, only because he profits by them. He paints him either as a character who prostitutes his understanding to his interest; or as one whose powers of mind are not of a size to grasp anything great and noble; who cannot see above five yards before him; and who must therefore be utterly unable to take in the views of the enlightened benefactor of mankind.

In this unamicable contest, the cause of truth cannot but suffer. The really good arguments on each side of the question are not allowed to have their proper weight. Each pursues his own theory, little solicitous to correct, or improve it, by an attention to what is advanced by his opponents.

The friend of the present order of things condemns all political speculations in the gross. He will not even condescend to examine the grounds from which the perfectibility of society is inferred. Much less will he give himself the trouble in a fair and candid manner to attempt an exposition of their fallacy.

The speculative philosopher equally offends against the cause of truth. With eyes fixed on a happier state of society, the blessings of which he paints in the most captivating colours, he allows himself to indulge in the most bitter invectives against every present establishment, without applying his talents to consider the best and fastest means of removing abuses, and without seeming to be aware of the tremendous obstacles that threaten, even in theory, to oppose the progress of man towards perfection.

It is an acknowledged truth in philosophy, that a just theory will always be confirmed by experiment. Yet so much friction, and so many minute circumstances occur in practice, which it is next to impossible for the most enlarged and penetrating mind to foresee, that on few subjects can any theory be pronounced just, that has not stood the test of experience. But an untried theory cannot fairly be advanced as probable, much less as just, till all the arguments against it, have been maturely weighed, and clearly and consistently refuted....

I think I may fairly make two postulata.

First, that food is necessary to the existence of man.

Secondly, that the passion between the sexes is necessary, and will remain nearly in its present state.

These two laws ever since we have had any knowledge of mankind, appear to have been fixed laws of our nature; and, as we have not hitherto seen any alteration in them, we have no right to conclude that they will ever cease to be what they now are, without an immediate act of power in that Being who first arranged the system of the universe; and for the advantage of his creatures, still executes, according to fixed laws, all its various operations.

I do not know that any writer has supposed that on this earth man will ultimately be able to live without food. But Mr Godwin has conjectured that the passion between the sexes may in time be extinguished. As, however, he calls this part of his work, a deviation into the land of conjecture, I will not dwell longer upon it at present, than to say, that the best arguments for the perfectibility of man, are drawn from a contemplation of the great progress that he has already made from the savage state, and the difficulty of saying where he is to stop. But towards the extinction of the passion between the sexes, no progress whatever has hitherto been made. It appears to exist in as much force at present as it did two thousand, or four thousand years ago. There are individual exceptions now as there always have been. But, as these exceptions do not appear to increase in number, it would surely be a very unphilosophical mode of arguing, to infer merely from the existence of an exception, that the exception would, in time, become the rule, and the rule the exception.

Assuming then, my postulata as granted, I say, that the power of population is indefinitely greater than the power in the earth to produce subsistence for man.

Population, when unchecked, increases in a geometrical ratio. Subsistence increases only in an arithmetical ratio. A slight acquaintance with numbers will show the immensity of the first power in comparison of the second.

By that law of our nature which makes food necessary to the life of man, the effects of these two unequal powers must be kept equal.

This implies a strong and constantly operating check on population from the difficulty of subsistence. This difficulty must fall somewhere; must necessarily be severely felt by a large portion of mankind....

CHAPTER X

Mr Godwin's system of equality—Error of attributing all the vices of mankind to human institutions—Mr Godwin's first answer to the difficulty arising from population totally insufficient—Mr Godwin's beautiful system of equality supposed to be realised—Its utter destruction simply from the principle of population in so short a time as thirty years.

The system of equality which Mr Godwin proposes, is, without doubt, by far the most beautiful and engaging of any that has yet appeared. An amelioration of society to be produced merely by reason and conviction, wears much more the promise of permanence, than any change effected and maintained by force. The unlimited exercise of private judgement, is a doctrine inexpressibly grand and captivating, and has a vast superiority over those systems where every individual is in a manner the slave of the public. The substitution of benevolence as the master-spring, and moving principle of society, instead of self-love, is a consummation devoutly to be wished. In short, it is impossible to contemplate the whole of this fair structure, without emotions of delight and admiration, accompanied with ardent longing for the period of its accomplishment. But, alas! that moment can never arrive. The whole is little better than a dream, a beautiful phantom of the imagination. These "gorgeous palaces" of happiness and immortality, these "solemn temples" of truth and virtue will dissolve, "like the baseless fabric of a vision," when we awaken to real life, and contemplate the true and genuine situation of man on earth.

Mr Godwin, at the conclusion of the third chapter of his eighth book, speaking of population, says, "There is a principle in human society, by which population is perpetually kept down to the level of the means of subsistence. Thus among the wandering tribes of America and Asia, we never find through the lapse of ages that population has so increased as to render necessary the cultivation of the earth." This principle, which Mr Godwin thus mentions as some mysterious and occult cause, and which he does not attempt to investigate, will be found to be the grinding law of necessity; misery, and the fear of misery.

The great error under which Mr Godwin labours throughout his whole work, is, the attributing almost all the vices and misery that are seen in civil society to human institutions. Political regulations, and the established administration of property, are with him the fruitful sources of all evil, the hotbeds of all the crimes that degrade mankind. Were this really a true state of the case, it would not seem a hopeless task to remove evil completely from the world; and reason seems to be the proper and adequate instrument for effecting so great a purpose. But the truth is, that though human institutions appear to be the obvious and obtrusive causes of much mischief to mankind; yet, in reality, they are light and superficial, they are mere feathers that float on the surface, in comparison with those deeper-seated causes of impurity that corrupt the springs, and render turbid the whole stream of human life.

Mr Godwin, in his chapter on the benefits attendant on a system of equality, says, "The spirit of oppression, the spirit of servility, and the spirit of fraud, these are the immediate growth of the established administration of property. They are alike hostile to intellectual improvement. The other vices of envy, malice, and revenge, are their inseparable companions. In a state of society, where men lived in the midst of plenty, and where all shared alike the bounties of nature, these sentiments would inevitably expire. The narrow principle of selfishness would vanish. No man being obliged to guard his little store, or provide with anxiety and pain for his restless wants, each would lose his individual existence in the thought of the general good. No man would be an enemy to his neighbour, for they would have no subject of contention; and, of consequence, philanthropy would resume the empire which reason assigns her. Mind would be delivered from her perpetual anxiety about corporal support, and free to expatiate in the field of thought, which is congenial to her. Each would assist the enquiries of all."

This would, indeed, be a happy state. But that it is merely an imaginary picture, with scarcely a feature near the truth, the reader, I am afraid, is already too well convinced.

Man cannot live in the midst of plenty. All cannot share alike the bounties of nature. Were there no established administration of property, every man would be obliged to guard with force his little store. Selfishness would be triumphant. The subjects of contention would be perpetual. Every individual mind would be under a constant anxiety about corporal support; and not a single intellect would be left free to expatiate in the field of thought.

How little Mr Godwin has turned the attention of his penetrating mind to the real state of man on earth, will sufficiently appear from the manner in which he endeavours to remove the difficulty of an overcharged population. He says, "The obvious answer to this objection, is, that to reason thus is to foresee difficulties at a great distance. Three fourths of the habitable globe is now uncultivated. The parts already cultivated are capable of immeasurable improvement. Myriads of centuries of still increasing population may pass away, and the earth be still found sufficient for the subsistence of its inhabitants."

I have already pointed out the error of supposing that no distress and difficulty would arise from an overcharged population before the earth absolutely refused to produce any more. But let us imagine for a moment Mr Godwin's beautiful system of equality realized in its utmost purity, and see how soon this difficulty might be expected to press under so perfect a form of society. A theory that will not admit of application cannot possibly be just.

Let us suppose all the causes of misery and vice in this island removed. War and contention cease. Unwholesome trades and manufactories do not exist. Crowds no longer collect together in great and pestilent cities for purposes of court intrigue, of commerce, and vicious gratifications. Simple, healthy, and rational amusements take place of drinking, gaming and debauchery. There are no towns sufficiently large to have any prejudicial effects on the human constitution. The greater part of the happy inhabitants of this terrestrial paradise live in hamlets and farmhouses scattered over the face of the country. Every house is clean, airy, sufficiently roomy, and in a healthy situation. All men are equal. The labours of luxury are at end. And the necessary labours of agriculture are shared amicably among all. The number of persons, and the produce of the island, we suppose to be the same as at present. The spirit of benevolence, guided by impartial justice, will divide this produce among all the members of the society according to their wants. Though it would be impossible that they should all have animal food every day, yet vegetable food, with meat occasionally, would satisfy the desires of a frugal people, and would be sufficient to preserve them in health, strength, and spirits.

Mr Godwin considers marriage as a fraud and a monopoly. Let us suppose the commerce of the sexes established upon principles of the most perfect freedom. Mr Godwin does not think himself that this freedom would lead to a promiscuous intercourse; and in this I perfectly agree with him. The love of variety is a vicious, corrupt, and unnatural taste, and could not prevail in any great degree in a simple and virtuous state of society. Each man would probably select himself a partner, to whom he would adhere as long as that adherence continued to be the choice of both parties. It would be of little consequence, according to Mr Godwin, how many children a woman had, or to whom they belonged. Provisions and assistance would spontaneously flow from the quarter in which they abounded, to the quarter that was deficient.* And every man would be ready to furnish instruction to the rising generation according to his capacity.

I cannot conceive a form of society so favourable upon the whole to population. The irremediableness of marriage, as it is at present constituted, undoubtedly deters many from entering into that state. An unshackled intercourse on the contrary, would be a most powerful incitement to early attachments: and as we are supposing no anxiety about the future support of children to exist, I do not conceive that there would be one woman in a hundred, of twenty three, without a family.

With these extraordinary encouragements to population, and every cause of depopulation, as we have supposed, removed, the numbers would necessarily increase faster than in any society that has ever yet been known. I have mentioned, on the authority of a pamphlet published by a Dr Styles, and referred to by Dr Price, that the inhabitants of the back settlements of America doubled their numbers in fifteen years. England is certainly a more healthy country than the back settlements of America; and as we have supposed every house in the island to be airy and wholesome, and the encouragements to have a family greater even than with the back settlers, no probable reason can be assigned, why the population should not double itself in less, if possible, than fifteen years. But to be quite sure that we do not go beyond the truth, we will only suppose the period of doubling to be twenty five years, a ratio of increase, which is well known to have taken place throughout all the northern states of America.

There can be little doubt, that the equalization of property which we have supposed, added to the circumstance of the labour of the whole community being directed chiefly to agriculture, would tend greatly to augment the produce of the country. But to answer the demands of a population increasing so rapidly, Mr

---

*   W. Godwin, *Enquiry concerning political justice*, 2nd ed., 2 vols (1796), ii, p. 504 [Malthus's note].

Godwin's calculation of half an hour a day for each man, would certainly not be sufficient. It is probable that the half of every man's time must be employed for this purpose. Yet with such, or much greater exertions, a person who is acquainted with the nature of the soil in this country, and who reflects on the fertility of the lands already in cultivation, and the barrenness of those that are not cultivated, will be very much disposed to doubt, whether the whole average produce could possibly be doubled in twenty five years from the present period. The only chance of success would be the ploughing up all the grazing countries, and putting an end almost entirely to the use of animal food. Yet a part of this scheme might defeat itself. The soil of England will not produce much without dressing; and cattle seem to be necessary to make that species of manure, which best suits the land. In China, it is said, that the soil in some of the provinces is so fertile, as to produce two crops of rice in the year without dressing. None of the lands in England will answer to this description.

Difficult, however, as it might be, to double the average produce of the island in twenty five years, let us suppose it effected. At the expiration of the first period therefore, the food, though almost entirely vegetable, would be sufficient to support in health, the doubled population of 14 millions.

During the next period of doubling, where will the food be found to satisfy the importunate demands of the increasing numbers? Where is the fresh land to turn up? Where is the dressing necessary to improve that which is already in cultivation? There is no person with the smallest knowledge of land, but would say, that it was impossible that the average produce of the country could be increased during the second twenty five years by a quantity equal to what it at present yields. Yet we will suppose this increase, however improbable, to take place. The exuberant strength of the argument allows of almost any concession. Even with this concession, however, there would be 7 millions at the expiration of the second term, unprovided for. A quantity of food equal to the frugal support of 21 millions, would be to be divided among 28 millions.

Alas! what becomes of the picture where men lived in the midst of plenty; where no man was obliged to provide with anxiety and pain for his restless wants; where the narrow principle of selfishness did not exist; where mind was delivered from her perpetual anxiety about corporal support, and free to expatiate in the field of thought which is congenial to her. This beautiful fabric of imagination vanishes at the severe touch of truth. The spirit of benevolence, cherished and invigorated by plenty, is repressed by the chilling breath of want. The hateful passions that had vanished, reappear. The mighty law of self-preservation, expels all the softer and more exalted emotions of the soul. The temptations to evil are too strong for human nature to resist. The corn is plucked before it is ripe, or secreted in unfair proportions; and the whole black train of vices that belong to falsehood are immediately generated. Provisions no longer flow in for the support of the mother with a large family. The children are sickly from insufficient food. The rosy flush of health gives place to the pallid cheek and hollow eye of misery. Benevolence yet lingering in a few bosoms, makes some faint expiring struggles, till at length self-love resumes his wonted empire, and lords it triumphant over the world.

No human institutions here existed, to the perverseness of which Mr Godwin ascribes the original sin of the worst men.* No opposition had been produced by them between public and private good. No monopoly had been created of those advantages which reason directs to be left in common. No man had been goaded to the breach of order by unjust laws. Benevolence had established her reign in all hearts: and yet in so short a period as within fifty years, violence, oppression, falsehood, misery, every hateful vice, and every form of distress, which degrade and sadden the present state of society, seem to have been generated by the most imperious circumstances, by laws inherent in the nature of man, and absolutely independent of all human regulations.

If we are not yet too well convinced of the reality of this melancholy picture, let us but look for a moment into the next period of twenty five years; and we shall see 28 millions of human beings without the means of support; and before the conclusion of the first century, the population would be 112 millions, and the food only sufficient for 35 millions, leaving 77 millions unprovided for. In these ages want would be indeed triumphant, and rapine and murder must reign at large: and yet all this time we are supposing the produce of the earth absolutely unlimited, and the yearly increase greater than the boldest speculator can imagine.

---

* Godwin, *Political justice*, ii, p. 340 [Malthus's note].

This is undoubtedly a very different view of the difficulty arising from population, from that which Mr Godwin gives, when he
says, "Myriads of centuries of still increasing population may pass
away, and the earth be still found sufficient for the subsistence of
its inhabitants."

Appendix C: Contemporary Reviews

1. *Analytical Review*, New Series, 1 (February 1799): 210–15

This novel professes itself to be an attack upon the system of the *new philosophy*. Whatever credit may be due to the motives which prompted the author to the undertaking, we are obliged to say that his performance falls much short of his object. Its literary merits, indeed, are so low, that were it not for the circulation which Mr. W's former character as a novelist is likely to give it, we should deem it entitled to a very trifling share of our attention. With this view, however, we think it incumbent to animadvert upon the apology which the author has prefixed for the mode in which he has devised his attack.

"Perhaps," says he, "a *novel* may gain attention when arguments of the soundest sense and most perfect eloquence shall fail to arrest the feet of the *trifler* from the specious paths of the new philosophy. It is also an attempt to parry the enemy with their own weapons; for no channel is deemed improper by them which can introduce their sentiments."

This assertion we apprehend to be greatly unjust: and we must remonstrate against it, as involving a charge more serious than the author appears to be aware of. Whatever be the real character of the doctrines of "Political Justice," our opinion of the human mind is not so narrow, as to make us apprehend danger from the influence of them, whilst they continue merely the subjects of closet speculation or of rational disquisition. It is only by exhibiting them, whether with a view to censure or approbation, in an unnatural, *practical* connection with modern characters, systems, and institutions, that they can be rendered mischievous or formidable.

None who have read the "political justice" of Godwin, and the novels of him and Holcroft with attention, can, we think, impute to them so pernicious a design: and we are persuaded that by far the greater part of those who have read the novels of these writers with delight and admiration, would be found amongst the avowed enemies of the system of "Political Justice."

A novel should be a description of things as they are; and a practical tendency of a novel should be to strengthen and interest the feelings by a sensible and bodily representation (if we may so call it) of those moral doctrines which the judgment is supposed to have already adopted. But who, that has bestowed the least study upon the principles of the new philosophy, can suppose that any but the most ill-judging advocates or the most ignorant antagonists of them, could choose a vehicle so partial and temporary, so in consistent with, and so unfavorable to abstract disquisitions, for displaying *their* merits.

It will be remembered that we are here speaking only of those parts of the system of "Political Justice" which [can] be called its characteristic doctrines. Most of them are doctrines common to it, with every liberal system of politics and morality which has appeared for many ages, and have been so long familiar to the understandings and study of mankind, and are so far practicable under the existing institutions of society, as to be safely and consistently exhibited in a picture of *present times*.

We needed not, however, to have made this distinction as a preface to the examination of the work before us. Mr. W. is by no means chargeable with an undue partiality in selecting the objects of his ridicule; on the contrary, it would be difficult to find any moral doctrine, not of the most universal currency, which is not involved in his sarcasms. In one place we find him ridiculing the author of "Political Justice," for exposing the absurdity of *duels*: in another, for the doctrine that our treatment of men should be dictated by a sense of their intrinsic moral worth, rather than of their external situation. In one page he endeavours to throw ridicule upon the doctrine of *universal sincerity*; and in another, directs a sneer at the general idea of the influence of philosophy, in arming the mind against wordly calamities.

Indeed, whilst we protest against the idea of ridicule being the test of truth, we are astonished that a work which lays itself so open to its lash, as does "Political Justice" in almost every page, should have afforded so poor a field for burlesque, to a writer of the discernment which Mr. W. has the credit of possessing. Yet so unsuccessful do his efforts acknowledge themselves in selecting from its objects of buffoonery, that he is obliged to have recourse to the most contemptible expedients for assisting him, in supporting the part which he has assumed: and the reader, after being introduced to the work as an attack upon the doctrines of the *new philosophy*, is surprised to find not only the names of Hume, Rousseau, Godwin, and Holcroft, but those also of Priestley, Buffon, Dr. Johnson, &c. jumbled together in the most unconnected and indiscriminate sarcasms. Nor does our author find even in these resources, a sufficient supply for the plenitude of his zeal or the deficiency of his wit; and to make up for his incapacity to discover real objects of ridicule in the system he encounters, he descends to the miserable artifice of supplying them from his own imagination.

Thus, not content with heaping inconsistently together in his personified representations of "Political Justice," all that he could collect, which is or has been thought extravagant in the abstract speculations of different modern philosophers, he goes on to describe the advocate of the new philosophy as a systematic gambler, as the leader and justifier of a furious mob, as a dogmatical atheist, as (still acting under the influence of principle) a highwayman and assassin.

In short, the object of his buffoonery, (for it can be called nothing else) is to be learnt only from his own preface; for the work itself might as well be called a burlesque of the Christian Religion, as of the "Political Justice."

Of his indecent and *brutal* sarcasms upon Mrs. Godwin, we shall say nothing: for nothing which we could say, could heighten the disgust which every one who reads them must feel towards their author.

We are sensible that we have already bestowed upon this work, infinitely more notice than it deserves: but the influence of books is not always proportioned to their importance; and Mr. W.'s name may introduce this into circulation as a novel, amongst many who would be neither disposed to attend to it, nor prepared to judge of it, as what it really is. The dirty cloak of a *Vagabond* may conceal infinitely more mischief than even the specious disguise of a *Monk*.[1]

Among what class of people does Mr. W. expect the influence of his book to operate? Its readers must be those who either are or are not acquainted with the principles of the *new philosophy*, which he pretends to attack. If they be unacquainted with them, and if his book be able to excite any interest, it can only hold out to them a temptation to seek for the tree of forbidden fruit; and upon those who have been previously informed of the doctrines which he abuses, what influence (but the inspiring of indignation and disgust) can be expected from his foul and gross misrepresentations of them?

Mr. W., however, addresses his work only to *triflers*—and so much

---

[1] *The Monk* (1796), by Matthew Lewis, was one of the most scandalously salacious Gothic novels of the period. A sensational success when it first appeared, *The Monk* was reviled in the conservative press, which regarded it as an exponent of Jacobin moral depravity—causing Lewis to discretely but rigorously bowdlerize later editions of the novel.

for his style of compliment: we were really in hopes that some of Mr. W.'s former productions might have entitled him to anticipate a more respectable audience. Mr. W. seems a great advocate for "*common-place reason:*" but Mr. W. should have reflected before he sat down to revile "Political Justice," or presumed to dedicate his labours to the BISHOP OF LANDAFF, that, however well *common place reason* might have served as a substitute for the new philosophy, it will make but a poor figure when brought into the field as its antagonist. We hope, however, that Mr. W.'s own stock of *common-place reason* will prove a satisfactory consolation to him if his present production should fail of procuring him the title of philosopher.

Indeed it might have been more consistent with the claims of our author to have said less concerning the *matter*, and more respecting the *manner* of his production. Mr. W. attempts to burlesque not only the doctrines, but the language of the writers of the *new school*. Probably, however, his readers in general will give him more credit for success, in this respect, in his former attempts to *imitate*, than in his present efforts to *ridicule*, the style of his *quondam* copy-masters. We would wish to give a specimen of his exertions in this way: but there is so little of that contrast which is necessary to even the semblance of burlesque, to be found between the language which we are to suppose him using himself, and that which he puts into the mouths of his straw men—(except indeed in one page, where he makes up a speech for one of them out of the sesquipedalian Vocabulary of Johnson)[1]—that it is not an easy matter to select one.

Let our readers judge between the accents of the puppet-master and his puppets.

The following is a description of the moral sublime from the mouth of Stupeo, his personified representation of "Political Justice."

"When truth, like a volcano, bursts forth and the darkness of night, its thunders shall awaken the dormant senses of mankind. Its lightning shall glitter in their eyes like the brilliant morning of science: its lava shall bear down all opposition, overwhelming all the puny barriers of state; and its cinders will scatter destruction upon its enemies; and the devastation it spreads, like a revolution, shall be momentary, giving place to a tenfold fecundity."

---

[1] Samuel Johnson (1709–84) was an authoritative English lexicographer, essayist, poet and moralist. His monumental *Dictionary of the English Language* (1755) was the standard dictionary for the English language until Noah Webster's dictionary of 1828. His literary style—Latinate and formal—was known as "Johnsonese."

As parallel to this, we will give a specimen of what may be called the author's own diction, being pronounced after he has thrown off his mountebank cloak, and in the conclusion of a passionate address to his native country.

"May then thy fair face never be blasted by the insidious attacks of self-interested and ignorant *empirics*; may the mania of impracticable political dreams, be dispersed by the surges of thy rocky shores; and may thy fair daughters know, that modesty and maternal feelings are the chief ornaments of a celestial mind. Experience has qualified me to judge of learning, whose researches have taught me the paucity of the human mind; taught me that in this age of reason, in the eighteenth century, I may exclaim with the learned and polished Socrates—*"All that I know is that I know nothing."*

This specimen will be a sufficient apology for omitting any criticisms upon our author's style.

Perhaps Mr. W. will have better success in drawing a smile from most of his readers when he attempts to be serious, than when he aims at being witty. He appears to have found a very considerable difficulty in tacking a happy and satisfactory conclusion to his story. He had sent his *philosophers* rolling down the abyss of folly at such a rate, and with such a load of crimes and absurdities upon their backs, that, before he could get to the middle of his second volume, they had almost got beyond the reach of his redeeming power; and he is obliged to use the most violent means to pull them back again into the road of salvation. Nay, one of them had gone so far as to be absolutely irreclaimable, and our author is reduced to the painful necessity of burning him alive—not in the infernal regions, but before an Indian bon-fire. The disgust of this exhibition is, however, compensated by the happy witticism with which our author concludes his narration of it.

"Such was the termination of that enlightened great man, who while he lived, endeavoured to kindle the world, and set society in a flame, but expired himself in the midst of a blaze."

His fellow disciples are at length recovered, after going through a most dreadful purgatory; tossed about by a storm at sea, and shaken about by an earthquake at land. Nor is our author wanting in his efforts to reclaim them by instruction, as well as by punishment. In the midst of the sea-storm, they are prevailed upon by a female saint, who sets the example, to sing psalms, for the sake (as we are told) *of preventing reflection*: and in the midst of the earthquake, whilst a "thick haze overspread the face of the heavens, through which the sun appeared, one moment purple, and the next violet—and the earth undulated like a moving lake," we are entertained by one of the most serious of the party with an elaborate discourse, seven or eight pages long, upon the geographical history of the world, and the Witch of Endor; which, together with the earthquake, and the subsequent bonfire, gives the *finishing blow* to the doctrines of the NEW PHILOSOPHY.

2. From the *Anti-Jacobin Review and Magazine; or, Monthly Political and Literary Censor* 2 (February 1799): 137–40

The object of this work is to place, in a practical light, as the author tells us in his preface, "some of the prominent absurdities of many self-important reformers of mankind, who, having heated their imaginations, sit down to write *political romances*, which never have, and never will be, practical." In the execution of this design there is so much of just and lively satire conveyed in the following manner:

[The reviewer subsequently offers a four-page summary of the plot—spliced with colorful quotes from the novel—paying particular attention to the more scandalous, lascivious aspects of Walker's representation of the doctrines of the new philosophy. The critic ends the review with:]

These are the outlines of the story. Some of the adventures, especially in America, are extravagant and improbable; but it is, on the whole, a lively sketch of the *more obvious* absurdities, follies, and wickedness of the new philosophy. As such we recommend it to our readers; at the same time we have the pleasure to announce to them that a much more comprehensive exposure of the ravings of Wollstonecraft, Holcroft, Godwin, Paine, Thelwall, and other abettors, principal or subordinate, of the new philosophism [sic], is the subject of a Novel of four volumes, now in the press, by that zealous Anti-Jacobin, Dr. Bisset.[1]

---

[1]   The reviewer is referring to *Douglas; or, The Highlander* (1800), a novel by Robert Bisset, one of the most prominent and vitriolic reviewers for *The Anti-Jacobin Review*. Bisset waged a bitter war against what he regarded as the enemies of Christianity, natural religion, monarchy, property and morality. High on Bisset's hate list was Mary Wollstonecraft, who is derided in *Douglas* in the character of "Lady Mary Manhunt."

3. New London Review 1 (April 1799): 406

Here is a kind of republican retaliation; as Godwin, the great and redoubted champion of morality without principle, politics without religion, and creation without a maker, is exposed to the ridicule of his contemporaries, as a reasoner without logic, a philosopher without science, and a visionary without enthusiasm. All this is very well, by why dedicated to a Bishop? Will not his Lordship think, this more in need of an apology than even his Bible? A novel and a mitre, fiction and prelacy, the new philosophy, and an old bishop, are, to say the least of them, ominous conjunctions! And in truth, George Walker, thou hast no thanks to expect from a political convert of the new school, either for their indications or retrospections!

4. Critical Review, New Series, 26 (June 1799): 237

It appears that this work was written "with a desire of placing, in a practical light, some of the prominent absurdities of many self-important reformers of mankind, who, having heated their imaginations, sit down to write political romances, which never were, and never will be, practical." To this end, our author has interwoven, in a tale of adventures, certain sentiments advanced by the tribe of *new philosophers* (as they are improperly called), and, it must be allowed, has occasionally introduced them with the happiest effect; but there are some objections to his work. His story is highly improbable. To correct extravagance by extravagance, and absurdity by something as absurd, is not the mode which a wise man would follow; and to push principles to an extent beyond the intention of their author, is an attempt to prove too much, which always fails. We approve Mr. Walker's views; but he is destitute of humour, and therefore incapable of fixing ridicule upon the reveries of the new philosophers. As *he* represents their sentiments, they are too horrid to be supposed to influence the minds of their disciples. His young philosopher commits all those enormous crimes which shock the reader in themselves, without any consideration of the principles which led to them. We admit that the writer claims some praise for having exhibited the dangers of the new philosophy; but he has supposed only extreme cases, and such perversions as are not deducible from the principles of Rousseau or Hume. For the purpose of combating the late pernicious theories in a fictitious narrative, we would prefer the humour of a Cervantes to the invective of a Burke.

5. Monthly Magazine, Supplement, 7 (20 July 1799): 542

We cannot speak in terms sufficiently indignant and contemptuous of Mr. Walker's *Vagabond*: this piece of folly, malevolence, and buffoonery, is a professed attack upon what is called the system of *new philosophy*. Mr. Walker, armed cap-a-pie, enters the field to destroy the doctrines of "political justice:" it would be uncandid to suppose that he had never read the work which excites his wrath; but it is certainly most true, that he does not understand it. Not satisfied with exposing his ignorance, however, by an indiscriminate attack upon those doctrines which are common to "political justice," and to every system of morality which we have yet seen or heard of, namely, the absurdity and criminality of duelling, the doctrine of universal sincerity, &c. Mr. Walker descends to characterise the advocate of the modern philosophy as an atheist, a highwayman, an assassin, and every thing that can be conceived bad. To complete the whole, he has made his work infamous by some allusions to Mrs. Godwin, of the most indelicate and brutal kind.

6. Monthly Mirror 9 (March 1800): 158

"The following work is written with a desire of placing, in a practical light, some of the prominent absurdities of many self-important reformers of mankind, who, having heated their imaginations, sit down to write *political romances*, which never were, and never will be practical; but which, coming into the hands of persons as little acquainted with human nature, the history of mankind, and the proofs of religious authenticity, as themselves, hurry away the mind from common life, into dreams of ideal felicity; or, by breaking every moral tie (while they declaim about morals) turn loose their disciples upon the world, to root upon and overthrow every thing which has received the sanction of ages, and been held sacred by men of real genius and erudition."

The absurdities of what is called the *new philosophy* are exposed, by Mr. Walker, in this novel, with infinite humour and ingenuity. The system of *Political Justice*, and the tenets of those mad philosophers who have been insulting common sense, and confounding the ignorant with their wild theories, about the *rights of nature*, and the *equalization of property*, are completely overturned. Though this has been effectually done already, by means of essays, treatises, and ponderous and elaborate disquisitions, there are so many readers who turn away, with disgust and contempt, from a dissertation, that Mr. Walker, we think, has employed his talents as usefully as judiciously in representing the impracticability, and the mischievous tendency, of the innovations proposed by Messrs. Godwin and Co through so popular and entertaining a medium as that of a novel.

The author has certainly executed his task with great ability; he illustrates his design by numerous examples, and, though the subject does not seem to be very favourable to the nature of a production of this kind, it must, in candour, be acknowledged that the author has contrived to interest the curiosity of his readers sufficiently for his propose, and that, independently of the drift of the work, he has rendered his characters and incidents in the highest degree amusing.

7. British Critic 15 (April 1800): 432

The principles of Jacobinism and Democracy are successfully delineated in these volumes; we would nevertheless have wished, that scenes and circumstances of horror had been introduced more sparingly. The same idea had already been prosecuted by Mr. Pye, in his publication called the Democrat; of which see an account in the British Critic, vol. vi, p. 669.[1] The favourable reception which both these publications have met with from readers of every description, decisively announces the triumph of true patriotism and social order over the detestable principles of Democracy and Jacobinism. The title-page informs us, that the Vagabond has already passed through three editions.

8. From the British Critic 16 (October 1800): 439–40

The Vagabond, written by Mr. Walker, and formerly commended by us (Brit. Crit. Vol. xv, p. 432) and this Novel of the Modern Philosophers,[2] are performed upon the same design; that of ridiculing

---

[1] The Democrat: Interspersed with Anecdotes of Well-Known Characters (1795), an anti-Jacobin novel by Henry James Pye. The novel's hero, Jean Le Noir, is a Jacobin leveler who travels to America to assist the Americans in their struggle against Britain and to put his "theory of equalization" into practice there.

[2] The present review was occasioned by the publication of Memoirs of Modern Philosophers, an anti-Jacobin novel by Elizabeth Hamilton (London: G.G. and J. Robinson, 1800).

the extravagances of several pretenders to wisdom in the present times, particularly, of Mr. Godwin. The wild and almost incredible absurdities of that author's Political Justice (exposed by us with some care in our first volume, p. 307, &c.) afford so fair and open an subject for ridicule, that no man possessing any share of humour could fail to raise a laugh, if so disposed, at the expence of the fanatical speculator. In this respect, both these publications are abundantly successful; though we cannot but think the humour of the Vagabond the more delicate and refined. Bridgetina in the present Novel, is such a caricature as [to] exceed all probability, and almost all patience; and Mr. Glib talks only the cropped cant of the Road to Ruin, and such stuff; the pleasantry of which consists in leaving out articles and pronouns. Mr. Myope greatly resembles the sublime Stupeo, but is drawn with less vigour. On the other hand, the villainy of Vallaton is well designed, and highly finished.[1] As a regular novel, the present has much more plot and more interest than the Vagabond. The good characters are given with admirable skill, and form a useful and striking contrast to the bad. Many of the serious parts are of high merit. The catastrophe of Julia in particular is tremendous, but touched with a most judicious hand. Yet the triumph of the amiable girl over the superficial philosopher, in the Vagabond, gave us more pleasure, and has in our opinion more probability, than the strange and unaccountable lapse of Julia.... The Modern Philosophers appear to us to have attracted the public attention more than the Vagabond; we have therefore been careful to compare them. Were we to add another feature to the comparison, we would say that Mr. Walker more completely exposes the authors he attacks than the present writer. His account of emigration to America is useful, because touched with truth; and his imaginary society of philosophers is managed with a vein of high humour. Both novels however will be read, and both deserve it.

---

[1]   Bridgetina Botherim is one of the novel's three heroines (the other two being Julia Delmont, who sympathizes with the new philosophy, and the virtuous Harriet). Bridgetina is a fairly crude caricature of the radical novelist Mary Hays, a feminist and ardent disciple of Mary Wollstonecraft, and author of the Jacobin novels *Memoirs of Emma Courtney* (London: G.G. and J. Robinson, 1796) and *The Victim of Prejudice* (London: J. Johnson, 1799). Vallaton, Mr. Glib and Mr. Myope are three new philosophers—the latter being a caricature of William Godwin. *The Road to Ruin* is a Jacobin play by the radical writer and activist Thomas Holcroft, first performed in London in February 1792.

Select Bibliography

Works by George Walker

The Romance of the Cavern; Or, The History of FitzHenry and James. 2 vols. London: Printed for William Lane, at the Minerva Press, 1793.

The Haunted Castle, A Norman Romance. 2 vols. London: Printed for William Lane, at the Minerva Press, 1794.

The House of Tynian. 4 vols. London: Printed for William Lane, at the Minerva Press, 1795. Further editions: Dublin, 1796 (two separate editions).

Theodor Cyphon; Or, The Benevolent Jew. 3 vols. London: Printed for B. Crosby, 1796. Further editions: Dublin, 1796; German translation, Hildburghausen, 1797–98; French translation, Paris, 1800; Alexandria, VA, 1803.

Cinthella; Or, A Woman of Ten Thousand. 4 vols. London: Printed for B. Crosby, 1797. French trans. Paris, 1798.

The Vagabond, A Novel. 2 vols. London: Printed for G. Walker, No. 106, Great Portland Street, and Lee and Hurst, No. 32, Paternoster Row, 1799. Further editions: London, 1799 (2nd and 3rd eds.); Dublin, 1800 (1 vol.); Boston, 1800 (1 vol.); French translation, Paris, 1807; Harrisonburg, VA, 1814 (1 vol.).

The Three Spaniards, A Romance. 3 vols. Printed for G. Walker and T. Hurst, 1800. Further editions include: Dublin, 1800; New York, 1801; Dublin, 1802; French Translation, [n.p.], 1805; New York, 1817; Baltimore, 1825; Exeter, NH, 1826, 1832, 1837, 1839; New York, 1827; New York 1833; Baltimore, 1834; New York, 1881 (dime novel); New York, 1882; New York, c. 1890; Chicago, etc., [n.d.].

Flowers of Harmony: Being a Collection of the Most Celebrated Catches, Glees and Duets, Some Entirely New and Many Extremely Scarce ... Printed music; 4 vols. in 2. London: Printed for G. Walker, [between 1800 and 1818].

Don Raphael, A Romance. 3 vols. London: Printed for G. Walker and T. Hurst, 1803. Further edition: New York, 1803.

Poems, on Various Subjects. Philadelphia: Printed by T.L. Plowman, 1804.

The Adventures of Timothy Thoughtless; Or, The Misfortunes of a Little Boy Who Ran away from Boarding-School. London: Published and sold by G. Walker, 1813.

The Travels of Sylvester Tramper Through the Interior of the South of Africa: With the Adventures & Accidents that he Encountered in a Journey of More Than Two Thousand Miles Through These Unknown Wildernesses, Constantly Exposed to Danger from Beasts of Prey, and the Attacks of Savages. London: Published and sold by G. Walker, 1813. Further editions: 2nd ed., 1813; 3rd ed., 1816; 4th ed., 1817.

The Battle of Waterloo. A Poem. London: Printed for G. Walker, 1815.

Contemporary Reviews

Analytical Review, ns, 1 (February 1799): 210–15.

Anti-Jacobin Review and Magazine 2 (February 1799): 137–40.

British Critic 15 (April 1800): 432.

Critical Review, ns, 26 (June 1799): 237.

Monthly Magazine, suppl., 7 (20 July 1799): 542.

Monthly Mirror 9 (March 1800): 158.

New London Review 1 (April 1799): 406.

Other Primary Sources

Anon., "An Explanation of the Word Equality." [London], [1795?].

———. Letters on Emigration. By a Gentleman, Lately Returned from America. London, 1794.

———. The Periodical Press of Great Britain and Ireland: or, an inquiry into the state of the public journals, chiefly as regards their moral and political influence. London: Hurst, Robinson & Co., 1824.

———. "Proceedings of the Friends to the Abuse of the Liberty of the Press." [n.p.], 1793.

———. Truth and Treason! Or a Narrative of the Royal Procession. London, 1795.

Anti-Jacobin Review and Magazine. London, 1798–1810.

Aratus [pseud.]. A Voyage to the Moon Strongly Recommended to All Lovers of Real Freedom. London, 1793.

Barruel, Abbé Augustin de. Memoirs, Illustrating the History of Jacobinism. A Translation from the French. Trans. Robert Clifford. 1795. London, 1797, 1798.

Burke, Edmund. Reflections on the Revolution in France. 1790. Ed. L.G. Mitchell. Oxford: Oxford UP, 1993.

Godwin, William. An Enquiry Concerning Political Justice, and Its Influence on Modern Morals and Happiness. 1793. In Political and Philosophical

Writings of William Godwin. Vol. 3. Ed. Mark Philp. London: Pickering & Chatto, 1993.

——. *An Enquiry Concerning Political Justice, and Its Influence on Modern Morals and Happiness.* 1793. 3rd ed., 1798. Ed. Isaac Kramnick. Harmondsworth: Penguin, 1976.

——. *An Enquiry Concerning Political Justice: Variants.* 1793–1798. In *Political and Philosophical Writings of William Godwin.* Vol. 4. Ed. Mark Philp. Gen. ed. Mark Philp. London: Pickering & Chatto, 1993.

——. *Considerations on Lord Grenville's and Mr Pitt's Bills, concerning treasonable and seditious practices and unlawful assemblies, by a lover of order.* 1795. In *Political and Philosophical Writings of William Godwin.* Vol. 2. Ed. Mark Philp. Gen. ed. Mark Philp. London: Pickering & Chatto, 1993.

——. *Memoirs of the Author of a Vindication of the Rights of Woman.* 1798. In *The Collected Novels and Memoirs of William Godwin.* Vol. 1. Ed. Mark Philp. London: Pickering & Chatto, 1992.

——. *Thoughts occasioned by the perusal of Dr. Parr's Spital Sermon, preached at Christ Church, April 15, 1800: being a reply to the attacks of Dr. Parr, Mr. Mackintosh, The Author of an Essay of Population, and others.* 1801. In *Political and Philosophical Writings of William Godwin.* Gen. ed. Mark Philp. London: Pickering & Chatto, 1993.

Hazlitt, William. *The Spirit of the Age or Contemporary Portraits.* 1825. Oxford: Oxford UP, 1928.

Holcroft, Thomas. "A Plain and Succinct Narrative of the Late Riots and Disturbances in the Cities of London and Westminster, and the Borough of Southwark...." London, 1780.

Hume, David. *Treatise of Human Nature, Being an Attempt to Introduce the Experimental Method of Reasoning into Moral Subjects.* 1739. Buffalo, NY: Prometheus Books, 1992.

——. "Idea of a Perfect Commonwealth." 1752. In *Utopias of the British Enlightenment.* Ed. Gregory Claeys. Cambridge and New York: Cambridge UP, 1994.

Imlay, Gilbert. *A Topographical Description of the Western Territory of North America; Containing a Succinct Account of its Climate, Natural History, Population, Agriculture, Manners and Customs....* London, 1792.

——. *The Emigrants, or, The History of an Expatriated Family.* 1793. Ed. and intro. W.M. Verhoeven and Amanda Gilroy. New York: Penguin, 1998.

Le Mesurier, Havilland. *Thoughts on a French Invasion, with Reference to the Probability of Its Success, and the Proper Means of Resisting It.* London, 1798.

Locke, John. *An Essay Concerning Human Understanding.* 1690. Ed. Peter H. Nidditch. Oxford: Clarendon Press, 1975.

Malthus, Thomas Robert. *An Essay on the Principle of Population.* 1798. In *The Works of Thomas Robert Malthus.*Vol. 1. Ed. E.A. Wrigley and David Souden. Gen. eds. E.A. Wrigley and David Souden. London: Pickering & Chatto, 1986.

Mathias, Thomas James. *The Pursuits of Literature: A Satirical Poem in Four Dialogues.* London, 1798.

Paine, Thomas. *Rights of Man, Part I.* 1791. Ed. and intro. Henry Collins. Harmondsworth: Penguin, 1969.

———. *Rights of Man, Part II.* 1792. Ed. and intro. Henry Collins. Harmondsworth: Penguin, 1969.

Pigott, Charles. *A Political Dictionary.* London, 1795.

Playfair, William. *History of Jacobinism, Its Crimes, Cruelties, and Perfidies, from the Commencement of the French Revolution, to the Death of Robespierre....* London, 1795.

———. *Peace with the Jacobins Impossible.* London, 1794.

Polwhele, Richard. *The Unsex'd Females: A Poem.* London, 1798.

Porcupine, Peter [William Cobbett]. *Observations on the Emigration of Dr. Joseph Priestley.* Philadelphia, 1794.

Price, Richard. "A Discourse on the Love of Our Country." 1798. In *Political Writings,* ed. D.O. Thomas. Cambridge: Cambridge UP, 1991.

Priestley, Joseph. *Disquisitions Relating to Matter and Spirit.* [1777] 2nd ed. Birmingham and London, 1782.

Robison, John. *Proofs of a Conspiracy against all the Religions and Governments of Europe: Carried on in the Secret Meetings of Free Masons, Illuminati, and Reading Societies.* London, 1797.

Rousseau, Jean-Jacques. *Discourse on the Origin of Inequality.* 1755. Trans. Franklin Philip. Ed. and intro. Patrick Coleman. Oxford and New York: Oxford UP, 1994.

———. *Julie, or the New Heloise: Letters of Two Lovers Who Live in a Small Town at the Foot of the Alps.* 1761. Trans. Philip Stewart and Jean Vaché. In *The Collected Writings of Rousseau.*Vol. 6. Ser. eds. Roger D. Masters and Christopher Kelly. Hanover, NH, and London: UP of New England, 1997.

———. *The Social Contract.* 1762. Trans. and intro. Christopher Betts. Oxford: Oxford UP, 1994.

———. *Confessions.* 1781, 1788. Trans. Angela Scholar. Ed. and intro. Patrick Coleman. Oxford: Oxford UP, 2000.

Thale, Mary, ed. and intro. *Selections from the Papers of the London Corresponding Society, 1792–1799.* Cambridge: Cambridge UP, 1983.
Thelwall, John. *The Tribune, a Periodical Publication, Consisting Chiefly of the Political Lectures of J. Thelwall.* 1795. In *The Politics of English Radicalism: Writings of John Thelwall.* Ed. Gregory Claeys. University Park, PA: Pennsylvania State UP, 1995.
Wollstonecraft, Mary. *A Vindication of the Rights of Woman.* 1792. In *The Works of Mary Wollstonecraft.* Vol. 5. Eds. Janet Todd and Marilyn Butler. London: Pickering, 1989.
———. *Letters to Imlay.* Ed. C. Kegan Paul. London: C.K. Paul, 1879.

Secondary Sources

General Studies

Andrews, Stuart. "Fellow Pantisocrats: Brissot, Cooper and Imlay." *Symbiosis* 1:1 (1997): 35–47.
Barrell, John. *Imagining the King's Death: Figurative Treason, Fantasies of Regicide, 1793–96.* Oxford: Oxford UP, 2000.
Brailsford, H.N. *Shelley, Godwin, and Their Circle.* London: Williams and Norgate, 1913.
Butler, Marilyn. *Jane Austen and the War of Ideas.* Oxford: Clarendon Press, 1975.
———. *Romantics, Rebels and Reactionaries: English Literature and Its Background, 1760–1830.* Oxford: Oxford UP, 1981.
Castro, J. Paul de. *The Gordon Riots.* London: Oxford UP, 1926.
Crossley, Ceri, and Ian Small, eds. *The French Revolution and British Culture.* Oxford: Oxford UP, 1989.
George, M. Dorothy. *London Life in the Eighteenth Century.* 1925. Harmondsworth: Penguin, 1965.
Gregory, Allene. *The French Revolution and the English Novel.* New York and London: G.P. Putnam's Sons, 1915.
Grenby, M.O. *The Anti-Jacobin Novel: British Conservatism and the French Revolution.* Cambridge: Cambridge UP, 2001.
Heilman, Robert Bechtold. *America in English Fiction, 1760–1800.* Baton Rouge: Louisiana State UP, 1937.
Keane, John. *Tom Paine: A Political Life.* London: Bloomsbury, 1995.
Keen, Paul. *The Crisis of Literature in the 1790s: Print Culture and the Public Sphere.* Cambridge: Cambridge UP, 1999.

Kelly, Gary. *The English Jacobin Novel, 1780–1805*. Oxford: Clarendon Press, 1976.

———. *Women, Writing and Revolution, 1790–1827*. Oxford: Oxford UP, 1993.

Klancher, Jon P. *The Making of English Reading Audiences, 1790–1832*. Madison: U of Wisconsin P, 1999.

London, April. *Women and Property in the Eighteenth-Century English Novel*. Cambridge: Cambridge UP, 1999.

———. "Clock Time and Utopia's Time of Novels in the 1790s." *Studies in English Literature* 40 (2000): 539–60.

———. "Novel and History in Anti-Jacobin Satire." *Yearbook of English Studies* 30 (2000): 71–81.

Lorraine de Montluzin, Emily. *The Anti-Jacobins, 1798–1800: The Early Contributors to the Anti-Jacobin Review*. Houndmills, Hamps.: Macmillan Press, 1988.

McCann, Andrew. *Cultural Politics in the 1790s: Literature, Radicalism and the Public Sphere*. London: Macmillan, 1999.

Marshall, Peter H. *William Godwin*. New Haven and London: Yale UP, 1984.

Park, Mary Cathryne. *Joseph Priestley and the Problem of Pantisocracy*. Diss. University of Pennsylvania. Philadelphia: Delaware County Institute of Science, 1947.

Philp, Mark, ed. *The French Revolution and British Popular Politics*. Cambridge: Cambridge UP, 1991.

Rudé, G. *The Crowd in the French Revolution*. Oxford: Clarendon Press, 1959.

Simpson, David. *Romanticism, Nationalism, and the Revolt Against Theory*. Chicago and London: U of Chicago P, 1993.

Spurling, Paul Merrill. *Rousseau in America, 1760–1809*. Tuscaloosa: U of Alabama P, 1969.

Thomis, Malcolm I, and Peter Holt. *Threats of Revolution in Britain, 1789–1848*. Houndmills, Hamps.: Macmillan Press, 1977.

Thompson, E.P. *The Making of the English Working Class*. 1963. Rev. ed. Harmondsworth; Penguin, 1968.

Tompkins, J.M.S. *The Popular Novel in England, 1770–1800*. London: Constable & Co., 1932.

Watson, Nicola J. *Revolution and the Form of the British Novel, 1790–1825*. Oxford: Clarendon Press, 1994.

Studies related to *The Vagabond*

Allen, B. Sprague. "The Reaction Against William Godwin." *Modern Philology* 16:5 (September 1918): 57–75.

Gregory, Allene. *The French Revolution and the English Novel.* New York and London: G.P. Putnam's Sons, 1915. 135–44.

Harvey, A.D. "George Walker and the Anti-Revolutionary Novel." *Review of English Studies* ns, 28:111 (1977): 290–300.

London, April. *Women and Property in the Eighteenth-Century English Novel.* Cambridge: Cambridge UP, 1999. 172–79.

MacMullan, Hugh H. "The Satire of Walker's *Vagabond* on Rousseau and Godwin." *PMLA* 52:1 (1937): 215–29.

Verhoeven, W.M. "New Philosophers in the Backwoods: Romantic Primitivism and American Emigration in the 1790s' Jacobin and Anti–Jacobin Novel." *The Wordsworth Circle* 32.3 (2001): 130–33.